The Tiger's Claw

THE TIGER'S HEART
VOLUME 2

The Tiger's Claw

THE TIGER'S HEART
VOLUME 2

Lewis Orde

PIATKUS

Copyright © 1988 by Lewis Orde

First published in Great Britain in 1988 by
Judy Piatkus (Publishers) Ltd of
5 Windmill Street, London W1

British Library Cataloguing in Publication Data

Orde, Lewis
 The tiger's heart.
 Vol. 2: The tiger's claw
 I. Title
 813'.54[F]

 ISBN 0 86188 743 3

Phototypeset in 11/12pt Linotron Times by
Phoenix Photosetting, Chatham
Printed and bound in Great Britain by
Billings Ltd, Worcester

Prologue

Central Park looked just like a bride that morning. A snow shower shortly before dawn had left the strip of green in the centre of New York swathed in a gown of shimmering white, as pure and beautiful as any girl walking down the aisle on her father's arm.

Gazing through the living-room window of her apartment on Central Park West, Pearl Granitz was not surprised to find herself making such a comparison. Only the previous day she had seen Joseph, the older by seconds of her twenty-two-year-old twin sons, married to his childhood sweetheart, Judy. Weddings were on Pearl's mind today, and since when had there been anything wrong with that? Where were Joseph and Judy now? she wondered. Still in the Waldorf suite where they had spent their wedding night? Pearl turned from the window to look at the carriage clock on the mantelpiece. Eight-thirty. Charitably, she hoped that her son and his new wife were in bed. On a cold January morning like this, what better place was there to be? Especially – Pearl's heart-shaped face broke into a gentle smile – for a couple of newlyweds. They'd better be up soon, though. They were flying to Europe, starting their honeymoon in Switzerland.

The streets were nowhere near as pristine as the park. Early morning traffic had taken care of that, transforming clean snow into grimy slush. Pearl stared down, glad to see more and more new cars. For so long, there had been nothing but pre-war automobiles. If you owned a ten-year-old Lincoln, you were in great shape. Now, the motor industry was in full swing again. In January 1950, America was getting back where it belonged: on wheels.

Pulling her blue dressing-gown tightly around her petite figure, Pearl left the living-room and walked along the hall until she reached a closed door. She knocked on it, and called out: 'Leo, are you getting up this morning?'

A minute later the door opened. The younger twin emerged, blue pyjamas rumpled, eyes gummy with sleep. Pearl's twin sons were fraternal, not identical. Whereas Joseph was tall and slim, with melting brown eyes, Leo was shorter and stocky, black-haired, his face etched into a permanent scowl. His appearance was made even more threatening by the fierce eyebrows that almost joined above his large, fleshy nose. Beneath their heavy brows his eyes were a light hazel. Pearl had learned to use those eyes as a barometer of her younger son's feelings. Hazel – he was relaxed and happy. But when a toneless grey crept in, be careful. Another of the many differences between her twins, Pearl reflected. Whereas Joseph was calm, reasoning, Leo possessed an easily triggered, raging temper. And the colour of his eyes was always a clue to the state of his feelings.

'Good morning, Ma.' Leo kissed his mother, unashamedly fond of her. At five feet exactly, Pearl was eight inches shorter than the younger twin. He had to stoop considerably. His breath was sour, but remembering what had happened the previous night, Pearl was not surprised. If anything, she was surprised to see him up, looking so lively and healthy.

'Make sure you dress warmly today, Leo. It snowed before.'

Leo regarded his tiny mother affectionately, accustomed to being fussed over by her. He would not have it any other way.

'And I want you to drive extra carefully in the snow.'

'I'll drive like an angel, Ma. Would I ever do anything to worry you?'

He kissed his mother again, and Pearl recalled the events of the previous night. He had worried her then, all right, but she was certain he had never intended to do so. He had been upset, that was all. Leo had been his twin brother's best man, entrusted with the ring. Somehow, he had lost it through a hole in his trouser pocket. Rather than face his brother's anger, he had run away, not returning home until early in the morning, long after everything was over. On top of that, disturbed at losing the ring, he had drunk far more than he should have. At first, Pearl had been furious with him, but now she felt more forgiving. Leo was so highly strung – it was all to do with the bad attack of diphtheria he had suffered as a child – that she knew she had to make allowances for his behaviour.

'Go take your shower, Leo, and I'll make you breakfast.' She watched him walk towards the bathroom, and wondered whether she spoilt him too much. He was twenty-two. Shouldn't he be out on his own, as his twin brother was? Then Pearl thought of herself. What would she do without Leo to look after? She was forty-four, a widow for almost ten years. With Joseph gone, Leo was her life now. If the younger twin left, what reason would she have to get up in the morning?

Before going to the kitchen, she looked out of the living-room window one more time. A grey Studebaker was pulling up in front of the apartment block's entrance. A man carrying a large, flat box climbed out and walked into the building. Wondering who could be getting a delivery so early in the morning, Pearl busied herself with Leo's breakfast.

The messenger went to the apartment directly below Pearl's. He knocked once. The front door swung open. A compact man with greying hair and hard blue eyes stood in the doorway, dressed in a conservative dark suit.

'The wedding photographs, Mr Levitt,' said the man from the Studebaker. 'First thing this morning, just the way you wanted them.'

Lou Levitt took the box and handed the deliveryman fifty dollars. 'Here's something extra for being so quick about it.'

'Thank you, Mr Levitt, sir!' But Levitt was already back inside the apartment, the door closed. He took the box into the living-room, stripped the string and wrapping free, and opened the wedding album which had been prepared over-night. The first photograph he saw was a group shot. Everyone was there. Pearl, himself, Joseph, Judy. . . . Everyone except the best man, except Leo. Levitt felt his stomach knot as he remembered how upset Pearl had been over her younger son's disappearance, and thought how much more

3

upset she would be if she ever learned the truth about it. Why he had run away, and what exactly he had gotten up to. Thank God Leo had possessed enough common sense to call for help from the one person who could be guaranteed to come to his aid with no questions asked – Levitt himself.

He lifted the telephone and dialled the number of the apartment above. Pearl answered. 'I've got a big surprise for you,' Levitt told her.

'Please, Lou, no more surprises!'

'This one you'll like, I promise you.' He hung up the receiver and left the apartment, carrying the album. He walked up one flight of stairs and along the carpeted hallway to Pearl's apartment. She opened the door, still in her dressing-gown, and Levitt handed her the album.

'I wasn't expecting this until the end of next week,' she exclaimed when she realized what she was holding.

'I paid the photographer to work right through the night. After yesterday, I figured you needed a pick-me-up.'

'Thank you, Lou. Thank you.' She hugged him, kissed him on the cheek. 'Come inside. Have breakfast with Leo and me.' Then, as an afterthought, 'Are the photographs good? How do I look?'

'Like the belle of the ball! You outshine even the bride.'

Pearl pushed Levitt with her hand and said, 'Get out of here,' but she was pleased with the compliment.

Leo came out of the shower as Pearl was setting plates on the table. His hair was wet and sleek, and he wore a terry robe. Levitt looked him up and down before asking: 'You feel well enough to go to work today?'

'I feel just fine, Uncle Lou.'

Levitt said no more. He simply stood looking at Leo, nodding his head slowly.

'Get dressed!' Pearl called out. 'Breakfast will be ready in five minutes.' She cracked eggs and beat them into an omelette to which she added pieces of smoked salmon. By the time Leo returned, wearing a dark grey suit like Levitt's, Pearl was dishing out portions of the omelette on to three plates.

'You hear from Joseph yet?' Levitt asked Pearl.

'For God's sake, Lou, it's only nine o'clock. Give them a chance to wake up.'

4

While Leo and Levitt ate, Pearl leafed through the album, admiring the photographs of the wedding celebration. She had not realized that wedding albums could be put together so quickly. Obviously, Levitt had worked his customary magic to get things done. Where would she be without him? Especially during the trying times, Levitt had always been there, right from schooldays. Perhaps it was because Pearl had been the first person to befriend him that he had repaid her so many times. As a young boy, Levitt had come with his family to New York from Poland. Children at the school on the Lower East Side had made fun of his heavy accent but Pearl had stood by him, demanding to know if the mothers and fathers of his tormentors had spoken so perfectly when they first arrived in the country. From that day, Levitt had been Pearl's friend.

Not that he had really needed her help. No one at school had laughed at him once he had demonstrated how intelligent he was, running away with every test, always there with the right answer. And figures, so smart with figures; he was like a human adding machine. And no one laughed at him now, either. No one dared.

Pearl looked from the album to Leo, as he wiped his mouth with a napkin. The wedding had gone off even without the best man and the ring. She had fully forgiven him, and showed it by asking: 'How much longer are we going to have to wait until you get married?'

It was not Leo who answered, but Levitt. 'Pearl, give the boy a break. He's only twenty-two.'

'So is Joseph.' She noticed Leo's face darkening. Was he blushing? Had she embarrassed him? Leo should know better than to feel embarrassed; his mother meant it all in good fun.

'What's good for Joseph isn't necessarily good for Leo,' Levitt pointed out. 'Now leave him alone, he's got a day's work to do for me.'

Pearl could not resist making a final teasing remark. After all that Leo had put her through the previous day she felt entitled to. 'When you do get married, darling, we'll make sure there are no holes in the pockets of the best man's trousers. We don't want to lose another ring, do we?'

Leo's eyes turned that peculiar angry shade of grey. He

5

shoved himself back from the table, and jumped to his feet. 'Okay, I messed up! I know I did. I don't need you or anyone else reminding me.' He swung around and walked quickly from the room. Moments later, his bedroom door slammed.

Pearl looked at Levitt. 'What did I do?'

'Leave the boy alone, Pearl. He feels miserable enough about last night without having it shoved down his throat.'

'But I was teasing, that's all.'

'Just leave him alone,' Levitt cautioned.

Pearl heard the warning note in his voice. 'All right.' She cleared plates from the table, and Levitt pretended to look through the album. Fat chance Pearl would ever have of seeing Leo married, and Levitt knew the reason why. Just as he knew the real reason Leo had run off the previous day. There hadn't been any hole in his trouser pocket through which to lose the ring. There hadn't been any fear of the bridegroom's anger. There had been nothing but sheer bloody-minded fury at being betrayed by his own twin brother.

Twins . . .! Never mind that they were fraternal. Since they were children, Leo had found a special bond in being a twin. He had wanted nothing to come between him and Joseph. He gave complete loyalty to his twin, and he expected it in return. When it failed to happen – when Joseph put someone or something between himself and Leo – the younger twin raged. In Leo's eyes he had been betrayed.

The previous day had brought the greatest betrayal of all: Joseph's marriage to a girl Leo hated. A girl who had forced herself between Joseph and Leo from the day they were old enough to walk. Unable to watch his twin brother go through with the ceremony, Leo had just taken off, keeping the ring with him in the irrational belief that without it there could be no wedding. Joseph and Judy had married anyway, borrowing Pearl's wedding ring which she still wore although Jake had died so many years before.

When Leo still did not return, Levitt had tried to calm Pearl by assuring her that the younger twin would turn up when his temper had run its course, but even Levitt had been surprised to see no sign of Leo by the time the party was over. Levitt had brought Pearl home. She had invited him in for coffee.

6

And then the telephone had rung. It was Leo. Not asking for his mother, but wanting to speak to Levitt.

'I'm in terrible trouble, Uncle Lou,' Leo had said. 'Please come quickly.'

Without worrying Pearl, Levitt had driven down to Greenwich Village. Leo was waiting in his car. He told Levitt how he had fled from the wedding ceremony at the synagogue, driving aimlessly around for hours before ending his journey at a bar on Sixth Avenue in the Village. There, a young man named Tony had befriended him. Together, they had gone back to Tony's flat in Bleecker Street, above a hardware shop, where, for the first time in his life, Leo had made love. Made love with a man, and never felt so right about anything. It was only later, when Tony had asked for money, that Leo realized he had been betrayed again. He had strangled Tony, and rushed blindly from the apartment. Later, thinking clearly, he had called on Levitt for help.

In turn, Levitt had summoned another man, Harry Saltzman from New Jersey, who had performed certain specialist services for Levitt in the past. This time, Saltzman's task was to cause a gas explosion in the apartment where Leo had left the dead man, destroying the building and all evidence of murder. Then Saltzman had silenced the bartender who had seen Leo with Tony, serving them before they had returned to Tony's flat. When Levitt eventually arrived back at Pearl's home, with Leo, he had a story all ready to account for the best man's disappearance and subsequent panic-stricken call. Leo had lost the ring and run away; had gotten drunk and been arrested. Levitt had fixed the police, just as he always fixed everything. As he would keep on doing, because there was no way he would allow trouble to come home and roost on Pearl's doorstep. She had already been through enough in her life; she didn't need any more grief.

Twins . . . Levitt thought again. That was some link. Both getting laid for the first time on the same night. Joseph with Judy, and Leo with some male whore who'd picked him up in a bar. Only Leo went one further: he killed his first lover.

How could Leo have thought that running away with the ring would stop the ceremony? Any ring would do, even the one Levitt had downstairs in his own apartment. The dia-

7

mond ring he had wanted to give Pearl last night as the final, fitting cap to a wonderful day. Levitt had never married because he had been in love with Pearl ever since they were children – since the day she had stood up for him. Twice he had asked her to marry him. The first time, when they were young, she had told him that she was in love with Jake Granitz, another of the neighbourhood boys. The second time was after Jake's death. Then Pearl had answered that it was too soon to think about marrying again. She needed time. Last night, Levitt had thought, would be the perfect occasion to ask her again. He had carried the ring with him, ready to present it to her. Then Leo had called and the moment had passed. But Levitt did not hate Leo for wrecking the day. He understood Leo's quirks, perhaps better than anyone else did.

Pearl finished cleaning up. Levitt thanked her for breakfast and said it was time for him to go to work. Leo slipped on a heavy coat, kissed his mother goodbye, and followed the little man out of the apartment. Through the window, Pearl watched them leave the building together to drive to work on the West-side of Manhattan where, in an office above a taxi company called Jalo Cabs, Levitt controlled a massive bookmaking and numbers operation.

After a few minutes, Pearl returned to the album, leafed through the pages. There was Benny Minsky, standing in for the bride's father, his curly hair now streaked with silver, his face as dark as ever. Minsky and Levitt were the only two of the old gang left. The two survivors of the original four – Benny Minsky, Lou Levitt, Jake Granitz and Moe Caplan, Judy's father, who had died within a few days of Jake himself. Just two left now, Minsky and Levitt who had hated the sight of each other since schooldays. Levitt was dismissive of Minsky, sure he was nothing more than an ignorant ape. Minsky felt that Levitt overrated his own cleverness. Strange, though, they seemed to get along better now than they had ever done, as if being the two survivors – being responsible for their dead partners' families – had quietened the enmity. To a degree, at least. . . .

Looking at the wedding pictures – thinking about what was and what had been – Pearl was engulfed by a sweeping wave

8

of sentimentality. She left the living-room and walked to her bedroom. An old-fashioned oak bureau dominated the room. She opened the bureau's bottom drawer and pulled out another picture album. This one was older, and stuffed full. She started at the front, examining photographs that were discoloured with age. Her father, Joseph Resnick, after whom the older twin was named, and her mother, Sophie, standing in front of the restaurant they ran at the bottom of Second Avenue. Pearl had been born there in November 1905. It had been a wonderful little restaurant, with red-and-white checkered tablecloths, cosy booths, and mouth-watering food. That was where Pearl's love affair with cooking had begun.

Another faded picture, this time of the young Pearl standing next to a taller girl. Pearl blinked back a tear at the sight of ginger-haired Annie Moscowitz. Annie had been dead almost ten years, but when this picture was taken she had been the child whose parents had run the bakery next door to the restaurant owned by Pearl's mother and father.

No, that wasn't quite true. The Moscowitzes might have owned their bakery, but Pearl's parents had really been nothing more than tenants, trying to pay off a usurious loan to a fat pig of a moneylender named Saul Fromberg and his bodyguard, Gus Landau. They were not in the album, but Pearl had no problem picturing the way they sat in one of the booths and conducted business with the unfortunates who had fallen into their web. What swine they were! Even when Pearl's father had died in an accident in the kitchen, Fromberg had not allowed Pearl and her mother to close the restaurant so they could observe the week-long *shivah*. Their friends had stepped in, though.

Annie and her mother had cooked. And the four boys – Jake, Lou Levitt, Moe Caplan, who was then Annie's boyfriend, and Benny Minsky – had waited tables and swept floors.

Pearl looked at another picture. The group as they had been in those days. Poor Benny Minsky. With his tightly curled hair and swarthy complexion, he did look as though he was part Negro. Children at school – those same tormentors who had mocked Levitt's accent – had nicknamed Minsky

9

'Nig'. He had hated the sobriquet, and still reacted violently when anyone referred to the darkness of his skin.

With prohibition, Fromberg and Laundau moved into clubs – speakeasies, where New Yorkers could illegally quench their thirst. Prompted by Levitt – and financed by money from gambling he had organized – the four boys followed a similar course. Pearl perused an interior shot of the Four Aces, their first club, in the huge basement beneath the Resnick restaurant on Second Avenue. A tiny stage, tables jammed together, and a gambling den in the back where Levitt, in tuxedo and bow-tie, ran his empire of figures and odds. Pearl smiled as she imagined herself and Annie in the club, little girls in long dresses. And the boys – Lou, the youngest by two years, Benny, Jake and Moe – all in tuxes. They had all looked so young they could have been masquerading at a fancy-dress party. Instead, they had been on their way to fortunes.

Pearl's gaze moved to the edge of the picture, to the blonde inside the hatcheck booth. Kathleen Monahan, a manicurist with a husky voice, to whom Benny Minsky had taken a shine. He had claimed he could get her a singing spot at the club, as long as she shared his bed. In speech, Kathleen's voice grated; but in song, the deep, vibrant huskiness was nothing short of electrifying. She became a favourite in each of the clubs opened by the boys, and from there she moved to Broadway, playing the lead in a hit show called *Broadway Nell*. By then, the four partners had also moved on to greater things. Levitt's drive had led him to Scotland where he had made deals for good off-the-boat Scotch, to be picked up outside American territorial waters and brought ashore by a fleet of speedboats. Cut with good grain alcohol, rebottled, and then distributed to clubs along the entire Eastern seaboard, it had brought in millions.

Pearl studied a photograph of a party at Sardi's to celebrate the opening of *Broadway Nell*. Then another picture. A double wedding. Herself to Jake Granitz, and Annie to Moe Caplan, childhood sweethearts all. They had even taken apartments next to each other on the lower section of Fifth Avenue. Lou Levitt's had been the only bitter face at the wedding, beaten to the girl he loved by

Jake. Still, it had not affected their friendship, or their partnership.

She turned from the wedding picture to a photograph of herself and Annie in Washington Square. Both pregnant, with Pearl two months ahead of her friend. There was joy on their faces, but in Pearl's case the happy expression had hidden doubt and fear. One time she had made a mistake, and she knew it would haunt her for the rest of her life. She and Jake had been trying so hard for a child, then disaster had struck. Jake had been involved in a car crash, and Lou Levitt had come to Pearl's home to break the news. Jake was alive, but badly injured. Levitt had taken Pearl to see him, a mess of bandages and splints and stitches. She had returned home shaken, and begged Levitt not to leave her alone. He had stayed, and he had brought comfort to her the only way he knew: by making love to her.

When Pearl learned she was pregnant, she could not, in her heart of hearts, be sure of the father's identity. Both Jake and Lou had made love to her within hours of each other. Only God knew which man had made her pregnant. Levitt, though, was certain he was the father of the twins. The expert in figures had worked it all out. Pearl told him that if he ever mentioned what had happened, she would kill him. He had assured her he would not, but a coolness developed between them that would last until after Jake's death.

Pearl's great concern had always been that Jake and his friends would overreach themselves. Small, with just a club or two, they were no threat to anyone. But under Levitt's shrewd guidance, they became very big. And when Levitt launched a borough-wide bookmaking and numbers racket, he drew the attention of other sharks, the same sharks who had kept Pearl's parents in penury – Saul Fromberg and Gus Landau. They tried to force their way into a partnership with the four young men. Rebuffed, they sought allies, linking up with a Boston-based Irish bootlegger named Patrick Joseph Rourke. For a fat fee, Rourke sent killers to New York to fight Saul Fromberg's war. They failed. The four partners and their families went into hiding, to the home of Harry Saltzman in New Jersey. In hiding, Lou Levitt mapped out a plan to hit back and get rid of Fromberg and Landau for good.

11

Pearl remembered that time in hiding because of the pressure it had put on them all. Her with the twins; Annie with her daughter, Judy; and Kathleen, now married to Benny Minsky, having to care for their young son, William, in cramped unfamiliar surroundings. That was when Leo had come down with diphtheria. Hospitalization was impossible. Once they showed their faces outside the security of the safe house, Fromberg's hired killers would track them down. A doctor, kidnapped from his office and brought blindfolded to the house, had supplied medicine and Pearl had cared for the sick child herself.

After Fromberg's murder by fake tax inspectors coached by Levitt, and Landau's disappearance, the fugitives returned to their own homes. While Pearl took Leo for proper medical treatment, Jake organized a revenge raid on Patrick Joseph Rourke in Massachussetts, who had sided with Fromberg. The idea was to hijack a convoy of whisky and make the Irishman pay through his pocket. The raid went terribly wrong. Twelve of Rourke's men were massacred. Pearl remembered her shock at being told, the terrible fear that she and her family would never be free of this mantle of violence.

A further chapter was written just days later when Gus Landau tried to avenge his former partner's death by killing Jake and Lou outside the restaurant owned by Sophie Resnick. Opening fire from across the street with a machine-gun, he missed both. Instead, he killed Pearl's mother. Before he could be caught, he disappeared once more. . . .

Pearl remembered that she, more than anyone, had been grateful when Prohibition had been repealed. Jake and his three partners could go legitimate now, or so she hoped. But Lou Levitt, who continued to make the major decisions, had other ideas. A legitimate front, yes, but Levitt wanted the edge that crime gave. Behind respectable businesses, the four men continued their illegal gambling enterprise. The nerve centre was above a taxi company called Jalo Cabs, jointly owned by Jake and Lou and taking its name from theirs. Benny Minsky had gone into trucking, refurbishing the vehicles that had once carried bootleg liquor. Moe Caplan had hidden himself behind a construction company. Convincing respectable fronts were put together with Lou Levitt's uncanny skill.

In 1940, as war engulfed Europe, Pearl's twin sons prepared for their *bar mitzvahs*. Benny Minsky's son, William, baptized into Kathleen's Catholic faith, was eleven. When he heard about the Granitz twins preparing for their *bar mitzvahs*, Minsky started to show signs of yearning for the heritage he had casually tossed away in his pursuit of Kathleen.

Pearl recalled seeing the nasty side of Levitt then. Little Lou Levitt, the only one of the four men who had ever placed any importance on being Jewish. It was he who had stressed to Pearl and Jake that the twins should be *bar mitzvah*ed. Levitt had said it was because of what was taking place in Europe, but Pearl suspected the truth was that Levitt thought of Joseph and Leo as his sons, and he wanted them brought up properly. When Levitt heard that Benny Minsky was asking about the possibility of having his son – his baptized son – *bar mitzvah*ed, he sneered, poked fun at the dark-skinned man for this sudden change of heart.

Sorry for Minsky, and angry with Levitt, Pearl had taken Minsky's side. With Kathleen away on the West Coast, making a film version of her big hit *Broadway Nell*, Pearl invited Minsky and his son over to her home for Friday-night dinner, with candles and wine and all the trimmings. On Saturday morning, Minsky took his son to a reform synagogue to get a feel for Judaism. When Kathleen returned unexpectedly to learn that Minsky was trying to make her Catholic son into a Jew, she flew into a rage. An awful fight ensued. Minsky finished by beating up Kathleen and throwing her out of the apartment. She returned to the West Coast to live with a film producer and never came back. Left alone to raise the boy himself, Minsky had done a fine job. Pearl remembered William's *bar mitzvah* – Minsky had every reason to be proud.

There were no photographs in the album of the twins' *bar mitzvahs*. No pictures of them giving speeches, dancing with their mother at the party. There had been no party, because celebration had turned to tragedy. Outside the synagogue, waiting in a car, was the man who had escaped the partners twice before: Gus Landau. He used a sawn-off shotgun on Jake, blowing the father of the *bar-mitzvah* boys to pieces in front of their eyes, before driving away.

There was some consolation, Pearl reflected, in the fact that he had not escaped for long. They had caught up with him a couple of days later, hiding in a condemned apartment building in the Bronx. But in death, Landau caused even more grief by taking Moe Caplan with him. Lou Levitt and Benny Minsky, the survivors – the two men who had always hated each other – came to Pearl, herself in mourning, to ask her to tell Annie. They were not brave enough. When Annie learned the only man she had ever loved was dead, she killed herself. She failed to take her daughter, Judy, with her only because Joseph performed a heroic rescue, climbing along a narrow window ledge to break into the apartment and turn off the gas before Judy too was overcome.

And that, Pearl thought, was when Lou Levitt really took over her life. He moved her, the twins and Judy into an apartment on Central Park West, directly above his own home. He became a father to the boys in everything but name, the father he had always believed himself to be. Guiding them. Advising them. When Leo left high school he went to work in the gambling business, starting as a runner on the streets, taking over bookmaking territory. Joseph, on completing college, went to work in the main office, using the education Levitt insisted he get. Even the honeymoon Joseph and Judy were taking had been carefully planned by Levitt as part of Joseph's further education. Levitt wanted him to see how money was taken out of the country, deposited abroad to avoid American taxes and awkward questions about its origin. When Joseph and Judy reached the airport for their flight later that day, a brief case with one hundred and fifty thousand dollars would be waiting.

Closing the album with all its memories, good and bad, Pearl continued looking through the bottom drawer of the bureau. Her hands closed around a heavy walnut presentation box. She lifted it from the drawer and set it on the bed. Opening it, she saw a card covered with scrawled handwriting: 'If you've got to protect yourself, protect yourself with style.' Beneath the card, resting on velvet, were a

14

matching pair of ivory-handled revolvers. The guns had been a twenty-fifth birthday gift to Jake from Benny Minsky. Even now Pearl could hear Jake saying: 'Will you look what that lunatic's given to me? Everyone else gives me a tie or a pair of cuff-links, and he brings me these.' But Jake had liked Benny all the same. Even his frequent irrational actions had not turned Jake away from him.

Pearl looked at the guns but did not pick them up. She hated the feel of the weapons. The only time she had ever handled one was during her mourning period for Jake. Late one night, she had hit the bottom of the pit. Then she had come to this bureau, removed a revolver and held it to her head. Squeezing the trigger, she had wondered just how much pressure was needed to end it all. The bang that echoed through the apartment was not the gun firing but the hammering of fists on the front door. It was Benny Minsky and Lou Levitt with their news about Gus Landau and Moe Caplan. They had saved her life so she could be the one to tell Annie that Moe was dead.

Sighing, Pearl replaced the presentation box in the bottom of the drawer, and vowed that one day she would get someone – Lou, of course, who else would know how to accomplish such things? – to throw the guns away.

BOOK 1

Chapter One

Joseph called his mother from the airport before he and Judy caught their flight to Europe.

'Any word on Leo?'

'He came home early this morning. He was arrested by the police for drunken driving. Uncle Lou had to fix it.'

'Why did he run away?'

'Joseph, he lost the ring. He was too embarrassed to come back without it. He's really upset.'

'So am I.' Joseph had not wanted his brother to be best man. He had wanted a guy with whom he worked, Philip Gerson, a worldly young businessman whom Uncle Lou found an excellent front for any illegal enterprise. But Pearl had pressured Joseph into making his twin brother best man, claiming he would feel neglected if Gerson were asked. Joseph had given in, and still there'd been trouble.

He hung up and rejoined Judy, who was sitting in the waiting area. 'Leo got arrested last night for drunken driving. Lost the ring, then went out on a bender.'

'Too bad he didn't drive into a brick wall,' Judy answered, and Joseph did not feel inclined to argue the point. He picked up a newspaper he had bought and leafed through it, barely registering two short stories that were set out side by side. One concerned an explosion caused by a gas leak on Bleecker Street. Fire had gutted both the apartment and a hardware shop beneath it; one charred corpse had been pulled from the ashes, a man identified as twenty-eight-year-old Tony Cervante. The other story was about a knifing in the West Fourth Street subway station. The victim was a John

Blackman, who had been on his way home to Elmhurst after finishing his shift as a bartender.

The flight was called. As they stood up, Judy said, 'What about the briefcase you're expecting from Lou Levitt?'

'Jesus Christ!' Joseph slapped his forehead. He'd forgotten all about it. 'Hold on.' He ran to a pay phone and hastily dialled the number of Jalo Cabs. 'Uncle Lou, the flight's almost ready. Where the hell's that briefcase?'

Levitt's voice was annoyingly calm. 'Relax, will you? I'm not going to let you walk through customs and passport control with it. Just don't worry about it.'

Joseph returned to Judy. 'He said to relax.'

'Then do as he says.'

He tried, and failed. As passengers filed on to the aircraft, Joseph hung back, hoping against hope to see someone with a briefcase calling his name. Judy finally dragged him on to the aircraft, as certain as Joseph that there had been a foul-up in Levitt's scheming. She was not unhappy. It showed the little man was human after all, prone to make mistakes just like anyone else.

Strapped in, they felt the aircraft lumber to its take-off point, pick up speed and climb into the sky. When the seat belts were undone, Judy said with a certain satisfaction: 'Now we'll be able to enjoy our honeymoon without any responsibilities, won't we?'

Joseph was annoyed. Despite Judy's misgivings, he'd wanted to take the briefcase full of money and meet the contacts in Switzerland. He felt that he'd been cheated.

'I bet the messenger ran off with the money,' Judy whispered mischievously.

'Mr Granitz?' The purser stood by Joseph's seat. 'I think you left this in the lounge.'

Joseph looked at the well-worn briefcase the man held, the baggage label with his name. 'Thank you.'

'You're welcome, sir.' Leaving the briefcase with Joseph, the purser walked away.

'Open it,' Judy said.

Placing the case between his feet, Joseph undid the clasp. It was filled with fifties and hundreds, neatly stacked and banded in shallow piles. At the top was a scrap of white paper.

Written in Levitt's tiny hand was the figure 'One hundred and fifty thousand dollars'.

Joseph refused to let the case out of his sight. He and Judy passed through Swiss customs without incident. When they took a taxi for the journey to the Hôtel Savoy Baur en Ville on the Bahnhofstrasse, he pulled the case roughly away from the driver who wanted to put it in the boot with the rest of the baggage. The same happened at the hotel when a porter carried their cases to their room. Joseph was prepared to take no chances whatsoever.

'What if no one contacts us while we're here?' Judy asked. 'We're only supposed to be in Zurich for a couple of days.'

'I know.' Joseph had the itinerary imprinted on his memory. Monte Carlo was the next stop, then Rome, Paris, and finally London. 'Uncle Lou said the case would be delivered, and it was. He said we'd be met, and that's good enough for me.'

Judy pulled back the drapes and looked out of the window at the wide avenue lined by lime trees. 'At least put it in the hotel safe or in one of the banks along this street. I'm sure we passed two dozen or more on the journey here.'

'It's staying with me,' Joseph said stubbornly, and he meant it. When they went out to eat, he carried the case firmly in his right hand. And when they went to bed that night, Joseph wedged a chair beneath the door handle to prevent anyone from breaking in. Between bursts of laughter, Judy told him he was becoming paranoid.

'Are you coming to bed with me,' she asked, 'or are you going to sit up on guard duty all night long?'

'Are you worth a hundred and fifty thousand dollars?'

'You know damned well I am!'

Shoving the briefcase under the bed, Joseph slid beneath the downy quilt with her.

When they went down for breakfast the following morning, they were met at the restaurant entrance by the *maitre d'hôtel*. 'Herr Granitz, I regret that we are unable to give you and your wife a table to yourselves this morning. There has been some confusion in the restaurant seating. Could I prevail upon you to share a table with another charming American couple?'

21

'This is turning out to be some honeymoon,' Judy murmured. 'You're handcuffed to that damned case, and now we've got to share a table. They'll probably be big fat mid-Westerners with rainbow clothes.'

They followed the *maitre d'hôtel*. Halfway across the restaurant, Joseph stopped in shock. Seated at a table for four by the window were Phil Gerson and his girlfriend, Belinda Rivers. Gerson rose as Joseph and Judy approached.

'I bet you're going to be glad to get rid of that case, aren't you?'

'You're our contact?' It all fell into place for Joseph. Gerson had been his friend and mentor, introducing him to Lou Levitt's intricate web of business interests. With his fresh-faced good looks and Harvard education, Gerson had the ability to blend chameleon-like into any setting. Levitt used him where an appearance of the utmost respectability was needed.

'I'm the regular courier,' Gerson answered. 'Sit down, have some breakfast. There's no point in making your first deposit on an empty stomach.'

'What are you doing here?' Judy asked Belinda.

'I'm between shows. Phil thought it would be fun for us both to come, maybe even make up a foursome if you don't mind sharing your honeymoon with a couple of strangers.'

'You're hardly strangers. Have you got a deposit to make as well?' Joseph asked Gerson.

'Twice as big as yours.'

'Where is it?'

'In my room, of course. I'm not as insecure as you are, carrying it with you wherever you go. Did he take it to bed with him last night, Judy?'

'He tried to. I told him that three was a crowd.'

'So I got out and the case stayed,' Joseph added, to laughter.

Belinda turned to Judy. 'Why don't you and I go shopping while they do their banking business? You can buy some marvellous things here.'

Judy looked at Joseph. He nodded, grateful for Belinda's unexpected presence in Zurich.

Directly after breakfast, Judy and Belinda went shopping

along the Bahnhofstrasse. Joseph and Gerson, each carrying a case, walked in the opposite direction until they reached a building with an imposing black marble entrance. Written in raised gold letters was the single name: Leinberg.

'This is it?' Joseph asked, glad to be at journey's end with the briefcase. He took a step towards the entrance. Gerson pulled him back.

'Not so fast. We use Leinberg's back entrance.' He guided Joseph past the building to a narrow street. Halfway along was a heavy wooden door, very mundane in comparison with the main entrance. Gerson rang a bell. The door opened and the two men stepped inside. Joseph found himself in a narrow corridor. Utterly lost, he followed Gerson to a lift which took them to the third floor. They emerged into an office area. A woman sitting behind a desk smiled at them.

'Herr Leinberg is expecting you, Herr Gerson.'

'Thank you.'

The woman knocked once on a heavy oak door, then swung it back to reveal what looked to Joseph like a company boardroom. A wide oak table ran down the length of the room. Six chairs were placed on either side of it. Only the chair at the very top was occupied, by a tall, grey-haired man wearing thick horn-rimmed glasses, a morning coat and grey-striped trousers. The man rose as Joseph and Gerson entered.

'Joseph, meet Walter Leinberg, the president of Leinberg Bank.'

'How do you do, sir.'

Leinberg accepted Joseph's handshake. 'Is this a social call, or do you have a deposit for Blackhawk?'

'Blackhawk?' Joseph looked to Gerson for an explanation.

'That's the code name for the account your godfather and Benny Minsky share.'

Once, Joseph thought, it would have been his father, Jake, and Judy's father, Moe Caplan, as well if they hadn't been wiped out so cruelly. In a way, he and Judy were restoring the balance of the partnership, keeping the family alliances alive.

Phil continued, 'The Swiss might be the most discreet people in the world where money's concerned. Even so, it's asking for trouble to open the account in your real name.' He hoisted a small suitcase on to the polished oak table. 'There's three hundred and fifty thousand dollars here, and another hundred and fifty thousand in my friend's briefcase.'

Leinberg pressed a buzzer. Inside a minute, two men entered the boardroom. They were dressed identically to Leinberg in black jackets, stiff-collared shirts and striped trousers. Without a word, they sat down at the table, divided the money between them and began to count with a speed that made even Lou Levitt's book-keepers seem arthritic. The total came to exactly half a million dollars.

'Correct as usual,' Leinberg said, with a thin smile.

'My employer doesn't make mistakes,' Gerson answered. 'Not when it comes to money anyway. Let's go,' he said to Joseph. 'Our business here is finished.'

Before Joseph knew what was happening, he was back in the lift. 'Don't you get a receipt?'

'We don't need one. Lou Levitt and Walter Leinberg know exactly what's been deposited.'

'How do you keep track of interest payments and everything else?'

'A statement for the Blackhawk account is prepared every month. Sometimes I bring it back with me, at other times it's mailed in a plain envelope to a post-office box your godfather keeps under a false name. The statement's just a list of figures, no identifying words on it. But Lou Levitt knows exactly what it means.' They reached the narrow street that ran along the side of the bank. 'Let's go and have a cup of coffee while the girls finish their shopping,' Gerson suggested. 'Then I'll put you right in the picture like I was asked by your godfather.'

Over coffee, Gerson related the history of Lou Levitt's ties with Walter Leinberg. They stemmed from Gerson's own family's investment business. Gerson's father had dealt with Leinberg Bank, salting money away in Switzerland against any eventuality of his own business going bankrupt. When it had done so in 1935, there was more than enough set aside to keep the family living comfortably. 'That included seeing me through Harvard Business School. When I graduated and went to work for Lou Levitt, I saw this fortune in gambling profits. Your godfather couldn't afford to show it, not unless he wanted the revenue people and the police after him. He

24

had to get rid of it. Walter Leinberg's late father was president of the bank then, he was the founder. My own father went to see him, set up the courier deal. When my father died, I took it over. Except for the war, of course, it's been a regular trip.'

'Don't all those stamps in your passport raise any suspicion?'

'Frequent trans-Atlantic crossings? No. When we leave here, I'll show you why not.'

From the restaurant they took a taxi to the outskirts of Zurich. Their journey ended in front of a drab two-storey factory. 'This is A.G. Kriesel,' Gerson explained, 'an engineering company owned by Lou Levitt and Benny Minsky. It's never made a nickel. That's why I, as vice-president, keep coming over here, to shake it up. Want to go inside and look around?'

'Not particularly.' Joseph had no interest in engineering companies. He was more concerned with the business that the company fronted for. 'How much is in the account now?'

Gerson smiled in anticipation. 'Around thirty million dollars.'

Leo whistled in surprise. 'You trust Leinberg with that kind of money?'

'As much as I trust anyone. Leinberg's a shrewd bastard. Before the war he took money from Jews who could get it out of Germany. And during the war, he did the same service for Nazi bigwigs who could see what the end would be. Leinberg probably pays half the bills in Buenos Aires.'

'Can anyone put money into Blackhawk?'

'Absolutely anyone. But only two signatures can get it out. One's your godfather's. The other belongs to Benny Minsky. I imagine that one day in the not too distant future your signature, your brother's and William Minsky's will perform the same miracle.'

Thirty million dollars. The sum was staggering. 'Has any been taken out?'

'Little sums so far, small investments in the States. But your godfather's got his eye on a big scheme soon, down in Florida. He wants to build a couple of hotels down there, real fancy places, and run casinos from them.'

'Why not Las Vegas where it's legal?'

'Too much competition there already. Don't you know Lou Levitt well enough by now? He likes that little extra edge. Anyone can build a casino in Vegas, but only a really sharp cookie can do it in Florida where it's illegal. Besides, if you were a high roller, where would you rather play? In the middle of some desert, or in a sub-tropical paradise?'

Joseph considered the information. He had little doubt that Levitt had instructed Gerson to impart it. Was that where he was meant to go? Take Judy with him to Florida to oversee the building of the hotels? Spread money around to police and politicians so the gambling could continue unhindered, creating even more money to be smuggled out of the country to Switzerland where it would rest in Walter Leinberg's vaults, side by side with the illegal funds of fugitive Nazis?

Phil Gerson and Belinda Rivers accompanied Joseph and Judy from Zurich to Monte Carlo, staying in adjoining rooms at the Hôtel de Paris. When they entered the casino on their first evening there, Gerson tugged at Joseph's arm. 'Before you go in, get a feel of this place. This is what Lou Levitt's thinking about for down in Florida. None of the meat-market approach that they use in Vegas. He wants a real classy place with dress rules – '

'I can't see everyone wearing a tuxedo in Florida.'

'Not necessarily a tux. But dressed properly, not in those strident plaid sports jackets and clashing striped trousers you see the suckers wearing in Vegas. He wants a place that reeks of class. And when they eventually legalize gambling in Florida – at least, in South Florida – we'll have a head start.'

'Will they ever make it legal? Remember it's the South.'

Gerson chuckled. 'South Florida's different, Joseph. Dade, Broward and Palm Beach Counties . . . to get to the real redneck South from there, you've got to go north.'

Gerson and Belinda Rivers stopped by a roulette table to play. Joseph and Judy watched for a while before moving away. Neither had any desire to gamble. To do so would be too much like a working vacation.

'Did you know Phil's married?' Judy asked out of the blue.

'Who told you that?'

'Belinda, while we were out shopping.' Judy gave a triumphant smile; she'd known something he had not. 'I asked her how long she and Phil had been seeing each other. When she said three years, I asked why they didn't marry.'

'Nosy, aren't you? You're lucky she didn't tell you to mind your own business.'

'I think she was looking for someone to talk to. Phil's got two daughters. They live with his wife in Riverdale. Estranged wife, I should say. He gets to see them once or twice a week.'

'Why don't they get a divorce?'

'She won't give him one. He's left her, he's playing around with Belinda, so he has no grounds to sue for a divorce. Plus, his wife's told him, apparently, that if he ever pushed for one, she'd make damned sure he never saw the girls again.'

'Sounds like a real shrew.'

'You may be right. So in the meantime Belinda lives with Phil, goes everywhere with him between her singing engagements and is his wife in everything but name.'

Joseph slipped his arm around Judy's waist. 'And there was I, getting jealous of him because I thought he was a happy-go-lucky bachelor. Proves how wrong you can be, doesn't it?'

'Sure does. Let's go back and see how they're doing.'

They returned to the roulette table. Gerson had a huge pile of chips in front of him. When he saw Judy and Joseph, he gave them a beseeching look. 'I'm the equivalent of five thousand dollars ahead. Belinda wants to risk the whole lot on one number. Tell her she's nuts from me, will you?'

'Isn't there a house limit?' Joseph asked.

'They'll lift it for one bet. They only use it to stop people doubling up until they win.'

'It's seven,' Belinda said. 'My birthday. Seven, seven . . . the seventh of July. I just know it's going to come up!'

'With a number like that, you should be shooting dice instead,' Joseph remarked.

Belinda stroked Gerson's cheek. 'Come on, honey. Your five thousand multiplied by the house's thirty-five to one odds. Please. . . .'

Joseph saw Judy give him an almost imperceptible nod.

27

Neither of them had the slightest doubt that Gerson would accede to Belinda's wishes.

He let out a resigned sigh. 'All right, but God help you if you're wrong.' He shoved the pile of chips into the centre of the table. '*Sept, s'il vous plaît.*' When the bet was acknowledged, he winked at Joseph and Judy. 'I know just enough French to play the tables and order food in a restaurant. But when you're on vacation, what else do you need?'

The wheel spun. The ball dropped and rattled around the numbered slots. At last it lay still. '*Vingt-trois rouge,*' intoned the croupier. Gerson's pile of chips was raked in with the other losing bets.

'Sorry, baby,' Belinda whispered.

Gerson tried to look angry, but the scowl changed to a big, happy grin. 'Ah, what the hell! Easy come, easy go, eh?' Turning from the table, he hugged her. 'How about we find somewhere to dance?'

'Around her little finger,' Judy whispered as she followed with Joseph. 'Manipulate him any which way she wants to.'

'Are you jealous? Is that how you want me to be?'

'I'd shoot you if you lost money like that. Even if it wasn't yours to begin with.'

Joseph laughed. 'You wouldn't have to. I'd blow my own brains out first.'

Instead of writing to Pearl, Joseph telephoned her from the room that evening. He told her that Gerson and his girlfriend were with them, talked about the weather, the food. Pearl listened before changing the topic to Leo.

'He's really upset over what happened with the wedding, Joseph. He's been very quiet, very subdued. I can hardly get a word out of him.'

Joseph was in a generous mood. He and Judy were enjoying themselves too much to feel any other way. 'Tell him we forgive him, Ma. He made a mistake. If he's genuinely sorry, that's okay.'

'You mean that? I think it's important to him.'

'We mean it, Ma.' When he'd finished the call, he told Judy. 'I said to Ma that we both forgive Leo.'

'Only on one condition.' Sitting on the bed, Judy patted the

28

space next to her. When Joseph sat down she held him tightly.

'What . . .' he kissed her '. . . is that?'

'That if we – ' the words were cut off as Joseph kissed her a second time – 'ever decide to get married again – ' another kiss – 'Leo won't be asked to be best man.'

In that instant, Judy realized just how happy Joseph had made her. If she could joke about Leo, she could forgive anyone for anything.

Chapter Two

Lou Levitt's plan for organizing gambling on a luxurious basis in South Florida received a setback before it even got off the ground. While the money to be used to finance the venture continued to gather interest in Zurich, a senator named Estes Kefauver rose to national prominence. Levitt forced himself to wait patiently while Kefauver's anti-organized crime circus paraded around the country. He knew that the public would eventually tire of the constant hearings and exposures. When they did, he would be ready to move.

It wasn't until January 1953, after the election of the Eisenhower Administration, that the move was finally made. A corporation was formed. Its name was the Palmetto Leisure Development Corporation, and its expressed intention was to build hotels. Listed as chairman and chief operating officer of Palmetto was Philip Gerson. He travelled south to Florida to inspect sites for the hotels the corporation would erect. He found two that he liked. The first was in Hollywood. The second, a mile further south, was in Hallandale. Both sites could be approached by either land or water. That was essential. The big gamblers Gerson envisaged patronizing the casinos that would operate from the hotels were just as likely to arrive by luxury yacht as by Lincoln. Armed with a seemingly inexhaustible grease account, Gerson approached law enforcement officials and politicians at local, county and state level; all recently elected to office, they would be in power for a long time.

Within three weeks of travelling down south Gerson returned to New York excited by the prospects. There would, he reported to Levitt, be no foreseeable problem in either the construction of the hotels or the running of casinos from them. Levitt listened approvingly. The move to Florida was a giant step away from the environs of New York where the business had been conceived, born and nurtured. Gerson's success with the local authorities proved that the same tactics that worked in New York worked in Florida as well. Levitt had harboured little doubt that they would. Every man had his price, whether he was a slick New York politician or a redneck councilman. It was just a matter of finding that price, and deciding if it was worth paying.

'Phil, get together some ideas for – ' Levitt looked at the wall calendar – 'Friday.'

'That's only three days.'

'It's long enough to jot some thoughts down. We'll have a general meeting on it then. I think it's about time that the next generation took a more active role in the running of this enterprise. I want to hear their opinions as well.' Levitt had been musing on such a move for a while. The twins were now twenty-five. Minsky's son, William, was two years younger. It was time for them to shoulder their share of the responsibility. They had all been carried for long enough.

The meeting was held at five o'clock in Levitt's office. He sat at his desk, a large-scale map of Broward County spread out in front of him. The twins, Benny and William Minsky, and Phil Gerson sat crowded around the desk on chairs that had been brought in from the main room.

'Phil, the floor's yours,' Levitt said. 'Go ahead.'

The chairman and chief operating officer of Palmetto Leisure Development Corporation circled two places on the map, both along Highway A1A, the coastal road running north and south between the Atlantic Ocean and the Intracoastal Waterway. 'Two hotels, that's what we're going to build down there. The Monaco in Hollywood, and the Waterway in Hallandale. These are quickly commissioned artist's sketches, just to give you a rough idea of what I'm talking about.' He passed out sheets of paper to the men around the table. Levitt, who had already seen the sketches, glanced at his disinterestedly.

31

While the others studied the drawings, Gerson read out specifications. 'The hotels are going to be similar. Luxury hotels, each one six storeys, about three hundred rooms. We'll be booking great shows, providing superb restaurants with top chefs hired from Europe, a ballroom, even conference facilities. And on the top floor of each hotel, reached by a restricted access lift service, will be the casino.'

Benny Minsky looked sceptical. 'How much are these hotels going to cost?'

'For land, construction, building materials . . . somewhere between four and eight million dollars apiece.'

'Somewhere between?' Minsky's eyes had narrowed but the question came from Joseph. 'That's a hell of a spread. Why can't we get a better handle on the price?'

Levitt jumped in immediately. 'We're still groping in the dark. We haven't made an offer on the land yet, we haven't contacted builders, we haven't gone into anything. What Phil's giving is a ball-park figure, the low and the possible high.' Levitt was pleased at Joseph's instant question. The older twin was thinking along the right lines, worried about price, the lack of firm information. But then Levitt had never doubted he would react in any other way.

For the past eighteen months, Levitt had given Joseph complete control over the book-keepers who managed the financial side of the gambling empire. Simultaneously, he had appointed Leo to be in charge of the messengers who picked up and delivered the bets and the money. Both young men had slotted right into their new positions. Joseph was as sharp in his work as Levitt had ever been, constantly checking that every single cent was accounted for. Leo, Levitt was glad to see, was just as conscientious. He was regularly out on the street, watching the messengers, ensuring that all payments to the police were being made. Between them they ran the operation very smoothly. But the young, despite their admirable ambition and drive, needed an older hand – his hand, he thought grimly – to guide them.

At fifty, thoughts of retirement were far from Levitt's mind. The business might have begun as a partnership between the four original members but Levitt knew that it was his brains, his vision and sheer lowdown cunning that had made all their fortunes. He wasn't through yet – not by a long way – but he was nothing if not a realist. More than thirty years of feuding, fighting and violent death among enemies and associates alike had taught him that if a business were to survive and prosper one strong man must assume control of it. While he lived, Levitt would be that man but if, God forbid, he was taken before his time, which of the Granitz twins – *his* twins – would be best suited to succeed him?

Levitt sat back in his chair, his face inscrutable, and watched how each of them in turn handled himself. To the third youngster at the table, Minsky's son William, he gave no thought at all. So far as Levitt was concerned, when the brains were handed out Minsky had been shortchanged. He wouldn't even consider his boy as a possible head of the business.

Gerson continued with his presentation. 'These places are going to be something special. Every penny they cost will come back tenfold from the high rollers we'll get in there. I'm talking about the finest materials: marble floors from Italy, exquisite art on the walls – '

'Never mind all the fancy trimmings,' William Minsky broke in. 'What kind of a payback period are you talking about?'

If Levitt was surprised by the astuteness of the question coming from a Minsky he gave no sign of it. William, after all, had a footing in the business world.

In this evaluation, however, Levitt had for once underestimated his man. Straight from high school William had gone to work for his father at B. M. Transportation. For two years he had worked on the trucks, loading and unloading the merchandise that Minsky's fleet carried for Garment Centre companies. Now, at twenty-three, he was looking at the business with a wider vision. He understood that B. M. Transportation was just a respectable front, a façade that carried on its books men whose real work was in gambling. But that was no reason, he stressed to his father, for the firm not to expand into other areas. B. M. Transportation should stand independently, be a highly profitable concern on its own. Minsky had given the boy his head.

William had contacted furniture and appliance manufacturers, worked out terms to get their custom. Soon, he intended to negotiate for new premises, wanting to move the company out of Manhattan to a much larger – and cheaper – depot in Long Island City.

Levitt concurred wholeheartedly with the proposed expansion. The bigger B. M. Transportation became, the more men it could carry. He tried to remember Benny Minsky at twenty-three: a swarthy, short-tempered lunatic who loved women and danger. His son did not take after him, that was for damned sure. William, with his *Goyishe* good looks – his fair skin and light brown hair – enjoyed working as much as his father had liked to hang around the cloakroom of the Four Aces and make eyes at Kathleen.

'We haven't had adequate time to work out a payback period yet,' Gerson said in answer to William's question.

Before he could say more, Leo hit him with another. 'These high rollers you keep talking about – where are they going to come from? Are you going to advertise in the *New York Times* what you're up to?'

'Word of mouth.' Gerson looked to Levitt for help. Levitt had thrown him to the wolves, made him face a barrage of questions without enough time for complete preparation.

'If Phil's going to be tied up in Florida,' Joseph said, 'who's going to make the Zurich runs?'

'You will,' Levitt answered instantly. 'You know the route, you know Leinberg. Phil can resign his fake position with A.G. Kriesel and you can succeed him. That'll give you reasons for travelling there.'

'When will we have more concrete figures on these hotels?' Minsky asked as he checked the sketches again. 'The Monaco and the Waterway?' He was concerned about the vast sums of money that Gerson had so casually mentioned. They'd worked damned hard for all that money, earned it when Gerson was still a snot-nosed kid in his diapers. Minsky had never shared the faith in Gerson that Levitt had. The guy had been born into wealth; he couldn't possibly appreciate it like a man who'd worked and bled for it.

'When I've had time to look into it more,' Gerson answered. 'I only got back from Florida three days ago. I looked at sites, I cleared the way with the local bigwigs – '

'Okay, Phil, relax,' Levitt told him. He turned to the others. 'This thing'll get us out of New York, give us a whole new perspective. Phil's keen on it and he's the man we need up front. It'll mean his moving down there to supervise construction and run the hotels. What we have to do now is vote on whether we withdraw some of our money from Leinberg in Zurich to finance this thing. What Phil's spent already – the incorporation of Palmetto Leisure Development, the grease – is peanuts. From now on, we start getting into the big bucks.'

'Lou, how come William and the twins are here?' Minsky asked. Usually, a vote was just him and Levitt.

'I was wondering when someone would ask that,' Levitt answered with a smile. 'I think it's about time they stopped being our employees and became our partners instead. Don't you?'

Minsky wasn't certain. It meant that Levitt, with the twins, would gain two votes to Minsky's one.

After the meeting was over, Levitt and the twins drove to Pearl's apartment on Central Park West for dinner. Judy was already there, having come straight from her job at the dress firm where she had been employed since leaving school. During the three years since her marriage, she had risen several rungs. In the kitchen, where Pearl worked with a busy cheerfulness, small plates of chopped liver were set out on a counter, a saucepan of chicken soup bubbled merrily on the range, while in the oven a chicken was in the final stages of being roasted. The entire apartment smelled of Friday night.

This was the night of the week that Pearl looked forward to the most, when her entire family was together for dinner in her home. Just like it used to be. Since Joseph's wedding three years earlier, the apartment had seemed empty, the family no longer a strong, single unit. Although her son and daughter-in-law lived just across Central Park, Pearl often felt as though a high wall had been erected. Judy offered a dinner invitation at least once a week, but Pearl always went by herself. Leo never accompanied her. He refused to step inside Judy's home; he had as little to do with her as possible. Even when Judy and Joseph came to Central Park West on a Friday night Leo would stay just long enough to eat dinner before disappearing for the evening, to return long after

35

everyone had gone. He only stayed for dinner, Pearl knew, for her sake. In his odd manner of rationalization, he still blamed Judy for breaking up the family. Both Judy and Joseph had seemingly forgiven – if not forgotten – his peculiar behaviour at their wedding. Only Leo could not pardon so easily. Pearl guessed that he even held Judy responsible for the one time his mother had hit him.

That Leo went out at all was a consolation for Pearl. She had always worried that he spent too much time at home, especially after the wedding when he had barely ventured out. Gradually, though, he had become more outgoing, more sociable. He told Pearl that he had joined clubs, made friends with whom to spend his leisure hours. Pearl sensed that working for Levitt had helped. He had given the younger twin responsibility and trust, and Leo's confidence had bloomed. Deep down, Pearl hoped that he was seeing a girl. That was what Leo needed, a nice girl who would show him the love and kindness she had always given to him. Love and kindness . . . they were the best ways to make him respond positively.

When darkness fell, Pearl lit the Sabbath candles and made the blessing. Levitt, sitting at the head of the table, poured wine into silver goblets, broke a slice of freshly baked bread and passed the pieces around. As Pearl served the hors d'oeuvre of chopped liver, Levitt said: 'You should be proud of your sons, Pearl. Today they became equal partners in the business.'

'Oh?' She looked at Joseph and Leo.

Levitt started to talk about Palmetto Leisure Development Corporation. 'We're moving into a totally new area, a new direction. Big respectable hotels.'

Pearl disagreed. 'Lou, it's the same area, the same direction. It's still gambling. Only instead of having everything tied up in small shops and restaurants, it'll be in some fancy hotels. What happens,' she asked, 'when they have the next elections down there? When the officials Phil Gerson bribes are voted out of office?'

Levitt smiled. 'By the time that happens, we'll be so strong that we'll finance the campaign of candidates who'll know how to pay us back once they're in office. If we play our cards right, we can wind up owning all of Broward County.'

'Indeed? And what about when the next Estes Kefauver turns up?'

Levitt dismissed the Senator with a wave of the hand. 'We won't get touched because we're not involved in inter-state crime like those characters who were called up by Kefauver. We're strictly gambling, and we keep our noses clean.'

The moment dinner was finished Leo stood up. He went to his bedroom, returning ten minutes later after having changed into a fresh suit and shirt. 'I'm going out,' he said to his mother. 'I'll be home late.'

Joseph ran his eyes over his twin. 'What's her name?'

Leo's face froze. 'What's it to you?'

'Come on, Leo, you can tell us,' Pearl said. Tonight she had allies, she could press the younger twin on his social life. 'Two or three nights a week you're out. She must be someone very special.' If everyone at the table cajoled him, Leo might finally admit something.

'Leave the boy alone,' Levitt said sharply. 'If he doesn't want to share his girl with the rest of us, he doesn't have to. Go on, Leo, go out and enjoy yourself.'

Leo kissed his mother on the cheek, took a coat from the hall closet and went downstairs to his car. As he drove south, he felt a spontaneous burst of warmth for Levitt. The little man had assumed the role of father in Leo's life. He had shown Leo trust by giving him responsibility in the firm; he'd shown reliability by extricating him from that situation on Bleecker Street and destroying any incriminating evidence. Most importantly, Levitt had shown him love. The love of a man, which Leo could understand and appreciate.

After Bleecker Street, Leo had been terrified to leave his mother's apartment in the morning in case he should be drawn to another bar, meet another man like Tony. Every time he closed his eyes he could see Tony's face in front of him, turning red as he applied the pressure to his throat, the tongue rolling around the corners of his mouth. He remem-bered the fear that had followed, while he'd waited in the car for Levitt to come and save him. No one else but Levitt would have come that night. No one else could have arranged every-thing so neatly. Uncle Lou, Leo believed, loved him as much

37

as his mother did, had always understood and forgiven him right from when he was a kid.

Who but Levitt, for instance, would have had the brains to work out what really happened to the puppy he had given the twins, and the wisdom to say nothing after finding its battered body shoved head first into the garbage can where Leo had left it? He had made a mistake in listening to Joseph's pleas and giving the twins a puppy Leo did not want. But, having acted in error, he abided by the consequences, covering up for Leo when the truth would have caused a painful rift from his brother.

He needn't have done any of it. He needn't have stood up for Leo as he had done only this evening when his mother and brother had questioned his comings and goings. Levitt must know the truth, Leo decided; the little man had to be aware that the incident with Tony was not just a solitary experience. But he loved Leo enough to protect him. Or was it that Levitt loved Pearl too much to allow her to know? Leo remembered his godfather's exhortation never to let Pearl learn the truth. That was it. Levitt loved not only Leo but Pearl as well.

Slowly Leo's fear had passed until he was left with only the memory of the pleasure, the release, that Tony had offered him that night. He even forgot the feeling of betrayal when Tony had asked for money. Love, like anything else, was a commodity. Sometimes it had to be bought.

Leo parked his car near Washington Square. It excited him now to return to the Village, walk past the bar on Sixth Avenue where he had met Tony, wander along Bleecker Street and see the repair work that had been done on the hardware shop and the apartment above it. In that moment, Leo had held life in his hands, just like when he had swung the German Shepherd puppy on its leash against the wall. He had held life in his hands and extinguished it, like Harry Saltzman had done with the bartender. It made Leo part of an elite society: those who had taken life. The events on Bleecker Street gained a new perspective. It was the night Leo had become a man. He had made love like a man, and he had killed like a man.

This time, however, he did not walk past the bar on Sixth Avenue or the building on Bleecker Street. Instead, he

38

entered a four-storey block of apartments on MacDougal Street, climbed to the top floor and let himself in. The apartment was fully furnished with an accent on antique pieces. Leo liked antiques; they gave him a sense of permanence.

After hanging up his coat, he turned the radio to a classical station. Humming along contentedly to a Chopin Polonaise, he sat down to wait.

In the summer of 1953, Phil Gerson was transferred south to Hallandale, living in a luxurious rented house on the Intracoastal with Belinda Rivers who had given up her stage career to accompany him. With Gerson went twelve million dollars that had been withdrawn from the Leinberg Bank in Zurich, the final estimate he'd come up with for the construction and furnishing of the Monaco and Waterway hotels. He had completion dates from the builders of February for the Monaco, and the following August for the Waterway. Within a week of each completion Gerson expected to have the casinos working, the money flow across the Atlantic reversed.

Gerson revelled in his role as head of the Palmetto Leisure Development Corporation. This was what a Harvard degree entitled him to, not book-keeping for a gambling czar or shuttling across the Atlantic with cases of contraband money. Not that those days hadn't served their purpose. They'd added to Gerson's education, provided a learning experience that was beyond the scope of any university. Although Gerson understood that the real power of the corporation lay with its two hidden partners – Levitt and Minsky – it did not stop him from enjoying the respect his new title merited.

When the foundations for the Monaco were laid in Hollywood, Gerson celebrated with a party at his rented house. He invited the builders, local dignitaries, and his New York backers. Belinda acted as the gracious hostess, only too pleased to show the guests around the large house she'd had redecorated, the fifty-foot yacht that was moored to the dock in the back. 'It comes with the house,' she told everyone. 'That's why we rented this place, because it had such a big boat as part of the deal. Phil doesn't know how to drive it yet, but he's learning.'

'Sail it,' a member of the mayor's office corrected her. 'You sail a boat, you don't drive it.'

'Whatever.' The easy reprimand didn't bother her; she was having too much of a good time to worry about it. 'Who cares just as long as it goes in the right direction and doesn't sink?'

Gerson introduced Levitt and Minsky to members of the country commission, high-ranking officers in the sheriff's department and the local police force. The two New York partners smiled and shook hands automatically, made small talk. The moment they were alone with Gerson, though, Minsky's attitude changed dramatically. He pushed the younger man roughly against the side of a grand piano that Belinda had installed when redecorating the house. 'Are you running some goddamned popularity contest down here, or are you putting together a couple of hotels for us?'

'One goes hand in hand with the other, Benny.'

'When you're playing around with our money, Phil, you get the work done first. How much did this joint set you back? Hell, how much is it going to set *us* back for the year?'

It was a throwback to the Minsky of old, the man who would strike or shoot first, ask questions later. Lou remembered his crazy jealousy over Kathleen, the violent rages in which he had severely injured one rival admirer and murdered another . . . although that was their secret, for as long as it suited Lou.

'Take it easy, Benny,' Levitt hissed. 'There are people here who work with Phil and respect him. Don't make him lose face.'

Minsky released his grip, but not without adding another warning. 'Don't ever forget you're down here to work for us, Phil.'

'The foundations' been laid on schedule, hasn't it?'

'Sure, but that's only the start. Finish the Monaco and the Waterway, and then you can play all you want. You can be the sailor on the big fancy yacht, you can be the famous hotel owner, gladhanding everyone at the door, throwing all the goddamned parties you and Belinda like. But until you've done what you came here to do, you work. Understand?'

On the return flight to New York Minsky was silent. He could see that Gerson was on schedule. The foundations for

40

the Monaco had been laid right on time. It was the wasted money that bothered him, the way Gerson was throwing it around like it was going out of style. Who the hell decorated a rented house so lavishly? Who rented so big a house anyway? Why did Gerson need it, with a boat yet! Gerson shouldn't have the time to learn how to sail. He should be busting his butt every waking hour, accomplishing what he'd been entrusted to do.

'Lou,' he said at last, 'you figure that Rivers broad has got her hooks real deep into Phil?'

Levitt smiled bleakly at Minsky. 'Like Kathleen had hers into you?'

'Forget Kathleen,' Minsky said angrily. 'She never had me blowing our money the way Phil's doing.'

Oh, didn't she? Levitt thought. If Minsky had gotten his way, he'd have spent every cent on which he could lay his hands on Kathleen. His money and everyone else's. Only Levitt had stood in his way.

Still, Minsky's concerns did bear thinking about. 'We took this house,' Levitt recalled Belinda saying, 'because it had such a big boat as part of the deal.' The line stuck in his mind. This wasn't the first time that he had drawn a comparison between Belinda and Kathleen. The situation was similar. A Jewish guy who worked with Levitt being hung up over a blonde *shiksa*. It was almost the same as Minsky and Kathleen, but not quite. The big difference was that Gerson had more brains than Minsky had ever shown. And important connections. Minsky could not have been entrusted with ferrying the money to Switzerland; he'd have found a way to get caught. Besides, the Leinberg Bank was a Gerson family connection to begin with; using Leinberg had been Phil's suggestion. Likewise, Minsky could never have sought out and found the right men to approach and pay off in Florida.

Because Levitt liked the Harvard graduate, respected him, he was more tolerant. Belinda didn't stick in his craw like Kathleen had done. Or was it, he asked himself, that he had grown mellow with the passing of the years? He did not honestly know.

He thought some more about Gerson. Everything about the man was so right. His background. His appearance. His ability to get on with people when it mattered the most. He was the perfect guy to hold up the front end while others worked and schemed at the back. But now Levitt experienced the first nagging worry that perhaps he had made a mistake in trusting Gerson with quite so much.

With Gerson working in Florida, Joseph made the regular courier runs to Switzerland to bank the New York gambling profits. When he was away, Judy was at a total loss. Her job occupied her during the day, but in the evening she felt miserable without him. Since they were children, they had seen each other every day. To be married to him and not see him for three or four days at a time was unbearable. Even if he did come back with his arms loaded with gifts, it was small recompense for the loneliness when he wasn't there.

Before leaving on the first trip Joseph had made Judy promise that she would stay close to Pearl. 'She'll be hurt if you don't eat over there every night,' he'd said. 'You know what Ma's like. She won't understand you wanting to stay home alone to cook for yourself. She'll expect you.'

Judy had promised to go. She was glad that she did, because in Pearl she found a sympathetic ear for her complaints about Joseph's absences.

'You're going through exactly what your mother and I went through,' Pearl told her daughter-in-law. 'Your father and Jake were frequently away for long periods of time, just like Joseph is now. You should just be thankful that his work isn't as dangerous as theirs was.'

Judy smiled. 'Knowing he's sitting on a plane or sitting in some fine hotel – and not guarding a truck full of whisky – doesn't make me any less lonely, Ma.'

'There's a cure for loneliness, young lady.'

'Oh?' Judy wondered what her mother-in-law was going to suggest.

'A baby . . . not a secret boyfriend,' Pearl said with mock disapproval. 'Shame on you, Judy, for even thinking that I could mean such a terrible thing.'

'Are you that desperate to be a grandmother?'

'You and Joseph take your time, darling. You're both in a better position to know when the time's right than I am.' She

42

remembered trying so hard with Jake for children, all those failures until that one eventual success . . . or had it been an immediate success with Lou the one and only time that Pearl, half-crazy with worry, had fallen into his eager arms?

'You're both all right, aren't you?' She asked Judy tentatively. 'You know what I mean . . . physically.'

'We're both fine. When the time comes, you'll be the first to know.'

Despite Pearl's understanding attitude, Judy still had to cope with her brother-in-law during the visits to Central Park West. When Joseph was present he acted as a barrier between Judy and Leo. Joseph had pardoned his twin's behaviour at the wedding. The brothers now got on as though no disagreement had ever taken place. They both held responsible, if different, positions within the business; they were equal. Consequently, in Joseph's presence, Leo acted in a civil if cold manner towards his sister-in-law. When Joseph was away, though, the barriers were down. All of Leo's dislike for Judy simmered just below the surface, ready to break out into open hostility.

If her visit occurred on a night he stayed in he would simply finish dinner and then lock himself in his room. He had a new interest to complement his taste for biographies. He had discovered the melodrama of opera; its intricate love stories and harsh violence appealed to a newfound sense of theatre within him. He had installed a phonograph in his room, and while Pearl and Judy would sometimes watch television after dinner, Leo sat in his bedroom and listened to his records. Occasionally he would venture out to request that the volume of the television be turned down because it was interfering with his listening. Once Judy countered by complaining that his music, played at deafening volume, was drowning out the 'You Bet Your Life' show that she and Pearl were watching.

'If you had any brains, you wouldn't be watching this mindless slop,' he answered back. 'You'd be appreciating something decent instead.'

Mistakenly Judy allowed herself to be drawn into an argument. 'Groucho Marx,' she stated firmly, 'is not mindless slop.'

'No? What would you call him then – an intellectual?'

'He's a damned sight more intellectual than that caterwauling you're listening to.'

'Married to a university man, and she thinks that Groucho Marx and the dumb quiz shows are smart,' Leo sneered before returning to his room.

The times that Leo went out after dinner inspired both relief and curiosity in Judy. While Pearl was content to assume that Leo had a girlfriend he did not want to share, Judy was more inquisitive. She told herself that she didn't give a damn about Leo. At the same time, she did not want to believe that something as normal as a secret liaison with a girlfriend could be possible of her abnormal brother-in-law. She wanted to know exactly where he went, why he was so secretive.

The next time that Joseph carried the currency-filled case to Switzerland Judy had a plan all worked out. Joseph would be away for four days. Surely on one of those nights when she had dinner with her mother-in-law Leo would go out. For the first two nights he disappointed her by staying in with his books and records. On the third night, as dinner finished, he went to his room to change. The moment he had gone, Judy turned to Pearl. 'Would you mind very much if I didn't stay, Ma? I think I'm coming down with a cold.'

Pearl was instantly concerned. 'Would you like me to call a doctor?'

'It's not necessary. I'll go home, go to bed. Make sure it's gone before Joseph gets back. God forbid I should give it to him.'

'Of course, darling. Do you want – ' Pearl gestured at all the food left on the table; Judy had deliberately eaten little, as though she was really sickening – 'to take something home with you? I've got plenty of chicken soup left over in the refrigerator.'

'No, thanks. It's sweet of you, though.'

When Leo returned, he seemed surprised to see Judy preparing to leave. 'Aren't you going to keep Ma company while she watches television?'

'Why don't you?'

'I have other things to do.'

'I forgot – television's too dumb for you to watch.'

'Leo, why don't you drive Judy home?' Pearl suggested.

'She doesn't feel well.'

'It's all right, Ma. I'll take a cab.'

Outside, she found a taxi immediately, checking to be certain that it was not a Jalo cab with a driver who might know Leo. Instead of telling the driver to take her across the park to Fifth Avenue, she instructed him to wait. 'See that red car over there?'

'The Oldsmobile?'

'That's the one. I want you to wait until the driver comes down in a few minutes. Then I want you to follow him.'

'Where to?'

'If I knew that, I wouldn't need you, would I?'

The cab driver wondered why. All kinds of ideas crossed his mind before he decided that the red-haired woman was trying to catch her boyfriend or husband cheating on her. 'I don't like being involved in some follow-that-car routine, lady.'

'Will this make you more co-operative?' She offered twenty dollars.

'For a while.'

Leo came out of the building five minutes later, close enough to the taxi for both Judy and the driver to see his face clearly as he passed beneath a street lamp. He climbed into the red Oldsmobile and headed south on Broadway, switching to Sixth Avenue at Herald Square. The taxi stayed close behind, anonymous among the crowd of similar vehicles that plied the streets. At last, Leo turned off on West Fourth Street into Washington Square. He parked the car, got out and strolled along the sidewalk.

'Now what, lady?' the driver asked.

'Please see where he goes.' She passed across another twenty dollars.

'Stay here.' The taxi driver followed Leo twenty yards behind. Ten minutes later, he was back. 'Your friend went into an apartment building on MacDougal Street.'

'Which apartment?'

'I wasn't going to follow him inside.'

'Take me there.'

45

When the taxi parked outside the building Judy debated what to do. Was this where Leo's friends lived? She'd never thought of him as being the Village type. A restaurant in the Village perhaps, but not friends. They wouldn't be his kind of people. They might, God forbid, even like Groucho Marx.

'What do you want me to do, lady?'

'Just sit tight for a while.'

'It's your money.'

The cleaning woman had been there that day, using the key Leo left with the building superintendent. The air was full of the scent of lemon oil. He breathed in deeply, liking the fragrance. He went from one piece of antique furniture to the next, checking that the woman had done a good job. He detested dust. It gave a home an uncared for appearance; even if it was a home he used for just a couple of evenings a week.

Fifteen minutes after Leo had entered the fourth-floor apartment, he heard a double knock on the door. Outside stood a rosy-cheeked, curly-haired teenager. 'Leo?' the boy asked.

'You must be Alan.' Leo's heavy face beamed with pleasure as he held back the door for the boy to enter. 'Come in, I've heard wonderful things about you.' He took the boy's coat and hung it alongside his own. The evening stretched ahead of him like a journey through paradise. 'Sit down on the couch over there. Tell me all about yourself.'

One day, he mused, he would no longer have to rely on the escort service he had discovered. He did not object to spending money on the boys the service sent around to the Mac-Dougal Street apartment, he just wanted something more out of the relationship. He wanted love as well, the genuine love that should exist between two people. He wanted someone who would always be there, not a boy with whom he had to make an appointment.

He looked around the apartment. Some boy would be delighted to live here. Be kept like a mistress. That notion made Leo smile. Could a homosexual have such an arrangement, or only a married man, like Phil Gerson and his Belinda? It was discrimination against homosexuals, Leo

46

decided, probably conceived by those same cretins who had popularized the terms *fag* and *fairy*. Leo loathed those words. He wasn't a fag or a fairy. He wasn't some queer who paraded around in women's clothes and played the submissive role. He was a proud homosexual.

'Lady, we've been sitting here a half hour already,' the cab driver complained. 'Are you planning to stay here all night?'

Judy looked at her watch, amazed at how much time had passed. She still did not know what to do. Common sense told her to go home, but her own inquisitiveness forced her to stay. She damned well wanted to know about Leo's friends – this girlfriend Pearl was convinced he had.

'I want to find out what apartment he's in,' she said.

'Why don't you hire a private eye instead of an honest cab driver?' Turning around in his seat, the man looked at Judy. He noticed the engagement and wedding rings on her third finger and decided that the man inside the building was her husband after all, and not her boyfriend. Did the woman have a gun in her purse? Was she about to administer her own brand of justice? Christ, that was all he needed. 'Lady, if your husband's two-timing you, why don't you just accuse him of it when he gets home? You can even throw the address of this place in his face for good measure.'

Husband? Two-timing? Judy hid a smile as he followed the cab driver's line of thought. God, what a disgusting idea – being married to Leo, let alone having him cheat on her! She decided to build on the cab driver's mistaken belief. 'I have to know who's with him. I have a girlfriend who's always made eyes at him, even before we were married. I wanted to know if it's her.'

Is this where she lives, this girlfriend of yours?'

'No, I don't know who lives here. But they might have rented a place where they could meet.'

'What does your girlfriend look like?'

'Tall, with wavy platinum hair and brown eyes,' Judy answered, projecting an image of Belinda Rivers. She could think of no one else on whom to model her fantasy girlfriend.

The driver turned forward again, gazed through the windshield. 'How much money you got on you, lady?'

47

'Another fifty dollars.'

'Let me have it. I'll find out for you.'

'How?'

'I'll bang on every door and asked who called a cab. If your husband opens the door, I'll try to see who's there with him.'

Judy handed over the money. The driver left the taxi and entered the building. Checking the mail boxes, he saw that there were sixteen apartments, including the superintendent's. That one he ignored. He pounded with his fist on the door of the first apartment. Moments later a middle-aged woman in a housecoat peered out. 'You call a cab, lady?' The woman closed the door in his face.

By the time the taxi driver reached apartment 4B on the top floor, he had seen seven doors closed in his face. Four had not been opened at all. Only one man had been polite enough to say that he had not called a cab. Anticipating another surly reply, the driver knocked on the thirteenth door. There was no response. He heard music coming from inside and knew that someone was home. If he was going to earn fifty dollars, he was going to earn it honestly. He knocked again.

The door swung back. Leo stood framed in the doorway, face glowering, the solid eyebrows knitted into a vee-shaped line. He was barefooted and wearing a cotton dressing gown. 'What the hell are you banging on my door for?'

The driver answered anger with anger. 'I'm trying to find out who ordered a goddamned cab in this building!'

'It wasn't me!'

'That's all I've heard from everyone . . . it wasn't me! Have you got anyone else in this place who might have wanted a cab?' He tried to see past Leo into the living-room.

'I told you that no one ordered a cab!'

'Jesus Christ!' the driver exploded. 'There's a law against giving false alarms to the fire department. There should be a damned law about giving false calls for a cab!'

Another door on the landing opened, an apartment the cab driver had tried before Leo's. When he'd knocked before, it had stayed shut. The cab driver swung around. 'Was it you who ordered a cab, buddy?' he asked the man who looked out curiously.

Leo grabbed the driver's shoulder and jerked him around.

'Didn't you hear what I said? No one ordered a goddamned cab!' And there, over Leo's shoulder, the cab driver saw a bedroom door crack open. He got the quickest glimpse of a rosy face and short, dark, curly hair. Then Leo slammed the door with a crash that almost deafened the cab driver.

The man trudged down the three flights of stairs to the street, muttering to himself about inconsiderate bums who called in false orders for a cab. The moment he was outside the building, his attitude changed. He took his seat behind the wheel, started the engine and drove away.

'Well?' Judy asked.

'Apartment 4B, lady. That's where your husband is.'

'Who was with him? Was it my girlfriend? Did you get to see her?'

The driver swivelled quickly in the seat to look back at Judy. 'Lady, your husband's not up there with *your* girlfriend. He's up there with *his* boyfriend.'

The discovery of Leo's homosexuality shocked and elated Judy. At last she had the weapon with which to wound Leo, disgrace him in front of his mother. No matter how much Pearl adored Leo – how much she spoiled him – she would be horrified to know that his secret assignations were not with a girl but with a man.

A man? A boy! That's what the cab driver had told her, a boy still in his teens. Did that make it criminal as well as immoral? Yet, in Judy's mind, the story about the boy somehow fitted together neatly with Leo's behaviour from childhood. Not for him the happy, relaxed comradeship, like puppies in a basket, that Joseph and Judy had shared as children. Leo had seemed always to dislike her, just for being a girl.

And as they grew older, and Joseph and Judy began to play more adult games, Leo's hatred of her seemed to intensify. On that never to be forgotten night on which he had broken down the door to find them together half-naked in Judy's bedroom, she had been stunned by the violence of his reaction. With a woman's intuition she had detected more to it than just the shock of betrayal he would inevitably feel when his twin turned to someone else. No, she had sensed then and knew now that Leo felt a deep physical loathing for

49

her, and anger with his brother for wanting her as a woman. That was something Leo would never be able to feel.

She should have made the connection at the time. Had Leo been seeing someone even then? Another boy like the one the cab driver had found him with? No . . . Leo had been little more than a boy himself at the time. Probably, he had not even recognized his own perverted sexual drive. It had just spilled out in his hatred of her.

Judy waited until Joseph returned from Switzerland. To show how pleased she was to see him home she prepared a special dinner. They went to bed immediately afterwards, leaving the dishes on the table to be cleared in the morning.

'I should go away more often,' Joseph said. He lay back and stared at the bedroom ceiling through half-closed eyes as Judy's long fingernails traced an exquisite pattern across his chest.

'You go away more often, and I'll find someone else to make candlelit dinners for.' Did she tell him now, before they made love, or did she wait until later when they would lie sleepily in each other's arms?

'Did you visit Ma while I was away?'

'Two nights ago, for dinner.'

'Was Leo there?' When Judy nodded, Joseph asked, 'Did he run off on one of his secret dates again?'

Judy felt more relaxed. Joseph was making this easy for her. Of course he was as curious about his twin brother's comings and goings as she had been. 'They're no big secret anymore.'

'No?' Joseph raised a querying eyebrow. 'Don't tell me he finally admitted something.'

'Not a chance, but I played detective.' She waited to see the response.

Joseph started to smile, and then he burst out laughing. 'What did you do? Follow him?'

'In a taxi.'

'Where did he go?'

'Down to MacDougal Street in the Village.'

'To a club?'

'No. To an apartment. A fourth-floor apartment.'

'And he never spotted you?'

50

Judy shook her head, trailing long red hair across Joseph's face. 'I got the cab driver to do the legwork for me. I didn't have to get out of the cab.'

'Let me see, what kind of a girl would my brother go for? Was she a brunette, a blonde, a redhead? I know . . . she'd have auburn hair like Ma had before it started turning grey. Leo would pick someone who looked like Ma.'

'Wrong, wrong, and wrong again.'

'What else is there? Don't tell me she was bald.'

'Joseph.' Judy's voice turned soft and earnest as she stared down at her husband. 'Leo wasn't with a girl, he was with a boy.'

'What?' Joseph sat up in bed so abruptly that Judy was flung back. 'What the hell do you mean he was with a boy?'

'Exactly that.' Suddenly Judy knew she'd made a mistake. It was all right as long as Joseph believed that she'd followed Leo to find out about his secret girlfriend, but not when she'd found out that his lover was a boy.

'Judy, do you have any idea what you're saying?'

It was too late to back out now. 'I know what I'm saying.'

'Why did you follow him?' Joseph's voice took on a note of hostility that frightened her.

'I just told you – to find out his big secret.'

'Is that the truth? Or did you follow him in the hope that you could find something to hurt him with? To hurt us all with?'

Judy's answer was brutally blunt. 'I wanted a chance to pay him back for every stinking rotten thing he's ever done to me, from jumping on my doll's house when we were kids, to breaking into my bedroom and then trying to wreck our damned wedding! And, by God, he presented it to me on a silver platter.'

'Wait a minute. You said the cab driver went into the building?'

'That's right.'

'So you never saw Leo inside the building yourself?'

'The cab driver did.'

'But you didn't. And you didn't see the boy either?'

'No.'

'Then how do you know the whole damned thing wasn't

51

dreamed up by the taxi driver so he could look like he was earning the money you were paying him to spy on Leo?'

'For Christ's sake, Joseph! The driver wouldn't make up something like that!'

'How do you know?'

Judy looked away, unable to hold Joseph's eyes. From being amused that she would take it upon herself to follow Leo he had become furious with her. She understood why. Faced with a choice between his twin brother and his wife, Joseph was siding with his twin. Because of the way he and Leo had been brought up, Joseph would rather believe that his wife was a troublemaking liar than that his brother was a pervert.

'Well . . . how do you know the driver didn't lie? You haven't even thought about that, have you?' Joseph demanded. 'You believed the damned driver because you *wanted* to believe him!'

Judy slipped out of bed, threw a robe around herself and opened the door. Joseph called out to ask where she was going. 'To do the damned dishes!' she fired back before slamming the door with such force that the entire apartment reverberated with the shock.

As she began to collect the dirty plates from the dining-room table, she heard the bedroom door open. Moments later, she felt Joseph's strong arms around her. 'Put down the plates,' he whispered, 'and come back to bed.'

'What for?'

'I believe you about Leo.'

She replaced the dirty plates on the table and turned around to face him. 'Sudden, isn't it? A few seconds ago you were calling me a liar.'

He shook his head. 'You wouldn't lie.'

'What about following him?'

'You've got every reason to hate Leo, every reason to try and find out something you can use against him. But Judy. . . .'

'Yes?' She knew what was coming.

'Judy, if you ever tell Ma. If you ever tell her about Leo . . .'

He left the sentence unfinished, but Judy did not need to

hear any more. She knew exactly what he meant. The only way truly to hurt Leo would be to expose his black little secret to Pearl, and Judy could not do that without breaking Pearl's heart.

Judy had wanted a high-powered rifle with which to pick off Leo from a distance. Instead, she'd been handed a shotgun whose widespread blast would injure others, take down Leo and everyone close to him.

It was the bitterest irony Judy had ever known. At last she had a noose around Leo's neck and she dared not pull it tight. She was no better off than she'd been before. On the contrary, her position seemed even more hopeless.

Chapter Three

Benny Minsky threw a party in the offices of B. M. Transportation's new depot when it opened in Long Island City near the end of 1953. The party was as much to honour his son, William, as it was to commemorate the opening. William wasn't university-educated like Joseph Granitz, yet in Minsky's eyes he had proven himself every bit as capable.

When Jake had been alive, Minsky had never harboured any jealousy of the Granitz twins. Jake had been his friend. Because of that, Minsky would never have begrudged Jake's children anything. But the moment that Levitt assumed the responsibility of raising the twins, guiding them in predestined directions, Minsky's attitude changed. He diverted some of his inbuilt animosity towards Levitt to the twins. It became a competition between the two men to see which of the boys was the smartest, the Granitz twins or William Minsky. Benny Minsky was fully aware of how Levitt looked down on William – the progeny of a maniac and a *shiksa*! He was determined to prove that William was as good as anyone else. So what if Leo organized the street end of the bookmaking and numbers racket? And if Joseph handled the business end, made the trips to Switzerland, juggled the money and made it come out right? All the twins had done was pick up where someone else had left off, carried on operations that had always run smoothly. William had achieved much more than that. He had created something. He had taken a small trucking company and, through his own hard work and endeavour, had made it big and prosperous. Even if Levitt did not appreciate the work that had gone into it, he knew

54

how valuable a front it was. There was no taking that away from the little man, Minsky thought sourly; he always had an eye for where a quick buck could be turned.

From the start in Long Island City, William worked until past ten every night. He only saw the Riverside Drive apartment he shared with his father for as long as it took him to fall into bed and sleep, then wake up, shower and dress the following morning before returning to the new depot. William felt comfortable living with Minsky. He loved his father deeply, and understood how much he owed to him. Minsky had brought up the boy singlehanded after his mother had left, making sure that he wanted for nothing. From what William could remember now of his mother, he doubted that her presence during his formative years would have added anything positive. Mostly, that final raging argument stood out in his mind, when Kathleen had come back from the West Coast to find Minsky taking William to the synagogue on Saturdays. Years later Minsky told William exactly what had happened that day, about the beating he'd given Kathleen. William had understood.

He loved to walk around the new depot, especially during the evening when most of the trucks were parked for the night with almost military precision. B. M. Transportation had purchased three dozen new trucks to complement the old fleet. William liked to inspect them, a commanding officer checking out his troops. He would rub a dust spot off the shiny paintwork with the sleeve of his jacket, kick some of the massive tyres. He was, he knew, like a child playing with a new toy. He would talk with the night watchmen as they made their rounds. Only then, satisfied that his toy was in safe hands, would he leave for the night.

Late one afternoon, during the third week at Long Island City, William's secretary came into his office. 'There are two men outside to see you.'

William checked his diary: it was blank. 'Get rid of them, Susan. Tell them to make an appointment like everyone else.' He was too busy going over despatch records to see anyone.

'They're very insistent on seeing you.' Susan Mendel had worked for William for six months, ever since he'd decided that he needed a secretary of his own. He had not hired her

55

because of references or qualifications. Straight out of secretarial school, she had few. Plainly and simply, he had been immensely attracted to her. Every other secretary who had applied for the job had been middle-aged and crusty, as though such looks and attitude had been prerequisites for the position. Susan's warm brown eyes, wide smile and shining short brown hair had made up William's mind even before she'd spoken a word.

'Insistent?' he asked.

'Would you prefer rude? They told me they wouldn't leave until you'd seen them.'

Before she could add anything else, the two visitors entered the office. One was middle-aged with a dark, lined face and oily hair. The other, William guessed, was around his own age, nattily dressed in a grey coat and grey hat, razor thin, a gaunt face with gleaming black eyes that remained ice cold despite the smile that played around the lipless mouth.

'I am Frank Scarpatto,' the older man said, 'and this is my nephew, Tony Sciortino. We have a business proposition for you.'

'I'm busy,' William answered curtly. 'If you want to see me, make an appointment with Miss Mendel here.' He looked down at the despatch sheets again. A hand encased in a grey suede glove whipped them away and scattered them across the floor.

'I think you'll see us now,' Scarpatto said.

Tony Sciortino looked at the secretary. 'Take a long coffee break.'

Susan gazed uncertainly at William, who nodded. When the door closed behind her he said to the two men, 'What do you want?'

Scarpatto motioned to his nephew who bent down to collect the despatch records from the floor and replace them on William's desk. 'A regrettable accident, Mr Minsky. Unfortunately, such accidents can always happen when one is not careful.'

'I asked what you wanted. What's this business proposition?'

'Insurance. Against bigger, more costly accidents taking place. Like your pretty new trucks, for instance.'

56

'Or your drivers,' Sciortino added for good measure. He removed one of his gloves and slapped it against his hand. 'Or even the expensive merchandise you carry for your customers.'

'I've got all the insurance I need.'

Sciortino's thin face sharpened. Scarpatto held up a hand, as though restraining his nephew. 'There is insurance and there is insurance, Mr Minsky. Just as there are trucking companies and trucking companies. Some are more reliable than others.'

'You want to run a business around here,' Sciortino said, 'you run it on our terms. You buy our insurance on your trucks, on your drivers, on your premises and on your loads. Otherwise nothing moves.'

William jumped up from behind the desk, grabbed hold of Sciortino's arm and twisted it behind his back. 'Get the hell out before I break your goddamned arm!' With one hand he pulled back the door. With the other he shoved Sciortino out of the office. The Italian sprawled on the floor in front of Susan Mendel's desk. His grey hat flew off, his face ground into the carpet. Hoisting himself on his hands and knees, he turned his head and glared at William.

'You'll regret this, Minsky.'

William took one step and lashed out with his foot at the man's raised posterior. Sciortino flew forward again, landing on his hat and crushing it. 'Come back again and you'll see how much I regret it!'

When the two men were gone, William rested his hands on the secretary's desk, breathing heavily. 'I'm sorry, William,' Susan began.

'Not your fault. Maybe it's mine. I might have expected something like this, new kid on the block and all that.'

'Will they do anything?'

'I doubt it. They're probably small-time hoods who just try it on every newcomer to the district. Some give in, I suppose, and that's where they get their money.'

'And you won't give in?' she asked admiringly.

He smiled at her. 'Damned right I won't. My father would eat those two clowns alive and not even have to chew over them.'

'That's reassuring. Mind you, seeing you in action just now I don't think your father would even be needed.'

'Are you trying to make me blush?' He drew her into his arms and kissed her.

'Me? I don't think anyone could make you blush.' She fingered the narrow dimple in the centre of his chin and looked up into his eyes. 'Will we be working late tonight?'

'No. We've just about caught up.'

'Thank God for that. For once we can have dinner without having to come back here afterwards and earn it.'

William chuckled. Every night that he had stayed late, Susan had kept him company. Once the office staff had left, they had gone for dinner before returning together to work on cutting down the backlog of paperwork created by the move. William had never asked Susan to work overtime. She had volunteered. When he'd tried to pay her, she'd refused. 'Buy me dinner,' she'd told him, 'and drive me home afterwards, otherwise my parents will worry.'

On the third night of working late together, when William had parked outside the Jackson Heights home in which Susan lived with her parents, he'd handed her a slender box. 'There's your overtime.' Inside was a slim gold watch. 'Now you can keep a check on all those extra hours you're putting in.'

'It's beautiful! Thank you!' Without thinking, she'd flung her arms around his neck and kissed him. The next moment she'd drawn back, eyes wide, mouth puckered in embarrassment. 'I'm sorry. . . .'

'Why?'

'Well, I shouldn't have. . . .'

'Shouldn't have kissed the boss's son?'

'Shouldn't have kissed the boss.'

'It's my father's company. Those initials, B. M., they're his.'

'But he's hardly ever there anymore. You run it.'

'He has other interests.'

'Either way, I'm still sorry.'

'Don't be. I was hoping you'd do exactly that.'

'Would you like to come in? Have a cup of coffee, meet my parents? I'm sure they'd like to meet you.'

To Susan's disappointment, he'd refused. 'I have to get home. Another time.'

Since then, she had asked him in every night after he'd taken her home. Each time he had refused. 'Is it because you're frightened that my parents might think there's something between us?' Susan had asked.

'Isn't there?'

That night, after throwing out Frank Scarpatto and his nephew, William decided that he would accept Susan's invitation. They would be earlier than usual, going to Jackson Heights straight from dinner.

'Coming in?' she asked automatically as he stopped outside her parents' home.

'Sure.' Before she could register surprise, William was around her side of the car, helping her out. As she entered the house, she called out that she'd brought a visitor. William forced a smile on to his face and followed her into the front room. Hettie and Benjamin Mendel were sitting in front of a television set. Only her father was watching the programme. Her mother, by the light of a small table lamp, was knitting a long, shapeless yellow form which William took to be a scarf. The scene warmed him. This was something he'd never really known – a family where both mother and father sat at home, comfortable in each other's company.

'This is my boss,' Susan announced.

Benjamin Mendel switched off the television set. Hettie put down her knitting. 'Welcome to our home,' Mendel said. 'Susan's told us everything about you.'

'She has?'

'She said you were a gentleman, and in my book that's all that needs saying.'

'Sit down, please,' Hettie said. 'Can I get you something?'

'A cup of coffee would be nice.' He dropped on to a couch. Susan sat next to him, her thigh pressed against his as if to give him confidence.

'That's quite some place you've just opened in Long Island City,' Mendel said.

'You know it?'

'I see it from the subway each day when I go to work in Times Square.'

William nodded; the elevated tracks passed within fifty yards of the depot. 'What do you do there?'

'I work in the advertising production department of the *Times*.'

Hettie Mendel returned with coffee and cake. William answered questions from Susan's father, while her mother continued with her knitting. But he noticed that her eyes kept darting to him; he was sure she didn't miss a thing. Mendel was interested in the trucking company and William explained how his father had started during the Depression. He phrased the story carefully. Instead of admitting that Benny Minsky had converted rum-running trucks to take garments, he told Mendel that his father had bought the trucks secondhand. Somehow, he did not feel that Susan's family's acceptance of him would be quite so warm if they knew that his father's wealth derived from bootlegging and gambling. And he found that he wanted her parents to think warmly of him.

After a second cup of coffee he decided it was time for him to go home. 'A pleasure to meet you, young man,' Mendel said, shaking William's hand. 'Come by any time.'

Susan saw him to the car. 'They were impressed with you.'

'Because I'm your boss's son?'

'Boss,' she countered. 'No, that had nothing to do with it. They liked you because you're one hell of a nice guy. The same reason I like you.'

He kissed her good-night and got into his car for the journey to Riverside Drive. He wondered if his father would be home. He hoped so. William wanted to tell Minsky that he had fallen in love. Then he remembered what had happened earlier, the two unwelcome visitors. Should he tell his father about Scarpatto and Sciortino as well? Or was he confident enough that he had killed any trouble before it could start?

By the time he reached home, William had decided to tell his father only about Susan. Minsky knew the girl already. It was time that he stopped looking on her as just a secretary, and started to regard her as a possible daughter-in-law. It was not worth dampening the moment, William decided, by mentioning Scarpatto and Sciortino as well. He doubted that they would be back anyway.

*   *   *

60

Months after learning of Leo's homosexuality, Judy was wishing that she had never found out. Knowing such potentially damaging information about her brother-in-law, and being frightened to use it, was wrecking her peace of mind.

Each time she saw Leo at Pearl's apartment, she had the wild fantasy of confronting him with her knowledge. She could ask, casually, how his boyfriend was keeping. Or, more subtly, she could say she'd seen his absolute double entering the apartment building on MacDougal Street. But when she thought about Pearl and Joseph, she knew she could not go through with it. Before, Judy had been frustrated by being powerless to strike back at Leo, repay him for the abuse he had heaped on her. Now she was equally frustrated because she knew how to square accounts but didn't dare to. She was uncertain which situation was worse.

Then something happened to take her mind completely off Leo and the old antagonism. New Year's Day fell on a Friday. That evening, she and Joseph went to Pearl's apartment as usual for Friday-night dinner. Leo was there, as was Lou Levitt. Judy waited until the meal had been eaten and Leo had left to keep his appointment downtown. Then, holding Joseph's hand beneath the table, she said: 'How's this for a New Year's surprise? I'm pregnant!'

The most surprised was Joseph. 'When did you find out?'

'When you were away in Zurich last week.'

'Why didn't you say anything earlier?'

'I wanted to save it for today, start out the year with some good news.'

Joseph kissed her. 'You succeeded! Happy New Year.'

Pearl rose from her seat to kiss both her son and daughter-in-law. 'Now maybe you won't feel so lonely when Joseph's away,' she told Judy.

'How about you? Will you feel different, being a grandmother?'

'How about someone asking how I feel?' Joseph broke in. 'I am the father, after all.'

'We all know how you feel,' Pearl told him. 'Immensely proud of yourself because you think that no one's ever done it before. Well, I've got news for you – the only person we

61

should be concerning ourselves with is Judy, because she's the one who's going to be doing all the work. Before and after the baby arrives.'

'How much work can there be? You didn't have much trouble with Leo and me.'

'Sure I had no trouble with you two,' Pearl said sarcastically. She looked at Levitt, sitting at the head of the table. He had been oddly quiet, not even congratulating Joseph and Judy on their news. 'Lou, tell them how easy they were to look after.'

Levitt seemed to consider his answer for a long time. Finally he said, 'Joseph, if your mother had had four pairs of hands she still would've been short two pairs. You and Leo were murder. You'd split up, go in different directions and leave your mother standing there, getting giddy while she decided which one to chase. And Judy, throw in what you and your mother were like when you were young, and you've got the bloodlines for a real lively kid.'

Pearl wagged a finger at Joseph and Judy. 'You're going to have a child who'll be just like the pair of you were.' Suddenly she started to laugh. 'I must sound just like my mother, that's what she wished on me. She wished it on your mother as well, Judy. She wanted us both to have children like ourselves.'

Pearl smiled fondly at the thought of Annie as a red-haired, freckle-faced livewire of a child. She was always the first to lead her friend into mischief, but the first, too, with heartfelt sympathy and offers of support when they were needed.

Soon after, Joseph took Judy home, leaving Pearl alone in the apartment with Levitt. She sat watching him for several seconds, unable to understand why tonight he was so quiet, so withdrawn. The news of Judy's pregnancy should have made him overjoyed, but he'd shown barely any reaction at all.

'What's the matter, Lou?' she asked at last.

'Why should anything be the matter?'

'I know you too well. You look like someone whose best friend just died, not a man whose godson is about to become a father.'

A slight smile lit Levitt's face. 'I'm sorry. Joseph and Judy having a kid is probably the only news guaranteed to cheer me up. It makes even me feel like a grandfather-to-be.'

She held his gaze. 'You're entitled, Lou. You helped bring the kids up. Now what's the problem?'

The smile disappeared behind a veil of gloom. Levitt rested his chin on his hands and stared glumly at Pearl. 'Florida's the damned problem. I've been on the phone with Phil Gerson all afternoon, trying to find out what the hell's going on down there. He's running up bills like money's no object. That six million bucks we budgeted for the Monaco in Hollywood now looks like going up to eight or nine million. And what's going to happen when he starts on the Waterway in Hallandale? How much will he go beyond the estimate with that?'

'What's causing the extra expenses?'

'That damned woman, Belinda Rivers. Benny spotted it long before I did, but I suppose he had the experience of living with Kathleen to go on. Belinda's got Phil dangling from a string. He's given her all the responsibility for the decorating and she's going nuts. Never mind those marble floors from Italy that Phil talked about – those were in the original budget. But they're getting in the most expensive furniture – genuine antiques, can you believe that? They're putting carpets in the halls and bedrooms that you'd be frightened to walk on if they were in your own home. The finest crystal, English gold-rimmed china and engraved silver flatware for the restaurants. We'll have to frisk everyone who eats in the damned restaurants to make sure they don't walk out with the cutlery! This Belinda, she's been touring Europe, buying the finest and the best, and then getting it air-freighted back here.'

'What did Phil say about it when you asked him?'

'He says that Belinda knows exactly what she's doing, and if we want the best place imaginable, we've got to pay for it.'

'Are you short of cash?'

'Of course not. I just don't like being taken for a fool.'

'What about Benny? What does he have to say?'

Levitt laughed grimly. 'What do you think? He wants to take the extra two million or whatever straight out of Phil's hide.'

'When were you last down there?'

'Five weeks ago. We're flying down there again for a few

days, the pair of us, and it's going to take all my persuasion to stop Benny from killing Phil.'

Phil Gerson met Levitt and Minsky at the airport three days later. The first thing they noticed was Gerson's deep suntan. After the bitter cold of a New York winter, Gerson looked remarkably fit and healthy. That made the two visitors from New York even angrier.

'What the hell is going to be the finishing price for the Monaco?' Minsky rasped the moment they were seated in Gerson's car. 'At the rate you and your girlfriend are going, the only way we'll ever get our money out is for a hurricane to flatten the place and the insurance company to pay us off.'

'Just relax, will you?' Gerson replied. 'When you see what we've done to this place even since you were last here, you won't have a worry in the world.'

'I don't want to relax,' Minsky fired back. 'I want to see those two hotels open. And I want some concrete reasons for all the damned expenses.'

'What was the place like when you were down here last, Lou?' Gerson aimed the question purposely at Levitt who, he knew, was more sympathetic to him than Minsky.

'The building was almost complete.'

'Right, but the grounds were a mess, none of the amenities were finished. Wait until you see what it looks like now. Then you'll appreciate the investment.'

They arrived at the Monaco just as the setting sun struck it full from the west. Gerson turned off the A1A Highway and passed through a portcullis-style entrance into the hotel grounds. Minsky and Levitt sucked in their breath. Built Spanish-style and painted the palest shade of pink, the hotel resembled a shimmering palace. 'Everything's finished but the inside,' Gerson said, 'and I've got double crews working overtime to get that ready for next month.' He drove right around the hotel. 'Three swimming pools, all finished. Tennis courts, all finished. And the dock – ' he braked the car by the edge of the Intracoastal – 'all finished.'

'You could park an aircraft carrier here,' Levitt said drily.

'Maybe we will one day, if the Navy decides to become our customer.'

'Let's look at the inside,' Minsky said impatiently. 'I want to see the big hole that all the dough's been poured into.'

Gerson drove from the dock and pulled up outside the hotel's main entrance, slipping his car in between three trucks that were unloading their cargoes. Workmen carefully carried a consignment of furniture into the hotel, treading on thick strips of matting that had been laid across the gleaming marble floor of the lobby. The three men followed the furniture inside. Standing in the centre of the vast lobby, dressed in tight slacks and a cotton blouse tied around her waist, was Belinda Rivers. One hand held a clipboard. The other directed a group of men who were pushing a trolley on which rested a gigantic, ornate crystal chandelier. When they almost collided with the work crew moving in the furniture, she screamed at them: 'Careful! For Christ's sake, be careful! That chandelier cost twenty thousand dollars!'

'Since when did she become one of the staff?' Levitt asked Gerson. 'You brought her down here as your girlfriend. No one objected to that. We didn't take into account that she was going to tear up the plans and write her own set.'

'That's because I never realized how talented she was. She's had some great ideas.'

'Yeah, we've been seeing the bills for her great ideas,' Minsky muttered. 'I don't eat off Royal Doulton and silver tableware at home.'

'Maybe you should,' Gerson told him. 'Proper presentation makes the food taste better.' He cupped his hands to his mouth. 'Belinda, come over here! We've got visitors!'

She turned away from the men moving the chandelier. 'Hi, I heard you were coming. What do you think of it?'

'The outside looks gorgeous,' Levitt replied. 'But this is where I don't like it.' He pulled out his wallet. 'Two hotels at this rate, and this is going to be empty.'

'Gangway!' a voice yelled from behind. Levitt stepped aside and two men pushed a pile of cartons past them. 'Where do you want these?' one of the men asked Belinda.

'What are they?' She checked the labels. 'Lace tablecloths, take them through to the laundry. They've got to be unpacked and pressed before they go to the restaurant.'

'Lace tablecloths?' Levitt repeated. He looked at the label.

The shipment was from a company in Switzerland. He felt grateful that the price wasn't listed. 'What the hell's wrong with linen tablecloths?'

'Everyone and his brother eats on linen,' Belinda explained. 'Lace adds something.'

'Sorry I asked.'

Gerson broke into the conversation. 'I know what'll make you happy. Upstairs is all finished.'

Leaving Belinda in the lobby, the three men rode the special lift to the top floor. Plush carpet greeted their feet. High, arched ceilings gave a feeling of spaciousness. The walls were panelled in rich, restful oak. Set across the floor were ten tables for craps, blackjack and roulette. Above each table hung a chandelier identical to the one Minsky and Levitt had seen downstairs. Another two hundred thousand dollars, Levitt calculated.

'What kind of furniture's that?' Levitt pointed to dainty chairs and occasional tables set every few feet around the walls.

'French . . . some king or other, I forget exactly which one,' Gerson answered. 'Belinda did remarkably well at estate sales in Europe.'

'Don't even think of telling me how much each piece cost.'

'You'll make it back and more. This place will be able to hold its own against the great casinos of Europe.'

Levitt gave a slight shake of the head. Twenty grand chandeliers, French antique furniture, solid silver tableware, a view of the ocean on one side and the Intracoastal on the other. And just down the road, hundreds of acres of tomato fields! Levitt did not know whether to be flabbergasted or impressed. 'Phil, when I was half your age, I was making a fortune on one craps table in the back of a joint on Second Avenue, underneath a restaurant Pearl's mother used to own. You do as well here as I did there, and we'll overlook the extra money . . .'

'. . . but God help you if you don't,' Minsky added.

The first week of the New Year was especially pleasing to William Minsky. Every truck in the fleet was out, hauling merchandise from manufacturers to retail stores to back up

66

New Year promotions. He could not have opened the new depot, expanded the business, at a better time. Nor, he congratulated himself, could he have chosen a better time to fall in love.

Since meeting Susan Mendel's parents William had taken her home every night. Twice he had eaten dinner with the family. He was even considering having his father meet them once he got back from Florida. He knew that such a meeting would make his relationship with Susan virtually official, and that suited him fine.

'When you advertised for a secretary, were you really looking for a secretary or were you looking for a girlfriend?' Susan asked him as they finished work for the evening.

'I could ask you the same thing – when the agency sent you here, were you looking for an employer or a boyfriend?'

'*Touché*. When's your father coming back from Florida? What's he doing down there anyway – wintering?'

'He wishes he was. He's checking out a hotel his company's building.'

'A hotel?' Susan was impressed. 'He's got a lot of different interests, hasn't he?'

'Can you keep a secret, especially from your parents?'

'A big, dark secret?'

'Nothing so romantic. Those trucks my father started out with twenty years ago: he didn't buy them secondhand like I told your father he did. He converted them from trucks he and his partners used for running bootleg liquor. That's where he got his start.'

'Your father was a racketeer, like those people in the Kefauver hearings?'

'He was never a racketeer. He never stole from anyone.'

'Why are you telling me this, William?'

'Because I love you and I think it's only fair that you should know.'

'Does he . . . does he still involve himself in anything?'

'He has gambling interests. So do I, Susan. I'm partners with him and his associates.'

Susan stared at the floor. 'I don't know what to say.'

'Just say that it doesn't make any difference between us.'

67

'But you work so hard here. I've watched how hard you work. You can't be involved in things like that.'

'My father worked damned hard during Prohibition as well. He had to, if he wanted to get on.' When she continued to stare at the floor he wondered if he'd made a mistake by telling her. 'Would you rather I'd kept you in the dark?'

At last she lifted her eyes. 'I'm glad you told me. It's just a bit of a shock, that's all.'

'Does it make any difference between us?'

Susan shook her head and smiled. 'If you hadn't told me – if I'd found out some other way – it might have done. But you've been honest. I appreciate that.' The smile faded. 'I'm not sure that my parents would, though.'

'That's why I lied to your father when he asked me about the company.'

'Then we'll both have to lie in the future, won't we?' She looked at the wall clock. 'We'd better hurry if we're going to have time for dinner before the movie starts. It's six o'clock already.'

While Susan tidied her desk, William made his last inspection of the depot. More than half of the trucks were still out. The security guards were patrolling their beats. In the service bay, two mechanics were cleaning up after having changed a faulty transmission on one of the older trucks. When William returned to the office, Susan was ready. They got into his car and headed toward the Queensboro Bridge into Manhattan. Snow was beginning to fall, and as William flicked on the wipers he felt a pang of jealousy of his father. South Florida sounded good at this time of year.

'William, watch out!' Susan shouted.

Ten yards ahead, a van pulled out from the side of the road and stopped dead. William stamped on the brakes. The car slid in the fresh snow and skidded to a halt less than a yard from the side of the van. Before William had time to recover and vent his anger at such reckless driving, the rear door of the van flew open. Three men jumped out and rushed towards the car. William's door was yanked wide open. Strong hands pulled him from the car. He heard Susan's screams, tried to struggle. A massive fist exploded in his face. His arms were grabbed from behind. Helpless, he was shoved forward on to the battering fists of the man who had first hit him. A knee slammed into the base of his spine and he fell to the ground. Feet smashed into his stomach, his ribs, his back. From a great distance he heard a man's voice shout: 'That's enough, let's get out of here!' Before he blacked out he saw, in the dim light from a streetlamp, a thin figure in a grey coat and grey hat.

'William, are you all right?'

Susan's voice penetrated dark waves of pain. William opened his eyes, forced them to focus. He was lying on the sidewalk, head cradled in Susan's arms. The snow was falling faster, covering his coat and legs. 'How long . . .?' Speech hurt. He raised a hand to his mouth; it came away bloody. 'How long have I been like this?'

'A minute. Can you move?'

One by one he tested his limbs. The greatest pain came from breathing. His ribs felt like they were on fire.

'I'll help you to the car,' Susan offered, 'and drive you to the hospital. Then I'll call the police.'

'No . . . no police. I don't need them. No hospital either.'

'Of course you need the police! I recognized one of the men, the one giving the orders. It was the man you threw out of the office, Sciortino, the nephew. He was telling the other men what to do.'

'And I'm telling *you* what to do. Just drive me home. Wait a minute. . . .' He touched the left side of her face. The skin around her eye was red and puffy. 'What happened to you?'

'I tried to stop them. One of them hit me. It's nothing.'

'What do you mean – it's nothing?'

Refusing to answer, she helped him into the passenger seat of the car. While she drove, he held a handkerchief to his torn lip and debated what to do. He thought he'd quelled any problem by throwing Sciortino and his uncle out of the office. He'd been wrong. He hadn't stopped it at all; he'd just declared war.

William knew what he could do now: the simple thing, tell his father and let Benny Minsky's friends handle the whole affair. Only William wasn't interested in the simple route. He turned his head to look at Susan. The injured side of her face was hidden from him as she drove. Whatever had to be done,

69

he swore, he would do by himself. If he was big enough to build up B. M. Transportation, then he was damned well big enough to take matters into his own hands and deal with any problems that accompanied expansion.

Once in the apartment, Susan went to the medicine cabinet where she found iodine and bandages. William winced as she dressed his split lip, bathed a graze on his temple. 'Do you think your ribs are broken?' she asked him.

'Just bruised. I didn't hear anything go snap.' He held her face tenderly. 'Who told you to be the brave one?'

'I couldn't sit there and watch you get beaten up.'

'Look, maybe you'd better go on home. Take my car, or I'll get you a cab. I'm going to have to make some calls.'

'To your father in Florida?' she asked, while holding a cold, damp cloth to her swollen face.

'No. I'll handle this on my own.'

She thought about it for a while. 'I'll stay here with you. I told my parents that we had a date tonight. What'll they think if I turned up at eight o'clock? Especially with my face looking like this.'

'That we had a fight and split up. Are you sure you want to stay?'

'I'm sure.'

William did not argue. He reached for the telephone. Before he could lift the receiver, it rang. 'Mr Minsky,' a soothing voice said. 'I just heard about your terrible accident this evening. You can't know how sorry I am.'

'Who is this?'

'Frank Scarpatto. We met the other day to discuss insurance for your company. Perhaps you've changed your mind about your decision.'

'I don't know about any accident,' William said. 'If you mean about me and my secretary getting driven off the road and then beaten up. . . .'

'I'd prefer to describe it as an accident, Mr Minsky,' Scarpatto said placatingly. 'We'll be by your office tomorrow evening to discuss the terms of the policy which I'm sure you'll wish to take out with us.' He hung up.

William turned to Susan. 'I don't want you coming into the office tomorrow.'

70

'Why not? This will be better by then.'

'I don't want you coming in, all right?'

'What's going to happen?'

'It's not necessary for you to know.' Before she could protest, he switched his attention to the telephone. His father and Lou Levitt were the only two survivors of the old generation. He was a member of the new, and his natural allies were the Granitz twins. Which one, though, did he call on for help? Did he approach Joseph, the figures man, the university graduate who worked with a pen and a briefcase? Or did he call Leo, the street man who had not even turned up for his own brother's wedding? William's fingers spun the number of Pearl Granitz's home.

Pearl answered. William fought down both pain and impatience to ask how she was. She had always considered him such a nice, polite boy, he could act no other way towards her. He even managed to make a joke about being jealous of his father and Lou Levitt sunning themselves down in Florida. 'They're probably playing golf all morning and swimming all afternoon,' he said. At last, he asked if Leo was home.

Leo came on the line. Immediately William dropped the chatty tone. In terse terms he explained what had happened. 'Leo, I don't want to wait for my father to get back from Florida. Those two guys are coming by the office tomorrow evening, and I want to handle this myself.'

'No problem,' Leo answered. 'There's no point in involving your father and Uncle Lou, not when we can take care of the matter ourselves.'

Leo breathed in deeply, felt the blood begin to flow faster in his veins. He kept his voice deliberately cool and unemotional, belieing the excited tremor of his hand around the telephone receiver.

'Meet with these guys, William. Agree to whatever they want. It'll be the only time.'

He replaced the receiver and walked into the kitchen where his mother was washing up after dinner. 'What did William want?' she asked.

'Nothing much, Ma. Just some information.' He put his arms around Pearl and kissed her on the cheek. He felt happy. Tonight he had a new boy coming to the apartment on

71

MacDougal Street. He'd asked the agency to find him something different. They'd come up with an eighteen-year-old Swedish-American boy named Gustav, with platinum blond hair and crystal blue eyes. Leo wanted to experiment, to learn what kind of youth, which looks, stimulated him the most. Only then would he dispense with the agency's services and find his own boy. His own mistress to love.

Before he left the apartment that evening to drive to the Village, he telephoned Harry Saltzman in Fort Lee. Gave orders just as he had heard Lou Levitt do.

Susan Mendel defied William's order by turning up for work the following morning at the regular time. 'I thought I told you not to come in today,' William greeted her. He saw that her left eye was almost closed. 'What did your parents have to say about that?'

'I told them we'd been in an auto accident, and that you were in even worse shape than I was. Too banged up to be left alone in the office,' she added meaningfully.

'I won't be alone.'

'Listen to me, William. I've got a piece of this company to worry about just like you do.'

'You have? What piece?'

'You, you idiot. And you're more important to me than all the trucks put together.'

William was torn. He didn't want Susan in the office because he had no idea what would happen, what Leo was planning. Nor did he want her to leave. She was his sole contact with sanity in a world that had suddenly gone quite insane. What would Leo do anyway? Surely nothing here, when mechanics and drivers would be all over the place? Whatever he had in mind, it would be accomplished secretly. 'All right, Susan, you can stay. But any trouble, and I want you out of that front door in one big hurry. Get me?'

'Got you.'

Just after midday, Susan entered William's office. 'There are two men to see you.'

Already? Scarpatto had said that he and his nephew would not be back until early evening. William hadn't even heard from Leo yet. He wasn't prepared.

72

'Not those two,' Susan said. 'But two others, just like them.'

William came out of his office. Waiting in the reception area were Leo and Harry Saltzman. 'Give us overalls and a spare truck,' Leo said. 'We're going to sit outside the front, where this Scarpatto and Sciortino will pull in.'

'What are you going to do with them?'

'When you go to a doctor with a cold,' Saltzman said, 'do you ask him what's in the pills he gives you?'

Susan stared at the two men. She'd want neither of them as a doctor. Were these associates of William's father? Both looked menacing. Middle-age hadn't softened Saltzman at all. Little of the solid muscle he'd had in his youth had turned to fat; he worked out regularly at a gym to avoid that. The hairline was still as low as ever, although the sides had begun to recede, leaving him with a widow's peak so pronounced as to be comical. But it was Leo who caught Susan's attention most. Shorter than Saltzman, but just as muscular, his heavy eyebrows lent a coarse expression to an already unattractive face. These two men frightened Susan even more than the Italian uncle and nephew had done.

'What happened to you?' Saltzman asked, pointing to Susan's face.

'I was with William last night when it happened.'

'We were going out for dinner,' William explained.

Saltzman grinned mirthlessly. 'Looks to me like someone slipped a knuckle sandwich on the menu. Okay, to business. We'll be outside in the truck. When these two characters arrive, William, your secretary can signal to us. Just stand by the window, honey, pull out a handkerchief and blow your nose. Me and Leo'll take care of the rest.'

'Harry – ' William's voice was low, urgent – 'my father doesn't know about this. I don't want him to.'

Saltzman hid a smile. The first thing he'd done after hearing from Leo the previous evening was to contact Lou Levitt and Benny Minsky in South Florida. He didn't make a move without their approval, especially Levitt's. If Levitt had told him to leave it alone, he would never have gone near the Long Island City depot. Instead, Levitt had instructed him to work with Leo, assist him in whatever he needed. Levitt had made the next generation equal partners. Now he wanted to keep tabs on the way they reacted under stress.

It was dark by the time Frank Scarpatto and Tony Sciortino arrived at the B. M. depot. Flurries of snow whipped up to obscure vision, and disappeared just as abruptly as the wind dropped. The Lincoln in which they were being driven pulled into the small parking lot in front of the company offices. Save for one truck parked by the side of the building and William's own car, the lot was empty.

'Wait here for us,' Scarpatto instructed the driver. Pulling up the collar of his coat, he walked towards the building entrance. Sciortino, still wearing the grey coat and hat, followed. Inside the Lincoln, the driver pushed his hat to the back of his head and lit a cigarette. As an afterthought, he started the engine and swung the car around so that it pointed towards the street.

Scarpatto and Sciortino reached Susan's desk together. 'I believe Mr Minsky is expecting us,' the older man said.

Susan looked from one face to the other. Something like a smile flashed across Sciortino's dark eyes. 'Walk into a door?' he asked.

She didn't answer. 'Your two visitors are here,' she told William. She held the door open for them to enter, closed it after them and walked to the window behind her desk. The cab of the truck in which Leo and Saltzman were sitting looked right into the office. She took out her handkerchief and dabbed her nose with it. The truck doors swung open and she walked away.

In William's office, the two visitors made themselves comfortable. 'Think of the trouble you could have avoided if you'd accepted our offer, Mr Minsky,' Scarpatto began.

'How much do you want?' William asked. He regretted the quickness of the question immediately. Was he rushing the meeting? He had no idea how much time Leo and Saltzman needed.

'Two thousand a month.'

'That's preposterous! We don't have that kind of money.'

'You've got more than sixty trucks. Are you telling us that you can't afford to spend a lousy five hundred bucks a week for insurance? That's just over eight bucks a truck.'

'Eight dollars a truck, like hell! More like four hundred dollars per truck per year.'

'So do what everyone else does,' Scarpatto said disarmingly. 'Pass it on to your customers.'

'I give my customers good rates. I don't rob them to pay other robbers.'

'Two thousand a month or you don't move a truck out of here,' Sciortino stated flatly. 'Pay that, and you can call us whatever you like.'

'What if – ' William leaned back in his chair – 'I pick up this phone and holler "Cop"?'

Sciortino stood up. 'You look like a sensible man, Minsky.' It wasn't lost on William that the 'mister' prefix had been dropped. 'In fact, you look a damned sight more sensible today than you did when we first came in here. If you call the cops, you'll need the fire department as well, because your depot will burn down, with all your shiny trucks inside. And you'll need ambulances for all the drivers who'll have accidents. After a while, they won't even want to work here – your accident record will be too high.'

'Take your choice,' Scarpatto said. 'Two thousand a month and you stay in business. Cut us out, and you'll have no business.'

William opened a desk drawer. Sciortino was at his side instantly, a hand gripping William's wrist like a vice. When he saw that there was nothing in the drawer but money he relaxed. 'Glad to see you're going to do the right thing.'

William counted out two thousand dollars in twenty-dollar bills, slipped the money into a large envelope. 'Thank you,' Scarpatto said as his nephew pocketed the money. 'That clears your account until the end of January.'

'We're already a week into January!' William protested.

'Our accounts run from month's beginning to month's end. We signed you up as of New Year's Day.' Scarpatto nodded to his nephew and the two men walked towards the door. Susan was still sitting at her desk outside William's office. She didn't look up as Scarpatto and Sciortino passed her.

A brisk flurry greeted the two men as they opened the front door, a sheet of fine snow picked up by the wind virtually

75

blotting out visibility. As it fell away, they saw the Lincoln waiting, smoke trailing from its exhaust as the driver ran the engine to keep himself warm. They walked towards the car, passing a tall, middle-aged workman who listlessly pushed a snow shovel in a losing battle to keep the parking lot clear.

Sciortino entered the back of the car from one side, his uncle from the other. As they closed the doors, the driver swung around, a gun pointed between the two men. 'Should have been you two guys who took out the insurance,' Leo said, grinning at them.

'Where's our driver?' Scarpatto asked.

'Taking forty winks in the back of that truck.'

The front passenger door opened and the snow-sweeper climbed into the Lincoln. Saltzman had discarded the shovel in favour of a heavy revolver. 'Back up the car,' he told Leo. 'Get it close to the truck.'

Leo put the Lincoln into reverse, guided it slowly until the rear doors were level with the back of the truck. Saltzman got out first, pulled open the back door of the car. 'Out.'

Hands in plain sight, Scarpatto and Sciortino left the Lincoln. When Leo threw open the loading door of the truck they saw their driver lying on the floor, hands and feet tied, a gag stuffed into his mouth. 'Step right in,' Saltzman ordered.

Scarpatto and Sciortino entered the truck, moved right to the front as Saltzman prodded them forward with the revolver. 'Lean forward, spread your legs and place the flats of your hands against the front wall. Take your weight on your hands.'

As the two men obeyed, Saltzman stood behind one, Leo behind the other. Both men held their weapons in their left hands. With their right hands, they each took a leather-covered blackjack from their coats. The blackjacks arced through the air simultaneously. With nothing more than a surprised grunt, a harsh escaping of breath, Scarpatto and Sciortino collapsed on to the floor of the truck. Leo and Saltzman picked up lengths of heavy string that lay on the floor, bound the arms and legs of the unconscious men, stuffed wads of rags into their mouths. Lastly Saltzman felt inside their pockets until he found the envelope containing the money.

76

'I'll take the car, you take the truck and follow me,' Saltzman told Leo.

The sound of the truck and car engines revving up could be heard inside the office. Standing with Susan, William looked out of the window. The Lincoln led the way out of the parking lot, followed closely by the truck. 'Will we ever know what happened?' Susan asked.

'Maybe we don't want to know.' It was one thing to decide on a certain course of action. It was quite another to know how that decision had been carried out.

'Take me home, please,' Susan said. 'I want to get out of this place.'

'So do I.' William said it as though leaving the depot would disociate himself and Susan off from what had happened to the two men who had tried to cut themselves in for a piece of the company. He knew it wouldn't. William had built up a legitimate trucking company, but in its first scrape with trouble, instead of going to the police as any legitimate businessman would have done, he had used his father's contacts . . . his own contacts . . . to overcome the problem. It was a decision from which there'd be no going back. He would never be troubled by Scarpatto or Sciortino again. At the same time, he would never be free of his father's past.

Saltzman checked continually in the rear view mirror to make sure the truck was still following as he headed towards the Queensboro Bridge. Once in Manhattan, he turned north on to the FDR. The truck stayed behind, all the way on to Harlem River Drive and then the George Washington Bridge into New Jersey. On the Palisades in New Jersey, he finally came to a stop, switching off the lights but leaving the engine running as the truck coasted to a halt behind him.

'Turn them off,' Saltzman told Leo, gesturing to the truck's lights, 'and move over into the passenger seat.' While Leo changed seats, Saltzman steered the Lincoln until it was pointing directly at the flimsy wooden fence on the edge of the cliff twenty yards away. He lifted the hood and jammed the accelerator linkage wide open. Slamming the hood closed, he reached in through the Lincoln's open window, jerked the gearstick from park into drive, and jumped back. The Lincoln

77

rolled forward, engine roaring as it picked up speed in a mad dash towards the fence. The fence shattered. A grinding crash of metal erupted as the car went over the edge, its underside scraping against clumps of rock. Then it was gone, toppling end over end into the trees far below, engine screaming at full revs. Then silence as the lubricating system failed to cope and the engine seized up, piston rings welded to bores, journals fused to bearings. Saltzman jumped into the truck, thrust it into gear and drove away. Only when he reached the road again did he turn on the lights.

'Where are we going now?' Leo asked.

'Paterson.' Saltzman removed his gloves; they weren't necessary anymore. The coldness of the steering wheel felt good to his hands. 'Then I'll show you how I got rid of a troublesome union man a few years ago.'

Leo fell silent. In school, the good students – boys like his twin brother, Joseph – had always been the quiet ones. They were too busy learning to talk, to play. Leo was learning now. He was studying with a master. Finally, he had found a subject he wanted to absorb.

Saltzman pulled the truck into the parking lot of a funeral home, cut the lights and steered around the back to where the hearses came and went. Only a small light showed in a window at the rear. After reversing up to a wide door, Saltzman killed the engine and jumped out. The door opened and a fat, bald-headed man peered out. Saltzman gave him the envelope full of money he had taken from Tony Sciortino. 'You all fired up in there?'

'Ready to go,' the fat man answered. 'How many?'

'Three.' Saltzman flung open the cargo door, picked up the body of the driver and carried it through the door into the building. Leo lifted Frank Scarpatto from the floor. The body writhed in his arms, almost dislodging his grip. 'Harry, this one's awake.'

'Too bad. Get a move on, it won't make any difference whether he feels it or not. Where he's headed it's going to be hot anyway,' Saltzman said as he returned for the body of Tony Sciortino.

Leo found himself in a chapel that was illuminated by a single lamp, the light he had seen from outside. The fat man led the way to a ramp where Saltzman had already deposited the body of the driver. As Leo set the wriggling Scarpatto next to it, Saltzman returned with Sciortino. 'Hit your button,' Saltzman told the fat man.

A low, steady hum filled the chapel. The ramp began to move. All three bodies were slowly transported towards a curtain that parted to give them passage. The first two bodies passed from view. The third, Scarpatto, writhed furiously as the conscious man realized the fiery fate that awaited him, his inability to do anything about it.

'Bet he wishes he didn't have such a thick skull now,' Saltzman remarked laconically. Nodding in satisfaction, he watched the curtain part and close for the final time.

Half an hour later, they were riding in the truck back to New York. Between Leo's feet rested a box containing the ashes of the three cremated men. Saltzman had suggested they give it to William Minsky as proof.

As they came off the Queensboro Bridge into Long Island City, a traffic light turned against them. Saltzman stopped. When the light turned to green, he put the truck in gear and pressed down on the gas. The drive wheels, stuck on a sheet of hard-packed snow, spun in place. Saltzman tried starting in a higher gear. The wheels continued to spin and the light changed back to red. Saltzman swore. 'Give me that damned box,' he said. Leo passed across the ashes. Saltzman climbed out of the cab and scattered the ashes beneath the drive wheels. He got back into the cab just as the light turned green again. Letting up the clutch, he gave the engine the tiniest squirt of gas. The drive wheels gripped on the ashes. The truck moved off.

Saltzman started to laugh. 'Those three dumb bastards were more use in death than they ever were in life, eh, Leo?'

Leo joined in, leaning against the door, his body shaking with laughter.

When he returned to Fort Lee that night, Saltzman telephoned Florida. 'Lou, it's Harry. The job went down okay.'

'How was Leo?'

'Behaved like a champ. Never had a better assistant in my life.'

79

'Thank you, Harry.' Levitt put down the receiver and smiled to himself. He'd been right all along. Take a streak of violence, channel it in the right direction and it can prove invaluable. Like Levitt himself, Saltzman was now middle-aged. How much longer would he be able to go on offering the services that Levitt had come to take for granted? It was time for an apprentice to be indentured. To be ready for that day when Saltzman was no more use. An apprentice who would evolve into a professional controlled absolutely by Levitt.

Chapter Four

Both Judy and Joseph agreed that an important ingredient had been conspicuously absent from their own childhood. To see grass, to throw a ball, to play on a lawn had meant visiting a park. They did not want their own child to be similarly deprived. An apartment was no place for a child to grow.

Within two weeks of Judy springing her New Year's Day surprise, she and Joseph started house-hunting. After a month of feverish activity, the field was narrowed down to two choices, both on the north shore of Long Island. One was a house in Great Neck; the other, in Sands Point, had been built by a film star in the 1920s, during Long Island's halcyon days.

One cold Sunday afternoon, Joseph and Judy called at the apartment on Central Park West. 'Ma, come for a ride with us. We need your advice on something.'

'On what?'

'You'll see. And wrap up warm.'

Pearl took a Persian lamb coat from the wardrobe and went downstairs to Joseph's car. 'Are you going to tell me where we're going?' she asked as they left Manhattan and drove through Queens.

'You'll see,' Joseph answered. The house was only part of the surprise. The other part belonged solely to Judy. She'd suggested it, and Joseph had quickly agreed.

At last, Joseph drove into the semi-circular driveway of a red-brick house in Great Neck. A brown Dodge belonging to the real estate agent was already there.

'You've bought this?' Pearl asked. 'Why do you need my advice if you've already bought a house?'

'We haven't bought anything yet. There's another one we're interested in as well.'

With Judy and Joseph, Pearl followed the real estate agent. The house had four bedrooms on the second floor, spacious rooms on the first floor and a long, sloping lawn that was surrounded by carefully cultivated rose beds. 'I don't know what advice you're expecting from me,' Pearl said. 'I've never lived in a house in my entire life.'

Judy and Joseph winked at each other. 'Get back in the car. We'll show you the other house.'

Pearl made the short journey to Sands Point in silence. She'd be lost in a house, she thought. Her life had been spent in apartments, first above her parents' restaurant, then at the bottom of Fifth Avenue, and finally on Central Park West. She was already forty-eight and she had lived in only three places in her life. What was it she had read once – that ninety per cent of people died within twenty miles of where they had been born? Somehow, it was a comforting thought, and at the same time a distressing one. She could count the times she'd been outside New York . . . outside Manhattan even. She had spent her life on a tiny, overpopulated island, hemmed in by concrete and steel. Envy gripped her at the prospect of Joseph and Judy living in such green luxury, the smell of trees, freshly-cut grass and the sea permanently in their noses.

'Here's the other place, Ma,' Judy said.

Pearl looked out of the car window. They had turned from a narrow road to pass between tall wrought-iron gates. A winding gravel driveway led up to the largest house Pearl had ever seen. She noticed a tennis court, a stable and a paddock where horses could be exercised. 'You'll need a map and a compass to get around this castle,' she said. 'Even with a baby, the place'll be like an echo chamber. It's much too big for three people. The other place is better, in Great Neck.'

'Who said anything about there being three of us?' Joseph asked.

'To begin with there'll be three. Unless, of course, you're expecting twins like I had.'

82

'No twins.' Joseph looked at Judy. The surprise was hers to impart.

'We want you to live with us, Ma,' Judy said.

'Me?' Stunned, Pearl pointed to herself. 'Why do you want me to live with you?'

'Why do you think?' Judy retorted. 'I'm going to need someone to help me with the baby, to do the cooking, the cleaning. And if you've got a few minutes left over at the end of the week, you can mow the lawns, clean out the stables and sweep the tennis court.'

'Have you lost your mind?' Pearl's amazement lasted only as long as it took Joseph and Judy to fall about laughing.

'We want you with us, Ma, because we love you. Is there any better reason than that?'

'That's different.' Pearl marched towards the front of the house. The estate agent ran quickly to get ahead of her and unlock the front door.

'Think she believed what I said about the cleaning?' Judy asked as she and Joseph followed.

'For a moment she did. It's a wonder she didn't tell you what to do with your invitation to live with us.' They quickened their pace when Pearl called them from the front door. 'What do you think, Ma?' Joseph asked. 'Here, or Great Neck?'

Pearl stood in the centre of a vast reception hall, staring at the wide staircase that curved gracefully to the second floor. 'How many bedrooms in this place?'

'Five upstairs,' the estate agent answered. 'Downstairs there's a formal dining-room, living-room, a library, and a recreation room with a full-sized pool table that comes with the house. There's also a room that can be made into a children's playroom, plus there's a separate self-contained guest wing.'

Pearl's eyes widened as she took it all in. She tried to remember the flat above the restaurant on Second Avenue . . . that place would have fitted into this entrance hall with space to spare. Yet hadn't she and her parents been thrilled to have such a home? 'I want to see the kitchen,' Pearl stated. 'Please show me where the kitchen is.'

'This way.' The real estate agent walked through the hall

into a large, airy breakfast-room that overlooked the gardens at the rear of the house. 'There's your kitchen.'

Pearl walked back and forth on the tiled floor. Heavy oak cabinets were fitted to the walls. She opened the doors, peeked inside, ran her hands across the wide counter tops. She pulled back the door of an enormous refrigerator that stood in the corner, inspected the huge range and oven. When she turned around to face her son and daughter-in-law, she was smiling. 'Now this is what I call a kitchen. Buy this house. Cooking here will be a pleasure.' Then concern replaced the smile. 'If I live here with you, how will I look after Leo?'

Before Joseph could say anything, Judy answered. 'Leo's a big boy, he's old enough to look after himself. He doesn't need his mother to fuss over him anymore.'

Pearl did not seem quite so certain. She still pressed Leo's shirts, cooked his meals, even made his bed each morning after he'd gone to work.

'Maybe if you stop taking such good care of him,' Judy added, 'he'll go out and find a girl to marry.' She saw Joseph glance at her. Was he frightened that she was going to spill Leo's secret to Pearl? Neither she nor Joseph had ever mentioned it since that night they'd fought over her following Leo. Judy was not even sure that Joseph fully believed her; for all she knew he might still be convinced that she'd fabricated the whole story. 'You've made Leo too comfortable, Ma. That's his trouble. While you fuss over him, he'll never want to leave.'

Pearl's smile returned. Judy was right. Hadn't Leo always treated her like she was his girlfriend instead of his mother? Leaving him to make his own bed, look out for himself, might just be the kick in the pants that he needed to go out and find a wife.

Touring the remainder of the house was an anti-climax. Even the bedroom that was designated Pearl's with its own dressing-room and *en suite* bathroom aroused little interest in her. She had been sold on the kitchen. If the kitchen had not been to her liking the house could have been a fairy-tale palace and she would have thumbed her nose at it.

As they prepared to leave, Joseph made an offer to the agent. 'If it's accepted, when do you think we can close?'

'Let me call you tomorrow,' the agent replied. 'By then I would have spoken to my principal.'

Instead of going to work the following morning, Joseph stayed at home by the telephone. At ten-thirty, the agent rang through to say the offer had been accepted. The closing could take place in four weeks. Joseph gave a yell of delight and hugged Judy who was standing next to him. Within ten minutes he was on the telephone to decorators, builders, painters, enquiring about estimates for the renovation of the house in Sands Point. He wanted to be in there in three months at the latest.

Leo was stunned when Pearl told him the news. 'You're going to move in with Joseph and Judy?' he asked in disbelief. 'What will I do?' Before Pearl could answer, Leo continued with his protest. 'How will I see you when you're all the way out there, Ma? Judy won't want me to come to *her* house. She talked Joseph into buying a house all the way out there so she could take him right away from me.'

'No one talked Joseph into anything, Leo. Buying that house is his idea. He wants a house in the country for when Judy has the baby.'

Leo did not accept that for a moment. It was yet another instance of Judy trying to draw Joseph further away from his twin brother, create a split between them that was totally irreversible. And then persuading Pearl to move in with them! That was compounding the evil! 'Why do you think they want you to live with them, Ma?' he burst out. 'It's her idea . . . Judy's! She wants to take you away from me as well!'

'Of course she doesn't, Leo. You're just imagining it,' Pearl said soothingly. Nonetheless, his wild accusation lodged in her mind.

Phil Gerson opened the Monaco in Hollywood at the end of February. The final cost was just over eight million dollars, two million more than had been budgeted for. Levitt and Minsky went down to judge what kind of return they could expect from their expensive investment.

They did not tell Gerson they were coming. Arriving at night, they took a taxi from the airport to the Monaco, walked into the sumptuous lobby – 'Goddamned twenty grand chandelier,' muttered Minsky – and asked for Gerson at the desk.

The clerk recognized them, picked up the telephone and made the call. Five minutes later, Gerson walked out of one of the lifts. Wearing a new hand-tailored tuxedo, he marched towards the two New York men, hand outstretched. 'I must have known you were going to pay me a surprise call. I've got the place packed out upstairs.'

'What about the rooms?' Levitt asked.

'Do you mean is there any place left for you two?' Gerson snapped his fingers. The clerk passed him the reservation book. 'Ninety per cent occupancy. Not bad for a first night, eh?'

'Not bad at all,' Levitt concurred. The grand opening of the Monaco had been well advertised, both in South Florida and in New York. Top entertainers had been engaged for the floor show. Additionally, word had gone out to big gamblers about the casino on the top floor. For a moment Levitt felt jealous of Gerson, standing there in his new tuxedo, the king of the casino. It reminded Levitt of earlier days, the sweetness of running his own show in the back room of the Four Aces. He still ran the show, but now he was in the position of a corporation head. He was removed, no longer on the floor where the real action was. 'Let's go upstairs and take a look.'

They took the special lift that served only the top floor. The moment the door opened, Levitt's senses heightened. The sound of rolling dice, the riffle of cards being dealt, the rattle of the ball against the numbered slots of the roulette wheel were like a shot of adrenalin to him. He felt that he'd come home. Bookmaking, numbers . . . none of them had anything on this thrill. 'How's the Waterway coming along?' he asked as he followed Gerson across the casino floor. From behind, he heard Minsky muttering sourly about more twenty thousand-dollar chandeliers.

'They're putting down the foundations next week. With what we learned from this place – mistakes, short cuts – we'll be able to move much faster.'

'Wait.' Levitt stopped to watch a dark-skinned man place a thousand dollars on twenty-two at a roulette table, just as the croupier called out 'No more bets.' The wheel slowed, the ball jumped from slot to slot, eventually settling in thirty-six. No one at the table had it. Levitt couldn't hide a smile as the dark-skinned man's thousand dollars joined the rest of the losing bets under the croupier's rake.

'Arab diplomat,' Gerson whispered. 'Came down from Washington for a couple of days.'

'Good. Hope he loses some more. We'll be generous with his money at the next Israel appeal.'

'Where's your girlfriend?' Minsky asked.

'Belinda? She had to go away for a few days. If we'd have known you were coming down for the opening, she'd have stayed around. You should have told us in advance.'

'Where'd she go?' Levitt asked. 'Off buying more stuff for the Waterway?'

Gerson laughed and slapped Levitt gently on the shoulder. 'I told you, we learned from building this place. The Waterway'll come in on budget, don't worry.'

Levitt backed off. He hated being touched. 'You just get two thousand more players like that Arab at the roulette table and you'll make up the deficit on this place.' It bothered him that Belinda Rivers wasn't on hand for the opening. It seemed so out of character for the blonde dancer. She had played the gracious hostess the entire time Gerson had been down in Florida. Mr and Mrs Bigshot Hotel, he'd thought of them. Now, when the action started for real, she took off. It didn't make any sense. 'When's she coming back?'

'Couple of days at the most. She had to make a trip.'

'Up north?'

Instead of answering, Gerson assumed a sudden interest in one of the blackjack tables, standing to the side to watch the dealer play against three men. 'What's the big secret with Belinda that he doesn't want to talk about her?' Minsky asked quietly.

'Beats me. You'd have thought she'd be here tonight, though. Grand opening and all that.'

'Maybe they split up.'

Levitt shook his head. 'I don't think so. But doesn't it bother you that when the Monaco is finished, when the builders are paid off, she disappears all of a sudden? Just

87

when all the final payments are made . . . when all the big bucks are on the table.'

'You think – ?'

'We've got our own ways of finding out, haven't we?' He broke off as Gerson left the blackjack table and rejoined them.

'If you're sticking around for a few days, I'll take you out on the boat. I finally took some sailing lessons.'

'When did you find the time?' Minsky asked.

'I made it. This place got finished on schedule, didn't it?'

'We'll take a raincheck on the boat ride, Phil,' Levitt said. 'Benny and I have to get back to New York. Another time, maybe. When Belinda's here as well.'

'Good idea . . . she does add something to the place, doesn't she?'

'Add' wasn't the verb Levitt would have chosen. He would have preferred 'subtract'.

Levitt and Minsky returned to New York. The moment Levitt reached home, he telephoned Joseph and instructed the older twin to meet him at a restaurant close to the Jalo Cab garage. As they sat down, Levitt said, 'I want you to go to Zurich, make another trip for Kriesel Engineering Company.'

'I was there last week,' Joseph answered, surprised at the demand. 'We've got nothing due for another three weeks.'

'I want you to see Leinberg. Not for a transaction but for some information.'

'What kind of information?'

'About Phil. I think he's been skimming money off the top, and that's why we're in so damned much of a hole over the Monaco.'

'What?' The single word was filled with Joseph's shock and revulsion at hearing such an accusation against Gerson.

'You heard me. All those trips Belinda's been making all over the place, buying up antiques in Europe, lace tablecloths from Switzerland. Every time she goes over there on a buying spree I think she's been socking money away in some account. Our money. And now, when the Monaco opens, she isn't even there.'

'So? What does that have to do with anything?'

'Joseph, have I got to spell it out for you? Everyone was

88

paid off this week, all the builders, all the contractors. There was a mountain of money flying around and no sign of Belinda. Benny and me, we asked Phil where she was. He wouldn't answer. I figure the reason she wasn't there was because she'd hightailed it to Switzerland again with what Phil's been skimming.'

Joseph shook his head emphatically. 'Uncle Lou, I just don't believe it. Phil and Belinda are friends. They wouldn't . . . wouldn't. . . .' Joseph broke off, unable to use the word 'steal' when it came to his friends.

'Joseph, you've got to realize, there are no friends where a couple of million dollars is concerned.'

Joseph remained defiant, as though his own stubborness could dissuade Levitt. 'What if I go to Switzerland? What if your accusation's true? Leinberg won't tell me anything. Even if Phil has stolen the money, even if Belinda's deposited it there for safekeeping, Leinberg won't admit it. Those Swiss bankers, they're sworn to secrecy about the accounts they hold. That's why you put Blackhawk there.'

'Leinberg will tell you if you use your common sense. That's why you spent all those years at Columbia, so you'd be smart.'

'Phil went to Harvard, that makes him smarter.'

'Don't you believe it. You've got too much of me in you to ever get outfoxed by anyone, Harvard or otherwise.'

'Too much of you?'

Levitt stiffened, realizing too late what he had said. Never, in all his years of jealously watching over the twins, had he so much as hinted at anything but an avuncular interest in them. To reveal the truth about himself and their mother would cause Pearl too much distress. Quickly he covered his tracks.

'You know what I mean. I've spent too much time making sure you went in the right direction. You don't get conned by anyone. By a Harvard graduate from a fancy family, or by a stone-faced Swiss banker. Get over there and find out what's been going on. It's your money as well as mine.'

Feeling troubled, Joseph returned home. He liked Gerson, liked him a lot. He'd even wanted him as best man at his wedding. Was Levitt's claim true? Had Gerson, through Belinda, been stealing from them? For once, Joseph wanted the little man to be wrong. He didn't want Phil Gerson to be exposed as a thief, a man they had entrusted with a fortune only for him to betray them. He didn't even want to travel to Zurich and meet with Leinberg. Yet he knew he must. When it came to loyalty, his family – and Levitt was a part of that family – had precedence over friends.

Judy was disappointed when Joseph sprung the news of his trip. 'I was hoping we could go out to Sands Point tomorrow, make some more decisions about what we're going to do.'

'We don't close for another two weeks.'

'Two weeks isn't long, Joseph. Besides, you went to Zurich only last week.'

'Business is good,' he joked. He saw no reason to tell Judy of Levitt's suspicions. Gerson and Belinda were her friends as well.

'Business is good,' she repeated, 'and this kid – ' she patted her stomach – 'is going to have a father who won't know whether he's on Eastern Standard Time, Greenwich Mean Time, or somewhere-in-between time!'

'You go out to the house. Take Ma with you. Between the pair of you, you can decide what should be done.'

Judy knew it was the best she could hope for.

Joseph faced Walter Leinberg across the boardroom table of Leinberg Bank. 'What you are asking from me,' the Swiss banker said slowly, 'is unethical and out of the question.'

'You shouldn't talk so glibly about ethics when you've got half the loot from the Third Reich stashed in your vaults,' Joseph retorted. 'We suspect that someone has had their finger in our till, and that the money – '

'Philip Gerson?'

Leinberg's instantaneous use of Gerson's name sounded a death knell to Joseph's faint hope that there might have been no truth to Levitt's claim. Of course it was true. As if there had ever been any doubt! Once Levitt said it was so, it was gospel. 'That's right, Phil Gerson. And that the money stolen from us has been brought over here and deposited in either this bank or another. What I want from you is information on whether an account has been opened here or in some other bank.'

'What occurs in other banks is none of my concern,' Leinberg replied tartly. 'And I doubt very much if other banks would allow me access to their records. You certainly would not want me to allow access to mine, would you?'

'Has Phil Gerson made any deposits here lately?'

'Philip Gerson has not been near our bank since you took over the courier run, Herr Granitz.'

'That isn't what I asked.' Joseph stood up and walked to the door. As he opened it, he looked back. 'I'll be at my hotel until midday tomorrow, after which time I will be flying home. Think about this. We have some twenty-five million dollars in Blackhawk. What's been stolen from us is two million at the most. You're a banker, you can work out balances. Which balance is more in your favour . . . our twenty-five million, or the missing two million?' He closed the door and left.

That evening, he telephoned Levitt in New York. 'Uncle Lou, I told Leinberg we'd stop doing business with him if he didn't help.'

'Good, that's a big hammer with which to hit someone over the head. Even a stoneface like Leinberg would feel it.'

'I gave him until tomorrow. But what if,' Joseph asked as an unwelcome idea crossed his mind, 'he threatens our secrecy?'

'He wouldn't dare. He'd blow his own bank to pieces if he did such a stupid thing. No one would go near him. And those more questionable accounts he carries – ' by that, Joseph knew that Levitt meant the Nazis on the run – 'they'd carve him up into little pieces and feed him to the fish in Lake Zurich.'

'If you don't hear from me tomorrow, you'll know I'm on the way home,' Joseph said.

All the following morning he waited by the telephone in his room. At one minute to noon, it finally rang. 'Herr Granitz, here is Leinberg. Would you come to my office, please?'

'I'd be delighted to.'

The two men faced each other across the boardroom table again. Joseph waited patiently while Leinberg searched through a file, eventually extracting a sheet of paper. 'The name of the account is Dancer.'

'How much is in it?' He tried to reach across the table for the sheet of paper. Leinberg swiftly withdrew it.

'Just over a million and a half dollars.'

'Who has signing rights?'

'Two people. Philip Gerson and Belinda Rivers. It was the woman who made the deposits.'

'I know. You will receive notification from us when Dancer is to be closed and the balance transferred to Blackhawk. You may arrange the documentation any way you like to account for the transfer.'

'As you wish, Herr Granitz.'

Five men sat around Lou Levitt's desk in the office above the Jalo garage: Levitt himself, Benny Minsky, the twins and William Minsky.

Levitt nodded at Joseph who began to relate details of his journey to see Leinberg in Zurich. Halfway through, as he mentioned the amount of money in the Dancer account, Minsky leaped to his feet. 'Why are we just sitting around here talking? That fancy Harvard guy robbed us blind. Him and his damned girlfriend, the interior decorator! We know what we've got to do, so why don't we just call up Harry Saltzman and let him get on with it?'

'Sit down, Benny,' Levitt said. 'And shut up.'

Minsky dropped into his chair, furious at Levitt for demeaning him in front of his son. The anger came out as biting sarcasm. 'Since when don't you care about a million and a half bucks? You're the only guy I know who ever squeezed a nickel so hard the goddamned buffalo screamed in pain!'

'I was entitled to squeeze it. I was the guy who made those nickels, and the dimes, and the dollars. Everything we have is of my making, and don't you ever forget it.'

'Sure, you're so smart that Gerson pulled the wool right over your eyes. He didn't pull no wool over mine. I told you right from the start that there was something down in Florida that wasn't kosher.'

Even to himself Levitt hated to admit that he'd been wrong and Minsky had been right. 'Let's take a vote on it.'

Minsky's decision was instantaneous. 'Hit him.'

'We know where you stand already, Benny. How about you, Joseph?'

92

Joseph sat there, uncomfortable as he weighed Gerson's friendship against the treachery. Finally he shook his head.

'That's right,' Minsky said. 'A university man stands up for another university man.' He'd harboured little doubt that Joseph would vote against killing Gerson. The older Granitz twin was too immature to know any better. He hadn't learned yet that sometimes it was the only way. Minsky did not have the same feeling about Leo. Leo had killed already, helped to burn the men who had tried extorting money from B. M. Transportation. Allied with William, whose vote Minsky was certain of, the decision would be in favour of killing Gerson. Joseph's dissenting vote carried no weight at all.

'You, Leo?' Levitt asked.

'He deserves whatever he's got coming to him.' If Saltzman was given the job, Leo was certain he'd go with him. He felt no loyalty to Gerson like Joseph did. The gifts that Gerson had given to Leo, the ties, the introduction to his own tailor, meant nothing against the enormity of stealing a million and a half dollars. Gerson was just another *schmuck* who'd let a woman make a fool out of him.

'Two for,' Minsky said, 'and one against.'

'I can count,' Levitt answered. 'William?'

'No.'

The single word of rejection hung in the air. Minsky swung around on his son, unable to believe what he'd heard. 'What the hell do you mean, no?'

'How do we know that the million and a half in the Dancer account is our money? We've got no proof of it. Every penny that's been spent on the Monaco has a receipt to go with it.'

'Receipt!' Minsky shouted. 'That's the oldest dodge in the world. That broad could have had doctored receipts for all the junk she bought! Are we going to send people over to Europe and check on every purchase? Phil could have pressured the builders to give him a kickback for getting the contract. All the builders have got to do is keep two sets of books, two sets of estimates, two sets of specifications. One for our benefit with figures that match what Phil's spent, and another set with the true figures for their own records and for the tax people!'

'I still don't want to see him killed,' William said. 'It's not necessary. We've got the money. Why kill him?'

'Two for, and two against,' Levitt cut in quickly. 'And my vote, the casting vote, is also no. You're outvoted Benny.' Levitt had not been surprised to hear Leo vote with Minsky. He thought he'd lost the motion on that vote alone. Then William had shocked him by going against his father.

'It doesn't matter whether we get the money back or not!' Minsky argued with his son. 'It's the damned principle of the thing. Phil robbed us and he should be punished for it!'

'When a man talks about principle,' Joseph said calmly, 'he really means money.'

'What?' Minsky turned his anger on Joseph. 'Is that something you learned during your four years at university?'

'Just something I heard once. A cute little phrase with a whole load of truth.'

Levitt rapped his knuckles on the desk. 'Listen to me. Phil's been valuable to us in the past. He had that courier run down pat. The whole thing was his idea anyway, his and his father's. He's saved us plenty more than the million and a half he's swindled. He's also in the middle of doing a big job for us down in Florida. The Monaco's up and operating at a profit. The Waterway's under construction now. Let him get finished down there, and then we'll decide what should be done.'

'Let him finish so he can steal more from us?' Leo asked.

'What does it matter how much Belinda ships over to Switzerland on her trips?' Joseph fired back. 'We've got a lock on that Dancer account. It might as well be in our names because Leinberg will do whatever he's told to do with it.'

'I don't care about the money,' Minsky said. 'This guy keeps stealing from us *carte blanche*, and I won't wait for Harry. I'll put Phil on ice personally.'

'That's because you're taking it so damned personally,' Levitt responded. 'Stop thinking with your heart, Benny. Think with your head. Use the little bit of grey matter you've got inside it. Even your son can see what's right and what's wrong.'

Minsky swung around to glare at William; he still couldn't accept that his son had gone against him. Like father like son . . . like hell!

'Let me say something,' Joseph broke in. 'I agree with Uncle Lou. Phil's done a lot of good for us, in Florida and before he went down there. I think that makes him deserving of a second chance. Let me go down there. I'll speak to him – '

'You'll tell him to his face that we know he's been robbing us?' Leo asked.

'No. I'll tell him, friend to friend, that the people up here are upset over the cost overruns. There's a feeling that there might be something strange going on. I'm not going to tell him that we know. I'm just going to hint, that's all. If I'm right, that'll be enough. He'll toe the line from here on in. When the Waterway's up . . . and it comes in on budget . . . we'll just take the Dancer account from him. We won't be out of pocket. And if you want to punish him, you can throw him out on his ear. Losing the job he has with us will be punishment enough.'

Slowly, Levitt nodded his head. 'Good logical thinking. Do we take a vote on Joseph's proposal?'

Minsky turned down the idea of a vote; he already knew what the count would be, the same as before. 'I want to know one thing, Joseph. What if he pulls the same crap with the Waterway, doesn't take a blind bit of notice of your hint?'

'How will we know,' Leo asked, 'unless we check every receipt?'

'Leinberg will inform us of any transactions on Dancer,' Levitt answered. 'I'll get on to him and make sure he relays news of any activity.'

'Well?' Minsky pressed. 'What if?'

Joseph had already considered that possibility when he made the proposal. 'Then you can do whatever you want with him.'

The deal on the house in Sands Point closed two weeks later. Joseph attended the closing at the lawyer's office with Judy, and then went to the house to meet with the decorators who were starting work the same day. Late that evening, he flew down to Florida to see Phil Gerson. He had purposely let those two weeks elapse between the discussion and seeing Gerson. He did not want his warning to come right on the heels of the visit to Florida by Levitt and Minsky. He needed Gerson to be at ease, free of the immediate worries of the hotel opening, receptive to some well-chosen words of caution.

Gerson met him at the airport. Joseph had telephoned ahead to say he was coming, although he had not given a reason. Nor did he mention one as they drove from the airport to the Monaco in Hollywood.

'What do you want to see first?' Gerson asked when they entered the hotel. He assumed Joseph had come south out of curiosity. 'The casino or the books?'

'Show me both.'

Gerson's office was on the top floor, through a door leading from the casino. As they passed between the gambling tables, Joseph saw Belinda. She was so intent on her game of blackjack that she didn't even notice him. 'Is that good policy, Phil, having Belinda play?'

'It's quiet right now. A little action can lead to more action, a domino effect. People who are just watching might get the urge to play themselves. Besides,' he gave a dry laugh, 'it keeps the dealer's fingers supple. Here,' he unlocked the office door, 'sit down and I'll show you what's what.' He set two ledgers on the desk in front of Joseph. One was full-sized, bound with a hard red cover. The other, smaller, thinner, with a flimsy blue cover, was more like a school exercise book. 'The red one, that's the real accounts for the hotel operation.'

Joseph flipped through the pages. Room occupancy was down to seventy-four per cent from the original ninety. That was to be expected, Joseph supposed. The novelty of a new hotel soon faded, even after only a couple of weeks, and the winter season, when South Florida made its money, was drawing to a close. The room rates would drop during the summer months, and the hotel would take in the vast bulk of its money from the top floor. In November, when the season started again, the rates would go up. By then, the Waterway would also be open. Another luxury hotel, another moneymaking casino.

'The blue book, that's for up here.'

Joseph opened it. There was not a single word, a single letter, written on its pages. Just figures, corresponding to a code that Levitt had devised. At the end of each week, when the casino profits were shipped to New York for the eventual journey to Zurich, the blue book accompanied them. Once Levitt had read the figures, the book was burned in the furnace with all the betting and policy slips. 'Over and above the pay-offs, how much have we made so far?'

'A hundred and twenty thousand, that's the take for the first two weeks. We're not – ' Gerson bathed Joseph with a wide smile – 'billing up here for any share of the hotel's overheads, of course.'

Joseph closed the book. 'Phil, I didn't come down here to look at the accounts, to see how business was doing. I came down here as a friend to do you a favour.'

'Oh?' Gerson pulled up a chair. 'What kind of a favour?'

Throughout the flight, Joseph had pondered how to approach this moment. He remembered Levitt's caution to Minsky: think with your head, not with your heart. The same applied to him. His heart urged him to come right out and tell Gerson that they knew what he'd been up to, beg him to quit, offer to give the money back on his own accord. His head overrode sentiment. He had loyalties to Levitt, to Leo, to the Minskys as well. He would only do exactly as he'd been detailed to do.

'New York isn't happy about the way this place went so far over budget, Phil. They've got a feeling – '

'Who's got a feeling?'

'Benny Minsky, mainly.'

'Not Lou Levitt?'

'No,' Joseph lied. 'It's Benny. He feels you've been deliberately inflating the costs to line your own pockets.'

'He's crazy. Every goddamned penny we spent is accounted for. What does he think I'm doing, overcharging and sticking it in my pocket?'

Joseph didn't answer.

'That's fine gratitude,' Gerson went on. 'I bust my ass down here and Benny Minsky's sitting up there stabbing me in the back. You know why he's got it in for me, don't you?'

'I've no idea.'

'Because I'm smart enough to have gone to university, the same as you. His kid wasn't bright enough to get in.'

Joseph recalled Minsky's sarcastic comment about university. If it were not for seeing Leinberg, for knowing about Dancer and Gerson's duplicity, Joseph might even have agreed with him. 'His son's no dunce. William just wanted to get out and work. He didn't want to study.'

The office door opened and Belinda walked in. Joseph could not help noticing how heavy the purse she carried was. It bulged so much that it looked as if the seams might split at any moment. 'Joseph, what a lovely surprise!' she burst out. 'When did you get in?' Too late she tried to hide the swollen purse out of sight behind her back.

Joseph riveted his eyes on her face, pretended he hadn't even seen the purse. 'Now I get the big greeting. Before, I walked by within three feet of you, and you didn't even notice me. You were too busy playing blackjack.'

'You should have said hello.'

'Did you win?'

She shook her head. 'I never win.'

'It's lucky she only plays minimum stakes,' Gerson added with a laugh. Joseph did not share in the laughter. He had seen a mountain of chips on the table in front of Belinda. If she had been gambling with minimum stakes, it would have taken her the rest of the night to go through that lot.

Belinda clapped her hands. 'Why don't we go out on the boat tomorrow?' she suggested. 'Phil could do with a break from this place for a few hours. How about it, Joseph?'

'Why not?' Maybe with no distractions other than the sun and the sea, he could drill some sense into Gerson's head before Benny Minsky got his way and drilled lead into it instead. . . .

The sun beat down the following morning, sending the temperature to eighty degrees by ten in the morning. By then, Joseph, Gerson and Belinda were aboard the yacht, anchored two miles off the coast. The sun, as it rose towards its midday zenith, bathed the coast in white. Joseph had no trouble in picking out the Monaco; it shone like a pink pearl.

'This is the life, eh?' Gerson said as he and Joseph sat in the stern of the yacht. Belinda was stretched out on a towel at the bow, sunning herself. For a fair-skinned blonde, Joseph thought, she tanned amazingly well. 'Now let's hear this again about Benny Minsky wanting my head on a silver platter,' Gerson said.

'If you don't come in on budget for the Waterway, he'll have it, Phil. You'd better keep a tight rein on the builders, and on Belinda. Right now, only Lou Levitt's standing in Benny's way. And he's doing that for services rendered in the past.'

'Lou's the only one I'm worried about,' Gerson answered. 'If he had me in his sights, I'd be wetting my pants. But Benny Minsky . . .? Pah!' He slapped the air with his hand. 'That guy hasn't got the brains he was born with. Lou's carried him the whole time. Believe me, if Benny had been in charge of this operation, the Monaco would be ten million dollars over the projected price and they'd still be waiting to set the damned foundation!' Steadily, as the tirade continued, Gerson's voice rose. 'He can't talk about me. He's got no right to. And you've got no right to come down here acting as a messenger boy!'

'I'm trying to do you a favour.'

'The hell you are! You're just relaying the message, that's all you're doing.' Gerson stood up, leaned against the rail and shouted at Joseph. 'You know what you can tell him from me? You can tell that dark-faced bastard to go screw himself. If he's got any messages for me . . . if he thinks I'm helping myself . . . he can come down here in the future and tell me himself. Face to face, like a goddamned man!'

'Let's go back,' Joseph said. 'I'll catch an earlier flight.' He had no wish to stay with Gerson any longer. He was betraying the man, even if Gerson had stolen from his friends to begin with. Betraying him by passing on a veiled threat when he could have told him the truth.

Joseph had no doubt that Gerson would bring the Waterway in for the right price. He wouldn't have to inflate it because he'd found another way to steal. With the Monaco casino open, he could help himself. How much did it take to bribe a dealer or two, especially when it was the manager who was doing the bribing? When no one was watching too closely, like last night, the dealer just paid out and paid out . . . to Belinda who filled her purse until it was fit to burst. Gerson had a pot of gold and he couldn't resist sticking his fingers into it. He thought that Levitt and Minsky would be satisfied with the one hundred and twenty thousand dollars

99

from the first two weeks; that they wouldn't miss the extra few thousand or so. Probably they wouldn't, Joseph thought. Only if Gerson continued to do his banking with his old family connection, the theft would show up in Switzerland instead of Florida.

As Gerson guided the yacht through the inlet into the Intracoastal, Belinda joined Joseph at the stern. She'd heard every word between the two men. 'You don't believe Benny Minsky and his crazy idea about Phil, do you?' she asked.

'If I did, I wouldn't have come down here to talk to Phil,' Joseph answered. He decided to give it a last try. He'd work through Belinda. If she really loved Gerson, she'd put him straight. 'Belinda, for Phil's sake, go easy on the spending for the Waterway. Buy a few less antiques. Buy a few less fancies that aren't really needed. Keep your decorating tastes less extravagant.'

'You're a nice guy,' she said and kissed him on the cheek. 'If you weren't you wouldn't have come down here to warn us. You'd have just believed Minsky and left it at that.'

'Friendship counts for something.'

When Joseph left for New York that afternoon, both Gerson and Belinda saw him off. They waited until the aircraft was airborne before starting the return drive to the Monaco. 'Joseph knows, doesn't he?' Belinda said.

'That we've been skimming from the building costs, giving in false receipts, padding the bills? Sure he knows. That's why he came down here, to warn us off. To tell us that everyone knows.'

'What'll we do?'

'Just sit tight and put up the Waterway for what it's supposed to cost. In the meantime, we can still milk the golden calf other ways. We put stooges in to play the tables, pay off a dealer, a croupier or two, and cash in that way.'

'They won't find out?'

'How can they? I'm the manager. Security's one of my responsibilities. They're so smart up there that they put a glutton in charge of the candy store. Of course he's going to eat the shelves clean, but he'll leave them enough to live on as well.'

'What about Leinberg?'

100

'Don't worry about him. His father and mine were buddies way back when. A connection like that is stronger than anything Levitt or Minsky can throw at him. I'll contact him anyway, make sure that no one's been asking awkward questions.' Suddenly he slammed a clenched fist on the steering wheel. 'Why the hell should I be a pauper when they're coining it in like they own the mint? I'm the guy who put Florida together for them. I'm entitled to a piece of the profits, a big piece.'

'That's right, honey.' She leaned across the seat and kissed his cheek. The front of the car twitched as Gerson responded. Like he'd told her, there were a million ways to milk the golden calf and not get burned. He'd only just started.

Chapter Five

The work on the Sands Point house was completed by the last week in April. Joseph and Judy moved in immediately. By then Judy was six and a half months pregnant. Both she and Joseph were anxious to be settled in their new home as quickly as possible. Pearl was to join them two weeks later.

As the time left before the move shortened, Pearl's trepidation increased. She compiled lists of what to take to Sands Point, what to leave at Central Park West for Leo who would continue to live in the apartment. Each time she drew up a list, she would scrutinize it, shake her head and discard it, and begin writing a new one. Joseph pestered her about how much she really *needed* to take with her. 'Ma, you don't have to drag all this stuff along. I'll buy you new.'

'Why waste money on new when the old is still good?' Her own words made Pearl laugh. She sounded just like Sophie Resnick. Thirty years earlier, Pearl had been annoyed with her mother for hoarding, for being frightened to spend money that was abundant. Now she was doing exactly the same thing.

'Ma. . . .' Joseph tried again. 'The moving men need to know how big a truck to allocate. Make up your mind!'

Finally, Pearl drew up what she termed her ultimate, irrevocable list. It was small, comprising only her bedroom furniture and the bureau where Jake had kept his valuables and important documents. These were familiar items she needed to see around her to make the transition easier. On the day before the move, a Saturday, she went through the bureau's drawers. Painful memories flooded through her. She recalled another time she had inspected the contents of the bureau. Thirteen years earlier, the night that Lou Levitt had come around to tell her that she had to be strong; the same night that she had seen Annie alive for the last time. Now she was preparing to move to the home of Annie's daughter who had survived that terrible night only because of the bravery of Pearl's son.

Purposely she left the bottom drawer until the very last. When she unlocked it, she saw the wedding and birth certificates. And there, beneath the documents, was the polished walnut presentation case that held Jake's twenty-fifth birthday present from Benny Minsky. She did not open the case. She simply sat there holding it, and wondered if she were breaking the law by having the pair of ivory-handled revolvers in her possession, with their ammunition. Of course she was. Should she get rid of them? It would be simplicity itself to ask Lou Levitt, or even one of the twins, to do it for her. She quashed the notion. Like the cuff links, the tie pins and collar studs that were still set out so neatly in the bureau, the two revolvers had belonged to Jake. She could not callously discard anything that had been his.

At ten-thirty on Sunday morning, Joseph arrived with the moving men. When Pearl opened the door, he said, 'Just in case you changed your mind about your ultimate, irrevocable list, the moving guys brought the biggest truck available. You can stick the whole apartment block in it.'

'Don't you be so fresh. When I make a last list, I make a last list.'

'Sure – until the next one,' he said fondly and kissed her on the cheek. 'You show the guys what's got to go.' While Pearl gave the moving men instructions, Joseph rapped on the door of his twin brother's room. 'Leo, are you awake?'

A minute passed. Still in pyjamas, Leo swung back the door. His hair was awry, eyes gummy from sleep. 'What do you want?'

'I'm getting ready to take Ma to Sands Point,' Joseph began, and Leo interrupted him with an enormous, uncovered yawn. 'Jesus, you must have had some night out on the town,' Joseph said spontaneously.

Leo's response was a wide, sleepy smile. He'd spent most

of the night with Gustav, the young Swedish-American boy whom he'd been seeing since the beginning of the year, and had not arrived home at Central Park West until just before dawn.

Joseph did not know what to make of the smile. Judy's accusation kept running through his mind. He tried not to think of it, but that smile forced him to. What had Leo's night on the town comprised? What had he enjoyed at that apartment that Judy said he had on MacDougal Street? Whenever Joseph saw his twin, he was torn apart by Judy's claim. Torn by a loving husband's desire to believe his wife, and equally torn by *not* wanting to believe that such a thing was possible of his twin. Homosexuality! It was something you made jokes about – men with lipstick and eye-shadow, twitching their butts like little girls. Homosexuality wasn't your twin brother!

'Tell Ma to wait a minute,' Leo said. 'I'll get dressed, come out to see her off.'

'What about driving out with us to Sands Point?' Joseph asked. 'You haven't been out to see the house. You haven't shown any interest at all.'

'My invitation's got to come from Judy, not from you.'

Joseph pushed past Leo into the bedroom and closed the door. 'Listen to me, Leo. You've got it all wrong about Judy. You can come out to Sands Point whenever you want to. To see Ma, to see us, to see the baby when it arrives. You don't need an invitation. Don't you understand that what happened at the wedding – and everything else before that – is all water under the bridge now? It's behind us.'

'Maybe it's behind you, but it's not behind Judy. She doesn't want me at her house. She never liked me, so why should anything change now?'

Joseph felt like grabbing Leo by the shoulders, shaking him hard. Did you ever, he wanted to yell, give Judy any damned reason to like you? With all of your craziness, was there ever the least likeable thing about you as far as Judy was concerned? Didn't you give her reason enough to want to find a way of hurting you? Despite the only answers that such questions could elicit, Joseph knew that Leo was still his brother. His only brother. His twin. An accommodation had

104

to be made, a compromise. By both Judy and Leo. Joseph had already told Judy that. Damn Leo's apartment in the Village, the boys he saw there, Joseph had said to Judy. If Pearl was to live with them in Sands Point, then Leo would have to be a welcome visitor. Judy had responded by promising to hide her antagonism towards her brother-in-law. Now it was up to Leo to make a corresponding move.

'For Ma's sake, Leo, you've got to make things change. If you don't come out to Sands Point, how the hell are you ever going to see her? She's not going to be riding up and down the Long Island Rail Road all the time to come and see you!'

'That's what Judy wanted,' Leo answered, gazing evenly at his brother. 'She wanted to take Ma away from me, and now she's done it.'

'You might believe that but no one else does. Do you think that if Ma saw it that way she'd have agreed to move in with us?' Joseph stared sadly at Leo for several seconds. 'For God's sake, you're my brother. I'm telling you that you're welcome at my home. Will you believe it from me? Because if you won't, when's the next time you're going to see Ma?'

Leo had an answer for that. 'A week from today, when William Minsky marries that secretary of his.'

In the rush of moving, Joseph had forgotten all about William Minsky's impending wedding to Susan Mendel. Now that he thought of it, it seemed ridiculous that the date could have slipped his mind. Ever since William had announced his plans to marry, just after the extortion attempt at the Long Island City depot, Benny Minsky had talked about nothing else. The marriage had even superseded Phil Gerson in Minsky's list of priorities. As a wedding present, he'd bought the young couple a house in Forest Hills Gardens, as if by doing so he could show that his son and daughter-in-law would live just as comfortably as Joseph and Judy.

'Fine,' Joseph said. 'So when someone gets *bar mitzvah*ed, married or buried, those are the times you'll see Ma. Is that what you really want?

'No.' Leo stared down at his bare feet protruding from his pyjama trousers. 'That's not what I want at all, and you damned well know it.'

'Then make up your mind to let bygones be bygones.

105

Whatever harm you *think* Judy's done to you, just forget it.'

A knock sounded on the bedroom door. Pearl stood outside. 'The men have taken down the furniture.'

'Want to take one last look around the place?' Joseph asked.

'I've looked all I want to.' She stared past Joseph. 'Leo, I'm going.'

A softness appeared in Leo's eyes as he walked towards his mother, a tenderness that Joseph could rarely recall seeing. It was as though his twin brother had a secret store of warmth and love that was reserved solely for his mother. 'Ma, if they don't take good care of you out there, you know you're always welcome back here. I'll keep a light shining for you in the window.'

'You keep it shining for some nice girl instead,' Pearl told him. 'You're going to find out that this apartment is a big, lonely place when you're all by yourself.'

'I didn't let you get lonely in it, did I?'

'No, you didn't.' It suddenly occurred to Pearl that perhaps the reason Leo had not married – or even considered it, as far as she knew – was because of her; he could not bear to leave her by herself. She could see so many things, so much goodness in Leo that seemed to be invisible to anyone else. She looked at Joseph, dismissal in her eyes. When he had walked out of the bedroom, she said to Leo, 'Will you come out to Sands Point to see me?'

No matter what he thought of Judy, Leo could not refuse his mother. 'Of course I will.'

'Every Friday night, so we can still have our family dinner together.'

'Every Friday night, Ma.'

Pearl smiled, her worries evaporating. 'And when you come, you bring me your shirts. I'll wash and press them just the way you like.'

'I can take them to a laundry here.'

'No laundry takes the care I do. You bring them to me. Leo . . .' She choked back a tear '. . . I'm going to miss you. And I'm going to worry about you being all on your own.'

'Ma, I can take care of myself. Don't worry about me.'

'Only when you find a nice girl,' Pearl said, unable to resist

106

getting her message across one last time, 'will I stop worrying about you.'

'One day, Ma.' He held her in his arms and kissed her, unwilling to break the embrace for he knew that when his mother walked out of the door, a period of his life would end.

'Don't forget to bring me your shirts,' Pearl said, forcing herself to break away. 'Just because you're on your own now, doesn't mean you can walk around looking like a down-and-out. That's not the way I brought you up.'

When Pearl left in Joseph's car to follow the moving truck out to Long Island, Leo stood staring through the living-room window. He was alone for the first time. The realization swept over him but it did not bring the terror he had once thought it would. He had no reason to fear being alone. He had his work. He had his boys. He might – the idea excited him – even be better off than before. Without his mother he would not have to be so careful about keeping his second life a secret, dreaming up stories to answer her questions about where he'd been, with whom he'd been. He would not even have to return to Central Park West at all if he found a boy he really loved. He could just keep the apartment as a base, spend as much time as he liked at MacDougal Street.

His mood brightened. Every hour he had spent in Mac-Dougal Street had been tinged with the fear that Pearl would find out. Now that she had gone to live with Joseph and Judy, there was absolutely no possibility of her learning the truth. As unashamed as Leo was of his homosexuality, he had been terrified that his mother would hear of it, that others might use his feelings as a weapon with which to turn Pearl against him. With Pearl's departure, that fear was gone.

During the journey to Sands Point it wasn't Leo who occupied Pearl's thoughts, but Lou Levitt. She was surprised that he had not ventured up from the floor below to see her off. It was not as though he would be saying goodbye to her for ever, but he should have been there to offer his best wishes on the move.

She voiced those thoughts to Joseph. 'You'd have thought Lou would have come by.'

'You figure he's upset because you're moving out?'

107

'I don't know. He is the one who made me take that apartment.'

'I remember. After Pa, and Judy's parents.' Joseph drove on in silence for a mile, the moving truck fifty yards ahead of him. 'Why did he do that, Ma? Did he just want to keep an eye on you? On all of us? Or was there more to it?'

Pearl gave a gentle smile. 'There's a lot about Lou Levitt that you don't know, Joseph.'

'Such as?'

She considered how much to tell Joseph, how much he'd guessed already. 'He asked me to marry him.'

'When?'

'A couple of times. Once before your father asked me – ' how glibly that term rolled off her tongue – 'and once after your father died.'

'You turned him down both times?'

'I had to. The first time I was in love with your father. I was waiting for him to ask me – he was a bit slow. And the second time . . . well, it was too soon after all the trouble. I told Lou I needed time to think.'

'That's more than thirteen years ago. He's given you a hell of a lot of thinking time.' News of Levitt's proposals came as a shock to Joseph. He'd never viewed the little man in that light; he'd always been a good friend of his father, a friend of his mother, a friend of the family. And his and Leo's godfather, of course. 'Maybe he figured you turned him down twice, and he wasn't going to set himself up for a third rejection.'

'You know . . .' Pearl touched Joseph's hand as it rested on the steering wheel '. . . I think he had it in mind on the day you and Judy got married. There was something about him that day, the way he fussed over us all before we left for the *shul*. I could sense that he was leading up to something.'

'And then Leo stuck in his two cents worth,' Joseph muttered. 'Do you love Uncle Lou?' He could sense his mother's hesitation and added, 'There's nothing wrong with being middle-aged and in love.'

'Thanks. I'm glad you're allowing your mother to have feelings,' she said, laughing. 'I don't know how I feel about him, Joseph, and that's the truth. I've never been able to

108

work it out to my own satisfaction. He's been like a father to you and Leo. He's done everything a father could have done.'

'And he's done everything he could for you. You really think he'd forget to come upstairs and wish you luck with the move?'

'That's what I don't understand.' She clutched at Joseph's arm, almost dragging his hand off the wheel. 'My God, do you think there could be something wrong with him? Maybe he's ill! Joseph, turn back!'

Joseph started to laugh. 'He's not ill. He didn't come up to say goodbye because he's waiting for you at the house.'

'He is?' Pearl's anxiety turned to delight.

'He came by first thing this morning. He wanted to be there to greet you, figured that saying hello would be more positive than saying goodbye.'

Pearl sat back, smiling. That sounded just like Levitt, the tiniest detail given careful consideration.

When they arrived at the house, Levitt was waiting on the front steps, holding the largest bunch of roses Pearl had ever seen. 'Welcome to your new home,' he greeted her. 'May it bring you as much pleasure as your old one.'

She took the roses and felt Levitt's lips brush her cheek. Had she found pleasure on Central Park West? Yes, she supposed she had. The joy of seeing the twins and Judy grow up – and anguish at the fighting that had torn them apart. But was that so different from what happened in other families? Perhaps the rows between the twins had been fiercer than those between other brothers, but they *were* twins and so their bond – their love and their passion – was so much stronger. Certainly those fights had finished now, the fiery emotions dying as the twins had matured. 'I'd given you up for lost this morning,' she told Levitt. 'I thought you'd washed your hands of me.'

'Would I ever do that?'

'No, Lou, I don't think you would. You, above anyone else, would always stand by me.'

'You never said a truer word. I've even got my eye on the guest wing here. Perhaps I can talk Joseph and Judy into renting it out to me.'

Although he made it sound like a joke Pearl sensed an

109

undercurrent. Like herself, Levitt was middle-aged; they were both closing in on fifty. She had Judy and Joseph, Leo. Who did Levitt have? It saddened her to think of him all alone. Since Jake's death he had taken care of her. Who, in turn, would care for him? Or was he so alone? He had a family he could always rely upon. Her family.

They walked together into the house, stood in the large entrance hall and watched the moving men carry the bedroom furniture up the curving staircase. 'How did Leo take it this morning?' Levitt asked.

'About my moving? Better than I ever imagined he would. He promised to come here every Friday night for dinner, just like usual. I was frightened that he might think I was deserting him.'

'He's past that stage now, Pearl.'

'He blew up when I first told him, when Joseph bought the house.'

'He's had time to think about it since then. He knows it's the best thing for you.'

'It might be best for him as well. Now that I'm not there – ' Pearl's favourite subject surfaced – 'he might start looking seriously for a girl to marry.'

Levitt shrugged his shoulders and smiled. Pearl was wrong there, dead wrong, but he was not going to be the one to tear her apart by telling her. It was just as well that no one else knew. Leo's secret was safe only with him.

Two days after Pearl moved into the Sands Point house, Joseph made the courier run to Zurich to deposit money from the New York operation, and the casino profits that Phil Gerson had sent up from the Monaco Hotel in Hollywood. It was Joseph's first trip in more than a month, and with Pearl in the house he was comfortable about leaving Judy.

Carrying the small suitcase he'd been given after boarding the aircraft at Idlewild, he left the Savoy Baur en Ville and walked along the Bahnhofstrasse to the Leinberg Bank. He used the side entrance, rode up the elevator to the third floor. Walter Leinberg was waiting in the boardroom. Joseph opened the case and set two separate amounts of money on the table. The bookmaking and numbers take came to a fraction under half a million dollars. The casino profit for the month was just over two hundred thousand dollars. Leinberg pressed his buzzer and the two black-coated book-keepers filed in to count the money.

Leinberg drew Joseph away from the table. 'We have had a deposit for Dancer.'

'How much?'

'One hundred and seventy thousand dollars.'

Joseph performed some rapid mental arithmetic. That was almost a third of what Phil Gerson had reported as total profit on the casino since its opening ten weeks earlier. Gerson had declared himself in as a partner . . . a silent, stealing partner. Was he still letting Belinda win at the tables, or had he found some other way to skim money off the top? They was no way they could check on him without installing a permanent watch, and it was Gerson himself who was supposed to be performing that security duty. Joseph grinned sourly; the bank vault was never safe when the guard himself was a safecracker.

The knowledge that Gerson was still stealing from the Monaco came as no surprise to Joseph. Only two weeks after he'd given Gerson and Belinda the warning, Levitt had heard from Leinberg that a letter had been received from Gerson. In it, Gerson had asked if any enquiries had been made from New York about dealings he might have had with the bank. On Levitt's instructions, Leinberg had replied that no enquiries had been made. To Gerson, that had been the green light to rob his employers blind.

'What do you wish us to do with the deposit, Herr Granitz?'

'Let it ride. Pay interest on it as you would for any account. Don't give Gerson any reason for suspicion. When we're ready, you'll receive instructions on disposition of the Dancer account.' He turned to watch the book-keepers flicking through the bills. 'Who made the deposit?'

'The woman. But she did not come here. Perhaps she was afraid of a chance meeting with you. She paid for one of our employees to meet her in Geneva. He transported the deposit back to the bank.'

Joseph's face blazed red with anger. It was one thing for Gerson to steal. They knew he was doing that and had made plans so that the money would not be lost. But to trust it to

111

an unknown party for the journey from Geneva to Zurich! No matter that the messenger was one of Leinberg's employees, he was still only a man living on a wage. What was to restrain him from succumbing to the temptation of walking away with the money?

Leinberg read Joseph's expression perfectly. 'Would you rather we refused to collect the money in future, Herr Granitz, and force the woman to come here to make the deposit instead?'

Joseph quickly shook his head. Such a move might alert Gerson. At the same time, though, Joseph did not want the stolen money at risk. 'You. . . .' He pointed a quivering finger at Leinberg. 'You pick up the money from the woman in the future. You I trust.'

'A bank president does not normally perform a messenger's duties,' Leinberg began. He saw steel in Joseph's eyes and his resolve wilted. 'But I would be more than happy to make an exception to accommodate you.'

'Thank you. I never doubted that you would.' To Joseph it was another demonstration of the power of wealth. No matter how you got it – through legitimate work or through illegal enterprise – money was still money. Even presidents of prestigious Swiss banks prostituted themselves for it.

Joseph arrived back in New York late on Friday afternoon. When he reached home, the dinner table was set. The house was full of the smell of cooking. His mother had not taken long to settle in.

Lou Levitt and Leo arrived together from the office above the Jalo garage. Leo's arms were full, clasping a suitcase in which were his week's dirty shirts for Pearl to launder and a large box of chocolates, wrapped with red ribbon tied in an enormous bow. Joseph waited for him to give the chocolates to Judy. Instead, he made a big show of presenting them with his dirty shirts to Pearl. It was obvious whom he had come out to Sands Point to see. He asked Pearl to show him around the house; he was especially interested in seeing her room, as if it were up to him to pass approval on the way she was being cared for. When he returned to the entrance hall, he was obviously satisfied.

112

'Some place you bought,' he told Joseph. 'You've got room for ten kids, never mind the one you're expecting.' He walked to the window and looked out over the stable and paddock. 'A place in the country . . . maybe I should buy one for myself. Get away from the rush of the city.'

'No one's stopping you,' Joseph said. Leo would have the stable operative in no time, learn to ride a horse and go cantering across his property like some feudal landowner.

Leo turned to his mother. 'If I bought a place like this, would you spend a few days a week with me?'

Pearl began to laugh. 'I've heard of divorced parents sharing custody of a child, but never of sons sharing custody of their mother. I'll tell you what, Leo – you get married and give me grandchildren. . . .'

Even before she finished, Leo had turned away to look out of the window again. He was becoming tired of listening to his mother harp on that subject.

After dinner, while Judy helped Pearl to clear the table, Joseph led Leo and Levitt into the ground-floor recreation room. There he told them what he had learned from Walter Leinberg in Zurich.

'It comes as no surprise,' Levitt said. He picked up one of the balls from the pool table and rolled it gently across the green baize. 'Once Phil sent that letter to Leinberg it was obvious that he intended to carry on screwing us. He just wanted to be sure the coast was clear.' He picked up another ball, rolled it slowly after the first, nodded in satisfaction as the two balls collided with a solid click. 'I'm afraid that your well-meaning advice to Phil fell on deaf ears, Joseph.'

'Did you get any figures on the Waterway while I was in Zurich?'

'It's coming in on budget, not a cost overrun in sight. But what did you expect? Phil thinks we'll have our eyes on that and we'll never notice the rest.'

'Almost a one-third share,' Leo mused. 'He thinks big.'

'There is no other way to think,' Levitt said, 'but he shouldn't think so big when he's handling our money. I'll tell Benny when we see him on Sunday at William's wedding.'

'He'll want to take care of Phil right away,' Joseph said.

'So he should,' Leo cut in.

Levitt looked sharply at the younger twin. 'You ever play this game?'

'Pool?' Leo shook his head.

'You should do sometime. You could learn something from it. Just because you've got a ball sitting on the edge of the pocket doesn't necessarily mean that you've got to sink it with your next shot. There might be other opportunities out there. You can always come back to the sitting duck when the time's right. The same goes for Phil. We know what has to be done. But before we sink him, let's get all the use out of him that we can. Let him put up the Waterway for us, get it running smoothly.'

Listening to Levitt, Joseph resigned himself to seeing his friend killed. Phil Gerson had broken the rules. Even after the most blatant warning, he had shattered the trust that had been placed in him. There was no alternative. Joseph could do nothing, even if he wanted to.

'Always going to be there, just waiting on the edge of the pocket,' Leo murmured, warming to the analogy that Levitt had created. He walked to the table, picked up the eight ball and rolled it into the centre pocket. 'And then, when we've had our use out of him, the big drop. And goodbye Harvard Phil.' Leo fished the eight ball out of the centre pocket, weighed it thoughtfully in his hand. Would Harry Saltzman get the job? Would he need help?

Judy went to bed that night at ten o'clock. When Joseph followed her an hour later, after Leo and Lou Levitt had left to return to Manhattan, he found her sitting up in bed, reading by the light on the bedside table.

'Baby keeping you awake?' he asked.

'No. I was waiting for you.' She set down the book and watched him undress. 'Your brother acted tonight like I didn't even exist.'

Joseph slipped into the bed, barely able to keep his eyes open. He was exhausted. The journey to and from Switzerland, the changing back and forth of clocks – it was all catching up with him. On top of that, he had to cope with the knowledge that his information had passed a sentence of death on Phil Gerson. 'Don't start now with Leo, darling,' he pleaded. 'I can't even think straight anymore.'

114

'Joseph, you asked me to accommodate him. I did. I let him come around here. The least he could have done in return was treat me with some respect. Did he thank me for dinner when he left? Hell no! He thanked your mother but not me. Did he ask either you or me to show him around the house? No – he asked your mother. He didn't come to my home tonight, to our home. He came to his mother's home.'

'Judy, it's only once a week. You can put up with that, can't you?' He rolled over on to his side, facing away from her.

'Why should I have to put up with it? Joseph, I wanted your mother to live with us. God only knows, she's earned the right to have things a little easier now. But I didn't count on Leo totally ignoring me in my own home.' She waited for Joseph to respond. When no sound came, she leaned over him and saw that his eyes were closed, his breathing slow and regular. He was fast asleep. She snapped off the light and lay awake in the darkness, her fury at Leo mounting. It was not long before it expanded to include Joseph and Pearl as well.

William Minsky and Susan Mendel were married the next Sunday. Leo had been invited to bring a girl to both the ceremony and the dinner-dance that followed. He came alone. When the dancing began, he ignored the single girls who were Susan's cousins and friends in favour of dancing with his mother.

Pearl was both flattered and flustered. 'Stop wasting your time with me,' she urged him. 'There are plenty of pretty girls here. Ask one of them.'

'I don't want to ask one of them. I want to dance with you.'

'Everyone wants to dance with me tonight. You, Uncle Lou, even your brother because Judy's in no shape to go stepping out.'

Leo stared over his mother's shoulder at Judy sitting at a table with Joseph. Unkindly, he thought that she looked like a fat red-headed cow. He had never liked her to begin with, and pregnancy had not altered his views. Her face had puffed up, her legs and ankles were swollen. 'Did you dance when you were expecting me and Joseph?'

Pearl tried to remember. All that came to mind about her own pregnancy was the constant worry about that single indiscretion with Lou Levitt. Besides, those had been busy days, too hectic to even think about dancing, what with the clubs and the never-ceasing convoys. Judy was far more fortunate, always knowing where her husband was, certain that he was safe. When Judy's time came, Joseph would not be riding shotgun on a convoy of bootleg liquor.

They bumped into someone. Pearl heard an 'Excuse me' and turned to see Benny Minsky dancing with his new daughter-in-law. 'How come you're dancing with your mother, Leo?' Minsky wanted to know.

'I just asked him the same thing,' Pearl said.

'Susan's got all these cousins sitting around like wallflowers,' Minsky went on. He looked at the bride. 'Can't you fix Leo up with one of them?'

'He's old enough to find his own girls,' was Susan's curt answer. She remembered Leo from the depot, with that other man who had also been invited to the wedding. Harry Saltzman, another of her father-in-law's business associates. She would not want her cousins dancing with either man.

'See, Ma,' Leo said. 'Only you're anxious about me. You're going to get more grey hairs than you have already.'

The two couples separated, danced their way towards different sides of the floor. 'You don't think too much of him, do you?' Minsky asked Susan.

'He enjoyed what he did that night at the depot. Him and that other man who's here – Saltzman.'

'They were doing a job, that's all. A job that had to be done.'

'Why couldn't William have gone to the police?' Susan had already asked William the same question; he'd avoided answering.

'The police are only good for writing traffic tickets. When it comes to trouble, we take care of our own.' Minsky held his daughter-in-law a little tighter. 'You're not thinking you made a mistake, are you?'

She shook her head. 'William's not on the same level as those other two men.'

'Damned right, he's streets ahead.' Minsky's eyes drifted across the floor to where Susan's mother and father sat, surrounded by members of their family. There had been very little mixing of the bride's side and the groom's side; it was as if each had recognized the other and decided to have no part. That was all right. William wasn't marrying the entire Mendel clan, just Susan. 'Do your parents know about that night?'

'Of course not. Do you think I'd tell them? I might be able to handle it, but they wouldn't.' They danced in silence for a few seconds, then Susan said, 'William told me how you got started with B. M. Transportation, converting the trucks you used to run bootleg whisky in.'

'A lot of respectable people got started the same way.'

'Name one.'

Minsky was taken aback. He had expected the girl to accept his statement as absolute truth without demanding that he validate it. Deep lines furrowed his brow as he concentrated. 'You ever hear of Patrick Joseph Rourke, a bigshot up in Boston?'

'The old ambassador?'

'That's the one.' During the war, Patrick Joseph Rourke had served a short term as the American Ambassador to Ireland, a reward for his staunch support of the Democratic machine in Massachussetts. Minsky remembered the day he'd read of the appointment. Levitt had shown it to him, and they'd both laughed until they ached at the way the Irishman had bent over backwards to become respectable. He'd invested his bootleg profits in real estate, buying up huge parcels of land at deflated Depression prices; he had even backed successful Hollywood movies, invested in utility companies, speculated successfully in engineering and automotive plants that surged to full production with the war. He had become a rich and powerful man, with every penny emanating from a legitimate source.

It hadn't been all roses for the Irishman, though, Minsky thought. Rourke had lost one of his three sons in the war, an armour captain in the Battle of the Bulge; he'd been one of the American prisoners of war murdered by the SS at Malmedy. Minsky tried to remember which son it was. The middle son came to mind . . . Joseph, the same name as the older Granitz twin. 'Old man Rourke had a big bootleg operation,' Minsky told Susan. 'The king of Irish whiskey. That's why he got that job in Ireland. All the *gontser macher* Micks had dealt with him before.'

117

'Did you know Rourke personally?'

'We did business with him, that was all.' Minsky decided that Susan need know nothing more. 'What else did my son tell you?'

'Everything.'

'Everything?' What did William know? How they'd hidden out from Saul Fromberg more than twenty years earlier? How they'd killed him? And how Jake had taken his revenge upon Patrick Joseph Rourke for siding with Fromberg? No . . . William had been a kid then, a baby.

'He told me about the bookmaking places you have, about the gambling in those hotels you're building in Florida. He said it was important that I knew everything before we were married.'

'Would you rather he'd kept you in the dark?'

'No. I'm not sure how I would have felt if I'd found out later on.'

'And how do you feel now?'

'Worried,' was the simple answer. 'William doesn't have to be involved in things like that. He's exposing himself to unnecessary danger. He can make a success of any business he tried. I've seen what he's done with your trucking company. He could do it with anything.'

'I know. That's what puts him one up on the Granitz twins,' Minsky replied, thinking of his own comparison. 'They just continued something that was already established. William created a business almost from the ground up.'

'That's exactly what I mean. So why does he have to be involved in those other things?'

'Just because you're in a straight business doesn't mean you'll have no contact with hoodlums, Susan. You saw that for yourself when those goons tried to muscle in on the new depot. It doesn't do any harm to have some muscle on your own side.'

The dance finished. Minsky returned Susan to William. When he turned away, he saw Levitt beckoning. The men walked from the hall to the washroom. Levitt checked the cubicles to be sure they were vacant. 'Leinberg told Joseph that Phil's girl made a deposit in the Dancer account.

'That's it then.' Minsky drew a hand across his throat. 'Old

118

friendships, past good deeds – they don't count for nothing now.'

'We'll let him finish putting up the Waterway first.'

'Okay, Lou. But don't think you can use that time to get him a reprieve. Once that hotel's up, Gerson goes.'

'You're glad, aren't you?' Levitt accused Minsky angrily. 'I can see that goddamned righteous I-told-you-so look plastered all over your ugly mug.'

'Yeah, I'm glad, because you were wrong. You were just stuck on the guy because he came out of some fancy university, good family and all that crap. You and Joseph both figured he could be straightened out.'

'That makes your own son wrong as well, Benny. He also voted for giving Phil another chance.'

Minsky's face clouded over at the reminder of William's treachery. 'He's entitled to a mistake.'

'So am I, Benny,' Levitt said, clapping Minsky on the arm. 'I don't make that many so I'm entitled to one now and again.' He led the way back into the hall. The two men separated. Minsky went to where his son and daughter-in-law stood while Levitt walked over to the Granitz table.

Midway through the evening, Judy began to complain of feeling tired. She had not enjoyed the wedding at all. The little food she'd eaten had lodged in her chest. The noise and excitement were making her irritable. Most of all she was still angry at Joseph for Friday night when he had stood up for his brother and tried to make her a party to a one-sided treaty of respect. Judy's only bright spot during the evening was a bitter amusement at seeing Pearl trying to persuade Leo to dance with one of the many single girls.

'Joseph, I'd like to go home,' she said.

'You feel all right?'

'Tired. The noise and the heat's getting to me.'

'Sure.' He looked around. 'Where's Ma?'

'Dancing with your brother, where else?'

'We'll wait until they've finished this dance, then we'll leave.'

Judy derived some satisfaction from that. At least she could take Pearl away from Leo. It was a victory of sorts. When Pearl returned to the table on Leo's arm, Joseph said they

119

were leaving. Leo appeared momentarily disappointed. Then he shrugged his shoulders and said he might just as well go home, too.

Joseph drove carefully, trying to pick out potholes in the glow of the headlights. He didn't want to jar Judy; with less than two months to go, he wasn't even sure that she should be in a car. In the back seat, Pearl kept up a steady conversation. She'd enjoyed William's wedding, just as she'd enjoyed his *bar mitzvah*. She felt that she had a stake in his well-being. Benny Minsky had sought her help with the boy, and her interest in him had continued. 'Sometimes I even feel that William's my third son,' she mused. 'Now if only Leo would find someone, then it would be three out of three.'

'He's not going to find anyone dancing with you all night long,' Joseph replied.

'He's too fussy, that's his trouble,' Pearl said. 'All those girls there tonight, and would you believe there wasn't one he liked?'

'Must we talk about Leo?' Judy asked. 'I feel lousy enough without having to listen to his love life being discussed.'

'Judy. . . .' Pearl's voice was full of pain. 'I thought that was all behind us.'

'The hell it is! He comes to my home and treats me like I'm a piece of furniture. Am I supposed to just sit there and say thank you very much? Joseph asked me to be courteous towards Leo. Okay, I was courteous. The least he could have done was give me some respect in return. Even thanking me for dinner would have been a vast improvement.'

'Judy . . . knock it off,' Joseph warned. 'We can work this out without dragging Ma into it.'

'Why didn't you try working it out on Friday night instead of turning your back on me and falling asleep?'

'I was tired, Judy. I'd just flown back from Zurich. I couldn't keep my damned eyes open.'

Pearl leaned forward to touch Judy on the shoulder. 'I'll speak to Leo. I'll tell him that he's upsetting you, all right? Next Friday, when he comes, you'll see the difference.'

'Satisfied?' Joseph asked.

'No, I'm not. I'm sick and tired of everyone standing up for Leo by putting me down. I don't know whether he got dropped on his head as a baby, but there's something wrong with him.'

'Judy, you've got to remember what happened when he was a child,' Pearl began.

Judy cut her off abruptly. 'The diphtheria? How the hell can I ever forget? Every strange action, every rotten thing Leo's ever done has its roots in that damned illness! It wasn't the diphtheria that made him the way he is, believe me! He was born like that!' The last remnants of self-control fled from Judy, leaving naked anger and frustration. 'You want to know why he didn't ask any of those girls to dance tonight Ma? Do you?'

Joseph flicked his eyes nervously from the road to Judy and back to the road again. He'd never seen her like this before, fury mixed with a total abandon. The need to spew it all out smashing aside consideration for anyone. He was terrified of what she was going to say. Of what she could only say! Yet the harder he tried to speak, the tighter his throat became, the drier his lips. The more swollen his tongue. It was all he could do to breathe, let alone speak to interrupt her.

'Well, do you want to know?' Judy demanded of her mother-in-law. 'I'll tell you. Leo doesn't like girls. He prefers little boys to girls, and that's the goddamned truth!'

'Judy!' At last Joseph found his voice. His angry roar filled the car as he jammed his foot down on the brake pedal. The car slewed to a stop.

'Judy, darling. . . .' Pearl's shocked whisper barely carried from the rear of the car. 'Have you any idea of the terrible thing you're saying?'

Judy tried to stop but couldn't. All the poison she'd harboured against Leo spilled out. 'I know exactly what I'm saying, and if you don't believe me I'll even give you the address of the apartment on MacDougal Street where he meets his little boys.'

'Shut up!' Joseph yelled. 'Not another word! We'll sort this out once we get home!'

Judy stared rigidly through the windshield as Joseph drove to Sands Point, his face taut, hands gripping the wheel like a pair of white claws. From behind, Judy could hear Pearl sobbing. Damn it . . she hadn't wanted to hurt Pearl. She hadn't wanted to hurt Joseph either. But dear God, didn't anyone give a damn about her?

By the time they reached the house, Pearl had regained her composure. Her face was streaked with tears when she confronted Judy in the entrance hall, but there was a resoluteness in her voice when she asked: 'Where did you hear this terrible thing about Leo? Who would spread such a slanderous story?'

'She heard it from some cab driver,' Joseph answered before Judy could say a word. 'She had a cab driver follow Leo one night – '

Judy held up a hand for silence. If she was being interrogated, only she would give the answers. To her own surprise, she was icily calm. Finally, the secret she had withheld from Pearl since the previous year was out in the open; a weight had been removed, tension dispelled. 'Do you remember when I left your home early one Friday night when Joseph was away?'

'You were ill, or you said you were,' Pearl recalled. 'I asked Leo to drive you home, and you said you'd take a cab.'

'That's right. I found a cab downstairs. I told the driver to follow Leo when he came out of the building. Leo led us to Washington Square. I gave the cab driver money to follow him when he got out of the car. The driver came back with the information that Leo had gone into a building on MacDougal Street.' Speaking evenly, Judy completed the story right up to the point where the driver had imparted his startling news.

Pearl looked at Joseph. 'You knew about this already?' Joseph nodded mutely. 'Why didn't you say anything?'

'There was no need for you to know.'

'No? I'm only Leo's mother, have you forgotten that? Or is it because you didn't believe Judy that you didn't tell me?' Without waiting for an answer, Pearl marched to the telephone in the entrance hall. Joseph asked whom she was calling. 'Leo,' Pearl answered. 'He left the hall when we did. He should have been home half an hour ago. If he's there, that should put paid to this story.' The telephone rang forever in her ear. She replaced the receiver and turned to Judy. 'Give me that address on MacDougal Street, the apartment number, everything. I'll get out of this long dress, and then I'll find out exactly what's going on.'

'For God's sake, Ma!' Joseph burst out. 'It's the middle of the night. I can't leave Judy alone here to take you to the Village.'

'Who asked you to take me? I'm perfectly capable of telephoning for a taxi.'

Joseph looked beseechingly at Judy. 'Tell her that just because Leo hasn't gone straight home, it doesn't mean that he's out with some little boy! Will you tell her that you made up this whole damned story?'

'Did you, Judy?' Pearl asked.

Judy fervently wished that she could tell her mother-in-law that the story was a lie. She wished now that she had never followed Leo, never tried to find a way to hurt him. Because Leo wasn't the one being hurt. It was all the people around him. Just like always! Wherever Leo went he scattered grief like a farmer planting seeds. Only Leo never harvested his own crop. Others were always left with that rotten job.

Pearl checked the directory for the number of the local taxi company and made the call. 'He'll be here in fifteen minutes,' she told Joseph, 'and maybe then we'll start to find out the truth.'

'Joseph, tell your mother to cancel the taxi,' Judy said. 'You take her if she's so insistent on going. I'll be all right.'

Pearl countermanded the order. 'Joseph, you stay right here. You can't leave Judy on her own.' She had a vision of herself telling Jake that she would be all right when he had wanted to cancel his trip to the South Jersey shore. At least she'd had her mother staying over, and poor Annie living just next door.

'What are you going to do once you get to the Village?' Joseph asked his mother.

'Learn if there's any truth to this horrible story.' Pearl left the living-room and walked up the long, curving staircase to her own room to change.

'Happy now?' Joseph demanded of Judy. 'You've got Ma running out in the middle of the night like there's some emergency. What in God's name made you come out with that garbage?'

'I didn't mean to come out with it, Joseph. You know I promised I'd never – '

'Some promise!'

Judy's anger heightened in the face of Joseph's sarcasm. 'If I'd meant to tell her, don't you think I would have done it the moment I found out about Leo? I kept it here – ' she beat her breast – 'because I *didn't* want to hurt her. Tonight it just slipped out because I was so damned mad. All I ever hear is Leo, Leo, Leo! I'm sick of the sight and sound of him, of always being reminded about his attack of diphtheria when he was a kid and how it's affected him, and how we should overlook his ugliness!'

In Judy's outburst, Joseph heard his own words. Hadn't he said just the same to Leo one night when the younger twin had accused him of not caring for their mother? Hadn't he accused Leo of making a career out of having diphtheria? Used it all his life to get his own way? 'Are you sure that cab driver told the truth?'

'You asked me that once before, Joseph. I told you then that the man had no reason to lie.'

Joseph reached out to hold Judy's hands. 'Then we'd better start figuring out a way to help Ma over the shock when she finds out about Leo for herself.'

From the wedding party, Leo went straight to the apartment on MacDougal Street. He had made many changes in the week since his mother had moved to Sands Point. He had transferred some of his clothing from Central Park West to the apartment in Greenwich Village: he'd put food in the refrigerator, stocked the bar. He intended to use the small apartment as a proper second home, not just as an occasional meeting place.

Leo had left instructions for Gustav to come to MacDougal Street at midnight. That gave him enough time to enjoy a leisurely shower, after which he rubbed himself down briskly with cologne and dressed in a pair of beige silk pyjamas and a robe. He poured himself a drink and set a record on the turntable. The thundering strains of Wagner's 'Ride of the Valkyries' rolled through the apartment, carrying Leo away on a tidal wave of danger and excitement. What better music could he play as an overture to his night with the young Swede?

At five minutes before twelve, he heard a knock on the door. Setting down the drink, he walked across the living-room. Gustav stood outside, tall and slim and platinum blond. Leo's heart leaped as he regarded his visitor. Of all the boys the agency had sent, Gustav was by far his favourite. Leo had paid willingly for him since the beginning of the year, adding generous tips to the fee charged by the agency. The dreams he'd nourished of keeping a boy as his mistress were beginning to take firmer shape. He would have to pay off the agency, come to an arrangement with Gustav; install the boy in the apartment, pay for his loyalty, his love, do away with the crass, commercial necessity of having to make an appointment like a man using a prostitute.

'Hi, Leo, how was your wedding?'

The voice was the only thing about the youth that grated on Leo. A boy with Gustav's looks, the Swedish name, should speak like a Swede, not with a mid-Western accent. Only Gustav's parents had come from Sweden. He had been born on a farm in Minnesota, from which he'd fled at the age of fifteen. 'The wedding was boring. I only got through it by thinking of you. What did you do this evening?'

'Saw a movie.'

Leo wanted to believe the youth. He didn't want to think that Gustav might have been seeing someone else on the agency's instructions. The only way to forestall that would be to take him over completely. Perhaps tonight he should broach the subject. 'Was it a good movie?'

'It was like your wedding. Boring.' Gustav's mouth curled in a sly smile. 'Like you, I only got through it by thinking of what would come later. Are we going to stand out here talking all night, or are you going to invite me inside?'

'Come in, of course come in.' Stepping back, Leo caught the faintest trace of some indefinable perfume as Gustav walked by him. It tantalized his senses. He'd have to ask Gustav what it was.

He was about to close the door when he heard the sound of footsteps ascending the stairs. Light steps, a woman's, and hurrying. Curious, he swung the door wide open and looked out . . . straight into his mother's amber eyes as she emerged from the stairwell. Leo's mouth dropped in shock. His sto-

125

mach twisted itself into a tight knot. A confused babble of questions burst from his lips.

'What are you doing here? How did you get here?' And finally, an anguished: 'Why?'

'What's the matter?' Gustav asked, thinking that Leo was talking to him. Too late, he saw Leo's hand frantically gesturing for him to hide.

Breathless from the stairs, Pearl marched up to the door and looked past Leo to see the slim, blond youth. 'So it's true,' was all she said.

'It isn't what you think – ' Leo's voice broke as, without another word, Pearl swung around and walked back towards the stairs.

'Who was that?' came Gustav's voice.

Leo whirled around, his thick eyebrows drawn together in one solid line. 'Shut the fuck up! Get out of here!' He rushed past the startled youth into the bedroom, ripped off the robe and pyjamas and clambered into trousers and a shirt. Tugging his belt tight, he raced after Pearl, clattering down the three flights of stairs like a runaway horse. He reached the sidewalk just in time to see her climbing into a taxi.

'Ma! Wait!' Leo's grief-stricken shout echoed along Mac-Dougal Street. The taxi inched away from the kerb, then stopped while another vehicle rolled past. Leo threw himself after the taxi, grabbed hold of the rear door handle and yanked it open. 'Listen to me, will you, Ma? It isn't what you think!'

'What do I think, Leo?'

He reached into the cab as if to pull his mother out. She drew back, for the first time in her life rejecting any contact with him. Leo's hand hung motionless in mid-air, unable to reach the huddled figure of his mother in the far corner. 'Who told you, Ma?'

'Does it really matter?' She watched as he withdrew from the taxi and closed the door. 'Take me back to Sands Point, please,' she told the driver. As the taxi moved off, she fought the urge to look back.

Standing on the sidewalk, Leo stared after the lights of the taxi. Lou Levitt's name roared through his mind. It could only be Levitt. His godfather. His Uncle Lou, who, he'd always

126

thought, loved him. Loved him and understood him. Was this Levitt's method of demonstrating that love? Telling Pearl, giving her the address so she could come and see for herself? He began to trudge back to the building. Wait, Levitt did not know about the apartment on MacDougal Street. No one knew about that. He'd been too careful. Damn it, he hadn't been careful enough. Someone knew. And that someone had told his mother, shattered her trust and love for him. But who . . .?

Gustav was still in the apartment when Leo reached it. 'What are you doing here?' he demanded. 'I thought it told you to get the fuck out!'

Bewildered, the blond youth hesitated. 'That old broad, who the hell was she?'

Leo smashed him across the face with the back of his hand. 'That's my mother! Get out, you little bastard! Don't you see what you've done?'

Clutching his face, Gustav fled.

In the taxi, Pearl sat back quietly, her breathing shallow, all emotion drained. Judy had been right. All those evenings Leo had been out, always refusing to divulge his destination or the names of his friends, he'd been seeing this blond-haired boy or one just like him. No wonder he'd brought no one to the wedding, ignored the single girls who'd been there, danced only with his mother. Pearl shivered at the memory. What had she done to deserve this? On top of everything else that had happened during her lifetime, why this?

Lights blazed in the house when Pearl reached Sands Point. Joseph flung open the front door the moment he heard the taxi drive up. He helped his mother out and paid off the driver. 'Well, did you see Leo?'

'I saw him. Judy was right, he was with a young boy. Is she still awake?'

'I told her to go to bed. She wouldn't.'

Judy was sitting in the living-room, feet up on a low stool. When Pearl walked into the room, Judy avoided her eyes. 'Don't look away,' Pearl admonished her. 'You've done nothing to be ashamed of.'

'Following Leo that night, spying on him, is nothing to be ashamed of?'

127

Pearl took hold of her daughter-in-law's hand and squeezed it gently. 'Then I'd have found out some other way. You'd better go to bed. Don't forget, you've got more than just yourself to think about.'

'Did Leo see you?' Joseph asked.

'Of course he did. I went up to the apartment.'

'What did he say?'

'What could he say?' She let go of Judy's hand and began walking towards the kitchen. 'I'm going to make a cup of tea.'

'Just make sure you don't start cooking a six-course meal,' Joseph called after her.

Pearl returned to the living-room with a tray bearing three cups. No one spoke for a full minute, as if each was waiting for one of the others. Finally Pearl broke the silence. 'It's my fault, isn't it?'

'How do you figure that?' Joseph asked.

'I spoiled him. I made him into a mother's boy.'

Now that the whole matter was out in the open, Judy could afford to be generous. 'You brought Leo and Joseph up the way you thought was best. Don't blame yourself for this. It would have happened no matter what.'

'Is that the truth, Judy? Or is that what you think I want to hear?'

'I believe it's the truth. You're not responsible for Leo's strange behaviour. That's just the way he is.'

Pearl felt grateful. Judy had suffered more than anyone from Leo's oddness. He'd treated her terribly, accused her of trying to drive a wedge between him and Joseph; he'd made her life a misery, especially after Moe and Annie had died and she'd become a part of the Granitz family. She'd found one chance to avenge herself, and then she'd been too terrified to use it for fear of hurting the people she loved. Until tonight, when everything had flooded out. 'Whether I'm responsible or not, Judy, I think it's about time I apologized for the hell Leo's put you through. I never blamed him, and maybe I should have done. I always blamed you.'

Joseph breathed a long sigh of relief. At least the immediate family unit had not been damaged. 'What are you going to do about Leo?'

'What should I do?'

128

'While you were out, Judy and I talked it over. No matter what, he's still your son, Ma. He's still my brother. There's no reason – as long as he keeps his private life to himself – why anything should really change.'

'If I know Leo,' Judy said, 'he'll be going crazy right now. He'll be trying to figure out how you learned the truth about him, but most of all he'll be torn apart thinking you don't love him any more. God only knows what he'll do.'

Pearl felt confused. Her emotions had been raked over tonight. First she'd been furious at Judy, sure she was lying about Leo. Disgust had followed, when she'd seen the truth for herself. Now she was being asked to find compassion.

'Ma,' Joseph said, 'I just told you that Leo's still my brother. Speak to him and show him that you're still his mother.'

'If he wants to come here to see me, would he still be welcome?'

Instead of answering, Joseph looked to Judy. 'Only if you'd want him to come,' she said.

'I do.'

'Then Ma had better speak to him before he does something stupid.'

Pearl finished the tea, washed up the cups and went to bed. Before she fell asleep, she decided to telephone Leo the following morning. What he was doing was wrong, God alone knew that, but she could not just cast him out of her life. She was responsible for him. Joseph and Judy might have been right, saying that Leo would have turned out the same, no matter how he'd been raised, spoiled or brought up strictly. But in the final analysis, Pearl knew the fault was her own. She was his mother – everything he did, everything he became, reflected upon her.

She would have to learn to live with it as she'd learned to live with everything else that had happened during her lifetime. It was just another obstacle to be surmounted.

Benny Minsky was the last person to leave the hall, waiting until the final guests had drifted off into the night. William and Susan had departed an hour earlier, spending their wedding night in a hotel before boarding the *Queen Mary* the following day for the voyage to Southampton, the first stop of a leisurely tour of Europe from which they would return six weeks later.

Minsky was delighted with the way the day had gone. Even paying the hall owner and the caterer had not dented his pleasure. He had wanted a much bigger wedding for his son than Susan's parents could afford, so he'd footed the entire bill himself. It didn't matter. He had only one son, and he wanted the very best for him; just as good as anything either of the Granitz twins had ever had. What made the day especially pleasing for Minsky was the knowledge that he'd been right about Phil Gerson. That was the icing on the cake. It put him one up on Lou Levitt who'd wanted to give Gerson another chance. No more chances now. They would let him finish putting up the second hotel, get it running smoothly, and then take care of him. Being wrong like that was a black mark against Levitt, and Minsky was not about to let him forget it.

He reached his home on Riverside Drive just before one o'clock. Without William, the apartment would be empty. Maybe he'd move, buy a place near the house in Forest Hills Gardens that he'd given to William and Susan. He wouldn't crowd them, act like some anxious, obnoxious mother-in-law. But it would be nice to stay close to his son. They'd always been close; no sense in letting marriage change anything.

Parking the car thirty yards from the building entrance, he strolled leisurely along the sidewalk. The air was crisp, one of those gorgeous May nights when the sky was clear and every star visible. Minsky noticed a woman standing concealed in the shadows. Her back was stooped, her clothing shabby. Resting by her feet was a worn cardboard suitcase. Poor bitch, he thought as he felt in his pocket. Some broad down on her luck, probably looking for a handout. Tonight, fate had brought her to the right place. He was in a generous mood, ready to give where normally he'd ignore a panhandler's approach.

'Here you are, honey,' he said, without looking into her eyes. 'Get yourself a meal and a place to sleep.'

The woman felt a bill pressed into her hand. She looked down and saw twenty dollars, then she lifted her head and stared after Minsky as he walked on towards the entrance and the uniformed doorman on duty there. 'Last of the big spenders, aren't you, Benny?'

Minsky stopped dead, turned around slowly. 'What did you say?' Four long strides took him back to the woman. He ripped off the scarf that covered her head. Greasy hair tumbled down to the shoulders of her coat; once the hair had been a shining blonde, now it was a stringy salt-and-pepper grey. 'Kathleen . . .?' Minsky murmured.

Heavy footsteps approached from behind. The doorman pushed himself in front of Minsky, picked up the woman's suitcase and started to carry it away. 'I told her to hit the road before, Mr Minsky, when she came asking for you. I thought she'd gone. Sorry you've been bothered.'

'Hold it right there!' Minsky rapped out the order. 'Bring that goddamned case back here and mind your own business!'

'Whatever you say, Mr Minsky.' Uncomprehending, the doorman dropped the case at the woman's feet and returned to the building.

'Always the gentleman, Benny. Always the gentleman.'

Minsky stared into Kathleen's face. The green eyes had been robbed of their lustre. They were flat, sunken. The face was gaunt and lined; folds of skin sagged at the bottom of her jaw. She looked as though she had lost twenty pounds the hard way, not by dieting but through starvation. 'Kathleen, what the hell happened to you?'

'Bad times happened, Benny.'

'So you came back to me?'

'I had nowhere else to go.'

A million times Minsky had played this scene over in his mind, what he'd do should Kathleen ever return to him. He'd always pictured her as begging to be taken back; that aspect of the scene had never altered. His own reactions had covered a wide spectrum. Sometimes he just slammed the door in her face. At other times he had paid her off, drawn a fistful of bills from his pocket and flung them at her, telling her to use the money to hide herself from him. And just occasionally, he was honest enough with himself to know exactly how he would react. No matter how she came to him, how she looked, he'd take her back.

131

'So you had nowhere else to go,' he repeated softly as he picked up her cardboard case. It was surprisingly light, as though it carried little.

'No one wants to know you when you're down, Benny.'

'No one but your real friends, baby.' He carried the case towards the building entrance. The doorman stared at him incredulously but was wise enough to say nothing.

'You've still got the same apartment,' Kathleen said in wonder as Minsky inserted the key in the door. 'I thought you would have moved.'

'It suited me. Come in.' He set down the case on the carpet just inside the door. In the bright light of the apartment, he got his first good look at Kathleen. What he'd seen outside was only a hint of how badly she'd fallen. Bones poked through paper-thin skin. The hands in which she'd once taken such pride were now like a pair of skinny claws, the nails dirty and broken. The clothes she wore, expensive when new, were badly worn and fitted poorly.

Minsky was scarcely able to believe that this scarecrow of a woman was the voluptuous good-time girl he had fought and killed for, the siren who had driven him to depths of craziness and heights of passion. But he had never, in all their tempestuous years of loving and loathing, pitied her as he did now.

Gently he helped her off with her coat. 'When's the last time you ate anything?'

'This afternoon, when the bus stopped somewhere in Pennsylvania.'

'Bus?' Minsky asked as he walked towards the refrigerator. He and William, both preferring to eat out, only kept bare necessities there. He found some bread, cheese and tomatoes that the cleaning woman had bought. She came in twice a week, stocked the refrigerator as she thought necessary and cleaned it out when the food started to turn.

'I took the bus from Los Angeles, and I had to beg, borrow and steal the money for the fare.' Hungrily, she watched him making a sandwich. 'Do you want me to do that?'

'Go ahead, I'll fix some coffee.' He found a tin of Nescafé, boiled water.

Kathleen carried the sandwich into the living-room where she waited for Minsky to bring the coffee. 'How's William?' she asked.

'William?' Minsky stared down at the tuxedo he was wearing. 'He got married today, Kathleen – that's why I'm all dressed up like this. I just came from the wedding.'

'William married . . .?' Kathleen's eyes turned misty and Minsky feared that the news might have been too great a shock. He could see she was weak – how much could such a frail body stand? 'What's she like, Benny? William's wife?'

'Susan's her name, a lovely girl. You'll see them both when they get back from their honeymoon. They've taken a cruise to Europe. Be back in about six weeks. I'll show you the big house I bought for them in Forest Hills Gardens.' He watched Kathleen begin to eat the sandwich. He could feel no animosity towards her. He could not even remember now how furious he'd been during their final fight. It all seemed so stupid. He'd wanted to see William *bar mitzvah*ed, and Kathleen hadn't. 'What happened with Hal Brookman?'

'Went bankrupt,' Kathleen answered between bites. 'Long time ago. Invested in a few bad movies. Some of them – ' she gave a bitter laugh – 'were even mine. I didn't have it any more, Benny, but it took us a few movies to find that out. Truth is, when I quit the first time, I should have stayed quit.'

'You left him?'

'Hell, no!' A spark returned briefly to the green eyes. 'I never got the chance. The sonofabitch left me. I woke up one morning and found he wasn't in the house. Not even a goddamned note. Just the sheriff's men downstairs, come to repossess everything . . . the house, the cars, every damned thing he and I owned.'

'Did you ever marry him?'

'No. Maybe that was the only smart move I ever made.' She finished the sandwich and took a sip of coffee. Suddenly her face turned ashen. She stood up, looked around wildly as if trying to remember the layout of the apartment. Then she ran towards the bathroom. Minsky followed, watching through the open door as she kneeled over the bowl and brought up the sandwich she'd just eaten. When she lifted her head her face was grey and soaked with sweat. Minsky helped her up,

133

guided her back to the couch she'd been sitting on. She leaned back, struggling for breath while Minsky stood by helplessly.

After a couple of minutes, she felt strong enough to speak. 'Maybe I left it too late, eh, Benny?'

'Too late for what?'

'To see William. To tell him I'm sorry.'

'I just told you – he'll be back in six weeks time. Him and Susan, they're on their honeymoon.'

Kathleen closed her eyes and let her head drop back on to the top of the couch. Her words were strangled, but their meaning held a startling clarity. 'I don't have six weeks, Benny. When they let me out of the hospital – '

'Hospital? What hospital?'

'In Los Angeles. They opened me up, took one look, and closed me again. Cancer, Benny. I'm riddled with it. They think it started as cancer of the throat or some such thing, and spread. They gave me three months tops then, and that was two months ago.'

Minsky's eyes burned with tears. 'I'll get you to a hospital here.'

Weakly, Kathleen shook her head. 'No more hospitals, Benny. No one's carving me up like a Christmas turkey again.'

Minsky snapped his fingers. 'William and Susan haven't left yet. They're catching their boat tomorrow. They're staying in New York for the night. I know the hotel – I'll call them.'

He'd taken no more than two steps towards the telephone when Kathleen called him back. 'Benny, I did my best to ruin that kid's life. Don't ruin his wedding night on my behalf, or his honeymoon.'

'Don't be crazy, you're his mother.'

'Some mother. You think I want him to remember me looking like this? Let him go, Benny. Perhaps if I'm still here when he gets back. . . .'

She left the sentence unfinished. Minsky sat down on the couch, wrapped his arms around her painfully thin body. He could smell the sickness. It was on her breath, oozing through the pores of her skin, yet he was not deterred. Despite their fights, despite the way she'd run out on him – and the way he'd treated her! – she was the only woman he'd ever loved. After

134

seeing William married, that meant even more to Minsky. 'Those quacks in Los Angeles . . . did they know what they were about?'

'Benny, it may have been a charity hospital, but the doctors knew what they were doing.'

A charity hospital, Minsky reflected bitterly. If Kathleen had stayed with him, he'd have made sure she had the best attention possible. Would it have made any difference, though? Cancer of the throat. He recalled the first time he'd seen her, when he'd gone to the barber shop on Jake's advice. That husky voice had attracted him like a magnet. When it was used for singing, how it had captivated the audience. Even that little squirt Lou Levitt had been enchanted by it – maybe the only thing outside of money to have that kind of an effect on him. Had something been wrong with Kathleen even then, a forewarning of this dreadful disease lending her that unusual vocal tone?

'Can I stay with you, Benny?'

'Of course you can, baby.'

Kathleen gazed around dreamily. 'You know, this was the only place where I ever had any happiness. This building. The other apartment I had first, and this place when I played mother for a few years, until that bastard Hal Brookman turned up on the doorstep. You should have thrown him out that first day, Benny. Why didn't you?'

'Because I wanted you out of the way, that's why. It was the only way I was going to get William *bar mitzvah*ed. With you on the West Coast, I could sneak him out for his lessons.'

Kathleen's brittle laugh turned to a choking rasp. 'Christ, you were a crazy bastard, weren't you, Benny?'

He gave a big grin, as though she'd just paid him the greatest compliment possible. 'You were some kind of a crazy bitch yourself, you know that?'

'How did William turn out? Crazy like both of us?'

'No. He's a good kid, just like I wanted him to be. Like you would have wanted him to grow up.' He gazed around the room for a photograph, spotting one that had been taken during the party to celebrate the opening of the Long Island City depot for B. M. Transportation. While Kathleen looked at it, he told her how William had built up the trucking

135

business, adding proudly how much smarter he was than either of the Granitz twins.

'You're all still tied up together then?' Kathleen asked.

'You, that half-pint imitation Lou Levitt, Jake and Moe?'

'Jake and Moe are dead. So's Annie.' He felt Kathleen's body stiffen in his arms. He cursed himself for being so insensitive. Kathleen was in no shape to be shocked.

'What happened?'

He brought her up to date. 'Poor Pearl,' Kathleen said when he'd finished. 'Everything fell on her. Poor Pearl, and that poor kid of Annie's. I remember her – cute little red-headed thing.'

'Perhaps I turned out to be the luckiest one,' Minsky said. 'I didn't lose anyone. My wife just ran away, found some fancy Hollywood producer and took off with him.'

'She found a jerk,' Kathleen countered. 'Which shouldn't be so surprising, seeing she was just as big a jerk herself.'

Minsky smiled. Kathleen had come back. All he cared about was making her comfortable, making her last days . . . Christ, it was tough to think in those terms . . . as easy as he could. He did not believe that she had come to him because she had nowhere else to go. She had come because, when all the cards were dealt, he was the only one she'd ever loved, the only one who'd ever loved her. Funny how forgiving you became as you grew older, as you realized that none of it was really important anymore.

Kathleen took another sip of coffee and swallowed a large tablet which she took from a brown bottle in her purse. 'Sleeping pill,' she explained when she saw the question forming on Minsky's lips.

Minsky just said 'Oh', refusing to show that he disbelieved her. 'Would you like to take a bath?' he asked.

'I'm not sure I could manage.'

'Don't worry. I'll help.' With a tenderness that surprised even himself, he assisted her from the couch to the bathroom. After filling the bath, he undressed Kathleen and helped her into it. The sight of her naked body was like a stunning slap in the face. Once he'd worshipped that body, now he was repelled by it. Her breasts were wizened and sagging like those of a woman of seventy. Livid scars, still fresh from the

136

surgery, criss-crossed her abdomen. Her arms and legs were withered. Only when he saw her naked did Minsky realize exactly how much weight she had lost. She resembled a parchment-coated skeleton.

'Sleeping pill working?' he asked as he helped her from the bath, wrapping a fluffy towel around her spindly shoulders.

'I'd like to go to bed.'

'You can have William's room. Do you have a nightgown in that case?'

'Nothing in there but a change of clothes, and I changed them already.'

'I'll get you a pair of my pyjamas.'

Kathleen was asleep the moment her head touched the pillow. For fifteen minutes, Minsky sat by the bed, watching anxiously. Her breathing was so shallow that her chest barely moved. Her skin seemed more transparent than ever, paper stretched taughtly across her cheekbones and forehead. Her hair, spread across the pillow, was lank and lifeless. He clenched his right fist and slammed it into the palm of his left hand. Damn it! Why the hell hadn't she come back to him when she'd first learned she was ill? A charity hospital! That was no place for the star of *Broadway Nell* to wind up. No place for the ex-wife of Benny Minsky, the mother of William Minsky! She should have come back, sought his help earlier on. She should never have waited just so she could return to die in his arms.

At last he stood up and tiptoed from the room. He opened the cardboard suitcase and removed the clothes. Like the ones she'd been wearing, they'd seen better days. Wrapping them in a bundle, he threw them down the incinerator chute. Tomorrow he'd buy her a new wardrobe, colourful dresses that would fit properly and help to disguise the aura of impending death. He picked up her purse, opened the clasp and looked inside. The brown bottle of tablets caught his attention. He read the label: the name of a drugstore in Los Angeles, Kathleen's name, pharmaceutical terms he didn't begin to understand, and lastly the directions – one to be taken every four hours, dosage no more than five a day. Sleeping pills like hell! They were pain-killers. God alone knew what agony she was going through.

137

Minsky spotted a long white envelope. He opened it and extracted a single sheet of paper. The name of the hospital was on the top; the date was seven weeks earlier. The word 'carcinoma' stood out starkly from the rest of the text. Other words – 'exploratory' and 'not treated' – jumped at Minsky's eyes. He shoved the sheet of paper back into the envelope and snapped the purse shut. Kathleen was carrying her own death warrant around with her.

He walked into William's room and sat down again. After Jake and Moe Caplan had died Lou Levitt had asked if Minsky appreciated irony – the two men who'd been at each other's throats being the only survivors. What was happening now qualified as irony in its truest sense. William's bed, in which he'd slept until last night, was now occupied by the mother he had not seen for fourteen years. Nor would he ever see her. If Kathleen and those doctors from that damned charity hospital were right, she'd be dead and buried by the time William and Susan returned from their honeymoon in Europe.

Tears started to dribble from Minsky's eyes. He leaned forward, elbows on the bed, head resting in his hands. That was the way he finally fell asleep. . . .

The sound of coughing woke him at seven-thirty. He sat up in the chair, back aching, mouth sour and dry. 'Benny. . . .' Kathleen's voice was racked with pain. 'Please, get me one of those pills in the brown bottle, and a glass of water.'

'Sure.' He ran from the room, returning moments later with the pill and a glass of water. With one hand he raised her head, with the other he held the glass to her lips. When she had swallowed the pill he put another pillow behind her head so she could sit up.

'I heard you crying last night, Benny. You were crying in your sleep. Was it for me?'

'Since when have you ever known me cry?' he asked in return.

She was touched by the way he tried to hide the moment of softness. She'd heard him crying all right, but if he wanted to deny it she wouldn't push the issue. 'You might have improved with age, you bastard, learned a little compassion.'

138

'If I'd turned compassionate, you'd never have recognized me. You want something to eat?'

'Later on, perhaps, when I feel strong enough to get up.'

He stood up and walked to the window. 'Looks like it's going to be a nice day. I'll put a chair out on the balcony for you. You can watch the river.'

'A view of New Jersey's sure to make me feel better.'

'You can't be that ill if you can make jokes. Those doctors must have been drunk when they said you were sick.'

'I wish, Benny. I wish.'

'So do I, baby.' As he left the room, he found himself wondering whether Kathleen would have come back to him had she not been ill, not been dying. He shook his head to dispel the notion. It didn't matter what had prompted her to return. The important thing was that she had.

Chapter Six

In the week since moving from Manhattan to Sands Point, Pearl had automatically assumed the responsibility of being the first to rise. She had always woken early on Central Park West, making breakfast for Leo, and before that for both of the twins and Judy, when they had gone to school and then to work. Moving out to the island had not changed her routine. Nor had the confrontation with Leo the previous night. Pregnant, Judy could not be expected to get up early and fuss over Joseph. It was Pearl's duty.

By six-thirty she was downstairs, listening to the radio playing softly as she made coffee and prepared breakfast. She liked this time of the morning best, when she had the house to herself. She still found the greatest peace in the kitchen. There, among pots and pans, dishes and cutlery – items which had a familiarity that took her back to her earliest childhood days – she could think most clearly.

Both Joseph and Judy had advised her to be forgiving towards Leo. Judy's benevolence towards her brother-in-law was especially surprising to Pearl. If anyone had reason to despise him, it was Judy. Yet she had urged Pearl to forgive. And if Judy could feel that way, how could Pearl feel otherwise?

At seven o'clock, she heard footsteps coming down the curving staircase. Joseph entered the kitchen. Although he was dressed for work, he would not be leaving the house for another hour and a half. Before the long drive into Manhattan he liked to take a long walk with the Labrador he'd bought a few weeks earlier when he'd moved into the house. The serenity of the country setting prepared him for the hectic pace of the city.

Sitting down at the breakfast-room table, he sipped the coffee that Pearl had poured for him. 'Have you spoken to Leo yet?'

'I was going to wait until later. He doesn't get up early.'

'I doubt if he even went to bed last night, he must have been so shaken up. Stop putting it off, Ma. Get on the phone to him right now. Don't forget –' he took another sip of coffee – 'he's supposed to be at work in a couple of hours. If he doesn't hear from you, God knows what he's liable to do.'

Pearl went to the telephone and dialled the number of the Central Park West apartment. It rang unanswered. 'Do you think he could still be at that other place?' Joseph asked. 'With . . . with his friend?'

Pearl shook her head adamantly. 'As I was going down the stairs, I heard him scream at the boy to get out.' And what language he'd screamed, she thought. She'd never heard Leo swear like that; it was a barometer of his anguish.

'Try, anyway. See if he's got a phone installed there.'

Pearl called directory. The operator informed her that there was no listing for a Granitz on MacDougal Street. 'Do you think I should call Lou Levitt? Perhaps he's heard from Leo.'

'Why should he?'

Pearl fell silent. Why should he, indeed? But where was Leo? Had she done right by confronting him? Would she have done better to leave him alone? What had gone through his mind when she appeared so unexpectedly to find him with that blond boy? And then the way she'd ignored him when he'd chased after her. She should have stayed, listened to him, understood. Never before had she rejected him like that.

Joseph finished his breakfast. Judy came down, her woollen robe blossoming out in front of her. 'Before you even ask,' Joseph said, 'Ma hasn't spoken to Leo yet. There was no answer when she tried just now.'

'Where is he?'

'That's what we've been sitting here trying to figure out.'

Joseph got up from the table and announced that he was going

141

out for his morning walk. He got as far as opening the front door before he came running back. 'Leo's coming up the drive.'

'Here?' Pearl asked.

'Where do you think I mean? Judy, go back upstairs. I'll slip out of the back way, let Ma be here alone.'

'Is that safe?' Judy asked.

'What's he going to do to me?' Pearl wanted to know. 'Besides, it's better if he thinks that no one else knows.'

Judy saw the wisdom in that. Carrying her cup of coffee, she climbed the stairs as quickly as her condition would allow. Joseph waited until he heard the slamming of a car door, then the ponderous bang of the heavy knocker on the front door of the house. As Pearl walked from the breakfast-room, and across the entrance hall, Joseph let himself out of the back door and whistled for the Labrador.

Pearl opened the front door. 'Leo . . . I've been trying to call you for the past hour.'

Leo looked terrible. Huge pouches hung beneath his eyes. His face was heavy with fatigue. A dark sheet of stubble covered his cheeks and chin. He hadn't slept at all. After his mother had appeared at MacDougal Street, and Gustav had fled, Leo had remained at the apartment all night, alternately sitting down, then pacing around as he debated what to do. He was living through a nightmare . . . his secret exposed, and the blond boy of whom he'd grown extremely fond gone. He had no doubt that Gustav would never return. No matter how much Leo pressured the agency, the youth would never consent to another assignation; getting slapped around wasn't part of the bargain. Leo cursed himself for his fiery temper, and for his stupidity. It was bad enough that his mother had come to MacDougal Street, that she had found out; he should have known better than to lose his temper so violently and blame Gustav for the catastrophe.

Slowly, the self-directed fury at losing Gustav had faded, leaving only the hopelessness of coming to terms with his mother's feelings. He tried to remember every second of the short confrontation, from the moment Pearl had appeared at the top of the stairs, to when she'd shrunk away from him in the taxi. She hadn't been angry with him. She'd been dis-

142

tressed, disgusted. She'd pulled away from him when he'd reached out to her in the taxi as though she'd wanted nothing to do with him. As though, damn it, he had the plague! He knew he could cope with the loss of Gustav. There would be more boys. But the withdrawal of his mother's affection was heart-wrenching. He'd always looked to her for support, encouragement; he'd made her his life. Without her, he wasn't sure what he'd do. He had to see her. Somehow he had to make her understand that what he was doing was not so terrible. And if she thought it was, whose fault was it that he had turned out this way? Certainly not his own. He was not responsible for his physical and mental make-up. Pearl was responsible for that. Pearl and his father. They had conceived him, given him life. Whatever he was, the blueprint was theirs. His father was dead, so Pearl carried the blame alone.

As dawn had filled the narrow streets of the Village with dim grey light, Leo had made up his mind to drive out to Sands Point. Pearl must be made to understand that she was accountable. She had created him, designed him. She could not wash her hands of him just because she had discovered something not to her liking. . . .

Leo stood in the doorway. 'Why were you trying to call me?'

'I want to talk . . . to discuss last night with you.'

He entered the house and walked through to the breakfast-room, noticing Joseph's dirty cup still on the table. 'Where's Joseph?'

'Outside, walking the dog.'

'And Judy?'

'She hasn't come down yet,' Pearl lied.

'Do they know?'

'About last night? No,' Pearl lied again.

'How did you find out?'

'It doesn't matter, Leo.'

'It damned well matters to me. Was it Uncle Lou?' All night he'd debated who'd pointed the finger at him. Never mind that Levitt didn't know about the Village apartment; the little man was still the only person who was aware of Leo's predilection.

Pearl was so astonished to hear Levitt's name thrown at her

143

that she could barely force herself to say, 'No, it wasn't Uncle Lou.' Why should Leo think it was? That could mean only one thing, and it shocked Pearl even more than learning about what Leo had done.

'Ma. . . .' Leo reached out and grasped his mother's arms. Tears burned his eyes as he felt her stiffen involuntarily. 'Whoever told you did so for only one reason – they wanted to hurt us, don't you see that? They wanted to turn you against me.'

Leo's impassioned plea brought back to Pearl with stunning clarity all those childhood moments when he'd come running to his mother for support in every crisis. She'd been incapable of refusing him then. This time was different. To give him comfort now would require an effort of will; there would be no heartfelt spontaneity. She tried. 'No one's going to hurt us, Leo. No one's going to turn me against you.'

Pearl's woodenness was evident. 'If you really loved me, you wouldn't have listened to stories about me . . . you wouldn't have come down to the Village . . . you wouldn't have sneaked up on me!'

'Leo, I do love you.'

'Then tell me how you found out.'

'It's of no importance.'

'I want to know who's trying to hurt us.'

'No one is. I wasn't hurt last night –'

'Of course you were. I saw you run away. You wouldn't speak to me, you wouldn't listen to me.'

'Leo, I was shocked. How else would I be? But since then I've done a lot of thinking. I love you, don't you understand that? However you want to live, I'll still love you.'

Pearl's tone betrayed her. She might say that she could accept what he was doing, but Leo knew otherwise. 'You're lying! I can hear you're lying!'

The door leading outside from the breakfast-room opened and Joseph appeared, with the Labrador tugging at the leash. He had been crouching just below the open window, listening to every word. When he heard Leo's voice rise, he knew it was time to make an appearance. 'I thought I heard a car,' he said, feigning surprise when he saw Leo. 'What brings you out here?'

144

Leo looked first at his twin brother, then at the dog which bounded towards him as Joseph undid the leash. Jumping back, he pointed a finger at the Labrador. 'Get it away from me!'

Joseph snapped his fingers and the Labrador returned to his side. He bent down and rubbed the dog's head. 'What's the matter with you? You can't find a more friendly dog than this.'

Leo could not take his eyes off the Labrador. 'I don't like dogs.' The memory of the German Shepherd puppy flashed before him, swinging it on the leash and smashing its head against the wall in the alley behind his parents' home. His fear of dogs hadn't abated since then; even a seemingly docile dog like the Labrador terrified him.

Judy chose that exact moment to come down the stairs. She, too, had been listening. 'Come to join us for breakfast, Leo?' she asked sweetly.

Leo swung around, flustered. How much had Joseph and Judy heard? If they hadn't know before – if Pearl had told him the truth – did they know now? How much could they deduce from what they must have heard? Without another word, he turned around, strode across the hall to the front door and slammed it behind him. A minute later, the rear tyres of his car spit gravel as he accelerated down the drive towards the road.

'Why should he think it was Lou Levitt who told you?' Joseph asked.

'I'd like to know the answer to that as well,' Pearl replied. 'Did Lou know all along about Leo's . . . Leo's . . .?'

'Homosexuality?' Judy offered. There was no point in avoiding the word.

'If he knew, when did he find out? Pearl asked. 'And if he knew, why didn't he tell me?' She started to walk towards the telephone. Joseph called her back.

'Don't call him up and ask him.'

'Why not? I'm entitled to find out what's going on.'

'You're entitled to nothing. However Uncle Lou knew – whenever he knew – it doesn't matter. Can't you see the reason he never told you? He figured your feelings would be hurt, and that's the last thing he wants to do. You told me

145

yourself that he'd asked you to marry him a couple of times. If he loves you like you think he does, would he tell you something like that about Leo? Or would he keep it to himself in the hope that you never found out?'

Joseph's calm logic made sense. If Levitt knew – and obviously he did – he'd tried to keep the secret from Pearl with the best intentions. The least she could do in return was show just as much consideration by allowing him to believe he had succeeded. If Levitt ever learned that she knew, the information would have to come from Leo; and she could not see her younger son boasting that his mother knew he was a homosexual.

'I tried to tell him I understood,' Pearl mused, 'but I couldn't put my heart into it. He knew I was lying.'

'We heard,' Joseph said.

'I don't understand, I never will. I don't see how a man can act towards another man like he should act towards a woman.'

'Some people are like that,' Judy explained. Women as well. They're mixed up, not all men and not all women.'

Pearl shook her head. 'No, it's not that way with Leo. If anything made him the way he is, it was the diphtheria. That's what made him like this.'

'Okay, Ma,' Joseph said, knowing that he could never change Pearl's mind. Whatever Leo did, it could always be explained away by remembering how ill he'd been. He wondered what excuse she could find if he ever developed such strange ways. After all, he'd never had diphtheria.

Benny Minsky did not go into work that day. He telephoned Lou Levitt at the Jalo office and claimed that he was feeling unwell. Levitt, believing it was the aftermath of the excitement caused by William's wedding, voiced sympathy.

Once he'd finished the call, Minsky returned to the apartment's second bedroom to check on Kathleen. She slept peacefully, spared pain by the pill she had taken on waking. Leaving a note for her on the bedside table, he went downstairs to his car and drove to Bloomingdales. There he asked a salesgirl to help him collect a wardrobe for Kathleen. An hour later, with bulging bags, he returned to Riverside

146

Drive to find Kathleen just awakening. When she saw the clothes he'd bought for her she clapped her hands like a small child receiving a birthday gift. She chose a light green cotton dress to wear that day. It hung on her emaciated frame, but she didn't seem to notice. Just the idea of wearing something new and colorful cheered her immensely.

After eating a slice of toast and drinking a cup of weak coffee, she sat outside on the balcony. Minksy left her there while he telephoned a doctor. Kathleen was still sitting outside, looking over the Hudson River to New Jersey, when the doctor arrived. Before taking him out on to the balcony, Minsky showed him the letter he had found in Kathleen's purse, and the bottle of pills.

'I'd like to examine Miss Monahan myself,' the doctor told him, 'and draw my own conclusions.'

Minksy walked on to the balcony. 'Kathleen, I've got a doctor here. He'd like to talk to you.'

'Talk to me, Benny, or examine me?'

'Both.' Minsky didn't hold Kathleen's eyes as he answered. Instead, he looked south along the Hudson, wondering if the *Queen Mary* was making her tug-assisted journey down to the bay yet. William and Susan were out there, listening to the bands playing, watching the streamers arcing from the dock to the stately liner, while only a few miles away William's mother was sitting on a balcony, trying to find some enjoyment in the spring sun as she lived her final days.

'Benny. . . .' Kathleen turned her head to look into the apartment. She saw the doctor standing there, a middle-aged man with a lined, compassionate face. 'Tell that fucking quack to take his little black bag and shove it up his ass. I don't want anyone treating me like I'm some damned guinea pig. Let me spend what's left with a little dignity.'

Minsky could not argue. He returned to the doctor and relayed Kathleen's wishes. 'We can't force her to undergo an examination or further surgery,' the doctor said. He wrote down the name of the Los Angeles hospital. 'I'll speak to the doctors who attended Miss Monahan, learn what I can from that.'

'Thanks, Doc.' Minsky saw the man out to the lift before returning to the balcony.

'Benny, I'm sorry. I didn't want to be rude. I know you're only thinking of me.'

He rested a hand on her painfully thin wrist. 'I know, baby. I know exactly what you mean. Hey, even if you don't want a doctor, how about I hire a nurse to look after you?'

'Full time?'

'Of course, full time. Wht do you think I am – too cheap to get a live-in nurse?'

'Benny, I know you've got to work during the day, but you'll be here in the evening, won't you?' She gazed beseechingly at him, and there was no way he could refuse what he knew was coming. 'I don't want a nurse here at night. I want you.'

'Okay.' He held her hand between his own. 'When the doctor gets back to me, we'll see about getting a day nurse.'

The doctor returned in the early evening, when Kathleen was asleep. He had spoken to the hospital in Los Angeles, discussed Kathleen's case with the surgeons who had operated. There was, he told Minsky, absolutely nothing to be gained from opening her up again. All they could do was make her last few days as comfortable as possible. The doctor prescribed a diet that Kathleen would find easy to digest. When Minsky asked about a nurse, the doctor arranged for one to begin the following morning.

'Towards the end, Miss Monahan's pain might become even more acute,' the doctor told Minsky. 'I'm going to prescribe a steadily stronger series of painkillers. These may, as they reach maximum dosage, render Miss Monahan almost unconscious. She will understand very little of what's going on, which is probably for the best.'

When the doctor left, Minsky entered the bedroom and sat watching Kathleen. Were his senses fooling him, or did she seem to be resting easier? Was there more colour to her face? Had the day in the sun, the feel and look of new clothes, breathed some life into her frail body? Minsky made himself believe it was so; he didn't have the courage to dwell on the certainty that she was dying.

After half an hour of sitting by the bed, he got up and left the room. In the living-room, he dialled the number of the house in Sands Point where Pearl now lived. Joseph answered. 'Is your mother there?'

148

'I'll get her for you.' Joseph spoke as though his mouth was full, and Minsky guessed that he'd interrupted their dinner. Moments later, Pearl was on the line.

'Kathleen came home last night, Pearl.'

'To your apartment?'

'She was waiting outside for me. She came home to die.'

'Oh, my God,' Pearl whispered, as Minsky related the events of the previous night. 'Where is she now?'

'In William's room, asleep.'

'Are you going to let her stay?'

'What kind of a question is that, for Christ's sake? Of course I'm going to.'

'Have you called a doctor yet?'

'He just left. There's nothing anyone can do. Just a nurse, that's it.'

'Do you need anything, Benny? What about yourself – you don't keep food in the place. How are you going to get out and eat with Kathleen there tonight?'

'Don't worry, I'll manage.' He heard a sound from the bedroom and turned to see Kathleen standing in the doorway; his voice had roused her. 'I've got to go, Pearl. I'll speak to you later.' He replaced the receiver and looked at Kathleen. 'Everything all right, baby?'

'I've slept enough, that's all. Who were you talking to?'

'Pearl.'

'Does she know I'm here?'

'She does now.' Minsky held out an arm for Kathleen to lean on, and guided her to the couch. Tonight he'd live on toast and cheese and tomatoes. When the cleaning woman came the following day, he'd get her to fill the refrigerator properly. Maybe he could pay either her or the nurse to prepare meals as well. He'd work it out.

In Sands Point, Pearl rejoined Joseph and Judy who were sitting at the dinner table. 'Kathleen's back. She was waiting for Benny outside his apartment building when he got home from the wedding last night.' The ripple of excitement caused by that news disappeared when she explained Kathleen's reason for returning to Minsky.

'I think I should go over there,' Pearl murmured. 'Benny

149

has a nurse starting tomorrow, but knowing him there's no food in the place. He won't go out to eat and leave Kathleen alone, so I'll take some of this.' She gestured at the table full of food.

'How are you going to get there?' Joseph asked.

'The same way I went into the city last night – by taxi. You stay here with Judy.' Without finishing her own meal, she went into the kitchen. She returned with a heavy saucepan into which she ladled a generous portion of the goulash she'd made for that night. There was more than enough to take to Minsky. Pearl always cooked too much, as though she were still catering for a restaurant full of people and not for a small family. 'Call a taxi for me,' she told Joseph, 'while I put together some more food for Benny and Kathleen.'

'Are you doing this to help Benny,' Joseph asked, 'or just so you can forget what happened here this morning?'

'Both,' Pearl answered candidly. Purposely, she had refrained from even mentioning the incident with Leo, but now that Joseph had brought it up, she asked, 'What was he like today at work?'

'I didn't see much of him. I work inside, he works the streets. Especially today, when we were a couple of runners short and he had to go out and make pick-ups and deliveries himself.'

'You wish you hadn't gone to the Village last night, don't you?' Judy said.

'I'm not sure what I wish any more. I wish you hadn't told me, but in a way I'm glad you did. I wish I hadn't gone, but I had to. I wish I'd seen him without him seeing me. And most of all, I wish to hell I knew why Leo brought up Lou Levitt's name – asked if it was through Lou that I'd found out.'

'He must have known all along,' Joseph said. 'That's the only answer.'

'Did you see them together at all today– Lou and Leo?'

'For a few seconds, that was all, when Leo first came in. They barely spoke. When Leo returned after picking up the bets and the money, he just dumped the whole lot on my desk and walked out.'

Pearl placed a lid on the saucepan of goulash. She returned to the kitchen and filled a dish with salad, another with

150

almond bread she'd baked that afternoon. 'Call the taxi,' she reminded Joseph.

By the time the taxi arrived, Pearl had two shopping bags full of food. She assumed that Minsky had a working stove where she could warm it. 'What time will you be home?' Judy asked.

'Whenever I get home. I'm visiting a sick friend.'

Joseph passed money to the taxi driver. 'Stay with my mother, wait for her and bring her back when she's ready.'

Pearl sat in the back of the taxi as it headed west towards Manhattan. She clutched the two shopping bags tightly, frightened that some of the food might spill. She could barely believe that she was taking her second hurried trip into the city in as many nights, first to learn the truth about Leo, and now this. Kathleen coming back! The idea was so impossible that all she would think of was Lou Levitt's prophecy that one day Kathleen would return and Benny Minsky would forgive her everything. Again the little man had been proven right, but in circumstances he never could have imagined.

The taxi pulled up outside Minsky's apartment block. Reminding the driver to wait, Pearl walked into the building. The doorman was away from his post, so she went straight up to Minsky's apartment and knocked on the door.

'I brought you a few things,' she said when Minsky opened the door to stare blankly at her. 'Is Kathleen awake?'

'Sitting in the living-room. We're watching television, can you believe that?'

'Sounds like an old married couple. May I see her?'

'Come in.' Only when Pearl stepped into the apartment did Minsky seem to notice the two loaded shopping bags. 'A few things?' he asked incredulously. 'Hey, Pearl . . . don't get a shock when you see Kathleen.'

'I'll try not to.' Despite the warning, Pearl was stunned when she stepped into the living-room and saw Kathleen sitting there. Even in the dim glow of a small table-lamp and the fuzzy glare from the television, Pearl could see her skeletal appearance. 'Hello, Kathleen.'

She rose slowly. 'Hi, Pearl, good to see you.'

'Am I interrupting a good show?'

'Nothing I won't miss. You look well, Pearl. Nearly being a

grandmother suits you. Benny told me,' she added when she saw Pearl's mystified expression. 'He's spent all of today bringing me up to date. I was sorry to hear about Jake, and the others.'

'It was all a long time ago, Kathleen.'

'So was everything.'

Pearl wondered what to say next. How did you converse with someone who only had a few weeks left to live? You didn't ask how they were – you didn't say they looked well, that was for sure!

Minsky saved her. 'What have you got in those bags?'

'You show me what you and Kathleen had for dinner, and I'll show you what's in these bags.'

Minsky took Pearl into the kitchen. A couple of crumb-spattered plates lay in the sink. 'I made us some toasted sandwiches.'

'Bread and cheese? For God's sake, Benny, no one can live on that.' Pearl hoisted her bags on to the counter and started to take out the food. 'There's goulash in this saucepan, vegetable soup in that one. Put them both on a low light. Here's some salad – '

'Pearl, I've got a nurse starting tomorrow. She can cook.'

'That's tomorrow. First you've got to eat today. What kind of help are you going to be to Kathleen if you get malnutrition?'

'One day without eating properly isn't going to stick me in a hospital. I'm glad you came, though. I hoped you would.'

'Are you going to tell Lou about Kathleen?'

'I'm not in the mood for his sarcastic little speeches right now.'

'I think he'd be sympathetic.'

'I don't.' Minsky was sure that Levitt would use Kathleen's return as a weapon with which to avenge himself for the humiliation of being wrong about Phil Gerson; he wouldn't be able to resist squaring the score. 'If I haven't even told William – and I could have gotten word to him before the *Queen Mary* sailed – why should I bother telling Lou?'

'Different reasons. You don't want William to see Kathleen like this. You don't want to ruin the boy's honeymoon. With Lou, you're frightened that he'll get a laugh out of it,

152

Kathleen coming back and you doing everything for her. He won't laugh. He's not like that.'

Despite Pearl's assurances, Minsky was not so certain. Pearl could recognize qualities in the little man that Minsky had never seen; but then, he reminded himself, she was looking at him from a different perspective altogether.

Pearl remained at the apartment for an hour. Minsky ate the goulash. Kathleen was able to eat only a small cup of soup. At nine o'clock, when Kathleen's eyelids began to droop, Pearl decided it was time to leave. Minsky saw her downstairs to the waiting taxi. 'Pearl, you don't know how grateful I am that you came.'

'Could you imagine me not coming?'

'You must have been some kind of mother to the twins.'

'Me?' She was delighted by the compliment. 'You're turning out to be some kind of an ex-husband to Kathleen. Don't forget, if you need anything just let me know. If I can't get into town, I can always send it with Joseph.'

'We'll be all right. You know, Kathleen really appreciated your visit. I think she looked on it as being forgiven, not just by me but by everyone. If you can find the time to come over again. . . .'

'I'll be back, Benny.' Pearl climbed into the cab, returned Minsky's wave of farewell and gave the driver directions. Instead of returning to Sands Point, she told him to take her to the apartment building in which she'd lived until eight days earlier. While in the city, she had other errands to run.

While the driver waited again, Pearl entered the building on Central Park West. Instead of going to her old apartment, however, she went to the floor below. There, she knocked on Lou Levitt's door. It was a call on the off chance; she didn't know whether he'd be home or not.

He was. 'Pearl, what are you doing here all by yourself?'

'Making the rounds. May I come in?'

'Of course.'

She stepped inside. Levitt's home had the same feel as the apartment she had just left, a place cleaned not with love but by a woman whose only incentive was money. There was something missing in such clinical cleanliness. Both Levitt's and Minsky's apartments were like hospital wards, every-

153

thing just so, laid out with precision. 'I just came from Benny's place,' Pearl said.

'What were you doing there – taking care of him because you heard he was sick today?'

'He wasn't sick. He was nursing a sick friend.'

'Benny doesn't have any friends.'

'How would you describe Kathleen then?'

'Kathleen?' Levitt threw back his head and roared with laugher. 'What rock did she crawl out from under?' Pearl told him the story and he continued to laugh. 'What did I always say, Pearl? Didn't I tell you that one day she'd come back, and that mug would be eating out of her hand again? Didn't I say it?'

'You said it,' Pearl agreed softly.

'What about his son? Did he go on honeymoon?'

'Benny never told him, he didn't want to wreck the boy's trip.'

'Considerate of him.'

'Maybe you could learn a lesson and show some consideration as well. Right now isn't the time to laugh at Benny's misfortune.'

Isn't it? Levitt thought. He's ready to rub my nose into it over Phil Gerson, and I shouldn't make fun of him for being a jerk all over again? 'What were you doing at Riverside Drive?'

'Benny called me with the news. I went over to see if I could help.'

'Patron saint of waifs and strays . . . nothing changes. Is she really dying?'

'If you saw her, Lou, you wouldn't have to ask such a question.' She gazed steadily at him for several seconds, plucking up the courage to go against the well-intentioned advice of Joseph and Judy. 'Talking of questions, Lou, I've got one for you.'

'Fire away.' He was still smiling about Kathleen.

'It concerns Leo.'

Amusement disappeared; tension took its place. 'What about him?'

'Have you known all along that Leo's . . .?' Words failed Pearl as she tried to think of a gentle way to describe her younger son.

154

Levitt offered no help at all. 'Leo's what?'

'He's not right, not well. He . . . he goes out with men,' she finally blurted out.

'Where did you hear that?'

'It's of no concern where I heard it. I just want to know if you were aware of it. You were, weren't you?'

Did he lie? Did he try to protect Pearl from the truth when it was obvious that she already knew it? 'I knew,' he answered simply.

'For how long?'

'A few years.'

'How did you find out?'

'Like you told me, it's of no concern. And before you ask why I didn't tell you, the answer's simple: one, it was none of your business what Leo did; and two – ' he reached out to hold her – 'I didn't want to see you hurt, Pearl.'

'I wasn't so much hurt as shocked, disgusted. But now, seeing Benny with Kathleen, it's made me take a second look at myself. If Benny can forgive Kathleen for what she did – '

'I always told you he would.'

Pearl was glad to see that Levitt's attitude had changed. No longer did he sound as if he were enjoying Minsky's misfortune. 'If Benny can forgive, then I can. Leo came around to the house early this morning – I found out last night, you see – and I think he wanted some sign from me, some words that I understood, that I could pardon him. I couldn't give him those words this morning, Lou, but now I think I can.'

'Pearl, who told you about Leo is your business. But how did you find out?'

'Leo keeps another apartment, in the Village. I went there last night and saw him with this boy.'

'He saw you?'

'Unfortunately.'

'When I found out about him – it doesn't matter where or how – I made him promise to keep it from you. I didn't want to see your heart broken.'

'Thank you. Now I think I'd better go up and see him. I learned something tonight from Benny, and I think Leo should be the beneficiary of it.'

'Before you go, Pearl, what made you think I knew?'

155

'Because he asked me if I'd learned from you.'

'Are you angry that I didn't tell you?'

'No. You did what you thought was in my best interests. You always seem to.'

'Go upstairs and see him.'

Pearl climbed one floor. As she walked along the corridor, she heard music coming from the old apartment. Since moving out, she hadn't been back, and she wondered what changes Leo had made. The obvious one was moving the phonograph out of the bedroom into the living-room. She thought about the neighbours. Had they complained? Or were walls thicker than doors?

She had to knock twice before Leo heard above the roar of the music. Annoyed at the interruption, he flung open the door and stared, bewildered, at his mother. 'Ma! Why are you here?' He looked up and down the corridor, expecting to see Joseph.

'I came alone, Leo. I want to talk to you. About last night, and this morning.'

'I thought you'd said all you had to say.'

'I've had time to think since then.' She walked past him. Inside the apartment, the music was deafening, a chorus of voices shrieking at each other as though they feared being drowned out by the thunderous orchestral backing. 'Could you turn that down, Leo?'

Leo took off the record. Silence returned to the apartment. 'Well?' he asked.

'Leo, I'm sorry about this morning. I had a big speech all prepared for when I saw you again . . . how I understood . . . that I'd love you come hell or high water . . . that whatever you choose to do is your own business. When you just turned up this morning, I hadn't had the time to rehearse it.'

He stared stonily at Pearl, offering no help.

'Perhaps if we'd been alone, just you and me, I could have made you believe me.'

'You sounded like you didn't believe a word of it yourself.'

'It was hard for me to, Leo. What you were doing was something completely outside of my world.'

'You demonstrated that pretty clearly. Your tone was enough – you didn't have to spell it out for me!'

156

'But that was this morning, Leo, only a few hours after I'd seen you in the Village. I needed time to adjust.'

'You've adjusted now?' Leo sound dubious.

'I had to make a choice. Either accept you as you are, or lose you. And you know I don't want to lose you. Leo, you're my son, just as Joseph is, and I love you both equally. It doesn't matter to me what you do, don't you understand that?'

Leo was quick to notice that Pearl's voice carried far more sincerity than it had done that morning. Something had happened to his mother. He had no idea what. All he knew was that she had been turned around, made more receptive to his way of life. It was time to plead his case. 'Ma, there's nothing wrong with loving another man.'

'There's never anything wrong with love, Leo. It's hatred that injures people, not love.'

'I tried to keep it a secret, Ma, because I do love you. If I'd told you myself, ages ago, would it have been easier for you?'

Pearl didn't answer immediately because she was uncertain how to. Benny Minsky's forgiving attitude towards Kathleen had opened her eyes. Without seeing that, the wall between herself and Leo would still have been just as high, just as unscalable. 'You just said it yourself, Leo. You didn't want me to know because you loved me. But now that I do know, it doesn't make me love you any less.' She gave him a gentle smile. 'You know, when I was a little girl, Annie and I played around with some hair colouring stuff. I went to school the following day with my hair looking like a rainbow.' She saw Leo start to smile as well as she narrated the story. 'All the other kids laughed at me, except for Uncle Lou. He told me that those who laughed were just fools, mocking someone who was different because they didn't know any better. Want to know something? What he said then is just as right today. There's nothing wrong with being a bit different from the crowd. Now . . .' Pearl's smile faded '. . . can you forgive me what I did last night?'

Leo's answer was to reach out and hug his mother. Of course he could forgive her. She was still the most important person in the world to him.

*   *   *

157

A nurse came to care for Kathleen early the following morning. Minsky stayed in the apartment until eleven o'clock, when he was satisfied that the woman was capable. After kissing Kathleen goodbye, he drove to the B. M. Transportation depot in Long Island City, where he would fill in for William.

At midday, Pearl telephoned to ask after Kathleen. Minsky reported that when he'd left her she had been sitting out on the balcony while the nurse prepared lunch.

Thirty minutes later, Minsky had a surprise visitor. The temporary secretary who was filling in for Susan knocked on his office door. 'There's a Mr Levitt here to see you. He doesn't have an appointment.'

Minksy was startled. Levitt never came out to Long Island City. Any business between the two men – and there was nothing between them but business – was always conducted at the Jalo garage.

'Is this a social call or business?' Minsky asked Levitt, once he'd been shown in.

'Social. Got time for lunch?'

They drove in Levitt's car acoss the Queensboro Bridge and down to the Lower East Side, stopping outside Ratner's on Delancey Street. As they sat at a table, Levitt said, 'Pearl told me about Kathleen.'

Minsky felt both angry and distressed. Had Levitt taken the time out for lunch, driven all the way down here, just to poke fun? So help him – if that were the case, Minsky would do murder right here in Ratner's, right in front of the waiter who was placing a basket of onion rolls on the table. 'So she told you . . . so what?'

Levitt ignored the hostility. 'Pearl said it was doubtful that Kathleen would still be here when William got home. That's tough. Look, Benny, I know you're stuck with minding the store while William's away, but if you want to take time off to be with Kathleen, I'll cover for you.'

Minsky stared blankly across the table. 'What do you mean?'

'I don't need to be over on the West Side. Joseph and Leo have got the bookmaking down pat. If you want, I can stand in at the truck depot for you.'

158

Finally, the impossible dawned on Minsky. Levitt was feeling sorry for him! In all the years he'd known the little man, Minsky could not recall him pitying anyone. No kind of emotion at all was etched into his character; only a sharp brain that did not pander to the same feelings others might have. Out of the blue, Levitt had learned about sympathy. 'What's with the sudden change, Lou? I'd have thought you'd be the last person to care about Kathleen.'

'Maybe we're all getting a little older, a little wiser. I never disliked Kathleen, Benny. I just thought she kept getting in your way. You weren't strong enough to draw a line where infatuation had to end and work had to begin.'

'But was I wrong? Did she have a great voice that time down in the Four Aces?'

Levitt laughed. 'You were right. I just didn't have it in me at the time to understand how any man would get so messed up over a woman like you did.'

'Now can you understand it . . . now that you're a little older, a little wiser?'

'I'm still not sure.' Levitt paused while the waiter took their orders. 'What's going to happen after it's all over?'

Minsky stared gloomily at the basket of rolls. 'After the wedding, on the way home, I was thinking about buying a place out in Queens, near the house I got for William and Susan. Now I'm not so sure. Maybe I'd like to get clean away for a while, out of town. William can run the trucking company, and you don't need me on the other side.'

'How would you like to run a couple of hotels?'

'Down in Florida? The Monaco and the Waterway?'

'Someone'll have to – once Phil, well, you know.'

Some of Levitt's sympathy rubbed off on Minsky. 'Lou, you want to let him off the hook, perhaps I'll go along with it.'

Levitt shook his head. 'That wasn't what I was after by seeing you today. The decision's already been taken regarding Phil. It's irrevocable. Someone's going to have to take his place, though. You think you can handle it – two hotels?'

'Florida,' Minsky mused. 'Yeah, it might be a good idea at that.' It would be something to tell Kathleen when he returned home that night. Talking about a move to Florida

159

would remove some of the coldness that lay ahead for both of them. Even if it was only Minsky who would be making the move.

For four weeks, Minsky's hopes regarding Kathleen remained on a plateau. He had not expected her to improve – barring a miracle, there was no possibility of that – but he was delighted to see that she had not weakened further. The care given to her by himself and the nurse, the new clothes he continued to buy for her, the lengthening stays out on the balcony as the weather moved through spring, were all having a beneficial effect. Even the doctor who visited Kathleen every couple of days expressed pleased surprise at the way she was holding up. Minksy became optimistic. He began to count the days until the return of his son and daughter-in-law. Kathleen would still be here when William got back; the young man would be able to see his mother.

At the beginning of the fifth week, Kathleen's condition suddenly deteriorated. From being able to eat light foods, she became incapable of keeping anything down. She complained constantly of pain – the drugs prescribed by the doctor seemed to have little effect. The dose was stepped up. The pain decreased, but so did Kathleen's awareness of her surroundings. She sat out on the balcony like a zombie, eating nothing, barely recognizing the nurse or Minsky. When Pearl came to visit in the evenings, while Joseph stayed at home with Judy, she was a total stranger to Kathleen. Once she even mistook Pearl for the nurse and said: 'Are you going to give me another pill?' Pearl left the apartment barely able to hold back tears. All the other times she had been associated with death, it had come in an abrupt yet merciful form. For the first time, she was witnessing a slow demise. She didn't know which was worse for the bereaved: the abrupt tearing away of a loved one – and she was in no doubt that Minsky still loved Kathleen – or being forced to bear witness to an agonizingly slow death.

Levitt came to the apartment just once with Pearl. Kathleen didn't seem to remember him at all. Neither his name nor his uniquely short stature meant a thing to her. She just smiled vacantly at him when he asked how she felt, and then

160

answered, 'I feel kind of tired, Irwin. Do we have to rehearse that number again?'

Levitt glanced at Minsky and Pearl. Kathleen's confused mind had mistaken him for Irwin Kuczinski. She could remember events from the past, but the present escaped her. Very gently, he rested his hand over hers. 'Not if you don't want to, star.'

'Thanks, Irwin.' She looked out over the Hudson again, her green eyes following a barge as it made its way up towards the George Washington Bridge.

Minsky went back inside the apartment with Pearl and Levitt. 'I was thinking she'd still be here when William gets home in ten days time. All of a sudden, I'm not so sure. And even if she were, would I want my son to see his mother looking like this?'

Pearl caught Levitt's eyes. Did the little man know the story of how Minsky had once held a gun to Kathleen's head? Or when he'd dangled her upside down out of the window? Was that going through his mind now? It was so difficult to tell what he was thinking; she had never seen him so distraught. He appeared as though he would burst into tears at any moment.

'I'd better take Pearl home,' Levitt told Minsky. 'She's got a very pregnant daughter-in-law to take care of.'

'I've got a daughter-in-law to worry about as well,' Minsky murmured. 'And a son. I've got to think how they're going to feel when they get home. Will they be better off seeing Kathleen like this, or not seeing her at all?'

'I wish I could give you an answer,' Levitt replied. Sadly, he guided Pearl towards the door.

That night, Kathleen didn't sleep at all. Despite the drugs, she lay awake, constantly crying in pain. Minsky sat on the edge of the bed, cradling her in his arms, burying her face in his chest so that her screams would not be so strident, so heart-rending. Every cry pierced right through to his brain, a red-hot knife that ripped and slashed at him. When morning came, and Kathleen lay sobbing weakly, Minsky telephoned the doctor.

'Those pills aren't working worth a damn, Doc. Haven't you got anything stronger?'

161

'I've prescribed the strongest safe dose, Mr. Minsky. Anything above that might kill her. Her body is in no shape to withstand more powerful medication.'

'Anything stronger might be an act of mercy,' Minsky grated.

'No, Mr Minsky. It would be murder.'

When the nurse arrived, Kathleen had finally fallen into a sleep of utter exhaustion, tossing and turning on the bed as her subconscious registered the pain that tore through her. 'She was awake all night,' Minsky told the nurse. 'Those drugs aren't doing the trick anymore. I spoke to the doctor, he said anything more powerful might kill her.'

'Have you given her anything yet today?'

'At seven o'clock this morning, just before she fell asleep. You can see and hear for yourself all the damned good it's done.'

'You know, Mr Minsky, it might be easier on Miss Monahan, and on yourself, if she were moved to a hospital for – '

'For her last days?' Minsky shook his head vehemently. 'Nothing doing. She's not going to get better, so why the hell should she be taken away from me? Why should I have to drag myself up to some hospital ward to see her die there when she can pass away with a little dignity right here?'

The nurse had no answer.

At midday the doctor visited the apartment. Kathleen was still asleep. Rather than wake her so he could conduct another examination that would tell him nothing he did not know already, he left her undisturbed. After speaking to the nurse, he took Minsky aside.

'I understand that the nurse suggested Miss Monahan be moved.'

'You understand right, and my answer's still the same. She's not going to die in some butcher's shop, surrounded by people she doesn't know. If she dies . . . *when* she dies . . . it'll happen right here. Get it?'

'A hospital has better facilities.'

'Sure, so they can prolong this existence – you can't call it life, can you? – a couple more days. Forget it, pal.'

'You're thinking with your heart, Mr Minsky, not with your head.'

162

'That's because my head's got me into trouble plenty of times. My heart's never been wrong.'

'It's your decision.'

'Damned right it is. Look, Doc, I'm sorry, I'm not trying to sound like some hard-nosed bastard. I just want to do what I think is best for her. Can you understand that?'

The doctor regarded Minsky sympathetically. 'I think I can. Should you need anything, or should you change your mind, please call me.'

'I will.' As Minsky escorted the doctor to the door, a firm resolve began to grow within him, a strength to comfort and support him through what had to be done. The doctor couldn't help anymore. No medical person could. Even God couldn't help, because if God cared a damn he would never have let this terrible illness befall Kathleen. God had washed his hands of her, just like he washed his hands of everything. In the long run, mercy was left to man himself.

The nurse, as she did every evening, left promptly at six o'clock. Kathleen was asleep again, painkillers and sleeping pills giving her a temporary relief. Minsky sat watching her for a few minutes before picking up the telephone. He called Pearl out at Sands Point. After answering her enquiry about Kathleen with a curt 'No change' he asked if Pearl had intended coming to visit that evening. When she said yes, he suggested that she forego the journey. 'She's sleeping right now, Pearl. It's best that no one comes. That way she won't be disturbed, and she might sleep right through the night.'

'Are you sure there's nothing I can do, Benny?'

'Nothing, Pearl.' His voice softened. 'I appreciate everything you've done so far, and Kathleen does too. She might not have seemed to recognize you these past few days, but I'm sure she did.'

As Pearl replaced the receiver, all she could think of was the chilling finality that had underridden the softness of Minsky's voice.

Kathleen slept until midnight. Minsky was dozing in an armchair he'd dragged into the bedroom when her cries woke him. He sat up, startled. She was calling his name and looking at him. 'What is it, baby?' he asked, after rushing from the chair to the bed. 'What do you want?'

'Hold me tight, Benny.'

He wrapped his arms around her and squeezed tenderly, scared that any greater pressure would snap her bones like twigs. He could feel her heart pounding, lungs labouring to bring oxygen to her failing body.

'How long is it until William gets back from his honeymoon?' she asked.

She understood what was going on around her! She remembered William being away! Minsky was elated until he comprehended the reason. She was overdue for another of the painkillers that the doctor had prescribed. She had exchanged the slight relief from pain that the drugs afforded her for clarity of mind. Should he give her another pill, when it was so evident how much agony she was in? Or should he try to soothe her pain with caresses while he formed a mental bond with her?

'How long, Benny? How long before he gets back?'

'Seven, eight days.' He wasn't sure anymore. It was midnight. Did that make it a day less, or didn't the new day begin until morning? His mind could not function properly enough to work out simple arithmetic.

'I'm not going to make it, am I, Benny? I'm not going to be around to say welcome home to William.'

'Sure you are, baby. If I have to carry you, you'll be down on that Cunard dock to give him one of the biggest, happiest surprises of his life.' Yeah, some surprise, he added to himself . . . seeing his mother looking like a survivor of a hunger strike. He didn't want William to see Kathleen like this. It was better all around that she faded away quietly before the honeymoon couple returned.

'You're full of shit, Benny. You never could lie a damn.'

He remembered her language from the old days, how he'd been excited when she screamed and swore at him. '*I* couldn't lie worth a damn? What makes you think that *you* ever did better?'

She moved her head back and forth knowingly. 'Every lie I ever told you, you believed. You were the easiest person in the world to tell a lie to.'

'Oh, yeah? Give me one example.' Minsky found himself enjoying the game. Kathleen was the most animated he'd seen her for days, the pain forgotten as she plunged into the argument.

'Remember that sapphire necklace – the one I said I got from my mother?'

'The sapphire necklace I threw out of the window?' Minsky started to laugh. That had been the night of the double wedding – Jake to Pearl, Moe Caplan to Annie. Minsky's eyes had been riveted to the necklace all evening long, certain that he hadn't given it to Kathleen. 'Then I threw all your clothes out of the window as well, didn't I?'

Kathleen's body began to tremble. For an instant, Minsky was terrified, until he realized that, like himself, she was laughing. 'And I pulled your gun from its holster – '

'And damned near blew my head off, you crazy bitch.' Even now he could see the flash from the muzzle of the automatic, hear the smack of the bullet as it ploughed into the wall three inches from his head. 'Remember how I held you out of the window?'

'I really thought you were going to drop me. You were a mad bastard, Benny, you really were. And look at you now, as gentle as can be.'

He kissed her forehead. 'What's all this got to do with you getting away with telling me lies?'

'That sapphire necklace – it wasn't from my mother.'

Minsky was in a dilemma. Did he admit to Kathleen that he knew? Did he tell her the truth, or did he just go along, pretend that he'd been taken in? Which alternative would be most beneficial to Kathleen?

'When you held me out of the window and I still yelled that it came from my mother, then you believed me, didn't you?'

'I never thought you'd have the guts to lie when you were a split-second away from being dropped on your head from five storeys up.'

'Guts had nothing to do with it, Benny. If I'd told you the truth – ' her voice grew weaker as if she were finding all this talking, all this remembering, tiring – 'you'd have opened your goddamned hands right away.'

'The truth? That David Hay gave it to you?' The name sprang to Minsky's lips. There was no way he could ever forget it, not until the day he died.

165

'David Hay. . . .' Kathleen's body went rigid. For a moment Minsky feared that he'd gone too far. Then she asked, 'How do you know about David Hay?'

Minsky chuckled. 'Tht night Jake smashed up the car, remember? I was supposed to go down to the Jersey shore that night, but I didn't. Instead I went to the club where you were singing –'

'I was at the King High that night.'

'You've got some memory. I went there but I missed you, and when I tried your apartment you weren't there either. So I figured something wasn't kosher and I waited. When that fancy chauffeur brought you home, I followed him. And that's how I found out about David Hay and his big palatial joint out on Long Island.'

'Were you mad?'

'Damned right I was mad! I didn't know who to go after first, you or that rich creep Hay. So much for lying to me, eh?'

Kathleen's eyes slowly opened wide as she understood the implications of Minsky's smug confession. 'Benny, just after that, David disappeared. He went out riding. His horse came back but he didn't.'

'I remember. I saw the story and his picture in the news-paper. I even pointed it out to you, just to see what your reaction was.'

'What did I do?'

'You taunted me. You had the *chutzpah* to ask me if I recognized Hay as the same guy who threw you a rose one night. And then I taunted you right back by asking if he was the guy you were seeing behind my back. Was that why you remembered him, I said, because he'd given you the necklace?'

'Benny, it was you, wasn't it?'

A wide smile spread slowly acoss Minsky's dark face. 'David Hay wound up as breakfast, lunch and dinner for the fish off the South Jersey shore. One shot right through the heart while he was out riding.'

Kathleen began to laugh again. 'And I thought . . . oh, God, I thought that he was so upset about me kissing him off that he just ran away somewhere.'

'You'd split up with him when I – ?'

'When you killed him? We had a huge row. I told him he wasn't man enough to wipe your ass!'

'Oh, baby, and all the time I figured that your punishment would be wondering what had happened to him! And you couldn't have given a damn! Oh, Christ if ever two people were meant for each other, it was us.' He held her with his left arm, while his right hand clasped the pillow, drew it slowly towards himself. 'I love you, Kathleen, you know that, don't you? I don't think I ever really stopped loving you.'

'I love you too, Benny,' she replied as he brought the pillow up and pressed it to her face.

At first she struggled. Minsky had no idea how long suffocation was supposed to take. On a healthy person it would require a few minutes at least. Kathleen wasn't healthy; she was a corpse looking for a grave. He wanted it to be over immediately; he didn't want her to suffer anymore than she'd done already.

Gradually, Kathleen's body relaxed in his grip. Exhausted by battling the cancer, her heart could not stand the additional strain of being deprived of oxygen. Tears fell freely from Minsky's eyes as he replaced the pillow on the bed and set Kathleen's head upon it. The flat green eyes stared up at him. He reached out and lowered the lids. She'd been right . . . one way or the other, she was not going to make it until William's return. She wouldn't have wanted her son to see her looking like this. Better that he remembered her as he'd known her in childhood – the blonde stranger who only came into his life when there were no other roles available. All in all, it was a less unkind memory.

For half an hour he sat looking at Kathleen. It was the first time since her return that he had seen peace in her face. The lines seemed to have softened, the bones had receded. Death's initial embrace was treating her less harshly than life had done.

At last, he stood up and walked to the telephone. 'Doc, it's Benny Minsky. Sorry to call so late but I just looked in on Miss Monahan. I think she's gone.'

167

Chapter Seven

The *Queen Mary* docked on the morning tide. Minsky was waiting to collect William and Susan and drive them to their new home in Forest Hills Gardens. During the journey, the returning honeymooners excitedly told him of their trip. Minsky listened and occasionally nodded. His own news would keep until they were in the house.

'Susan, while you're unpacking, I'm going to take William down to the depot,' Minsky said once they reached Forest Hills Gardens. 'We'll be back in an hour or so, then I'll give him the rest of the day off.'

'Keep him for as long as you like,' she answered cheerfully. 'I've got to get some food in the house as well.'

Instead of driving towards Long Island City, Minsky headed in the direction of Glendale. 'Where are we going?' William asked, puzzled.

'You'll see.' Minutes later, they entered a cemetery. After parking the car, Minsky walked towards a newly-opened section of the burial ground. Mounds of damp earth were piled high by open graves that waited to receive their occupants. At one graveside, a mourning party stood with heads bowed as a priest conducted the burial service.

'What are we doing here?' William demanded. 'We're supposed to be at the depot.'

Minsky held a finger to his lips before pointing it to a freshly-filled grave. There was no stone yet, just a modest wooden stake on which was written: 'Monahan/Minsky'. 'Your mother's resting there.'

'My *mother*?' William went to the grave, knelt down to get

a closer look at the stake. 'When did this happen? How?'

'She came back. On the night you and Susan got married, your mother came back to me. She was ill, she'd come home to die.'

'*Before* we left? Why didn't you get in touch with me? You knew where I was.'

'Your mother wanted it this way,' Minsky answered. 'I was going to call you – she wouldn't let me. She said she'd made a mess of your childhood, she didn't want to wreck your honeymoon as well.'

'What was the matter with her?'

'Cancer of everything. She found out about it in Los Angeles. Too late. The quacks cut her open and then sewed her up again right away.'

William picked up some of the earth, sifted it through his fingers. 'Why did she come back to you? Because she still loved you?'

'I guess.' There was no point in telling William about Hal Brookman and Kathleen's dire financial straits; let him think his mother died a respectable, self-sufficient woman. 'And I still loved her.'

'When did she die?'

'A week ago. She died in your bed.'

William brushed away a tear. 'You know, all these years the only memory I've had of my mother is that last fight between the pair of you. And now. . . .'

'Now what?'

'Why the hell couldn't she have lasted another week so I could have seen her? She came to you looking for two things – some love in her last days, and some forgiveness. I think she would have wanted my forgiveness too.'

Minsky wondered what William would do if he knew the truth – that his mother might just have survived had not Minsky taken matters into his own hands. Had he deprived his son of one last opportunity to see his mother, to forge a reconciliation? Or had he done William an enormous favour? Unless Minsky himself told William, there was no way the young man would ever know the truth. Kathleen's death had rated no inquest. She had been terminally ill, under the care of a doctor. The cancer had killed her; it was an open-and-

169

shut case. He sensed that other people guessed the truth, though. At the funeral, Pearl, who had come with Lou Levitt and the twins, had given Minsky the most piercing stare, as if she understood perfectly what he had done. Afterwards, she'd come up to him and said obliquely, 'Whatever you did, Benny, you did it out of love.' He had pretended not to understand what she was talking about.

'I told her you forgave her, William,' Minsky said to his son. 'Believe me, she went knowing that her own family loved her, and that was the most important thing in the world to her.'

William climbed to his feet, dusted dirt from his hands and started to walk back towards the car. 'Are you going to stick round in that apartment?'

'For a while, then I'll be moving down to Florida.'

William was surprised. 'Why?'

'To run those two hotels. You don't need me up here, so why should I put up with crappy weather any more?'

'It's still going on with Phil, is it?'

'Yeah, the smart Harvard boy's too damned dumb to take a hint.'

William returned to the car in silence. He'd come back from six weeks of love and tenderness to find his mother dead, and a death warrant drawn up for someone else. Welcome home.

A week after the return of William and Susan, Judy gave birth to a boy. The baby was named Jacob, after Joseph's father. Although delighted that Jake would be remembered through his grandson, Pearl could not help sounding a note of caution.

'Is Jacob such a good choice of name?' she asked when she went with Joseph to see Judy in the hospital.

'What's wrong with it?' Judy asked.

'What happens when you get mail that's just addressed to J. Grantiz? How will you know who it's for?'

Joseph started to laugh. 'We'll just do what we've always done. Judy'll open all the mail, no matter who it's addressed to.'

Although tired from her ordeal, Judy found the strength to wrench a pillow from behind her head and throw it at

170

him. 'You're a jerk!' she yelled at him. 'And that also begins with a J!'

In the first week of September, the Waterway Hotel in Hallandale opened. Unlike its sister hotel, the Monaco, which had gone two million dollars over the original estimate, the Waterway came in on budget. Phil Gerson had done some cost-cutting, depriving Belinda Rivers of her overseas jaunts to buy up antiques. Gerson was not as thrilled with the Waterway as he had been with the Monaco. The lack of twenty thousand-dollar crystal chandeliers and the other expensive fitments Belinda had purchased in Europe lowered the class. To compensate for this disappointment, though, Gerson knew that his employers in New York would not be able to pin any embezzlement on him. What he skimmed from the pot now came directly from the casino take; it didn't show up in construction costs.

Lou Levitt and Benny Minsky travelled down for the opening of the Waterway. With the coming winter season, the two men knew that both hotels would be competing with each other, but there was more than enough money to go around. Gamblers were a superstitous lot. They'd lose at one casino and think their luck would change if they tried the other one. Levitt, especially, blessed the superstitions and systems of gamblers. Without them, he knew he'd be little more than a book-keeper.

The first night at the Waterway, the casino was packed. Standing with Minsky, Levitt looked with satisfaction at the busy tables. When Gerson walked by, he pulled him over. 'Glad to see Belinda's here tonight. Her absence was a bit conspicuous when the Monaco opened, especially after all the work she put into the place.'

'She knew that if she missed this opening, there wouldn't be another one.' Gerson looked at Minsky. 'You happy now that this place came in on budget?'

'I'm happy,' Minsky growled in reply.

'Well, I'm not. You made me sacrifice class for a few bucks. Look at this place – it looks like any other hotel that's going up nowadays. The Monaco reeks of class, and this joint looks like Hilton threw it up.'

171

'If the customers aren't complaining,' Minsky said, 'why should you be?'

'Any imbecile can build a place like this. Only innovative talent can put up a class hotel like the Monaco.'

'Innovative talent and a complete disregard for the damned budet, you mean,' Minsky shot back.

'Still think I was skimming off the top, do you? Cooking the books?' Gerson had been in touch with Leinberg again; the banker had assured him that there had been no enquiries about him. He was confident that neither Levitt nor Minsky knew the truth. They might suspect . . . but suspecting and knowing for certain were two entirely different things. 'Joseph came down here and handed me that line of crap a few months ago. I almost told him to take the damned project and shove it. What gives you the right to treat me like I'm some kind of a cheap crook, after all the time and effort I've put into working for you?'

Levitt raised a placatory hand. He understood Gerson's manoeuvre. Reassured by Leinberg, he was putting on an act of injured innocence. 'Phil, we made a mistake, okay? Everyone's entitled to make a mistake now and then. We got sore because of those gigantic cost overruns and we just grabbed at the most obvious reason. It was the wrong reason, and we're sorry.'

'How sorry?'

'You've got nerve, you know that?' Minsky said. 'You stick us with a two million dollar cost overrun on the Monaco, and when you bring this place in on budget you expect some kind of a special reward'. This is what we're paying you to do. This is why we're picking up the tab on all your little luxuries down here.'

'You still sailing around in that boat?' Levitt asked.

'Maybe one afternoon a week, when Belinda and I can take time off.'

'That's a big boat, isn't it?'

'Sleeps six,' Gerson answered proudly.

'An afternoon trip in a boat that size must be like using a Caddy engine to run a lawn mower,' Levitt said, baiting the trap.

Gerson dropped right in. 'Belinda and I keep planning to

172

take a proper voyage in it, go to the Bahamas for a few days. We just haven't had the time.'

'Take some time. You deserve a break.' Levitt looked around the crowded casino, spotted Belinda in a long evening gown as she watched one of the blackjack games. He called her over. 'Sorry you got deprived of your shopping trips this time around.'

Belinda regarded him coldly. She hadn't forgotten how Joseph had come down to spread the word that she and Phil Gerson were suspected of helping themselves. 'You still think we've been dipping our fingers into your money?'

'We've just been through that with Phil. No, we don't think you've been robbing us. If we did, you wouldn't be here operating this place now.'

Gerson stepped in quickly. 'Honey, Lou's just offered us a few days off, a chance to get away to the Bahamas. What do we do – take it, or stand here arguing about some misunderstanding that belongs in the history books?'

Belinda wasn't sure. While she and Gerson were away, what would happen? Would others be moved in to fill their places? No, the idea was ridiculous. She and Gerson had nothing to fear. The New York men were in the dark. 'Let's take it.'

'Stay around for a few days,' Levitt said, 'until the first weekend is over. Take off on Monday. Benny and I'll come on back down to cover for you.'

'Just remember,' Gerson said, his confidence riding high, 'that there's a world of difference between these two casinos and the back room of a club in Pearl's mother's basement on Second Avenue.'

'We'll manage.' Levitt touched Minsky's arm and the two men walked away. They left the casino, but instead of going down to their rooms on the floor below they went to the parking lot. They drove north, eventually stopping outside a small, shabby hotel in Fort Lauderdale. Walking through the lobby, they banged on the door to one of the rooms.

'Harry, it's Lou. Open up.'

Held by a chain, the door cracked open and Harry Saltzman's left eye appeared. Recognizing his visitors, he

173

unhooked the chain and pulled the door wide open. The moment it was closed again, Levitt said, 'It's all set up for Monday.'

Saltzman rubbed hairy hands together. 'It'll be a piece of cake. I'm going to need help, though. I can't control the boat and do the other things at the same time.'

'You want Leo?' Levitt asked.

'Can Leo handle a boat?' Minsky wanted to know.

'He won't have to,' Saltzman answered. 'All he'll have to do is hold it steady for a minute or so. Yeah, Leo'll be fine. He knows what it's all about.'

'You sure you know Phil's boat?' Levitt asked.

'I drove along the other side of the Intracoastal and eyeballed it pretty good. I even took some pictures. Are you guys staying on down here?'

'No, we're going back tomorrow. We'll come down again on Sunday. Anything you need?'

Saltzman gave both men a crooked smile. 'Nice weather. Get the ocean to be like a sheet of glass that day. Not a ripple in sight, let alone a wave.'

'I'll try to arrange it,' Levitt said as he left.

On Saturday afternoon, Leo drove his car to the airport and left it in the parking lot. Removing a small suitcase from the trunk, he waited. Fifteen minutes later, Joseph drew up and removed a suitcase from the trunk of his own car. Together, the twins made the journey from the parking lot to the terminals. There they separated. Leo checked in for the internal flight to Florida. Joseph, passport in hand, checked on to the trans-Atlantic flight to Switzerland.

Harry Saltzman met Leo when he arrived in Florida and drove him to the small Fort Lauderdale hotel. Maps were spread across the floor of Saltzman's room and both men got down on their hands and knees. Leo watched intently as Saltzman's thick finger traced a route. 'Phil and his girlfriend are going to be coming out of this inlet. We'll be waiting here, scanning the inlet for them. Once they come out and head east towards the Bahamas, we'll just tag along, maybe a mile away. We don't do anything until we're at least ten miles out, with no other boats around.'

174

Leo felt excitement begin to burn within him as he listened to Saltzman's plan. 'How did you get the boat?'

'I hired it for a few days, nothing suspicious about that.'

'Where did you learn to sail?'

Saltzman sat down on the floor and laughed. 'Everyone from the old days can take a small boat out into the open sea. How do you think we used to bring in the booze? Magic? Snap our fingers and make it fly through the air from outside the territorial limit?'

'I forgot,' Leo said.

'All I want you to do is hold the wheel and keep us on a steady course. I'll give you some practice at it when we go out tomorrow. If you don't think you can do it, let me know now. There's still time to get someone else.'

'I can do it,' Leo answered confidently.

'Good, because if you screw up, we'll never see hide nor hair of Gerson and his girlfriend again. That boat they've got can outrun everything but a Coastguard cutter, and it carries damn near enough fuel to get them to Timbuctoo. We're only going to get one chance, and we've got to use it.'

On Sunday, while Saltzman and Leo practised on the hired boat, Levitt and Minsky returned to the newly-opened Waterway Hotel. Levitt carried nothing more than a small valise. Minsky had come prepared, with two large cases. When this was over, Levitt would be returning to New York. Minsky would not. Florida was about to become his home, and he looked forward to the change. Kathleen's death had soured New York for him. Even with William and Susan there, and the grandchildren he was sure he'd have one day, he no longer wanted to live in the city. None of the memories were kind.

That night, a tremendous thunderstorm smashed in from the west. Rain lashed down at crazy angles. Crashing explosions of thunder shook the windows of the Waterway. Lightning lit up the land for miles around. Gamblers left the tables to stand at the windows and watch.

'Will this take care of your boat ride?' Levitt asked Gerson.

'These things pop up all the time during the summer and early fall. They're usually afternoon or night-time affairs. By

175

the morning, when Belinda and I leave, it'll be clear.'

Levitt looked at his watch; it was past ten. 'You'd better get away then, make sure you're awake enough in the morning to sail in a straight line.'

'I didn't take navigation courses for nothing.'

'Take off, anyway. Benny and I'll handle it from here.'

'Thanks for standing in for me.' Levitt's hand was perfectly dry and cool as Gerson shook it. Like the old wives' tale he'd once heard about thick eyebrows that joined above the nose, he also knew of the story about judging a man by his hand-shake. Levitt's handshake just then was the crispest Gerson had ever felt; it was the handshake of a man you could trust with a million dollars.

Levitt watched Gerson and Belinda walk into the special lift that served only the casino. As the door closed behind them, he turned towards the window, as interested as anyone in watching nature's fury. He didn't dwell on the fact that he would never see Phil Gerson or Belinda Rivers again; he had already blotted them from his mind.

Downstairs, Gerson and Belinda ran through the rain to their car. 'How much do we have put away in Switzerland?' Belinda asked as Gerson drove away.

'Close to two million, maybe just over.'

'Don't you think it's time to cut and run?' Belinda was still unsure about the future. With both hotels up, was Gerson really needed anymore? He'd got them into operation, set up the infrastructure. It would be easy for someone else to step in now.

'You worry too much. We can keep milking this thing for ever. I know Levitt and Minsky. As long as they see a steady take coming in we've got nothing to sweat about. Now quit it, will you?' He reached out to squeeze Belinda's thigh affectionately. 'We're going to have a few lazy days on the boat, a great time in the Bahamas – and who knows? I might even come back and tell Lou that he should open a place in Freeport as well. If you think these politicians and cops are easy to bribe, wait until you see their Bahamanian cousins.'

'For Christ's sake, Phil, how many millions do we need to steal? How many before it's enough?'

'Don't use that word, Belinda,' Gerson said angrily. 'I'm

176

not stealing a dime. What I'm taking from those two scrooges is rightfully mine. Without me, they'd have nothing.'

They went to bed the moment they reached home. Outside, the rain continued to lash down, spilling from the tiled roof in waves. The noise was a stimulus, a swirling current with which to time their lovemaking. Tomorrow, under a baking sun, they would make leisurely love on the boat. Tonight, to the metronome of rain and thunder, they made love as though they were competing in a race.

Morning dawned clear and dry. While Belinda cooked bacon and eggs, brewed coffee, Gerson ran a check on the boat. He knew about the storms that cropped up out of nowhere this time of year. He wanted to be sure he could run before one if he had to.

At seven o'clock, they cast off from the dock behind the house and headed along the Intracoastal towards the inlet and the ocean.

From half a mile out to sea, Harry Saltzman trained a pair of high-powered binoculars on the mouth of the inlet. Boats emerged in rapid succession as weekend sailors took advantage of the fine weather. Suddenly Saltzman gripped the glasses tightly. 'There she is,' he said to Leo, who was lounging on a long padded bench that ran along both sides of the small hired boat.

'Let me see.' Leo took the binoculars from Saltzman. Gerson's boat jumped into clear focus. Leo could even make out Gerson's face as he piloted the craft into open water. Moving the glasses fractionally, he saw Belinda dressed in a swimsuit. She was standing at the rail, gazing down at the smooth water.

'Let's go.' While Leo continued to watch Gerson's boat, Saltzman opened the throttle and moved further offshore. His intention was to keep a mile between himself and the bigger boat. Gerson might also have binoculars. Should he sweep the area with them and spot Saltzman or Leo, he'd know immediately what the score was. Neither man was known as an avid boating fan, and neither of them was supposed to be in Florida.

'Stay out of sight, Leo,' Saltzman ordered. 'If he gives us

177

the once-over, he'll just see me at the wheel. And with this – ' he pulled a white cap down low over his forehead, shoved sunglasses on to his face – 'he shouldn't be able to make me out.'

For more than an hour the game was played. Gerson's boat, with Saltzman and Leo always a mile ahead, ploughed steadily eastward. Soon, the morning rush of boats out of the inlet was left far behind; no one else was making the Bahamas run. Saltzman scanned three hundred and sixty degrees with his binoculars until he saw nothing but Gerson's boat. He throttled back, turned the wheel to bring the boat around. The distance between hunter and prey lessened.

On the bigger boat, Gerson noticed the manoeuvre and thought nothing of it. Obviously a weekend sailor who had reached his limit, or a fisherman who'd found a good spot to drop his line. 'You see that boat?' he said to Belinda. 'That's the kind of tiny thing we'd own if we hadn't helped ourselves. Instead, we're flying high in this fancy craft.'

'We don't own this one either,' she reminded him. 'It comes with the lease on the house.'

Gerson laughed. 'One of my earliest lessons at Harvard. Own only what appreciates in value – everything else you lease and let someone else carry the depreciation. Come over here and give me a kiss.'

She stood next to him, both arms around his bare chest. Despite the heat, neither of them was sweating. The brisk breeze off the ocean kept them dry. She dropped her lips to his neck, then his shoulder and finally his chest, nibbling at the skin beneath the fair hair. Her left hand strayed down to the front of his shorts.

'Hey, I'm trying to steer this damned thing!' he protested.

'Let it steer itself for a while.'

'You want to give the people on that boat a front-row seat?'

'We're in international waters. There aren't any laws here.' The notion of making love in the gently rocking boat – in plain view of others – excited her. She'd been a dancer; she appreciated a good audience. Her hand moved to the waistband of Gerson's shorts, tugged them down.

'I'm steering!'

Holding him with her left hand, she used her right to cut the engines. 'Now you've got nothing to steer,' she said

178

triumphantly. 'From now on – ' she felt him grow harder in her hand – 'any steering's going to be done by me.'

Half a mile away, Saltzman watched in amazement through the binoculars as the upper halves of Gerson and Belinda disappeared below the rail. 'Leo! Quick, come and take a look!'

'What?' Leo put the glasses to his eyes. 'Where the hell are they?'

'Where do you think? They've stopped in mid-ocean to knock off a quick one.' He adjusted course to turn them directly towards Gerson's boat and instructed Leo to take the wheel. 'Just keep it steady.'

While Leo maintained course, Saltzman crouched down and inspected the six capped one-quart bottles he'd placed on board that morning. Each was filled with a mixture of gasoline and paint – the gasoline would explode and burn, the paint would make the flames stick. He unscrewed each cap and inserted a long rag, shaking the bottles to wet the wicks. This was going to be easier than he'd ever expected. If he'd known they were going to stop dead in the middle of the sea to tear off a piece, he wouldn't even have needed Leo. He glanced quickly at the younger twin. That would have been robbing him of a high, though. Saltzman understood Leo. He revelled in this kind of work. Saltzman had seen that at the B. M. Transportation depot. Like himself, the younger twin appreciated the qualities of fire. It was cleansing; done properly, it left no clues.

Finished with the wicks, he stood up. Only two hundred yards separated the two boats now. Saltzman pulled a Zippo from his trouser pocket, took it to the other side of the boat and flicked the wheel. Flames flared up and he nodded in satisfaction. 'Move a fraction to port so we come up alongside them.' Leo turned the wheel until Saltzman said, 'Enough'. The small boat coasted on a course that would take Saltzman and Leo off the starboard side of Gerson's boat.

Gerson heard the steady thud of an approaching engine and started to lift himself from Belinda. She clung to him voraciously, refusing to let him go. Her legs were wrapped tightly around his thighs, her arms crushed his ribs. 'Let them

179

watch!' she hissed. 'Let them take pictures if they damned well want to. Kodak'll never dare develop them.'

'Anyone home!' a voice yelled across the water.

'Shit!' Beinda swore as Gerson eased himself out of her grip. She lay back on the deck, feeling the sun bathe her body as Gerson stood up. Then she started to laugh. 'Put some clothes on! Look at yourself!'

Gerson glanced down at his erection. He grabbed a towel and wrapped it around his waist before turning his attention to the small boat. 'What do you . . .?' The question died as he recognized Saltzman standing by the rail, a bottle in one hand, the Zippo in the other. And Leo at the wheel. 'Belinda!' Gerson screamed.

'Got a case of the hots for each other?' Saltzman yelled across ten yards of water. 'Here's a little something to keep the fires burning.' The firebomb arced across the intervening space to explode on the rear deck. With machine-like precision and efficiency, Saltzman lifted the next, lit and threw it, and the next and the next, until all six bombs were gone, raking the boat from bow to stern. As the last one left his hand, he roared at Leo: 'Hit it!'

Leo gunned the throttle. The bow of the smaller boat lifted. Wake spilled out, speed increased. Saltzman stood in the stern, watching in satisfaction as fire engulfed the larger boat. Through the flames he saw Belinda, hands beating furiously at her blazing hair, dive screaming into the sea. Of Gerson, there was no sign.

Four hundred yards away, Saltzman yelled, 'Cut!' Leo killed the engine and came back to the stern to stand alongside Saltzman. A booming explosion tore through Gerson's boat as the fuel tanks went up. Pieces of flaming debris soared into the air, whirling like broken windmill blades to land sizzling in the sea. The two men watched impassively until, with a dying wheeze, the boat went down. Then they changed course and headed back towards the coast.

Leo and Saltzman were at the airport by the time a Coastguard cutter spotted floating debris in the early afternoon. When the story of the sinking – 'Probably a fault in the fuel system,' a Coastguard spokesman explained – made the news broadcasts, both men were halfway to New York.

Levitt and Minsky listened to the news together. When the short, initial bulletin was over, Levitt shook Minsky's hand. 'Congratulations on your new job. I hope you have more luck than your predecessor.'

'There's no point in me stealing – I'd only be taking money out of my own pocket.'

The following morning, a notice was sent to all staff at both the Monaco and the Waterway, hotel workers and casino croupiers and dealers. 'It is with great regret,' the notice read, 'that Palmetto Leisure Development Corporation has learned of the tragic death in a boating accident of its chairman and chief operating officer, Mr Philip Gerson. Effective immediately, Mr Benjamin Minsky will assume all responsibility for the day-to-day operation of both hotels.'

As the notices were received and read it was early afternoon in Zurich. Joseph Granitz had spent the entire morning in his room at the Hôtel Savoy Baur en Ville, waiting for one phone call. Finally it came. The message from Levitt was short: go about your business.

Immediately, Joseph walked along the Bahnhofstrasse to Leinberg Bank, entered through the side door and took the lift up to the third floor. In the bank's boardroom, he sat across the table from Walter Leinberg and told the bank president: 'Dancer is closed. Please see to it that all funds are transferred to Blackhawk.'

BOOK 2

Chapter One

The period following the birth of her grandson was the happiest time Pearl could remember since Jake had been alive. She felt that she had a purpose in life again, helping Judy to care for Jacob, bathing and dressing him, spoiling him at every opportunity. She experienced supreme joy as he passed those important dates on a baby's calendar: first smile, first word, first step. Nothing, it seemed to Pearl in those first two years of Jacob's life, could make her happier. She was wrong. Her happiness increased a thousandfold when Judy became pregnant again.

In 1957, when Jacob was three, Judy gave birth to a daughter, a tiny, wrinkled bundle with a thick thatch of bright red hair. Pearl laughed the first time she went to the hospital with Joseph to see her granddaughter. 'Little doubt whose child this is, is there?' she said to Judy. 'Or who her grandmother was.' She placed a finger in the baby's hand and felt tiny fingers grip with surprising tightness. 'Have you and Joseph decided on a name yet?'

'Anne,' Joseph answered. 'We're going to name her Anne after Judy's mother . . . Anne Granitz.'

'Another red-headed Annie,' Pearl said, and made a horrified face. 'God help us all.'

Judy regarded her mother-in-law crossly. '*Anne*,' she stressed. 'Annie sounds too much Second Avenue. Our daughter's Nassau County, not Houston Street.'

'Excuse me,' Pearl said, and turned to Joseph. 'You'd better be careful now. One redhead's trouble enough, but two . . .!'

185

Soon, the house in Sands Point, which Pearl had feared would be too big, too echo-ridden for just Joseph and Judy, was filled with the nonstop noise of running feet, the shouting and laughter of young, exuberant voices. Pearl had her hands full helping Judy to cope with two normally boisterous youngsters as they played, fought and constantly raced beneath her feet, and she would have had it no other way. Life, with its perpetual reversals of fate and fortune, had turned full circle to smile on her again.

Another source of pleasure for Pearl was William Minsky's family. William and Susan also had two children, both boys – Mark, a year older than Anne, and Paul, a year younger. William's sons were the closest Pearl's own grandchildren would ever have to proper cousins. Judy was an only child – there would be no cousins from her family – and there was no possibility of Leo ever marrying. Pearl was pleased that such a strong friendship existed between the two young couples. The Minsky's were frequent visitors to Sands Point, as were the Granitzes to William's home in Forest Hills Gardens. Sometimes Benny Minsky would be in New York for a short visit from Florida, where he continued to operate the Waterway and Monaco hotels, and Pearl would be delighted to see him as well. She had reached a stage of her life where contentment came easily, and she was grateful for it.

Contentment, yes . . . except when she thought about Leo. Adult, perfectly capable of taking care of himself, the younger twin still caused Pearl to worry. Time and again she asked herself if she would be so concerned if he were . . . were normal. Then she would become annoyed at herself for thinking of him as abnormal. Years after going down to MacDougal Steet and finding him with that blond-haired boy, years after telling him that she could accept whatever he wanted to do, however he wanted to live, she still could not bring herself fully to understand the manner of life he had chosen. Or had he chosen it? Had it been thrust upon him instead? If that were true, it was her fault because she had created him. And then her self-directed annoyance would be transformed into waves of guilt.

Pearl's anxiety about Leo was not eased when he bought a house out in Scarsdale. In the Central Park West apartment, he'd had Lou Levitt living below him, Pearl's trusted friend whom she could rely on to keep an eye on Leo, advise him should he ever seek counsel. In Scarsdale, Leo was by himself. Pearl understood why he'd bought the house. He'd been impressed with the home Joseph and Judy had bought in Sands Point, and he wanted to prove that whatever his twin brother had, he could have also. Those old rivalries again, Pearl thought. On Leo's side they were anything but dead; he was still convinced that he had to prove himself in his mother's eyes, demonstrate that he was equal if not better than his twin.

Several times Leo drove Pearl out to the house in Scarsdale, and she always left thinking the same thing – although it was not as large as Joseph's, the house was still far too big for one man to live in by himself. Especially a man who did not appear to have a large circle of friends. Leo's entire social life, as far as Pearl could ascertain, centred around a cinema he'd had built into the basement of the house. He would sit for hours watching old Bogart and Cagney movies, and then watch them again, speaking the dialogue with the characters, affecting their tough-guy accents.

'Leo, you can't spend all your time hidden away here,' she protested one Sunday afternoon as she watched *White Heat* with him. He'd picked her up at Sands Point, taken her out for lunch and then driven her to Scarsdale for the afternoon. 'It's not healthy.'

He chuckled at her concern. 'Ma, all week long I work hard, out on the streets for Uncle Lou. When the weekend comes, I need some rest. This is where I rest, right here. I enjoy these movies, they help me to relax. Here . . .! He grabbed her hand as the final scene of the movie unfolded on the screen. 'Made it, Ma! Top of the world!' he shouted along with Cagney, his voice taking on the actor's sharp twang. 'You see that, Ma? He's going to blow himself to Kingdom Come, and all he thinks about is his mother. Some guy, huh?'

Pearl hated the movies, the noise and violence, the totally unsympathetic characters with whom Leo seemed to find such empathy. 'You think I'm like that no-good's mother?'

'No.' Leo squeezed her hand, his eyes riveted to the screen

187

as Cagney disappeared into his own flaming hell. 'You're like no one else's mother, past or present.'

Pearl used the tenderness of the moment to ask another question, a far more searching one. 'Now that you're living here in this beautiful house, do you still keep that apartment on MacDougal Street?'

Leo's gaze left the screen. His heavy eyebrows lowered threateningly. Deep within him an angry spark glowed. He still needed to know who had turned his mother against him that time, who had wanted so badly to hurt his mother and himself. It was unfinished business. Just as quickly his anger disappeared. 'No, I don't keep the place on MacDougal Street anymore.' As an expression of relief began on his mother's face, he added, 'I moved uptown. I keep an apartment on East 59th Street now.'

Pearl turned her eyes to the screen to watch the credits roll by. She was sorry now that she had asked. Sometimes ignorance was bliss. Even partial ignorance. . . .

The start of the 1960s saw a long-held dream turn to reality for Pearl. To celebrate her fifty-fifth birthday, in November 1960, Lou Levitt arranged to take her out to dinner. Pearl, who had intended to commemorate the birthday by cooking a small family dinner at home – 'After all,' she said to Judy after Levitt's invitation, 'who celebrates turning fifty-five?' – was mystified by the sudden invitation, even more so when Judy and Joseph pushed her into accepting the dinner offer.

'Maybe being fifty-five won't seem so terrible if you're with someone who's just as old,' Joseph told his mother. 'You ever think of that?'

'And did you ever think that you're so big that I still can't give you a slap across the behind?'

'Have dinner with him,' Judy pressed. 'You'll enjoy being taken out more than you would cooking for us all – that's no special day for you.'

Suddenly it all became clear to Pearl. Levitt was going to propose to her again. And he had roped in Joseph and Judy – and, who knew, perhaps even Leo as well – to set it up for him. God, what man in his right mind wanted to propose to a fifty-five-year-old woman? The fact that Levitt himself was fifty-five made little difference. Men were different from

188

women. As they grew older, they grew in many ways more attractive. Grey hair or a lined face on a man were signs of character, whereas on a woman they were merely tokens of age. Physical appearance was nowhere near as important for a man as it was for a woman. An ugly man could always get by. For heaven's sake, just look at those actors Leo loved to watch. Bogart, Edward G. Robinson, James Cagney. They all had faces that only a mother could love, but no one ever described them as ugly. Strong was the word used to sum up Edward G. Robinson's face. God help the woman, though, who looked like that!

Pearl was still thinking how unfair it was when Levitt came to call for her on the evening of her birthday, a Saturday. As she opened the door, he kissed her on the cheek, said 'Happy birthday', and handed her a small, gaily wrapped package.

Was this the ring? she wondered as she accepted the gift. Wasn't he even going to wait until the candlelit dinner was over, until the gypsy violinists had packed up their instruments and gone home? Stop it, she told herself. She didn't even know where he'd made reservations for dinner. How did she know there'd be candlelight and violinists? Probably there wouldn't. Levitt wasn't the overly romantic kind.

'May I open this, Lou?' she asked.

'Why do you think I gave it to you? And while you're opening it, may I come inside? In case you haven't noticed, it's pouring out here.'

She looked past him to see rain bouncing off the bonnet of his car. 'Come in, I'm almost ready.'

'Fine. I'll go talk to Joseph while you finish off.'

Pearl stared at the package. He'd given her a ring and then walked away. She undid the wrapping to discover a flat, square box. Fingers trembling, she opened it. There was no ring inside, just a narrow diamond bracelet with a tiny card – 'One stone for every year. Love, Lou.' She ran after him into the living-room, where he was talking with Joseph and Judy. 'Thank you, it's beautiful.' Before she knew what she as doing, she threw her arms around his neck and kissed him.

'Next year I'll get you a bigger one.'

'Where am I going to wear something like this?' she asked,

slipping the bracelet on to her wrist and showing it to her son and daughter-in-law.

'Maybe it's time you started hitting a few of the high spots again,' Levitt suggested.

'After dinner tonight,' Joseph said, 'go dancing with Uncle Lou.'

'Oh, sure,' Pearl answered sarcastically. 'Can you imagine your fifty-five-year-old mother doing the wild and crazy dances the kids do nowadays?'

'We'd probably be able to find some place that plays old-time music,' Levitt said. 'Maybe a joint where you have to knock on the door and be admitted through some secret password. You know. . . .' He lowered his voice into a growl and, in a rare flash of humour, added, 'Charlie sent me.'

Pearl smiled. Those had been the days.

As they left the house, Joseph and Judy saw them to the door. 'You make sure you look after Ma,' Joseph called out to Levitt. 'You treat her like the lady she is.' Levitt waved back, and Pearl was even more certain that he had another package in his pocket, another piece of jewellery. The bracelet had been part of the sell; the clincher would be the ring.

Pearl's suspicions were strengthened by the seeming sentimentality that began to overtake Levitt as he drove. 'Mind if we go for a ride before we eat? I'd like to look around the old neighbourhood.'

Pearl gestured at the wipers swishing across the windshield. 'You could have picked a nicer day.'

Levitt's only answer was a gentle smile. Once he reached New York he headed south along the FDR. Soon, they were driving on Houston Street, and then north along the first few blocks of Second Avenue. He pulled up outside a restaurant with a Spanish name. 'I wonder if they've got a club going in the basement, Pearl.'

She stared at the door. Two dark-skinned men came out and ran towards a parked car, the collars of their jackets up against the rain. As the door closed slowly behind them, Pearl looked into the restaurant. The counter was still there, so were the booths, but the restaurant looked greasy and she wouldn't want to eat there. Remembering the wonderful food that had once been cooked on the premises by her mother and herself, she felt a wave of sadness sweep over her. Rain streaked the window but she could discern the gaudily written menu card stuck behind the glass.

'I made cabbage *borscht*, *lockshen kugel* and *latkes* . . . now they make hamburgers, french fries and hot dogs. And look at those prices, Lou! Where do they get the *chutzpah* to charge such prices?'

'If you could have gotten those prices thirty years ago, we wouldn't have needed the club, would we? Or the books, or anything else.'

They drove to midtown and entered an Italian restaurant close to where Seventh Avenue met Central Park South. Levitt told Pearl it was a restaurant he dined at frequently when he was alone; the fare was good, and it was within walking distance of his apartment. Pearl recalled walking past it when she had lived in the area, but she'd never been inside. The atmosphere was that of a family dining-room, tables crowded together, diners who ate and talked simultaneously, waiters who bumped chairs without apologizing. It wasn't the kind of place where Pearl would expect to hear a marriage proposal.

She never got to hear one. Levitt's talk continued along the same sentimental lines that Pearl had noticed during the drive in from Long Island. She had to strain to hear him above the Saturday night turmoil of the restaurant.

'I thought you'd get a kick out of seeing the old restaurant,' Levitt said. 'I knew you hadn't been down there for years.'

'I didn't get so much of a kick as feel sad, Lou. I had beautiful memories of that place, except for when – '

He reached out to cover her hand with his own. He remembered her father's accident, and later her mother dying under a hail of bullets fired by the madman Gus Landau. ''I understand.'

'But what they've done to it! Hamburgers and french fries.' Genuinely outraged, she shook her head and made a disgusted face.

'And the price,' Levitt urged. 'Don't forget the prices they've got the *chutzpah* to charge.'

Her outrage vanished. Leaving her hand lying beneath his, she gave him a fond smile. 'Did I really sound like my mother then, worrying about prices and money?'

191

'A little. Like I said, if you could have charged those prices, we wouldn't have needed the club in the basement, the handbooks, anything. Pearl. . . .' His hand tightened around her own. 'The clubs were the first things to go when Prohibition bit the dust. And now the handbooks have gone as well.'

'What?' She could not keep the shock, and pleasure, out of her voice. Then worry. 'How did it happen? The police?'

'No, not the police, although there are going to be a lot of cops who'll miss their weekly paycheques. We closed them down, that's all. Started about three months ago, phasing out one area after the other. Joseph and Leo were sworn to secrecy. I didn't want you to know anything until the operation was complete.'

'Lou, you don't know how wonderful that news is. I never thought – '

'That we'd close them? It was time, Pearl. We made a fortune out of those places, but there are other ways to go now.'

'What ways?' she asked fearfully.

'Legal, respectable ways. One. . .' Levitt touched his left index finger to the thumb of his right hand. 'Ever since Castro kicked the casinos out of Cuba, there's been a lot of activity in the Bahamas. We were never in Cuba, Pearl, just as we were never in Vegas; the competition was too cut-throat. But we're moving into the Bahamas.'

'We?'

'Benny and I, the twins, William. We're moving into legitimate casinos. England's another place we're investing. They've got legal casinos springing up there – '

'Since when?'

'This year. They passed some law called the Gaming Act. Now they've got above-board places. Gaming clubs, the Limeys call them. Got a lot more class than the Vegas places, much smaller, dress codes, and to play there you've got to be a member.'

'Do these London casinos make a lot of money?'

'Not as much as the places in the Bahamas will make, or even Florida. They're just a solid, silent investment.'

Pearl considered the information. It had all come so abruptly that it took a while to digest. No more handbooks, no more New York gambling. Levitt and her twin sons had become international. Did that mean that Joseph and Leo would be travelling often to those faraway places? Well, the Bahamas wasn't that far away, but London certainly was. She voiced the question and Levitt shook his head.

'We're silent partners there, Pearl. We just put up the money and we take what we're given.'

'What will Leo and Joseph have to do all day long?' She couldn't see them retiring at thirty-three. 'The Jalo Cab company isn't enough to keep them busy – that runs itself anyway.'

'There is no more Jalo Cab company.' Levitt's face was wreathed in a big grin. He was obviously enjoying all the surprises he was springing on Pearl this evening. And she had thought that he was going to ask her to marry him! 'At least, not as far as we're concerned. We sold it. We don't need the premises upstairs any longer, so why do we need the cab company?'

For some reason, that news caused sadness in Pearl. It took her several seconds to comprehend the reason. 'Jake's name was a part of that company. Now it's like a tie with him is dead.'

'I'm sorry. But if it'll make you any happier, Joseph and Leo won't be sitting around doing nothing. Benny Minsky's boy, William, has his trucking business. And a damned fine business he's turned it into as well.' Pearl wasn't sure, but she thought she detected a sour note in Levitt's voice when he spoke of William's achievement. 'Now the twins have got a business as well. Real estate. Granitz Brothers. They're going to buy up property in Midtown, rent it out for offices. Joseph can finally use that education he got. Now, how much more respectable can they be than that?'

'Where's the money coming from? Zurich?'

'Where else do we get such good rates?'

'You mentioned the London gambling clubs won't make as much as the Bahamas or Florida. Does that mean that you're continuing with Florida?'

'For the time being. It's a class operation. Besides, it makes Benny feel like he's important, being down there, running the places.'

At the moment, Pearl was not concerned with Minsky. She sat back, her meal forgotten. The hubbub in the restaurant seemed to die; the interruptions by the waiters went unnoticed. The twins in real estate. Granitz Brothers. The books gone. And everything had been hidden from her, a conspiracy to keep her in the dark about what was taking place until Levitt could present it as a *fait accompli*. From a lifetime of flirting with the law to total respectability. Well, almost. The only vestiges in the United States of the Granitz and Minsky families' unconventional past would be the two casinos in Florida. Levitt wanted those kept in operation. Not for Benny Minsky's sake, Pearl was certain of that. Nor was it for money. He wanted them kept as a memento of the old days. Although respectability might have its value, nostalgia also merited a place.

She didn't realize she was smiling until Levitt said, 'Does that big grin on your face mean you approve of what's been done behind your back?'

'I was thinking, that's all. You know, Jake made a boast once . . . a lifetime ago . . . when you and he and Moe and Benny started buying into legitimate businesses. He said that one day not only would the twins own the clothing manufacturers who made their suits, but also the mills where the cloth was spun. Now that boast has come true. The only pity is that Jake's not here to see it.'

'Pearl, you really think he doesn't know?'

'I'm sure he does.'

They left the restaurant for the return journey to Sands Point. Pearl felt sorry for Levitt. It was still raining, and after seeing her home he would have the long, lonely drive back to Central Park West, just walking distance from where they'd eaten. 'Why don't you let me take a cab, Lou?'

'You heard what Joseph said to me as we left the house – that I should treat you like a lady. A gentleman doesn't let a lady take a cab home.'

Pearl sat back as Levitt drove towards the Queens-Midtown Tunnel. She was thinking about the birthday gift from Levitt, and what she'd originally believed it to be. She began to laugh. 'Lou, you're going to think this is crazy, but the way you asked me out tonight, and the way Joseph and

Judy pushed me into going with you when I just wanted to make dinner at home – well, I thought you were going to ask me to marry you.'

The moment the last word was out, she clapped a hand to her mouth, scarcely able to believe what she'd said. Her eyes moved sideways to see how Levitt was reacting.

His face remained expressionless, eyes fixed on the road. 'And instead I laid the big secret on you. Are you telling me that you're disappointed I didn't ask you?'

'When I first thought that was the reason for the invitation, all I could think about was that no man in his right mind would ask a fifty-five-year-old woman to marry him. I never thought about being happy over the possibility or not.'

'If I had asked you, Pearl, how would you have answered?'

'I don't know, Lou, and that's the God's honest truth.'

'Pearl, many's the time I've thought about it. I've even got a ring at home. I was going to give it to you on the night – '

'That Joseph got married?'

Levitt looked startled. He swung his eyes off the road and stared incredulously at her. 'How the hell did you know that?'

'I guessed. And then that thing happened with Leo, where he ran away and you had to get him out of trouble.'

Christ, Levitt thought, did I ever get him out of trouble that night! 'A lot of times I've considered getting that ring out, dusting it off.'

'Why didn't you?'

'Maybe I couldn't take another refusal. You turned me down twice, Pearl. Once before you married Jake, and again shortly after he died.'

'Neither time was opportune.'

'No, it wasn't. And that third time, on Joseph's wedding, when Leo pulled his number, I just figured that perhaps I was being given a message. I realized that you loving me – '

'I do love you.'

'Let me finish. You loving me and being in love with me were two totally different things.'

'Lou, I love you like a friend, like I loved Annie. It took me a long time to realize the difference as well.' She saw an opportunity to switch subjects gently. 'You know, loving you like that, I often worry about you being all alone in that

195

apartment. What if something happens one night? God forbid that it should, but just supposing? Who would know?'

Levitt had frequently considered the same possibility himself, in those infrequent moment when he'd looked inward. He could fall ill and who would know until it was too late? 'I'm not alone, Pearl. I've got a family. Your family. I get as much joy out of them as you do.'

Too many memories had flooded through the gates tonight. First, the sight of the restaurant on Second Avenue. Jake's boast about being respectable. Levitt's proposals. And now this, which brought up the strongest memory of all. 'Lou, do you still think they're yours?'

'The twins? Only God knows that, Pearl.'

'I didn't ask if you *knew*. I asked what you *thought*.'

'Yes. I still think Leo and Joseph are mine.'

They drove the remainder of the way in silence, as if Levitt's admission had killed any contact between them. Only when they pulled into the driveway of the Sands Point house did Levitt speak. 'Pearl, I'm sorry if the big surprise wasn't what you were expecting. I hope it didn't ruin the evening for you.'

'It made the evening for me. I've dreamed for years of the day that all those places would be closed down. I'm just wondering if it's going to feel any different to be the mother of a couple of real estate magnates.'

'You mean you loved them less when they were just in the gambling?'

'No, I'd have loved them no matter what they did. You, too,' she said quickly. 'I'd have loved you just as dearly if you'd stayed running a crap game beneath my mother's restaurant. Lou. . .' She reached out a hand to him. 'I want you to know that if that apartment ever gets too lonely, there's a guest wing here where you'd be welcome to stay. I'm sure Joseph and Judy wouldn't mind you as a tenant.'

'Thanks, I'll remember that, Pearl.' He leaned across the car to kiss her good-night, watched as she walked quickly up the stone steps and swung back the door.

Levitt drove slowly back to Manhattan, his actions in controlling the car almost automatic. He went over the evening, from the moment he'd picked up Pearl at the house to the time he had returned her. She'd thought he was going to ask her to marry him! He bit back a grin. Like he'd told her, he was convinced that such an event was fated never to happen. He too had recognized the difference between loving and being in love. Perhaps too late, but he'd recognized it nonetheless. He supposed that after all these years he should be happy that she loved him as a friend. He considered himself well past the age where sexual fulfilment was important. In fact, he'd never had much interest in sex. He wasn't comfortable jumping into bed with someone just for the sake of doing so; there had to be some deeper commitment. Pearl was the only woman he'd ever felt that way about. Too bad that she hadn't felt the same. But he did have the satisfaction of being one hundred per cent certain that Joseph and Leo were his children.

He thought about the new life, the new career the twins would share. Levitt harboured little doubt that Joseph would slot right into running a real estate company. He had the perfect background, a business education and some tough hands-on experience in the hectic rush of the large room above the cab garage, shuffling money around, working with the hotels in Florida. It was Leo who troubled Levitt. Where would he fit into an operation like this? When the decision had been made to close the handbooks, Leo had been the only dissenter. He had enjoyed a certain position while controlling the streets. Consequently, he had been loath to relinquish such power for a more humdrum position. He had even talked about moving to the Bahamas or down to Florida to be in touch with the casinos activity. Levitt had told him firmly that his place was in New York.

Leo was an enigma as far as Levitt was concerned. Whereas he could often spot traces of himself in Joseph – the sharp mind, the attention to detail – he could recognize none of these traits in the younger twin. If anything, he could see Jake in Leo sometimes. Jake had possessed that swashbuckling attitude that Leo affected. And look at those movies he watched all the time. Was it just movie lover's fascination, or did Leo really see himself in those gangster roles, living in that violent, exciting era where Levitt, Minsky, Jake and Moses Caplan had first made their mark? Was Leo a man born thirty years behind his time?

Levitt was still trying to reach an answer when he pulled up outside his apartment block on Central Park West. Instead of entering the building, he walked south through the rain to a news stand and purchased the early edition of the following morning's *Times*. He didn't feel at all sleepy; he might as well just sit up and read.

He turned to the week-in-review section, scanned through those stories which had made news during the previous seven days. Much of the emphasis was on the General Election which had recently taken place. His blue eyes followed the lines of type automatically, taking in details of congressional and senate victories. He hadn't taken much interest in the election at the time. Now, with a need to do something until he felt sleepy, he decided to rectify that lapse.

Suddenly his eyes sharpened. A familiar name leaped from the page. Rourke. Patrick Joseph Rourke. A loud chuckle burst from Levitt's lips. That Irish son of a bitch had finally reached the peak of respectability. Being named Ambassador to Ireland during the war hadn't been enough for him. Now he had a son, Patrick Rourke Jr., who had been elected to the Senate.

Levitt read through the story more carefully. In a tight race, Patrick Rourke Jr. had been elected Democratic Senator for Massachussetts. There was even a photograph of Patrick, with his younger brother, John, who had acted as his campaign manager. The middle son, Joseph Rourke, Levitt noted, had been killed during the war, shot by the SS after being taken prisoner during the Battle of the Bulge. Levitt tried to guess how old Patrick Joseph Rourke was now. He had to be almost seventy. His son, Patrick Jr., the Senator, was in his mid forties. John Rourke was in his late thirties.

A third time Levitt read the story. John Rourke must have done one hell of a job as campaign manager for his brother, Levitt mused; a tough campaign with millions of dollars thrown into the fight by old Patrick Joseph Rourke. Millions of bootleg dollars. There was no mention of that, though, not that Levitt expected there to be. Bootlegging was the skeleton in the Rourke family closet. They'd keep damned quiet about it.

Levitt found a pair of scissors with which to clip the story

198

from the newspaper. He'd show it to the twins, let them know what had become of the man who'd contracted with Saul Fromberg to kill himself and Jake Granitz. Another thought struck him. He lifted the telephone and put through a call to Florida. Benny Minsky wouldn't read the newspaper, at least, not past the front page of the sports section. He might not even find out about this unless someone told him.

'Hi, Benny, how's business?' Levitt asked when he reached Minsky at the Monaco in Hollywood.

'Pretty good. Both hotels are full, the casinos are busy. The season's just starting.' Minsky's voice turned wary. 'Why are you calling up in the middle of the night?'

'I want to read you something, from tomorrow's *Times*.' Levitt read through the story, listening to Minsky's gasp of surprise. 'See, Benny, there's hope for us all. Maybe we should get the twins and William to run for some public office.'

'I don't have any grand ideas for my son,' Minsky answered. 'That Irish scumbag Rourke always did. Shall we send him a wire, congratulating him?'

'The hell with him,' Levitt said. 'I wouldn't waste the damned money. Besides, the son only won by a handful of votes. Maybe they'll have a recount and he'll lose.'

Minsky laughed. 'That sounds more like you,' he said before hanging up.

Before placing the clipping in his wallet, Levitt read it through a final time. Senator! What he had done with the twins, what Minsky had done with William, none of it added up to a hill of beans compared with this. Old man Rourke must be revelling in his son's success, and Levitt begrudged every iota of happiness he found.

Chapter Two

The next few years flew past Pearl like a fresh breeze on a stifling summer day, there one moment to be enjoyed and gone the next. Her grandchildren seemed to sprout a half inch each time she looked at them, until she became scared to look at all, terrified that Jacob and Anne would be fully grown and another generation would have slipped past. By the time he was eleven, Jacob was taller than Pearl, showing the first signs of the transformation from boyhood to manhood – a sprinkling of hair on his upper lips, hands and feet that were suddenly too large for the rest of his body. Pearl was grateful that Anne – Anne of Nassau County, not Annie of Houston Street – was still a little girl, carrying that flaming head of red hair like a torch in memory of her grandmother.

As if to emphasize the remorseless passage of time, Pearl witnessed the twins' real estate company – Granitz Brothers, that respectable, legitimate business which Lou Levitt had surprised her with when she'd expected a marriage proposal – leap off the ground with the swift sureness that was the hallmark of any concern in which Levitt was involved. The first office block had been purchased on Broadway, just south of 42nd Street. Further loans from Leinberg Bank in Zurich had followed during the next three years to facilitate the purchase of buildings on Madison Avenue, Sixth Avenue, West 57th Street and East 34th Street, across from the Empire State Building. At the start of 1965, the twins constructed their first building, a thirty-storey block on East 42nd Street called Granitz Tower, with the entire top floor given over to corporate headquarters. Pearl went there regularly to meet Leo for lunch. Always she would stand by the huge picture window in his office and look out across the East River to Brooklyn and Queens. If only Jake could see, as she did, this view over all of New York. What pride he would feel. . . .

When Granitz Tower was erected, Pearl expected the top floor to have an office with Lou Levitt's name on the door. It didn't. Nor was Levitt's name to be seen anywhere on the roll of company officers. As ever he preferred to remain in the background, always available to give advice but wanting none of the fame that came with fortune; he was content to let the twins enjoy that. The same was true in the Bahamas and London, where Levitt's and Minsky's money had found willing takers. For Pearl's sixtieth birthday, Levitt took her to London. They appeared to be two friends sharing a vacation. First-class travel on a TWA 707; separate rooms in the Connaught; a formal good-night with a chaste kiss on the cheek before retiring, and a happy greeting when they saw each other over breakfast the following morning.

In London, Levitt and Minsky owned shares in two gambling establishments, the Dominion Sporting Club in Knightsbridge, and the Embassy Club in the centre of Mayfair. But when Pearl visited these clubs with Lou, they both had to take out overseas memberships, the same as any tourist, in order to enter. Once inside, Levitt was just one of many members. No one paid him any undue attention. He was simply a little sixty-year-old man in a smartly pressed mohair suit with a grey-haired woman on his arm whom everyone assumed was his wife.

'You own a piece of this place,' Pearl said to him when they were in the Embassy, 'and no one has any idea who you are.'

'That's the way I like it to be.' He handed her a ten-shilling chip, the minimum stake, to place on the roulette table. When she dithered over which number to play, considering family birthdays and street addresses, the battle plan of any superstitious gambler, he whispered, 'Put it on odd and even or red and black.'

'But they only pay even money,' Pearl protested. 'A number's worth thirty-five to one.'

'An even-money winner is always better than a thirty-five

to one loser,' Levitt answered with simple, undefeatable logic.

Pearl placed the chip on red. Black came up and the croupier swept the single chip into the pile of losing bets. Levitt refused to risk any more money, even another ten-shilling minimum bet. 'Let them call me *schnorrer*,' he said to Pearl. 'In the morning when the receipts are tallied, I'll have the bigger laugh.'

'Does Benny ever come here?'

'What for?'

'Well, he's as much a partner in these places as you are.'

'So are the twins, so's William. None of us comes here. We just take the money and say thank you very much, like any stockholder in a company who's happy to see in the annual report that the dividend's been increased.'

Pearl had never regarded making money as such an impersonal venture. In the restaurant with her mother, her own sweat had contributed to the profits. In the twins' business, in William Minsky's transportation company, the principals were directly involved. When Jake, Levitt, Minsky and Caplan had operated the club beneath the restaurant they'd all been involved, with Levitt supervising the tables in the back. Now it was all done by automation – they put in money and they got more money in return. Dividends. Even Benny Minsky down in Florida with the two illegal casinos – he did nothing more than walk around every so often, a landowner inspecting his property.

Looking at Levitt, Pearl could sense that he missed the intimate involvement. Although he refused to risk another bet on the roulette table, he was watching the croupier intently. 'You're jealous of him, aren't you, Lou?'

'Damned right. That guy's making a hundred bucks a week or whatever these Limeys pay him in their pounds, shillings and pence. We're making millions. Yet I'd give my right arm to be on that side of the table for an hour.'

'You're incorrigible, you know that?' she said, linking arms with Levitt and drawing him away from the table. 'Besides, if you gave your right arm, how could you spin the wheel, drop in the ball and rake in all the chips?'

'Believe me, Pearl, I'd manage somehow,' he answered

202

with a grin, and Pearl knew that he would. No matter how wealthy Levitt became, he would always have a hankering to be back in that small room beneath the restaurant on Second Avenue, dressed up in a tuxedo while he managed his tiny gambling empire. Or before that even. He'd give back all the millions to be a teenager again, scrambling around in the dust of the basement floor like a little monkey while he operated a dice game. That had been the happiest moment of Levitt's life and, as she considered it carefully, she was uncertain that the same did not hold true for herself as well.

When Pearl turned sixty-one in November 1966, she made a Sunday luncheon for family and friends at the Sands Point house. Benny Minsky made a point of flying up for the weekend to stay with William, Susan and their two sons – Mark, now aged ten, and Paul, two years younger. They were the first to arrive.

Levitt turned up fifteen minutes later. For once, his greeting to Pearl was perfunctory. To her surprise he seemed more intent on speaking to Minsky and William, but with four children running around the house and the final preparations being made for lunch he had little opportunity. When Pearl asked if something was wrong, he shook his head and said, 'I don't get much opportunity to sit down and talk with Benny and William these days, that's all.'

Remembering Levitt's earlier antagonism towards Minsky, Pearl found that answer difficult to accept.

Leo was late. When he finally arrived, the other guests were preparing to sit down for lunch. Pearl answered the door to him. He kissed her before hanging his sheepskin coat in the hall closet and joining the others in the dining-room.

'We thought you'd got lost,' Levitt remarked lightly as Leo dropped into his chair and tucked a linen napkin into his shirt.

'Either that,' Joseph added, 'or you'd forgotten all about today.'

'Me forget?' Leo shook his head. 'Ma's birthday is one day I don't forget.' November was the most important month on Leo's calendar. Everything of note had happened for him – and for his twin brother – during November. Their birth, their father's death on the same day as their *bar mitzvahs*, and their mother's birthday. The remainder of the year amounted to little.

Across the table from Leo, Susan Minsky kept her gaze firmly down. She wanted nothing at all to do with the younger twin, not even spontaneous eye contact. He absolutely terrified her. She would never be able to forget him at the truck depot on the night that he and Harry Saltzman had thwarted the extortion attempt. Even her father-in-law's reasoned explanation of the necessity for such murderous force had failed to ease Susan's discomfort. The odd thing was that she liked Leo's twin brother. Susan believed that she recognized many similarities between Joseph and William. Neither of them seemed to have been tainted by their family's violent background. Furthermore, she liked Judy, feeling that she had much in common with the red-haired woman. They both had young children. Both had husbands who controlled successful corporations. Never for a moment did Susan doubt that it was Joseph alone who directed Granitz Brothers; Leo, she was certain, did not possess the intelligence. Despite the bond of friendship that she and William had created with Joseph and Judy, Susan could never feel easy about Leo. His air of glowering menace seemed to be everywhere, hovering like some malignant spirit. Involuntarily, she reached out to hug her sons, Mark and Paul, who sat on either side of her, as if to protect them from Leo's evil eye.

Lunch finished with the traditional presentation of a candle-studded birthday cake, which Judy had stayed up late the previous night to bake. 'Are there really sixty-one candles there?' Pearl asked in wonderment. 'How am I supposed to blow them all out in one go?'

'I'll help you, Ma.' Leo positioned himself beside his mother, an arm around her tiny waist. 'Ready? One. . .'

Pearl found security and comfort in Leo's embrace. He was so caring, so fond of her. She knew that Joseph loved her just as strongly as Leo did, but the younger twin was unafraid, unembarrassed, to openly display his affection.

'. . . two . . . three. . . .'

Under the joint assault, the mass of candles flickered and died. 'Happy birthday, Ma,' Leo said, hugging his mother tightly. 'And many, many more.'

Misty-eyed, Pearl gazed around the table. It was so easy to believe that all the young men were her own sons, that all the youngsters were her grandchildren. That was how close she felt to William Minsky. She had helped in his upbringing, assisted in making some of the major decisions of his life. She knew that he regarded her as more a part of his existence than his natural mother had been. Too bad about Kathleen, Pearl suddenly thought, and a tiny tear formed in the corner of her left eye. The maternal instinct had been sadly lacking in the blonde singer, only present during lulls in her career. And too bad about the hand fate had dealt to her as well, coming back to Benny Minsky just to die. Pearl remembered questioning at Joseph's wedding whether Minsky still carried a torch for Kathleen. Obviously, he had done, and from what she could see he would continue to carry it for the remainder of his life, until he eventually followed her. Just as she would do for Jake.

'Did you make a wish?' Judy asked.

'Of course I did. Who blows out candles without making a wish?'

'What did you wish for?'

'If I tell you it won't come true.'

'You can tell us,' Joseph pressed. 'It doesn't matter if you tell your family.'

Pearl smiled. 'I wished for all of us to live in health and happiness, okay?' Some wish, Pearl thought. But was it really too much to ask for? Neither of her parents had reached the age she was now celebrating. Nor had Jake. Or Judy's parents, Moe and Annie. Was Pearl fated to make up for all of them, to have a life that would be so long that it would compensate for the shortness of theirs?

When the cake was cut and passed around, Levitt held up a hand in refusal. 'I'd love to, but I'm stuffed,' he said, patting his stomach. His body was relaxed and Pearl noticed for the first time that he had a small pot belly. It made her want to laugh, the man with no spare flesh suddenly exhibiting a little plumpness. Levitt's middle-age spread had started late in life. Not at all like Benny Minsky, who had put on at least twenty-five pounds since he'd moved down to Florida twelve years earlier. His once muscular build was now soft, his

205

dark-skinned face hung with heavy, sagging chins, the tightly curled hair was thin and turning white. As Pearl looked from one man to the other she wondered exactly where all those years had gone. Children and grandchildren . . . and only yesterday Jake and Minsky had been running down the alley-way to rescue her from the Irish bullies. Would Jake, if he were still alive, have a pot belly like Levitt? Or heavy chins and thin, greying hair like Minsky? No, she could not imagine it. Jake had always kept in such good physical shape, his body lean and hard. A pot belly . . .! A double chin . . .! But she'd willingly settle for Jake with a pot belly *and* a double chin, even a Jake with a bald head, if he could only have been here today. He'd been dead for twenty-six years. The twins were thirty-nine and she was sixty-one. Again she asked herself where the years had gone.

'How about we go for a short walk to work off some of this food?' Levitt suggested in an easy manner to the twins, William and Minsky. 'Give the women a chance to clear up.'

'Sure,' Joseph answered immediately. Despite the casual-ness of the invitation, he had discerned the implicit order. The five men took their coats from the hall cupboard and walked out of the front door, strolling in a tight group along the gravel drive. The sky had clouded over and there was a strong hint of early snow in the air. Joseph pulled up his collar and huddled further into his coat.

As they turned around the side of the house, the barking of dogs shattered the silence. Bounding towards the group of men came a pair of Dobermans, a male and a female, which Joseph had bought when his last dog, the Labrador, had died two years earlier. Joseph glanced at his twin brother and saw Leo shrink back, face white with fear as he tried to disappear into his heavy sheepskin coat as though it might offer him protection. Joseph clapped his hands sharply and called to the dogs. 'Solomon! Sheba! Into the house!' Well trained, the two Dobermans loped away towards the kitchen door, to wait there until they were told differently.

'Thank you,' Levitt said to Joseph after the dogs had gone. He had important business to discuss, and did not need to be interrupted by one of Leo's cynophobic attacks. Leo and dogs! The image of the German Shepherd flashed before

Levitt's eyes. Leo wouldn't do the same with those two Dobermans, that was for damned sure. 'Any of you read the *Times* this morning, the big political feature?'

As one, the other men shook their heads.

'Then you'd all better listen carefully, because there might be a whole pile of trouble coming down the road.'

'What kind of trouble?' Minsky asked.

'To do with the next election.'

'The next election?' Joseph repeated. 'Only yesterday Goldwater got himself plastered all over the voting booths.'

'It was two years ago,' Levitt corrected the older twin. 'And there's only two years until the next one. Johnson's got himself so deeply embedded in Vietnam that those couple of years are going to kill him, either physically or politically. There's already talk that he won't run again, which leaves a wide-open race among the Democrats to see who takes his place.'

'Race? What wide-open race?' William wanted to know.

'It'll be Humphrey. Humphrey's his vice-president. It stands to reason that he'll get the nomination.'

Levitt shook his head. 'Nothing stands to reason. Humphrey's more of the same, and the Democrats know that they aren't going to win the next election with more of the same. So the kingmakers are looking for new blood, a fresh face that can spark some interest among the electorate and prevent a Republican victory in 1968. One of those fresh faces – possibly the only fresh face – belongs to Patrick Rourke Junior. There's a move to run him.'

'Rourke from Massachusetts?' Joseph asked.

'The Democratic Senator from Massachusetts. More importantly, he's Patrick Joseph Rourke's son, which might make it tough for us.'

Joseph mulled over the information in his mind. Levitt had not been this serious six years earlier when he had cut the clipping from the *Times* about the election to the Senate of Patrick Rourke Jr. He'd laughed about it then, the epitome of respectability for the son of an old bootlegger.

Levitt, certain that he had the undivided attention of the other four men, continued talking. 'Patrick Junior got elected six years ago because of the fortune that Patrick Joseph

Rourke spread around. Senator was the first step. Maybe that old bastard looked on 1972 as the year his son would run for the White House, because that would be the end of Johnson's second full term and he wouldn't be eligible to stand again. But now that Johnson's getting himself so bogged down in this Vietnam mess, the timetable's been brought forward by four years, to 1968. Also, the old man's in his seventies, so he might figure that he doesn't have the time to wait until 1972.'

'How old is Patrick Junior?' Minsky asked.

'Fifty-one. His younger brother, John, a lawyer, acted as his campaign manager when he ran for the Senate six years ago. He'll probably fill the same slot for a shot at the White House.'

Joseph tried to recall the clipping that Levitt had shown him six years earlier. 'Wasn't there a third son?'

'Yes, with the same name as you. Joseph Rourke. He got himself killed during the war, so he's of no concern. We're just interested in Patrick Junior and John, and what old man Rourke's got planned for them. And for us.'

'I don't like the way you say *us*,' Minsky complained. 'What exactly is *us* supposed to mean?'

Levitt heaved a silent sigh. Nothing changed except the dates on the damned calendar! He still had to spell everything out. 'Old man Rourke has probably got it all figured out that Patrick Junior, if he makes it to the White House, will appoint John as Attorney General, him being a lawyer and all that. But before they can take a crack at the presidency, they've got the minor matter of the Democratic nomination to take into account. And that's where we, I think, come in. As sacrificial lambs.' He waved his hands to draw the other four men closer to him. 'Patrick Junior isn't that well known outside of Massachusetts, outside of New England. He's sure as hell not a household name down in Arkansas or out in Utah, so he's got to be sold to the American public, and damned quickly. How much better can that be done than with a repeat of what Estes Kefauver did fifteen years ago? That's what was in the feature in today's *Times*. Another senate investigation on organized crime is being planned.'

Levitt gazed at his listeners, satisfied when he recognized the anxiety that appeared so suddenly on their faces. 'The way I figure it, a move like that'll kill two birds with one stone for the old man. It'll get Patrick Junior and his lawyer brother known, just as it did for Kefauver, so when the big push starts for the primaries the Rourkes'll have a head start on Humphrey and whoever else is thinking of running. Secondly, and more importantly, it'll give the old man the opportunity to do what he's always wanted to do. Hit back at us. At me. And – ' he pointed a finger at Minsky – 'at you. Because we're the only two left of the old group that almost bankrupted him.'

'You mean the night his convoy was taken,' Joseph said needlessly.

'That's right, the night Jake led a crew up to Massachusetts to pay old man Rourke back for participating in Saul Fromberg's plot against us. Rourke lost more than a shipment of booze that night. He lost twelve men. Those men had families, they had wives and scores of kids like all the Irish seem to have. Rourke had to pay out and pay out and pay out until he was tapped almost clean. He's been aching for some kind of revenge ever since. He couldn't hit back at the time with guns – he wasn't powerful enough, and he didn't want to court any more of that kind of trouble. So he went the respectable route instead. He waited all these years, and now that Patrick Junior's all set to make a run at the White House the old man thinks he can nail us. Destroy us in full view of the public and make a name for his son . . . for his sons . . . at the same time.'

Leo made his first contribution to the conversation. 'Then kill him before he can do anything. Kill Patrick Rourke Junior.'

Levitt whirled around, his eyes gleaming with anger. 'For Christ's sake, you don't kill United States senators and presidential candidates! Think of the uproar. The Rourkes aren't those two jerks who tried to muscle in on William's trucking firm. They're not Phil Gerson skimming money off the casino profits. They're respected public figures. You don't team up with a Harry Saltzman and knock them off like a couple of cheap hoodlums. Maybe it's about time you took a break from watching those damned movies!'

William broke in. 'If this senate investigation gets off the ground, what real damage can it do to us? The handbooks are closed, the people who ran them were paid too well ever to open their mouths. With the exception of the casinos in the Waterway and Monaco hotels, we're one hundred per cent legitimate. Our interests in the Bahamas and London are hidden well enough. What do we have to fear?'

'We are *almost* one hundred per cent legitimate,' Levitt contradicted. 'We've all taken a few liberties. Like I just said . . . remember those two jerks Leo and Harry took care of for you.'

Benny Minsky ran his index finger along his upper lip and sniffed at the crisp air. He did not like the New York cold, not when he could be sunning himself in Florida. 'What about Harry Saltzman, Lou? You're still in contact with him. Can he be relied on to keep his mouth shut? He's been involved in enough stuff with us. He even lent us the men to knock off Saul Fromberg, and for the raid on Rourke's convoy. He's been tied to us through the years.'

Not to mention helping to cover up the murder of a man named Tony Cervante, Levitt thought and glanced at Leo. Saltzman could drop them all right into the crap, but Levitt had what he considered sound reasons for not worrying. 'Harry wasn't directly involved with the convoy that night. He lent us the men for the raid, sure, but there's no way old man Rourke could have possibly known that. Rourke just figured it was us – you, me, Jake and Moe. We were the guys he'd contracted with Saul Fromberg to kill. And he was certain of it when his liquor started turning up in clubs we controlled. Forget Harry . . . Rourke doesn't even know he exists. Worry about us instead. The way I see it, once this investigation gets going, we'll be subpoenaed to appear. That might,' he said to the twins, 'include your mother.'

Leo was instantly anxious, not for himself but for Pearl. 'How will Ma be able to stand up in front of some investigation?'

'Don't sweat about your mother. She's tough.'

'Wait one minute,' Joseph said. He held a finger in the air like a scientist who has just solved a supposedly impossible problem. 'If Patrick Rourke Junior starts throwing barbs about the old days, surely he's going to incriminate his own

210

family right along with it. His father wasn't any better. He's not going to smear himself.'

'Wrong. The old man was a bootlegger, straight and simple. The one time he got involved in murder for hire with Fromberg turned out to be a disaster for him, and no one knows about that anyway. As a bootlegger, he was a popular hero, helping people to circumvent an extremely unpopular law. He made his pile and he got out, turned respectable. He didn't stay in the rackets – '

'Like we did?'

'That's right, like we did. We still like to think that what we did, what we do, with the gambling was on the same level as bootlegging. It's not. People are always going to want to drink, people are always going to gamble. But the two supply businesses are poles apart. Bootlegging's looked back on with fondness, the good old days when the guy who supplied you with the liquor was like some kind of Robin Hood. Drinking's legal now. Bookmaking isn't. It's called organized crime. And that's what I figure old man Rourke wants to see us hit with. Our past will be gone over with a fine comb. Just thank God we're out of business in New York, and we can pull the plug on Florida any time we want to. Those casinos can always be set up again.'

'We don't even need the money from them,' Minsky murmured. Any other time he might have argued the point with Levitt. He did not want to see his small empire in Florida emasculated, have himself made into nothing more glamorous than a hotel manager. Those two casinos gave him stature, but he was quick to see the problems that could be caused should they still be open during a Senate investigation. Buying cops and local officials in Broward County didn't carry much weight with a Washington investigation.

'Don't say anything to your mother,' Levitt cautioned the twins. 'It might never happen, so don't worry her unnecessarily.'

'Do *you* think it'll come about?' Joseph asked.

Levitt pursed his lips before answering. 'Yes, Joseph, I do think it will.'

The five men returned to the house. Only Leo did not replace his coat in the hall. He had to leave. He had paid his respects to his mother on her birthday, and now he had no other reason to remain in the home of his brother and sister-in-law.

Judy watched through a window as Leo climbed into a new white Cadillac convertible and started the engine. Despite the cold afternoon, the hint of snow in the low clouds, he had the roof down, the collar of his sheepskin coat up around his ears. All in keeping, so Judy thought, with Leo's character – a showman enduring a little discomfort just so he could be seen.

The Cadillac moved slowly down the driveway and Judy breathed a sigh of relief. Leo's visits to the house were always traumatic for her. He treated her like a doormat, and she tolerated him only for Pearl and Joseph's sake. She wondered what would happen when Pearl – God forgive her for even thinking about it – died. The death of the woman who meant so much to Judy would be tragic, but its silver lining would be the knowledge that Leo would no longer have cause to visit the house in Sands Point.

Hearing footsteps, she turned to see Joseph standing just beside her. 'Sometimes I'm almost grateful for your brother's little boys. They mean he doesn't stay here too long.'

'That's enough,' Joseph said sharply. If Judy had talked this way about any other man, he might have shared her feelings of revulsion. But Leo was still his twin brother, a loyalty continued to exist that intervened even between husband and wife. More importantly, should Pearl hear such criticism of Leo, she would be upset. She continued to blind herself to Leo's faults, his perversions. She would allow no one to speak ill of him. In her eyes, he remained the perfect, loving son. How could he be otherwise when he visited her so regularly, as a loving, dutiful son should do?

'You think I enjoy having Leo around here when I've got a young son to worry about?' Judy asked.

'Don't be so ridiculous! For Christ's sake, Jacob's Leo's nephew.'

'All right, but Susan's two boys aren't his nephews, and I can tell you that she wasn't the least bit happy about having Leo near Mark and Paul. Didn't you see her over lunch when she put her arms around the boys? Just having Leo look at

212

them – having him at the same table with them – scared the living daylights out of Susan.'

'Judy, Leo's not a child molester.'

'That boy your mother found him with wasn't much older.'

Joseph turned away and began to walk back to the living-room. When it came to his twin brother, Joseph understood that he and Judy shared little common ground. God knew, she had reason enough to hate him. He only wished she could find it in her to forgive.

Judy continued to stare out of the window as the Cadillac reached the end of the driveway, swung into the road and accelerated away.

The white Cadillac convertible was two months old. Leo had not bought it for himself. Instead it had been intended as a gift, purchased for a nineteen-year-old boy who had been Leo's lover for nine months. Originally from California, the boy had been referred to Leo through the agency. After a month, Leo had installed him in the apartment on East 49th Street. The relationship had developed into the longest, most satisfying union that Leo had ever experienced, as fulfilling, he was certain, as that shared by any couple. Three months earlier, though, the boy had started to talk of returning home to the West Coast, a victim of homesickness. Leo had pleaded with him to stay, showered him with gifts, all to no avail. One evening after work. Leo had gone to the apartment, all ready with a new ploy to change his lover's mind: the keys to a brand new white Cadillac convertible. The apartment had been empty. Nothing but a note on the dressing-table thanking Leo for nine months of generous affection. He had been heartbroken. For two months he had moped around his Scarsdale home, sitting alone in the basement cinema while he tried to conjure up some enthusiasm for his favourite gangster movies. Only now was he beginning to emerge from the depression. He had heard of a new restaurant in Midtown named Oscar's Retreat, and his appetite was becoming sharp again.

Instead of returning to Scarsdale, Leo drove to the apartment on East 59th Street. Decorated with the antique furniture he had removed from MacDougal Street, the apartment was exactly the same as it had been on that day two months earlier when Leo had discovered that his lover had returned to California. Even the letter from the young man thanking Leo for his affection and generosity still rested in the same place, tucked into a buff-coloured envelope on the dressing-table. Leo picked up the letter and read it through for a final time before tearing it into tiny scraps which he dropped into a wicker waste-paper basket. He was over his feeling of loss. Tonight he would go to Oscar's Retreat. Tonight he would find someone to take the young Californian's place.

At seven-thirty, Leo left the apartment. In place of the sports jacket he had worn for his mother's party he now wore a pair of twill trousers, a pale pink shirt and a cashmere sweater. A vicuña coat replaced the sheepskin, and he drove with the Cadillac's roof up.

From the outside, Oscar's Retreat resembled many other restaurants along the Midtown stretch of Second Avenue. High glass windows fronted the street, muted lights shone softly inside. The windows were frosted, cutting off vision from the street to allow diners privacy. Leo checked his coat and settled himself on a bar stool, using the time the bartender took to bring his drink to orientate himself. Of the fifteen tables in the restaurant, only three were occupied. The restaurant was still too new to have gained popularity. Leo decided that he would wait for half an hour. If the activity did not increase, he would go home to Scarsdale and watch a movie in his basement cinema.

The bartender brought his drink. 'Would you like to see a menu?'

Leo shook his head. 'I don't know whether I'm staying. Is it always this quiet?'

'It's early,' the bartender replied with a casual shrug of the shoulders.

Several times during the next thirty minutes the restaurant door opened and closed. Always Leo's eyes flicked over the newcomers before returning to the drink in front of him. Men together, men and women, women together. Leo saw nothing to interest him. He would leave. Perhaps he would return to this place some other time.

214

As he emptied his glass in preparation for sliding off the barstool, the restaurant door opened once again. Two men entered. One was middle-aged and paunchy. Long brown hair was carefully waved off his face. His hands were heavy with jewellery. Rings gleamed on his thick fingers; ostentatious gold cuff-links peeked out from his sleeves. Leo dismissed him and concentrated on his companion, a slim youth with olive skin, jet black curly hair and dark flashing eyes. Perhaps the evening would not be wasted after all.

After checking their coats, the two men passed close to the bar. Leo swung around on the stool to follow them with his eyes as they were shown to a table. The older man lit a cigarette and made a show of studying the menu. His companion, more interested in the surroundings, glanced around, sharp eyes darting here and there until, at last, they met Leo's. Slowly a smile appeared on the dark face, a taunting expression that both mocked and teased. Leo felt his pulse quicken. A sudden, giddy warmth began to spread through his body.

As if sensing what was happening, the older man lifted his head from the menu. He looked first at Leo, then at his companion. A few angry, muttered phrases ensued. Leo, unable to hear the words, could guess their gist. The older man was jealous, insecure enough to feel that any attention paid to his young companion represented a threat. Like some old fart with a pretty young girl, Leo could not help thinking with amusement, frightened that she might succumb to the charms of a younger, more virile man. What was the arrangement between the two, the old man and the young? Did the older man pay for his companion's friendship, his favours? Did he keep the young man in a fancy apartment as Leo had done with his Californian? And would this young man one day jump up and leave, return to his home wherever that was? Studying the youth, Leo doubted that he was American. Italian, probably. Perhaps Spanish. His clothes appeared to be European, the square-toed shoes, the narrow cut of his jacket, the tightly fitting black leather coat he had left at the front of the restaurant.

Again the older man caught Leo staring at the youth. Annoyance filled his gaze. For a moment, Leo considered walking over to the table where the two men sat and taking the youth away from his companion. He knew he could. He'd seen interest that matched his own in the youth's dark eyes; they'd flashed a challenge, dared Leo to stake his claim. Leo looked away, stared across the bar at the display of bottles. He didn't need to create a scene. There would, he was certain, be time later to make his move.

He ordered another drink, nursed it while surreptitiously checking on the table where the two men sat. A waiter carried a menu to their table, stood waiting while they decided what to eat. Leo noticed how the older man tried to dominate his companion, suggesting what he order. The youth seemed to take a delight in ignoring the suggestions. A tease, Leo decided, and wondered whether the young man was really worth pursuing. Was the invitation in his eyes a tease as well?

After placing the order, the older man rose and walked across the restaurant to the men's room. Leo swung around on the stool, locked eyes with the olive-skinned youth and inclined his head towards the door. Grinning, the youth stood up, folded his napkin and followed Leo out of the restaurant, pausing only to collect his black leather coat. Neither of them spoke until Leo stopped by the white Cadillac convertible.

'This is yours?' the youth said as Leo unlocked the passenger door. He spoke English with a harsh, almost guttural accent, and Leo felt jubilant that his assumption had been correct. The youth was not American. Guessing right seemed like a good omen.

Leo slipped into the driver's seat, inserted the ignition key but did not turn it. 'Who was your friend?'

'No one of any importance. He is just someone I see occasionally. When I have nothing better to do.'

Leo liked the answer. It meant that in him the youth had found a preferable alternative. He held out his hand. 'My name's Leo. What do they call you?'

The youth took Leo's hand. He had the softest skin Leo could ever remember feeling. It was like a girl's hand, a hand that had been lovingly manicured, a hand that had never been insulted by manual labour.

'Mahmoud,' the youth answered. 'Mahmoud Asawi.'

'What kind of a name is that?'

216

'An Arab name. I am from Jordan.'

Leo's hand remained gripping Mahmoud's. Inside his head two voices raged. One was Lou Levitt's, demanding to know what Leo was doing, shaking the hand of an Arab? The other voice, the voice that he chose to heed, was his own. Why should he care about Levitt and his prejudices? What place did they have in his life at this particular moment? He had been instantly attracted to this youth, so where did Levitt come off telling him whom he could and could not see?

Mahmoud gazed around the interior of the Cadillac with undisguised admiration. 'A Cadillac convertible! Fantastic! Ever since I came to America I have dreamed of owning a car like this. Of driving a car like this.'

'You want to drive it?' Without waiting for an answer, Leo opened the door and changed seats with Mahmoud.

Sitting behind the steering wheel, Mahmoud turned the ignition key, pressed the accelerator experimentally. Before driving away, he switched on the radio, selecting a station that was playing Beatles music. Leo winced at the choice but made no comment. He was content to let this slim Arab youth play whatever music he wanted to play.

'How long have you been in America?'

'Two years. My father – he lives in Amman – sent me here to study engineering at MIT. I preferred to have a good time, so I dropped out and came to New York. That was when my father cut off my funds.'

'How do you survive?' Leo asked, although he already knew the answer.

Mahmoud looked to his right. Even in the darkness of the car, his smile was visible. 'There are men more generous than my father, more understanding. They would rather see me enjoy myself than waste away my youth learning how to erect a power station.'

Leo recognized the outright proposition. Like the man . . . what was his name now? Tony, that was it. Tony who had picked him up in the Sixth Avenue bar on the night of Joseph's wedding. This youth, this Mahmoud Asawi, sold himself as well, but unlike Tony he was putting his terms up front. He was open about it, honest. There was none of Tony's deceit, the treachery that had caused his death, about

217

Mahmoud. He had a frankness, a knowledge of his place in the world, that appealed to Leo as much as his slim build and dark beauty did.

'That man before, what was he to you?'

'I already told you. Someone I saw when I had nothing better to do. For a date with me – ' Mahmoud spoke unashamedly about his way of life – 'he would be very generous. Sometimes as much as one hundred dollars.'

'And others?'

'Of course.' Mahmoud paused at traffic lights leading to FDR Drive. His right foot flicked the accelerator impatiently as he waited for the signal to change in his favour. When it did, he sent the Cadillac surging forward to leave the other cars behind in a mad dash on to the FDR. He drove like he was involved in a race, arms rigid, lips drawn back from shining teeth, eyes alight. Within seconds, he was doing sixty miles an hour in the outside lane.

Leo sat back. He had been entranced by this young man from the moment the restaurant door had swung open. Now he was jealous. He did not want to share him with other men. 'Where do you live?'

'I have a studio apartment on West 72nd Street.'

'Would you like to move from there?' The offer was made spontaneously, tossed out before Leo even realized he was speaking.

'Move to where?'

'To a beautifully furnished apartment on East 59th Street.'

'I will stay where I am. I like it there. East 59th Street . . . is that where you live?'

'It's one of my homes.'

'Where are the others?'

'I'll show you.' Leo gave Mahmoud directions for Scarsdale, proud of the opportunity to show off his home. The man who had brought Mahmoud to the restaurant, Leo was sure, would have nothing like this with which to bewitch a potential lover.

The Cadillac's headlights picked out a high brick wall and concrete pillars. Leo gave the order for Mahmoud to pass between the pillars. Floodlights in the garden illuminated the house Leo had bought. Although not as large as Joseph's home in Sands Point, the house had the formidable solidity of an ancient fortress – weathered stone, leaded windows, and a steep cupola on one side in which it was easy to imagine slits for archers. On Leo's instructions, Mahmoud parked the Cadillac in front of half a dozen wide steps that led to a massive oak front door.

There was awe in the young man's voice as he asked, 'You live here?'

'I live here.' Leo climbed out of the car and walked up the wide steps. He inserted keys in two locks and swung back the heavy door. Mahmoud followed, staring with admiration at the panelled entrance hall, the rich carpet and heavy crystal chandelier which hung from the centre of the sculpted ceiling.

'Who is that?' Mahmoud pointed to an ornately framed painting which hung on the wall directly facing the front door.

'My mother,' Leo answered.

Mahmoud studied the painting. Pearl had sat for it five years before as a birthday present for Leo who had insisted that was what he wanted more than anything else, his mother's portrait to grace the front hall of his new home. The artist had concentrated on Pearl's light brown eyes, imbuing them with a warmth and fire that totally dominated the painting. 'Your mother lives here with you?'

'No one lives here with me. My mother lives with my brother out on Long Island.'

Mahmoud turned slowly on his heel, taking in the entire entrance hall. 'Wow, some pad,' he said, and Leo smiled, amused at hearing the Arab youth use American slang. It seemed so incongruous, so charmingly unexpected. Leo glanced at the portrait and thought about his mother and Lou Levitt. What would they say, how would they feel, if they knew that he had brought this boy into his home? His mother, along with Judy, was active in Hadassah, or was it ORT? And Levitt always gave generously to Jewish and Israeli causes. They would have a fit, Leo thought, and he knew that whatever relationship he developed with Mahmoud would have to be kept secret. He did want a relationship. The knowledge that others would disapprove so strongly made the attraction even stronger. Like Adam in the Garden of Eden, the serpent

219

and the apple. Mahmoud Asawi was a temptation, the forbidden fruit. Leo was going to enjoy every bite.

'You like movies?' he asked Mahmoud.

'Are we going out to see one?'

Leo pointed to the floor. 'I've got my own theatre downstairs.' He led the way through a door, down a flight of carpeted steps to the basement. A large screen was fixed to one wall. A projection booth was built into the opposite one. Heavy leather furniture was scattered around the room. Again, Mahmoud resorted to American slang, as though incapable of expressing his admiration in any other manner.

'Man, this is some set-up!'

Leo slid open a door to reveal racks of film cans. The movie he chose was *White Heat*, the same one he had watched with Pearl. Of all the movies he owned, this was the one to which he could relate the most. Cagney's devotion to his mother was touching. Like Leo, Cagney understood who was the most important person in his life.

As images flickered across the screen, Leo and his newfound friend settled comfortably on a wide leather settee. Knowing every moment of the film by heart, Leo closed his eyes. His right hand strayed to his side, across the cool leather of the settee. His fingertips questingly touched Mahmoud's thigh, stroked the smooth fabric of his trousers. He wondered what kind of an arrangement this youth would want. Leo had little doubt of Mahmoud's independence. He had not been at all interested in the offer to move into the East 59th Street apartment. He wanted to stay where he was, in his West Side studio.

Leo made up his mind to accede to whatever demands Mahmoud made. He had never enjoyed a dark-skinned lover before. It would be fun, even more so when Leo understood that he had to keep it such a secret from everyone he knew. An Arab! But, after all, what did it mean? Only in the Middle East did heritage really matter. This was America. Biblical feuds had no place here. . . .

It was after midnight when Mahmoud returned from Scarsdale to Manhattan. Again, Leo allowed him to drive the white Cadillac, content to sit in the passenger seat and watch the Arab youth, enjoying the thrill Mahmoud so obviously felt at handling the luxurious convertible. Leo felt sated, more so than he had ever been with the boy from California. With any other boy. He knew that he had to reach an arrangement with this youth before they arrived at the studio apartment on West 72nd Street. Otherwise . . . the prospect chilled Leo . . . otherwise he might never see Mahmoud again. Leo could not risk letting Mahmoud escape from him, letting him go to someone else like the man with whom he had entered Oscar's Retreat earlier that night.

'Mahmoud, I do not want to share you with anyone. Do you understand me?'

Mahmoud took his eyes off the road just long enough to smile at Leo. 'That is up to you.'

'You want a car like this? You want this car?'

Mahmoud drummed long, slim fingers on the steering wheel. 'That would be very nice, Leo. But I cannot live in a car. I cannot eat a car. I cannot wear a car.'

'You sure you want to stay where you are?'

'I am certain.'

'I'll pay your rent – '

'And?'

'And a thousand a month.'

Mahmoud's eyes sparkled. 'Leo, I saw your house. I know about your other place on East 59th Street. You are a man who is accustomed to pay for the very finest. Two thousand a month.'

'From a hundred bucks a date to two thousand-plus a month, that's quite some jump.'

Mahmoud took one hand off the wheel and rested it on Leo's thigh. His palm made slow circular motions and Leo could feel his groin tighten. 'Leo, you always have to pay for exclusivity.'

'You promise me I'll get it?'

'I promise you.'

Leo rested his hand on top of Mahmoud's, pressed down. Mahmoud had him figured perfectly. Money was only useful for buying goods, and the rarer those goods, the more they cost. Leo did not object to spending money, just as long as he received fair value. And he was certain he would.

On the return trip to Scarsdale, his mind was full of Mahmoud. The secrecy would add a touch of conspiracy, a dash of excitement, to their relationship. Leo would pay him in cash, two thousand dollars a month, untraceable. He'd give him cash to cover the rent so the lease would remain in Mahmoud's name. Instead of this Cadillac, he would give him cash to buy one in his own name. There would be absolutely nothing to tie him to the Arab youth, no clues that might give him away to Levitt.

How would he work their meetings? Leo dared not be seen visiting Mahmoud's studio apartment. He would have to journey out to Scarsdale. The house was secluded. Once inside those high walls their relationship would remain a secret. From Levitt. From Pearl. From the world.

Always pay in cash . . . he'd learned that from Levitt. And now he would use what he had learned to keep Levitt in the dark, enjoy an affair that was so forbidden the very thought of it sent the blood bubbling through Leo's veins.

So enthralled was Leo with his plotting, he did not even spare a thought for Levitt's concern over the Rourke family.

Chapter Three

Christmas Day dawned bitterly cold in Boston. A brisk wind from the harbour ripped through the city to send the mercury plunging. Frost sparkled on windows and clung to trees, adding its own extra dimension of seasonal decoration. Automobiles trailed plumes of thick grey smoke as worshippers made their way to churches whose chimes hung on the frigid air.

In Jamaica Plain, to the south of the city, Patrick Joseph Rourke listened to those church bells from the comfort of an armchair placed by the drawing-room window. There, he could watch the wide boulevard that swept gracefully in front of his home, see the cars full of churchgoers all bundled up against the wintry weather. He was completely alone in the house, his chauffeur, butler and cook having left ten minutes earlier to attend services. He, too, would have liked to go, but his arthritis was particularly painful today. Even with a stick, he was barely able to walk half a dozen steps. The three servants, who had been with the family for more than thirty years, had been loath to leave him. He had waved away their concern, refusing to interfere with their Christmas Day observances. Nothing would happen in the hour or so they were away.

Glancing down at the hands which lay still on his thighs, Rourke gave way to self-pity. The joints of his fingers were twisted grotesquely by the arthritis, swollen and misshapen. His right hip was almost destroyed by the disease. Once he had been strong and vibrant, a mover of mountains. Now he was an old and crippled man who had to be helped to dress and undress, helped into a bath, helped into bed. Rourke was unafraid of death; he was simply irritated by the decay that preceded it.

Leaving the window and the view of the boulevard, he hobbled to another chair in front of a roaring fire. The warmth seemed to ease his pain more than any medication could, seeping into his joints to offer temporary relief. Behind thin wire-rimmed glasses, his watery blue eyes stared into the flames, then at the large, brightly lit Christmas tree that was set beside the fireplace. Gaily wrapped packages were scattered beneath, presents for his two sons, Patrick Junior and John, their wives, Grace and Rose, and Rourke's eleven grandchildren who would all be coming for the traditional Christmas dinner. The old house would shake with the sounds of laughter and enjoyment, corks popping, the rattle of dishes and silverware. The long table in the dining-room would be full, and the air would carry the mouth-watering smell of turkey and baked ham. And then, when Christmas was over and the family gone, the house would settle back into the heavy silence that Rourke knew best, nothing but the soft footsteps of the servants, the hushed voice of the butler checking that his master needed nothing.

Rourke's mind slipped back to the Christmas of 1956, ten years earlier. It had been his wife's last Christmas. She had known she was dying from cancer, but at Christmas time she had forced a smile on to her face and insisted on cooking the family dinner just as she had done every year since they were married. Two weeks later, she had gone into the hospital, never to come out. The following year, his daughter-in-law Grace, the wife of Patrick Junior, had said she would take over the responsibility for Christmas dinner. She was now the oldest Rourke woman. Rourke had told her that as long as he remained alive, Christmas dinner would continue to be served in his home. And so the tradition had continued.

Another memory arose, a Christmas twenty-two years earlier. Not a white Christmas, but the blackest of the black. His three sons were in the services. Patrick was a Navy pilot in the Far East. Joseph was an infantry lieutenant in Europe. John was a lieutenant in the Army Signal Corps. The Battle of the Bulge was taking place, Joseph's unit fighting in the very centre of the disputed area. Christmas dinner that year was tinged with fear. Then the throbbing anxiety when Joseph was reported missing. A cable confirmed him dead. And only later, much later, a terrifying account from a survivor of how Joseph Rourke and seventy other American prisoners of war had been cold-bloodedly butchered by SS soldiers in a field in the Ardennes Forest. Rourke stared into the fire and saw his middle son as he had last seen him. Still freckle-faced at twenty-six, an enthusiastic lieutenant all ready to be shipped to Europe in preparation for the invasion.

The picture slowly faded as Rourke's eyelids dropped. Lulled by the comforting warmth of the fire, he fell asleep.

'Sir . . . your guests, your sons and their families, are here.'

Rourke jerked awake, head snapping around to see the butler's lined face only inches from his own. Rourke had not heard the servants return from church. They were all back, and now his sons were here. He must have dozed for more than two hours. While he had slept, the city of Boston had gone to church to celebrate the birth of the Saviour. Now those same citizens were ready for their annual feast.

'Show them in, show them in.' He struggled to stand and the butler lent an assisting arm. Rourke wanted to look alert, erect, when his sons saw him. He did not want them worrying about his health. They had more important matters with which to concern themselves.

The doorbell sounded a heavy chime that echoed through the house. Leaving Rourke standing in front of the fire, leaning on his cane for support, the butler went to answer the summons. Rourke heard shouts of 'Merry Christmas!' and guessed that his sons were giving presents to the butler; all the servants were like members of the family. The drawing-room door burst open and a swarm of people rushed in. Rourke tried to separate the faces, the six children of Patrick and Grace, the five children of John and Rose. They all seemed so grown-up now, especially Patrick's two oldest girls, both married and both pregnant. The Rourke clan would be going strong for a long time to come.

'Merry Christmas, Dad!' Patrick and John reached their father simultaneously, enormous packages clutched in their hands. 'You want to open these now or should we stick them under the tree?' John asked.

'Put them beneath the tree. We'll open all the presents later.' Rourke gazed at his sons, thinking, as he always did, that there could be little doubt of their brotherhood. Patrick was much sturdier than John, but both men had unruly mops of thick, light brown hair, the same easygoing smiles on faces flushed with the cold. No doubt about their being Irish either. Rourke felt a twinge of regret when he realized that this would probably be the last family Christmas they would have, all together like this in the big house in Jamaica Plain. Next Christmas, Patrick would be unable to lead such a carefree life. He would be more than just a United States senator. If everything went according to plan, he would be a front-runner for the Democratic nomination for President.

Rourke's daughters-in-law, Grace and Rose, kissed him on the cheek, then the grandchildren took turns in wishing him a Merry Christmas. Halfway through the routine, Rourke had to sink back into his chair, suddenly tired.

The butler pushed a trolley full of bottles into the centre of the room. 'Sir,' he addressed Rourke first, 'would you care for a drink?'

Rourke eyed the bottles carefully. 'Jameson. For my sons as well. Nothing like good Irish whiskey to keep out the cold on Christmas Day, eh?'

The butler poured the whiskey into three highball glasses. When he made to add ice, Rourke waved him away. 'For God's sake, man, you should know better than to give an Irishman ice in his whiskey.'

The butler passed the glasses to Rourke and his two sons. Rourke pushed himself to his feet again, faced Patrick and John and raised his glass. '*Sliante.*'

'*Sliante*,' the two brothers replied before following their father's example of downing the whiskey in one swift gulp.

Rourke eased himself back into the chair. The fire and the whiskey and seeing all his family were doing him good. He'd do credit to the Christmas dinner the cook had prepared. And afterwards, while the rest of the family opened presents, he would lock himself away in the library with his sons. They had much to discuss. . . .

226

Noise failed to penetrate the library. The book-lined walls acted as a sound barrier. The drawing-room rocked with shouts of delight as the children of Patrick and John Rourke discovered what gifts their grandfather had bought for them, but in the library there was only silence. Rourke sat in a deep leather armchair. His two sons sat opposite, in straight-backed chairs. Between them on a table rested the bottle of Jameson and three glasses.

Rourke opened the conversation. 'If everything goes right,' he said to Patrick, 'this Senate investigation committee on organized crime is going to catapult you right into the nomination come convention time. The only thing that could stop you is Johnson and Humphrey bringing Vietnam to an end sometime in the next fifteen months, before the first Democratic primary. And we all know that's not going to happen. Vietnam's going to get a damned sight worse before it gets any better.'

Patrick gazed thoughtfully at his hands. 'I can't believe we start sitting in New York in six weeks' time. When I first sponsored the resolution for a special Senate committee on organized crime, it seemed like a million light years away. Now it's almost here.'

'Are you nervous about it?' Rourke asked.

'No.' Patrick gave his father a quick smile that news-papermen had termed a boyish grin. 'I'll have to feel my way the first few days in New York, but by the time we sit in Philadelphia I'll have the whole thing down pat.'

'I'm not interested in Philadelphia or any of the other places your committee will be sitting. I only care about New York. Who have you subpoenaed to appear in New York?'

'The names you gave us. Louis Levitt and Benjamin Minsky. Minsky's son, William. The Granitz twins, Joseph and Leo, and their mother. The subpoenas were served during the past week.'

Rourke smiled back at his son. 'That's what I call a Christmas present.'

'Subpoenas went to a lot of other people as well,' John cut in. Responsible for the campaign that had led to his brother being elected to the Senate six years earlier, and hopeful of repeating the feat when Patrick ran for the White House,

John had thrown himself wholeheartedly into the Senate investigation, working behind the scenes with law-enforcement officials. He understood that this investigation would be the make-or-break point for his brother's political ambitions. And his own.

'What other people?' Rourke asked sharply.

'Suspected mob figures. Italians with links to organized crime. We don't want to make it look like we're gunning for just one ethnic group.'

'I don't give a damn about the Italians. Those Wops, they never cost me what the Hebes did – Levitt and Minsky and their damned partners, Granitz and Caplan, may they rot in hell! Those bastards almost put me out of business that night. And they killed your cousin, John McMichael. Don't forget they did that.'

'We know,' Patrick said. He glanced uncomfortably at his brother. 'Dad, we've got to think about the Jewish vote. It swings a lot of weight in places like New York and California. We're going to need to win those states in the primaries and in the election, if we get that far, and we're not going to win them without the Jewish vote.'

'If we make a name for Patrick by going after mobsters,' John said quickly, 'exposing these so-called respectable businessmen to be nothing more than hoodlums, we'll win popularity. But if we make a name for just going after Jewish mobsters, it'll be too damned obvious where our priorities are. Not justice, but some kind of bigoted vendetta. It's one thing for this Louis Levitt to scream anti-Semitism when we're investigating gangsters of all faiths. If he does that, he'll be ridiculed. But if we're seen to be questioning only Jews and he waves the bloody flag of anti-Semitism, then people might start thinking that he's got a damned pertinent point!'

Rourke considered that. He knew his own vision was clouded by revenge. He couldn't give a damn about the Mafia, the Cosa Nostra, or whatever the hell the newspapers wanted to call it. Those Eyeties had never done to him what the Jews had done. Those damned Jews! All his life they'd cost him. First with that hijacking, a quarter of a million in booze and twelve families to support. Then the war, the Jews' war, that had taken his middle son, Joseph. Always they'd

228

been there, pulling the strings to cause him grief. And no one wanted to help him fight back.

'But don't you understand what they did to me?' The question to his sons was a whispered plea.

Again, Patrick appeared awkward. Ever since that terrible day more than thirty years earlier, when the convoy had been hijacked on the coastal road, he'd had to listen to his father spew this poison. The old man's reasoning was distorted by it. Patrick knew of the deal that his father had cooked up with Saul Fromberg to supply killers to solve a dispute between two New York Jewish gangs, but Rourke never mentioned that. He had conveniently forgotten his own part in the devastation that had befallen him; he was just consumed by hatred.

Both Rourke sons loved their father deeply. He had given them far more than most fathers could ever give their sons. Immense wealth through investments in steel, oil and railroads. Position. And now this, the opportunity to walk among the most powerful men in the world. *To be* the most powerful men.

Rourke had always been a staunch Democrat, able to see the power that could be wielded through political position. His appointment as Ambassador to Ireland during the war, before the invasion of Europe and the death of his middle son, had been repayment for his work on behalf of the party. He had guided his oldest son into politics, put millions behind him in his bid for the Senate. And all the time he had been plotting his revenge on the Jews who had cost him so much that lonely night on the coastal road. He had kept tabs on what they were doing. When Jake Granitz and Moses Caplan had died, Rourke had rejoiced. Now, through his sons, at last he had the opportunity to close out all accounts.

Neither Patrick nor John had inherited their father's zealous hatred, though. In politics, where the secret of success was never to slam doors, bigotry could prove an expensive indulgence. But the sons also knew they owed an immense debt to their father. His work, his foresight, had given them incredible opportunities. They had to repay him, even if it was by conducting a witch hunt against his old enemies. At the same time, however, they had to protect their own positions. Hit their father's enemies, by all means, especially when it would achieve the publicity necessary for a successful presidential campaign. But not in a way that would brand them as the anti-Semites they were not.

Rourke stared at his two sons, unable to believe that they found his hatred so incomprehensible. Didn't his blood flow through their veins? Was not his cry for vengeance also theirs? 'What have you got on them so far? On Levitt? On Minsky and his family? On the Granitzes?'

'We believe they own interests in overseas gambling ventures,' John answered. 'Two clubs in London, the Embassy and the Dominion Sporting Club. And a hotel casino in the Bahamas, the Belvedere.'

'That's not illegal.'

'No, it's not. But publicizing the connection might cause them discomfort. Their partnership is silent. I doubt if the British or Bahamian governments are aware of the connection. Also, they own two hotels in Florida – the older Minsky runs them – that have gambling.'

Rourke nodded in satisfaction. 'What about that bookmaking and policy racket they had going in New York?'

'There's no longer any trace of it. Our people have asked until they're blue in the face and they can't get one positive answer. People have been paid too well to offer information – the police, and the shopowners who ran those books and numbers drops.'

'Minsky's transportation company . . . the Granitz Brothers real estate corporation. . . .' Rourke sounded desperate. 'Surely there's something there.'

'Nothing. Everything's perfectly legal and above board. Except – '

'Except what?'

'They don't borrow money from any American financial institution. They use a Swiss bank, Leinberg, in Zurich. We're looking further into that.'

'Good.' Rourke felt easier. So what if his sons did not go after the two remaining members of the old group of four because they shared his hatred of Jews? All that mattered was that they went after them. He leaned forward and poured whiskey into the three glasses. Lifting his own, he said, 'It's

230

fitting that we drink this toast in Jameson. That cargo I lost that night was Irish whiskey.'

'What is the toast?' John asked.

'To the Senate committee investigation. To its success.'

'And to Patrick,' John said. 'To the next President of the United States.'

'And to Levitt and Minsky,' Rourke added. 'May their souls be damned for ever.'

While Patrick Joseph Rourke spent Christmas in Boston with his family, the families of the men he damned were in Florida, staying at the Waterway Hotel in Hallandale, where Benny Minsky occupied a suite of rooms on the floor below the casino.

During the day, the temperature was in the low eighties; at night it fell back to sixty. The four children of the Granitz and Minsky families frolicked in the hotel pool all day long while their parents sunned themselves, all except for Judy whose red hair and fair skin were ultra-sensitive to the sun's rays. For that reason, she kept a cautious eye on her daughter, Anne. This was a vacation, a break from the New York winter, and she did not want to spend it dabbing calamine lotion all over Anne's arms, legs and shoulders.

Neither Lou Levitt nor Pearl made use of the pool. Both agreed they were past the age when swimming was a pleasure. They seemed content to sit in the hotel lounge, either reading or sometimes joining other older couples in a game of cards. As in their trip to London, their stay at the Connaught, other people naturally assumed they were husband and wife.

Leo was the only one to feel restless. Although he visited the casinos at both the Waterway and the Monaco during the night, he rarely stayed around the hotels during the day. He hired a car, explaining that he wanted to explore the area, see what the other beaches were like. In reality, he drove south to a hotel in Miami to spend time with Mahmoud Asawi who, at Leo's suggestion, had travelled down to Florida to be close to his lover. In keeping with the shroud of secrecy which Leo had thrown over the affair, Mahmoud was not even registered under his own name. Leo was certain that no one knew of his connection with the Arab youth.

The purpose of the trip to Florida, however, was not pleasure. Pearl, the twins, Levitt, Minsky and his son had all been served with subpoenas to appear before the Senate Special Committee on Organized Crime when it sat in New York during the second week of February. The fear of only a month earlier had become reality.

The six people who had been subpoenaed met late one evening in Benny Minsky's suite. Above their heads, dice clicked, cards were dealt, roulette wheels spun, but for once Levitt's mind was not on the action taking place in the casino, or how much the house was making. It was the year's busiest season and he could not care less.

'When we return to New York,' he said, 'we meet with our lawyers. Benny, you'll come back with us. We've got to fight this thing as one, cover every question we might be asked and make damned sure we all come up with the same answers.'

'Do we have friends in the press who can throw some dirt on old man Rourke?' Joseph asked.

'We can try. We can get stories printed about Rourke's bootleg dealings, but I've said before that there are a lot of respectable people who started out that way. Bootleggers don't have any real skeletons in their closet.'

'What about his tie with Saul Fromberg?' The question came from Minsky, who was disturbed at having to leave the sun of Florida for the cold of New York. He'd come to appreciate warm winters and was loath to give them up. 'Surely that deal he made with Fromberg is pretty damning.'

'You mean the way he contracted with Fromberg to commit murder? To kill me and Jake? I'd love to use that, Benny, to be able to use it. But if that story leaked out, it would harm us more than the Rourkes. Old man Rourke never did commit murder. That crew he sent down to New York failed. In return we *did* commit murder, twelve times, the twelve men who were guarding Rourke's convoy.'

Pearl's complexion paled at the memory of that night. 'Jake came home from Massachusetts like he'd seen a ghost,' she murmured. 'He kept talking about those stupid Irish bastards, putting up a fight when they were so outnumbered. He couldn't believe what had happened.'

'Neither could I,' Levitt said quietly. He, too, remembered

232

clearly Jake coming down to the Four Aces the following day to tell him the news, to beg him to find a way of explaining it all to Pearl. And all the time, Gus Landau had been sitting in the front room of an apartment on the other side of Second Avenue, sighting into Pearl's mother's restaurant along the barrel of a machine-gun. Jelly roll . . . jelly roll . . .! Levitt had never forgotten Leo's comment on seeing the dead, blood-spattered body of his grandmother. Christ – get back to the reason for this meeting, he told himself. Don't dwell on that!

'This fight,' he continued, 'on the surface anyway – what the public will see and hear about – is between Senator Patrick Rourke Junior and us. It's not between old man Rourke and us. You can be damned sure the Senator – ' he dripped sarcasm on to the title – 'is going to tread carefully when he asks his questions. He won't expose his father's background if he can help it, so his questions are going to concern our more recent activities.'

'Should we close this operation down?' Minsky jerked a hand towards the ceiling. 'Here and the Monaco?'

Gloomily, Levitt nodded. He hated to do it, with the profitable winter season just underway, but he felt he had little option. 'Let the casinos run until New Year's Day, Benny, then shut them down. Have all the stuff moved out. Turn them into ballrooms or nightclubs. We can always go back into business again afterwards. And be sure that you keep paying off all the sheriff's men, the cops and local authorities you've got on the list. That way, we'll be able to open again with no problem once this thing is over.'

'How much will closing the casinos cost us?' William asked.

'Too much, but we've got to do it.'

Pearl sat fidgeting on her chair, clasping and unclasping her hands. 'What do you think they'll ask me?'

Levitt regarded her bleakly. He'd mentioned the possibility of Pearl being subpoenaed along with the rest of them, but he'd never thought it would actually happen. He remembered using the word 'might'. Pearl might be included in the list of subpoenas, he'd told the twins. And then he'd cautioned them not to let her know anything about it. He didn't want her worried sick. Well, she was worried now. The

233

moment she'd been served, she'd called Levitt. Between sobs she'd wanted to know what to do. He'd told her to relax. They'd plan strategy when they all came down to Florida. Damn the Rourkes! he thought viciously. Where the hell did those Irish bastards come off dragging Pearl into this? A woman in her sixties! What goddamned right did they have to parade her in front of television and the press, and brand her a criminal?

'They'll ask you what you knew about Jake's business connections,' he finally answered, putting as much gentleness in to his voice as possible. 'That's all. Maybe something about the New York book. I'm sure they know about it, but knowing and proving are two entirely different things. Believe me, Pearl, this thing might drag on for months, but in the end we're all going to walk away from it without a stain on our characters.'

'Have you been in touch with Harry Saltzman?' Minsky asked.

'He didn't get subpoenaed. I've told you before, Rourke doesn't know Harry exists.'

'I wish to hell he didn't know we existed either,' Minsky muttered. And then, without thinking, he added, 'Damn Jake for going up to Massachusetts that night!'

'Benny, shut your stupid mouth!' Levitt snapped. He swung around to look at Pearl, saw the shock on her face. He glanced at the twins. Joseph was sitting perfectly still, but Leo's eyes were undergoing that odd change of colour, that hint of grey. Quickly, Levitt stood up. 'We're all going to relax, okay? Senator Rourke's fishing, that's all. Fishing for the White House. This is not a criminal proceeding. He just wants to make a big name for himself by asking a lot of questions about organized crime, and he's hoping at the same time to show us up, square accounts for his old man. That's all there is to it. We're so clean, we squeak.' His gaze turned hard. 'And we stay clean!'

Without another word, he took Pearl by the arm and led her from Minsky's suite. 'Don't get upset over Benny,' Levitt said soothingly. 'You know that jerk doesn't think before he opens his mouth.'

'But he's right,' Pearl said softly. 'You begged Jake not to

234

go. You said it would cause trouble down the road.'

'I know. If I could turn back the clock, I'd find some way of stopping him. But that's not the way life works, Pearl.' Seeing her tears, he felt a terrible fury towards the Rourke family. When this was all over, he'd find some way of paying them back again, even if it was only to keep Senator Patrick Rourke Junior from making 1600 Pennsylvania Avenue his home.

He thought about Leo's remark at the house in Sands Point. Kill him. Kill Patrick Rourke Junior. He'd screamed at Leo . . . a United States Senator wasn't someone like Phil Gerson who'd been milking the till. You didn't send a Harry Saltzman after a man like Patrick Rourke Junior! Or did you? Only if you were desperate, Levitt had thought at the time, and he hadn't been desperate. He still wasn't. But he was mad enough to consider doing it. He'd consider killing anyone who caused Pearl this grief.

Like the men with whom he had been closely associated since the days of Prohibition, Harry Saltzman was now in his early sixties. Age had treated him far more generously than it had dealt with Lou Levitt and Benny Minsky. The abnormally low hairline which had been the bane of his schooldays, leading to the hated sobriquet of Simian Saltzman, had receded. For the first time in his life, Saltzman had a forehead. His hair, like that of Levitt and Minsky, had yielded its original colour to grey, but his body had not softened noticeably. Every morning, he worked out religiously in the basement of his Fort Lee home, that same basement where Pearl had nursed Leo's diphtheria. He had weights down there, a punching bag, a chin-up bar, even a set of wall-bars he had installed. In his sixties, Saltzman had lost little of the strength he'd had at thirty, or the confidence that such strength gave him.

Christmas and the days that followed presented nothing out of the ordinary for Saltzman. While the Rourkes celebrated in Boston by going to church and enjoying a warm family atmosphere, and the Granitzes, the Minskys and Lou Levitt bathed in the Florida sunshine, Saltzman spent each morning by working himself into a sweat in the basement of his home, finishing off a round of weight-lifting with a five-minute session of pounding the daylights out of the punching bag. He would have preferred to be in Florida, enjoying the hospitality of the Waterway or the Monaco. Indeed, he had planned to be there. But Levitt had called him the moment the subpoenas had been served with strict instructions to stay away from Florida, to avoid contact at all costs. Saltzman's name had evaded the scrutiny of the Senate investigating committee, and Levitt wanted to keep it that way. He did not want any connection between Saltzman and himself to be seen.

'I just don't way you to have to give testimony, Harry,' Levitt had told Saltzman. 'Even with a battalion of lawyers sitting behind you, you wouldn't know what to say.'

The rebuff had not offended Saltzman. He realized that his forte was strength, whereas Levitt's was brains. Saltzman eagerly anticipated watching the investigation on television, just like the Kefauver hearings fifteen years earlier. People running for public office always thought they could get some kind of a lift by dragging up horror stories about organized crime. Maybe the Rourkes could garner some popularity by tripping up some of the Italians they'd subpoenaed, but Saltzman was confident that Levitt would not get the Rourkes a single vote. He'd run rings around the investigation. By the time he was finished, Saltzman decided with a chuckle, the Rourke brothers would be investigating each other!

On Tuesday, two days after Christmas, Saltzman exercised as usual and took a long shower that finished with a sudden burst of icy water to set his blood tingling. He towelled briskly, dressed in a conservative grey suit – he'd learned from Levitt the importance of the right kind of clothing – and prepared to leave the house. If he could not spend Christmas week in Florida, that didn't mean he had to remain idle at home. There was always work to be done.

He drove into New York, stopping in front of a brownstone in Murray Hill. A tall, middle-aged man waited on the sidewalk, hat pulled low over his eyes, coat collar wrapped around his ears, hands thrust deeply into his pockets. Saltzman leaned across the car to open the passenger door. 'Hurry up and get in, Charlie, before all the heat escapes.'

Charlie Jackson climbed into the car and slammed the door. 'Merry Christmas, Harry.'

236

'Merry Christmas, yourself.'

'Is it this cold the other side of the Hudson?'

'Colder.'

Jackson opened his coat collar experimentally as if to check on the temperature inside the car. Satisfied that it was warm enough, he unbuttoned his coat and removed his hat, which he set on his lap. He looked like a man who would find extreme cold oppressive. His hands were long and bony, the fingers like skin-covered twigs. His brown eyes were deeply set in a face that was almost totally devoid of flesh. His cheek bones jutted dramatically. Saltzman often thought that Jackson resembled a walking skeleton. Six feet two, and if he weighed a hundred and fifty it was a lot. Even his hair appeared malnourished, thin, weak strands that lay lifelessly across his scalp.

'Christ, Charlie,' Saltzman muttered. 'Every time I look at you I have to wonder how the restaurants where you worked ever stayed in business.'

Jackson laughed, a dry, brittle noise that was in keeping with his looks. 'I haven't waited tables for many years, Harry. You know that.'

'Just as well. The bosses would be paying you to stay home sick, not to come in and put the customers off their food.'

Saltzman drove along East 34th Street towards Madison Avenue. As he neared the intersection he saw a dozen men and women walking in a circle on the sidewalk. They all carried signs that screamed of unfair treatment and workers' rights. The target of their demonstration was a restaurant named Antonio's. Patrons who tried to enter the place for lunch were confronted by placard-waving pickets. Rather than risk trouble, they turned away to find another restaurant. Ten yards from the demonstration, two patrolmen stood watching.

Saltzman parked the car, then he and Charlie Jackson walked towards the restaurant. The pickets broke ranks to allow them to pass. One of the men patted Jackson on the shoulder and shouted, 'Give him hell, Charlie! Give him hell!' Jackson grinned at the recognition of the power he and Saltzman wielded.

Pushing back the door, Saltzman entered the restaurant

with Jackson following. Antonio's did not cater to the office trade, clerks and secretaries rushing in for a sandwich and a bowl of soup. Its lunchtime business comprised executives on expense accounts, salesmen clinching a big deal, editors entertaining valued writers. In the evening, although it was well outside the theatre district, its tables were always filled. Today, the tables were set for the regular lunchtime trade. From the kitchen at the rear rose an appetizing combination of smells. Only there were no customers present. Nor were there waiters, busboys or dishwashers. Just one man was visible, and he stood in the centre of the floor, hands clasped behind his back while he glared hostilely at Saltzman.

'You've got some damned nerve coming in here, you bastard!'

Saltzman ignored the unwelcoming tone. 'It's Christmas week, Mr Berganza. I'm full of Christmas cheer, okay? I want to help you out.'

'I don't need your help,' Tony Berganza answered. 'What I need is my staff back in here. I don't open for lunch today, I've got food back there that goes rotten.'

'I understand that, Mr Berganza, and this whole unfortunate situation can be resolved in just a few minutes. You know each other?' Saltzman asked Berganza and Jackson. 'Mr Berganza, this here is Charlie Jackson. He's the president of the waiters' local.'

'They've got no reason to strike me. You know it and I know it. I pay good money, I don't take liberties.'

Saltzman placed a heavy arm around the restaurateur's shoulders. 'Mr Berganza, I've got a lot of pull, a lot of influence with Charlie here. He and I, we've been friends for a long time. Right, Charlie?'

Jackson nodded. 'Since we were kids.'

'Charlie's open to doing me any favour I want, Mr Berganza. If I asked him to, he'd go outside and tell those guys they've got to come back to work. He'd iron out your problems. But Mr Berganza, why should I ask Charlie a favour like that, put myself in his debt, when you won't do anything for me?'

'Like join your goddamned association?'

'The New York Guild of Restaurateurs and Victuallers.'

238

Saltzman reeled off the title proudly. He'd spent a lot of time dreaming up the name of the association he'd created two years earlier. A fancy title for a trade guild covering fancy restaurants. Fast food places and hamburger and pizza joints weren't worth worrying about; they didn't have the kind of money Saltzman charged as dues.

'Your guild's nothing but a protection racket,' Berganza protested.

'So's Blue Cross,' Saltzman answered with rare humour. Except he was better organized than Blue Cross. With power among the service unions, shaking down restaurant owners was a logical step. 'Your health insurance people, they give you a tatty paper card that you show to the hospital when you get sick. Me . . . the New York Guild of Restaurateurs and Victuallers . . . I give you this.' He pulled a gilded plaque from his pocket on which was stamped the guild's logo. 'Instead of showing this to the admission nurse at some hospital, you put it in your front window. Then, when you get a problem like you've got today, and if you're a member in good standing, all you do is contact me. It becomes my responsibility then, because I'm the president of the guild and you're a member.'

Berganza gazed through the window at the pickets. Even as he watched, more regular customers decided to eat lunch somewhere else that day. If this went right on to dinner . . . and then more of the same tomorrow . . .! Berganza shuddered. 'How much?'

'A joining fee of one thousand dollars. That's a one-off fee, Mr Berganza, to cover paperwork and administrative details. And a yearly fee, up front, also of one thousand dollars. That's what gets you your benefits.'

Berganza wanted to ask if it was tax-deductible, but he did not have the courage. Of course it wasn't. Extortion wasn't allowed by the IRS as a deduction, and this was nothing short of extortion. But if he fought it, how would he survive? His restaurant would be struck every week. He would encounter difficulties with his deliveries. And those were the mildest forms of persuasion. He gave a slight shudder as he envisioned the restaurant being consumed by flames, or himself being beaten up one night. 'Will you take a cheque?'

'Mr Berganza. . . .' Saltzman's voice was pained. It was unnecessary for him to say more.

'I don't carry that much cash so early in the day. I work with a small float, just enough to make change.'

'Then you'd better hurry to your bank before the lunchtime trade really picks up, Mr Berganza. Two thousand dollars.'

As he threw on his coat and hurried towards the door, Berganza reviewed the situation in a different light. Two thousand dollars was only forty dollars a week. He lost far more than that on the horses. And next year, after the one-time joining fee was paid, it would only cost him twenty dollars a week. Perhaps it wasn't so expensive after all.

Saltzman watched the door close behind Berganza, the pickets step back to let their employer through. 'You go out and talk to them,' he told Jackson. 'Get them back inside, show Berganza that the guild keeps its word. In the meantime, I'll fix this to the window.' Smiling in satisfaction, Saltzman glued the plaque to the inside of the glass.

Berganza returned ten minutes later clutching a white envelope. The restaurant was different from the way he had left it. The waiters were back at work, preparing for lunchtime; the busboys and dishwashers were at their positions. Even as Berganza handed the money to Saltzman, two regular customers entered Antonio's to honour their lunchtime reservations.

'See how useful the guild is, Mr Berganza?' Saltzman asked. He pocketed the envelope without bothering to count the money.

'Protection,' Berganza muttered. 'I'm paying you to protect myself from you.'

Saltzman rested a hand on Berganza's arm. 'You don't sound happy. The guild doesn't like its members to be unhappy.' There was more menace in Saltzman's voice than could have been contained in any outright threat. Berganza walked away to supervise the operation of his restaurant that was now a member of the New York Guild of Restaurateurs and Victuallers.

Saltzman and Jackson returned to the car. Inside, Saltzman opened the envelope and counted out five hundred dollars

240

which he gave to the union official. 'How many does that make, Harry?'

'Members of the guild?' Saltzman consulted a dog-eared notebook which he pulled from his jacket pocket. 'One hundred and thirty-five so far. Maybe we'll expand soon, take in northern New Jersey, Connecticut as well. Change the name and call it the Tri-State Guild.'

'We've got enough potential members in New York,' Jackson said. 'It's just a matter of getting everyone else into line.'

Saltzman nodded. The guild was not a spectacular fortune maker, but it was easy money and it gave Saltzman an entrée into the restaurant business. He understood that he could not squeeze the owners too tightly. If he levied unacceptable dues on them, they would go out of business and that would be the end of it. This way, he wasn't killing them. A thousand a year membership was affordable. Most importantly, it wasn't worth the trouble of going to the police.

'Who else is causing us problems?' Saltzman asked as he started the engine.

'Mickey's Deli over on Seventh Avenue. We pulled a strike there last week, got all the waiters out on the sidewalk just like we did at Antonio's.'

'And?'

'They fired everyone, closed up for the day and opened the following morning with a whole new crew.'

'That sounds like the kind of thing they'd do,' Saltzman growled, with just a hint of admiration in his voice. Mickey's Deli was a large, well-reviewed delicatessen that Saltzman had been trying to incorporate into the guild for three months. The owner, a former lightweight boxer named Mickey Phillips, had refused, saying that he'd seen his fill of crooks and thieves while he was in the fight game; he didn't need to run a restaurant to encounter more.

'You giving the order to stink the place out?' Jackson asked.

'Not yet.' Before Saltzman sent in men with butyric acid bombs, he wanted to try one more personal approach. Phillips was looked up to in the restaurant world. If he could be persuaded to join the guild, a lot of other hold-outs would fall into line. And if he continued to put up a fight, others would

241

take their lead from him. Perhaps it was time to offer the ex-boxer a loss leader. 'I'm going to take you home, Charlie, then I'll drop by Mickey's Deli for lunch. See if we can't work something out there.'

'I wish you luck.'

After dropping Jackson back in Murray Hill, Saltzman drove slowly to Seventh Avenue. The delicatessen was full when he entered, a mixture of shoppers in town for the post-Christmas sales, theatre people taking a break from rehearsals, journalists and sporting folk. Plastered across the walls were signed photographs of athletes and entertainers, all wishing Mickey Phillips well on the opening of his delicatessen ten years earlier.

Instead of choosing a table or booth, Saltzman seated himself at the counter that ran almost the entire length of the delicatessen. A waiter slapped a glass of iced water in front of him, following it with a menu. Saltzman let his eyes run down the cover of the menu – another photograph of an athlete, this one of Mickey Phillips in his prime, boxing gloves raised in a sparring stance. Below the picture was the story of Phillips carrying on a family tradition by opening the delicatessen. His parents, the story ran, had owned a small delicatessen on Delancey Street, and it had always been Phillips' ambition to follow them into the family business. Saltzman smiled at the sickly sentimentality of the story. Some public relations writer must have had a ball coming up with that connection. About the only similarity between Mickey's Deli and any joint Phillips' parents may have owned on Delancey Street was that they both sold food. This place was the Waldorf of delicatessens. Phillips' old-world parents would have felt as out of place here as they would have done at a hog barbecue.

Before the waiter could come back to take the order, Saltzman felt a strong hand grip his shoulder painfully. 'See that sign?' a voice asked. A finger alongside Saltzman's face pointed to the wall behind the counter. In the centre of the signed photographs was a sign that read: 'The management reserves the right to refuse admittance.'

'I see it, Mickey,' Saltzman said. He swung around on the stool and looked into Mickey Phillips' face. Despite the blue business suit, the white shirt and wine-coloured tie, there was

242

no doubting Phillips' fighting pedigree. His nose had been broken a couple of times, and scar tissue wove its way around his thin eyebrows. Much shorter and lighter than Saltzman, Phillips still possessed the aggressiveness of a professional fighter, moving on the balls of his feet, his body lean and hard. He looked as though he could step back into the ring at a week's notice and give a good account of himself.

'That means you, ape,' Phillips said. 'I'm the management, and I reserve the right to refuse you admittance. Now get the hell out of here before I toss you out.'

'Can't a man come in out of the cold for a cup of coffee and a pastrami sandwich?'

'I wouldn't serve you coffee if you were dying of the cold. Beat it, ape, before the zoo finds out you've escaped.'

Saltzman ignored the insult. 'I've got a proposition for you.'

'Join your guild? Forget it.'

'Honorary membership,' Saltzman said grandly. He pulled a guild plaque from his pocket. 'Stick this in your front window. No fee for joining, no membership dues.'

A flicker of interest crossed Phillips' face. 'Free membership, eh? And if I'm seen to join, how many others will also?' Before Saltzman could think of an answer, Phillips continued. 'If my being a member is worth that much, maybe you should be *paying* me to join. A free membership under those circumstances . . . why, that's almost an insult.'

'Maybe I could – ' Saltzman stopped speaking while he watched Phillips produce a gold lighter, hold the plaque in the air and set fire to it. As the flames licked his fingers, Phillips dropped the burning plaque into Saltzman's lap.

'You son of a bitch!' Saltzman yelled, leaping up from the stool to beat at his lap with his hands. The burning plaque fell to the floor and Phillips stamped on it.

'That's what I'm going to do to you, if you show your face around here again. Now get the hell out!' Phillips reached across the counter, felt beneath it and came up with a policeman's nightstick. Prodding Saltzman with the end, he shoved him towards the door.

Saltzman found himself out on the sidewalk, his trousers scorched, his pride shattered. He had hoped to get Mickey

Phillips to join for nothing, a gesture that would encourage others to pay up. Instead, Phillips had humiliated him in front of a restaurant full of customers. If word of this got around, the guild would be a laughing stock. Other restaurateurs would start burning their plaques, and Saltzman's comfortable little business would be in jeopardy.

He could not afford to let that happen. It was time to consider more drastic measures.

Chapter Four

The Senate Special Committee on Organized Crime convened in New York City the second week of February. The
chairman of the committee, briefed and assisted by his
brother John, was Senator Patrick Rourke Junior. The other
five members, all hand-picked as being outspoken opponents
of organized crime and supporters of a presidential bid by
Senator Rourke, were senators from New York, California,
Pennsylvania, Ohio and Florida. They each represented an
area where the committee would hold hearings, and all hoped
to reap political gain.

The committee was in session for a week, hearing testimony from figures with alleged connections to organized
crime, before any of the Levitt-Minsky-Granitz group was
called to appear. Their order of appearance was carefully
planned. Lou Levitt was to be the final witness of the group.
Senator Rourke did not want any of the others to take their
lead from Levitt's testimony.

William Minsky was first to be called before the committee.
Accompanied by a lawyer, William identified himself and sat
down to face the panel of senators. He was fully aware of the
television cameras upon him, the tape recorders running, the
reporters with pencils poised over their notebooks. With
Susan, William had watched the news reports of the hearing
the previous week. If anything, the questioning had seemed
easygoing, almost conversational, but William had little
doubt that once he and his associates appeared, the tempo
would quicken.

Senator Rourke opened the questioning. 'Would you tell

this committee where you work, Mr Minsky? Your position, and the nature of your work.'

'I'm president of B. M. Transportation Company in Long Island City.'

'B. M. stands for . . .?'

'Benjamin Minsky, my father. He founded the company.'

'When was that?'

'Back in the early Thirties.'

Senator Rourke inclined his head deferentially. 'That was quite a tough time for starting businesses, Mr Minsky. America was in the depths of the Depression. Businesses were going bankrupt, banks were being wiped out. Yet your father started what has become a well-known, highly successful company. In those hard times, where did he get the trucks? How did he afford to pay for them? And where did he find customers with goods to haul?'

William sensed the lawyer giving him a signal. He moved closer to the microphone on the table in front of him and said, 'I was a baby then. I didn't even know how to spell the word truck, let alone ask my father where they came from. You'll have to ask him yourself.'

'I intend to, Mr Minsky. I intend to.'

The Senator for Florida raised a hand. 'Do you have an interest in the Monaco Hotel in Hollywood and the Waterway Hotel in Hallandale?'

'Only by association. My father is chairman and chief operating officer of the Palmetto Leisure Development Corporation, which owns those hotels.'

'Could you describe the hotels for us?'

'They're just regular hotels, what else can I say?'

'You speak very self-effacingly about two of the most luxurious hotels in South Florida. Would that be because each hotel has a casino, an illegal casino, on the top floor?'

'Not to my knowledge they don't,' William answered evenly. 'Casino gambling is against the law in Florida. I would have thought that you, who represent Florida in our nation's capital, would have known that.'

Laughter erupted, and Senator Rourke pounded the table with a gavel. Not to be deterred, the Senator for Florida said, 'But casinos used to be there, right?'

William made no answer, and the Senator repeated his question. The lawyer leaned across to Wiliam. 'Regretfully, I must refuse to answer that question.'

William was questioned for another hour and then dismissed. Senator Rourke had never anticipated learning much from him, just as he expected to receive scant reward from questioning the Granitz twins. They, like himself and his brother, were of the second generation. The real answers lay with the first generation. With Benjamin Minsky, Louis Levitt and Pearl Granitz. He called Pearl next.

Despite the calm appearance she tried so hard to give, Pearl's stomach was churning. Her legs felt weak, and she was glad of the chair she dropped into. She did not know how long she could have lasted if she had been expected to answer questions while standing up. Nervously, she patted the fresh hair-do. Waved off her face and blue-rinsed – the first time she had ever coloured her hair since the escapade with Annie more than half a century earlier – the hairstyle made her look like a sweet, little old lady. It had been Levitt's idea, along with the dowdy brown dress and plain shoes she wore. Levitt had spent the entire weekend with her, trying to soothe her nerves, giving her assurances that she would waltz through the hearing.

'Mrs Granitz, you are the widow of Jacob Granitz?' Senator Rourke asked.

'I am.'

'How long ago did your husband die?'

'Twenty-six years ago.'

'It was on the occasion of your twin sons' *bar mitzvahs*, correct?'

'It was.'

'Would you explain to us how your husband died?'

Pearl wiped a tear from her eye. There was no need for acting here. Any time she thought of that terrible day, she started to cry. 'He was shot outside the synagogue, after the service.'

.'Shot by whom?'

'A man named Gus Landau.'

Senator Rourke understood the fragility of the line he trod. Any further questioning on the subject could bring an answer that might implicate his own father. He knew he had to elicit responses that would avoid doing that, while inflicting as much damage as possible on his father's old enemies. 'Do you know what happened to Gus Landau?'

'He was killed a few days later.'

'How?'

'He was shot by a friend of my husband.' Levitt had told Pearl that the questioning would certainly cover Jake's death. He had instructed her to tell the truh. There was nothing in it that could harm her or the family; it was all public knowledge, splashed across the headlines when it had happened.

'The name of this friend, Mrs Granitz?'

'Moses Caplan . . . Moe Caplan.'

'What happened to him?'

'He was killed by Gus Landau. They shot each other.' Pearl understood what Senator Rourke was doing – he was laying the groundwork for questioning that would come later from the other members of the committee. She decided to save him time by volunteering the remainder of the information she expected him to ask for. 'The following day, Moe Caplan's widow, Annie – a childhood friend of mine – committed suicide. I brought up her daughter as my own. She is now married to one of my sons.'

Senator Rourke smiled at Pearl's perceptiveness in answering the remainder of his questions. He looked to his colleagues to see who wanted to follow on. The Senator for New York took over. 'Mrs Granitz, what do you know about the Jalo Cab Company?'

'It was a business partnership between my husband and his friend, Lou Levitt. The name was derived from the first two letters of their first names, Jake and Lou.'

'I see. It was sold several years ago, I understand.'

'In 1960.' Pearl suppressed a smile as she recalled the day Levitt had imparted the news instead of asking her to marry him, as she'd anticipated.

The Senator for New York leaned forward, chin resting on steepled hands. 'There was a room above the Jalo Cab garage . . . a rather large room?'

'There may have been. I was never there.'

'Do you know what took place in that room?' When Pearl

248

was slow to answer, the Senator continued, 'Would it be safe to say that the nerve centre for a large bookmaking and numbers racket was located in that room above the Jalo Cab garage?'

Pearl felt her stomach move. How was she supposed to lie about this? She'd never been up there, but she certainly knew what had gone on. She felt the lawyer touch her arm. 'I'm afraid I must refuse to answer that question.'

The Senator for New York carried on as though he had not heard her. 'Would it also be safe to say that this highly illegal gambling operation was run through a chain of small mom-and-pop shops, cigar stores, restaurants, bakeries and the like? And would it furthermore be safe to say that the people employed in that operation were listed as employees of either the Jalo Cab Company or B. M. Transportation? Your son, Joseph, for example, who was employed as a deputy office manager for Jalo. And your other son, Leo, who was down on the books as a driver for Jalo.'

'Both of my sons went to work for Jalo when they finished their education.'

Senator Rourke lifted a hand to signify that he wanted the floor. Pearl watched him warily, certain that he was going to lead her down that painful avenue of death again. Her intuition was perfectly correct. 'Mrs Granitz, let's go back to Gus Landau. He killed your husband, and he killed your husband's friend. Did he not also have a hand in your mother's death?' Rourke consulted a report on the table. 'Your mother was killed in – '

'In the restaurant she owned on Second Avenue!' Pearl burst out. 'Why do you have to bring my mother into this? Isn't it enough that you've already dragged up my husband's death?'

Finally, Senator Rourke thought with a savage wrench of joy . . . finally he had reached Pearl, torn through whatever defences she had built up. 'There was a time period of seven or eight years between the deaths of your mother and your husband, yet they were both killed by the same man. What was the connection? What was the reason that Gus Landau would come back so many years after killing your mother to kill your husband?' He watched Pearl expectantly, waiting for an answer that never came. 'Or, Mrs Granitz, is the real reason that your husband was always Landau's target? That the intended victims on the night your mother died were Jacob Granitz and his friend, Louis Levitt? And Landau missed?'

Pearl burst into tears and Senator Rourke banged on the table with the gavel. The hearing would adjourn for half an hour, he said, until the witness had regained her composure. Led by the lawyer, Pearl rose and went outside. The twins and Levitt waited for her. Leo was seething, his eyes grey, the heavy eyebrows twisted into a tight line. He had seen his mother bullied, reduced to tears, and all he wanted to do was attack Senator Patrick Rourke Junior. Not with words, as the Senator had attacked Pearl, but with his fists. Levitt and Joseph worked hard to calm the younger twin.

'We've go to play the Rourkes at their own game,' Levitt stressed to Leo. 'We'll fend off their questions, give them nothing. And that way we'll defeat them.'

'Didn't you see what that bastard did to Ma?' Leo protested.

'He did what he's supposed to do,' Joseph said. 'We didn't expect him to do anything less. Ma handled him just fine.'

'She cried! No one makes Ma cry and gets away with it!'

Levitt had a sudden vision of Leo running amok during the hearing. All the careful work that Levitt had done, all the briefing of the witnesses, would come to naught if Leo managed to get hold of the Senator. A physical attack by him would do more damage than any of the questions could. 'I'll talk to him, Leo. I'll talk to Senator Rourke, okay?'

'You get him to lay off Ma, Uncle Lou.'

'I will.'

Before the hearing reconvened, Levitt sought out Senator Rourke. He found him cloistered in a small office with his brother, John. When Levitt was announced, the Senator showed surprise.

'I don't expect witnesses to see me beforehand.'

'And I don't expect a United States Senator to attack a defenceless woman the way you just did.'

'Are you trying to persuade the Senator to alter his line of questioning?' John Rourke asked.

250

Ignoring the younger brother, Levitt continued to stare angrily at Senator Rourke. 'You know damned well that Gus Landau was trying to kill me and Jake Granitz that night Pearl's mother was shot. And you know why! It was because of your father. He contracted with Gus Landau and Saul Fromberg to kill us. That failed, and we all know what happened after that, don't we?'

'No, we don't, Mr Levitt. I haven't the faintest idea what you're talking about.'

'Then let me put it another way. It's no skin off my nose if you want to carry on with this Landau business. Because when it comes to my turn to testify, I'm going to come back with the whole story. And all your gavel banging won't be able to shut me up. Your old man was a bootlegger . . . okay, that's nothing to be ashamed of these days. Lots of us started out the same way. But your old man's not going to look so smug and respectable once it comes out that he accepted a contract to kill people who were his good customers. We used to buy your old man's Irish whiskey, and he took money to bump us off. You think about that when you get back to questioning Mrs Granitz.'

'You wouldn't dare,' John Rourke said as Levitt turned to leave. 'You bring that up, and you'd better be ready to explain how twelve of my father's men got killed one night when a convoy was hijacked. Or how Saul Fromberg died.'

'Fromberg committed suicide because the IRS were going to nail him to a wall. His books were open on his desk when he jumped.'

'Sure he committed suicide,' John Rourke sneered. 'He jumped out of the window a split second after he was thrown out. And the IRS men were fakes. Your men, dressed and trained to look like IRS agents. You think we don't know all that?'

Levitt's blue eyes followed the quivering finger he pointed at Senator Rourke. 'You ask me whatever you like. You want to make some points for yourself, go right ahead and try to crucify me. But don't take cheapshots at Mrs Granitz. She's got nothing to do with any of this.'

'Were we right about you and Granitz being the intended targets on the night Pearl Granitz's mother was killed?' the Senator asked.

'You're right.'

'In that case,' John Rourke said quietly, 'how come only Granitz got killed outside the synagogue? Why didn't Landau go for you as well?'

'How the hell do I know? Maybe if I'd been standing with Jake, he'd have got us both. Landau was alone. He just fired the one shot and took off.'

'You could say you were very lucky that day, the same as you were when Mrs. Granitz's mother got killed.'

'I've learned not to question luck, just to accept it,' Levitt said. He swung around and walked quickly from the room, leaving the Rourke brothers to ponder his threat about exposing their father's past.

'Why are we doing this?' Senator Rourke asked at last. 'Are we doing it for Dad, to get his revenge? Or are we doing it for ourselves?'

'For ourselves,' John answered.

'That's what I thought. What we know and what we can use here are two different things. I'm going to adjourn for the day, give the Granitz woman a chance to get herself together again. When we start again tomorrow, we'll either ease up on her or we won't call her back. We'll decide which course to take tonight. We can always come down hard on her sons, this Benjamin Minsky and Levitt. They'll be able to defend themselves better, and we won't run the risk of having Dad embarrassed. Or ourselves.'

John nodded in agreement. The whole idea of the committee investigation was to gain popularity for his brother's run at the White House. No popularity ensued from making an elderly woman cry. Or having their own father's criminal involvement publicized. . . .

The hearing was reconvened just long enough for Senator Rourke to suspend proceedings for the day. Instead of going to their separate homes, the subpoenaed parties went to Granitz Tower. There, in Joseph's office, Levitt reviewed the day's proceedings.

'William, you handled yourself just great,' Levitt said. 'You didn't give those *mamzarim* a bone to chew on. I hope the rest of us do as well.' He turned to Pearl. 'What happened before to you was unfortunate, but believe me when I say it won't be repeated. I spoke to the Rourkes. I made a deal with them. They're going to leave you alone on the condition that they can ask me whatever they like.'

'That doesn't make what happened any better,' Leo broke in. 'That Irish bastard had Ma crying. For Christ's sake, everyone and his goddamned brother will watch it on television. You think I want people to see my mother like that?'

'I don't want people to see it either, Leo.'

'I want to pay them back.'

'Vote for Humphrey in the Democratic Primary,' Joseph quipped, 'and you'll have paid them back.'

Leo glared at his twin brother for a moment, and then he started to laugh. A vote for Hubert Humphrey . . . that was one way to pay back the Rourkes. But it wasn't enough by far.

Harry Saltzman felt disappointed in the television coverage of the Senate Special Committee. He had expected Levitt to be the first witness called to testify, and so far he had not been called at all. Saltzman found no pleasure in seeing William Minsky answer seemingly innocuous questions, or watching Pearl being reduced to tears. Levitt was the star of this spectacular. That was who Saltzman wanted to see tear the committee to pieces.

Regretfully, he turned off the television. He was expecting visitors that evening and wanted to be ready for them. Six weeks had passed since his disastrous visit to Mickey's Deli on Seventh Avenue. Once the offer of free membership had been rejected by Mickey Phillips, other restaurateurs had started taking courage from Phillips' defiance. It had to be stopped.

The doorbell rang. Saltzman admitted two visitors, men named Hymie Glass and Stan Kaye. He gave them money and a box that could have contained a pint bottle of whisky. Instead, it contained a stink bomb. Not the kind children bought at novelty stores and used as a practical joke, but a bottle filled with butyric acid, a chemical so strong that its vile odour of putrefaction seeped into carpets, furnishings, even into wood. Once there, it was impossible to remove. If Mickey Phillips wanted to stay out of the New York Guild of Restaurateurs and Victuallers, he would do so because he no longer had a restaurant.

253

Hymie Glass and Stan Kaye timed their arrival at Seventh Avenue that night to coincide with the closing of Mickey's Deli at midnight. The last of the customers were leaving as they entered the delicatessen. Waiters pushed brooms across the floors, stacked chairs and tables. Phillips stood by the cash register, totalling the receipts. The black nightstick lay next to the register, in easy reach. When he saw Glass and Kaye enter, he said, 'Sorry, fellows. We're closed for the night.'

'We're not here for a meal,' Glass answered with an easy smile.

'We're delivering a gift,' Kaye added. He pulled open the box and showed the pint bottle full of butyric acid.

Phillips moved with all the speed he had ever shown in the ring. Before Kaye could raise his arm to toss the stink bomb into the centre of the delicatessen, Phillips darted from behind the cash register. In one quick movement, he picked up the nightstick and slammed the end of it into Kaye's stomach. Kaye doubled forward. Phillips grabbed the bottle with his left hand, using his right to swing the nightstick in a wide arc that kept Glass away. One of the waiters rushed forward, a broom held like a lance. He rammed Glass in the back, sending him staggering. As he fought for balance, Phillips leaped forward, the bottle in one hand, the raised nightstick in the other. Glass gave nothing more than a whimper as the nightstick cracked against the top of his head.

Breathing hard, Phillips leaned back against the counter. Glass was unconscious on the foor. Kaye was on his knees, clutching his stomach. Phillips set the bottle down gently on the counter. He had little doubt what it contained. If it were going to be smashed, its contents spewed all over the place, it was not going to happen in the delicatessen he'd worked ten years to build up. He dropped the nightstick, stepped forward and lifted Kaye up by the lapels of his coat.

'Who sent you? Saltzman?'

Kaye groaned and Phillips slammed him against a wall. 'I'm going to ask you one more time, and then your head is going to start making a pretty stucco pattern on my walls. Who sent you?'

'Harry Saltzman!' Kaye's voice was a shriek as he felt Phillips' grip tighten.

'Where do I find him?' Phillips jerked his arms straight, and Kaye's head banged off the wall. 'Where?'

'Fort Lee. New Jersey.' Kaye sputtered out the address. Phillips memorized it, then dragged Kaye to the front door and threw him out on to the pavement. With the help of the waiter who had wielded the broom, he sent Glass after him.

'What are you going to do?' the waiter asked. 'Call the police?'

Phillips thought about it. 'What can the police do that I can't?' he asked with a grin. Carrying the bottle of butyric acid, he left the restaurant and walked to his car which was parked in a lot on West 54th Street.

Twenty-five minutes later, Phillips was in Fort Lee. He felt tense, excited and confident, just like the moment before stepping into the ring with a boxer he knew he could beat. Maybe he'd take some punishment during the bout, but at the final bell it would be his hand the referee held aloft, his ears in which the cheers of victory would ring. He found Saltzman's house at the end of a cul-de-sac. A large wrought-iron gate prevented him from driving further. Lights shone inside the house but no cars were parked in the driveway. Phillips guessed that Saltzman would be out, probably in company that would vouch for his whereabouts this night. Even if he had sent the men to stink-bomb Mickey's Deli, he would want an unshakable alibi of his own. That suited Phillips perfectly.

Letting himself in through the wrought-iron gate, Phillips walked along the driveway until he reached the front door. To make sure, he rang the bell. There was no answer. Satisfied, Phillips made a quick inspection of the outside of the house. All the windows were locked. Entrance was impossible without breaking glass. He did so, shoving his gloved hand through a large pane of glass in the living-room window. The sound barely carried as the broken glass fell on to soft carpet inside the house. Working carefully, Phillips picked all the glass out of the pane. He stepped back, wound up like a baseball pitcher and flung the bottle of butyric acid as hard as he could through the opening. The bottle sailed across the living-room and shattered against the opposite wall. Even as Phillips ran back towards the wrought-iron gate and his car he caught a whiff of the acid. The stench almost made him gag.

255

After tonight, Harry Saltzman would be more interested in looking for a new house than in increasing the membership of his crooked guild. . . .

Saltzman arrived home at three in the morning after playing in a poker game that would alibi him against any charges that Mickey Phillips might want to level. The moment he stepped out of his car, he knew that something was wrong. He could smell the butyric acid everywhere. Faint traces wafted across the grounds, carried by the light breeze, to hit Saltzman like the smell of a sewage farm from close up. He guessed immediately what had happened. Hymie Glass and Stan Kaye, the men he'd sent to soften up Phillips, had failed. Phillips himself had paid the return call.

The moment he opened the front door, the full force of the smell hit him like a bomb-burst. He staggered back, hands grabbing at his stomach as he threw up. The house was ruined. Every piece of furniture would have to be thrown out, burned. The house itself was a total loss. No perfume sprays, no coats of paint would ever hide that offensive odour. As he got back into his car he could smell the putrefaction sticking to his clothes. Leaning out of the window, he retched again and again, until his stomach was empty. And then he retched painfully on nothing at all.

Face covered with a cold seat, hands and body shaking, he drove like a wild man across the George Washington Bridge into Upper Manhattan. Stopping at the first pay phone he saw, he dialled Hymie Glass's home number in the Bronx. The telephone rang unanswered for fully thirty seconds. Saltzman slammed the receiver down on the rest. The dime dropped. He reinserted it and dialled Stan Kaye's home in Queens. Kaye answered.

'What the hell happened?' Saltzman yelled. 'I get back to my house and the place stinks like an overflowing shithole!'

'He jumped us, Harry.'

'What do you mean, he jumped you? There were two of you!'

'He jumped us with a nightstick. The waiters joined in. We never had a chance. Hymie's in the hospital. They're keeping him overnight for observation, possible concussion.'

'You get him out of that hospital and you meet me tomorrow night.'

'Where?'

Saltzman's mouth dropped. They couldn't come to his house; he didn't have it, couldn't use it. 'Wait until I get settled in a hotel, get myself some new clothes. Then you, me and Hymie are going to wait for Mr Phillips one night. You understand?'

'We'll be there, Harry. We've got a score to settle with him as well.'

'Not half as bad as mine,' Saltzman growled. He hung up the telephone, got back into the car and headed towards Midtown. What he had to do now was find a hotel where he could check in at three-thirty in the morning with no baggage and his clothes stinking of shit!

When the Senate Special Committee reconvened the following morning, Pearl was not called back to testify. The next witness was Leo, and his fury at Senator Patrick Rourke Junior was evident from the moment he opened his mouth to identify himself.

'Leo Granitz!' he spat out with such force and venom that Senator Rourke, playing to the press, mentioned facetiously that there was no need for the witness to shout as he had a perfectly adequate microphone on the table in front of him. Leo glared at the microphone, as though it were an extension of the Senator. He placed his hands on either side of it, clenched into hard, angry fists.

'Would you tell the committee where you work, and your position there?' Senator Rourke asked.

'Granitz Brothers. I'm a vice-president.'

'Responsible for what?'

'The day-to-day maintenance operations of our properties.'

'You give orders to the maintenance crews?'

'I do.'

Senator Rourke tapped the end of a pencil on the tabletop. 'When you left high school, you went to work for the Jalo Cab Company. What was it like to drive a cab?'

Leo looked at Senator Rourke as though he were mad. What kind of a question was that? What was it like to clean sewers . . . what was it like to sweep streets . . . what was it like to sew clothes or repair shoes? 'All right, I guess.'

'It's quite a switch from driving a cab to being vice-president of a thriving real estate company. I must congratulate you.'

The Senator for New York took over the questioning. 'While you were driving your cab for Jalo, did you make frequent stops at small restaurants, candy stores, places like that?'

'I stopped wherever I had a fare.'

'And were there many fares, every single day, at these small shops? Morning and evening?'

'I don't remember. It's been a long time since I pushed a cab.'

'Let me see if I can jog your memory,' the Senator for New York said. 'You weren't driving a cab. You've never driven a cab for hire in your life, although you do hold a licence to do so. You were going out every morning and every evening from the Jalo offices to pick up bets and betting slips and to deliver pay-out money. Is that true?'

'I drove a cab,' Leo reiterated stonily.

'Have you ever been involved with bookmaking?'

'I've placed bets at the track.'

'That does not answer my question. Have you ever been involved with bookmaking? Was a bookmaking operation run from the room above the Jalo garage? Were you a collector? Were you in charge of all the collectors? Is that where you received your experience in supervising, giving orders to other people?'

When Leo sat with his lips compressed in a thin, angry line, Senator Rourke told him, 'You must respond to the questions, even if only by saying you refuse to answer.'

After a brief consultation with his lawyer, Leo pleaded the Fifth Amendment.

'What do you remember about your father's death?' the Senator for New York asked.

'It was a long time ago.'

'What do you remember about your grandmother's death?'

'It was even longer ago. I was a small child.'

'Your mother, when she testified yesterday, could give us no connection between the same man shooting your grandmother and your father. Can you give us a connection, Mr Granitz?'

The fury, which had been bubbling just below the surface while Leo sat at the witness table, finally broke through. He shot to his feet and jabbed a fist in the direction of the committee. Immediately, two police officers hurried towards him. 'You had no damned business dragging my mother into any of this! What kind of a man are you, picking on a widowed woman?'

Senator Rourke watched impassively as Leo's lawyer hissed something to his client. Leo sat down before the two policemen could reach him. What with Levitt's visit yesterday after Pearl's breakdown, and now this, they certainly stuck together. An insult to Pearl Granitz was an insult to them all. Senator Rourke wondered if he would encounter the same fierce loyalty when Joseph Granitz was called to testify. Perhaps it would be just as well to lay off Pearl altogether. Her inclusion in this raised nothing but hostility. Besides, Senator Rourke already knew the answer to the question that had enraged Leo. Gus Landau had been after the same target both times. 'Mr Granitz, I promise that his committee will not mention your mother again.'

Joseph was next to testify. Senator Rourke led him through the background with the Jalo Cab Company, ascertained that he had been deputy office manager and, as he had done earlier with Leo, congratulated him on rising to such a prestigious position with Granitz Brothers. Joseph's face remained devoid of expression.

'I think we know all there is to know about the Jalo Cab Company,' Senator Rourke said, 'so we won't bore you any further with it. Let's talk, instead, about Granitz Brothers.'

'Talk about whatever you like,' Joseph invited the Senator.

'Thank you. Tell me, Mr Granitz, why do you finance your deals in this country through a Swiss bank?'

Joseph's eyelids flickered, but that was all. 'Because they offer us the most competitive rates.'

'I see. Leinberg Bank offers you the most competitive rates. You must like Switzerland as well. I understand that while you were deputy office manager for Jalo you made several trips there. Would you tell us the reasons for all these trips? Were they job-connected?'

Joseph took a deep breath. 'My first trip to Switzerland was for my honeymoon. Zurich was one of the many places my wife and I visited.'

'And the succeeding trips?'

'I was vice-president of an engineering company in Zurich called A. G. Kriesel.'

'Deputy office manager of a New York taxi company *and* vice-president of a Swiss engineering company. Quite a combination. I am impressed. Who owned this A. G. Kriesel?'

'Lou Levitt and Benny Minsky.'

'For the record, that is Louis Levitt who was a partner with your father in the Jalo Cab Company, and Benjamin Minsky, who founded B. M. Transportation and is now chairman and chief operating officer of the Palmetto Leisure Development Corporation. Have I got it all correct?'

'You have.'

'Why did you make such regular trips to A. G. Kriesel?'

'The company was experiencing difficulties. I was attempting to straighten out those difficulties.'

The Senator for Ohio raised a hand. 'Mr Granitz, what is the difference between a sun gear and a planet gear?'

Joseph stared dumbly at the Senator for Ohio; he might just as well have asked for the secret of eternal life.

'Does your silence mean that you don't know?'

'I don't know.'

'Isn't that rather odd for a vice-president of an engineering company not to possess such basic engineering knowledge?'

Joseph sought frantically to retrieve the situation. 'My degree is in business, not engineering. Kriesel's difficulties weren't concerned with engineering. Their problems stemmed from business mismanagement.'

The Senator for Ohio seemed not to hear. 'Isn't it also rather coincidental that this engineering company in Zurich, this A. G. Kriesel, should be so close to the Leinberg Bank, which has financed your real estate corporation? As it has also financed the Waterway and Monaco hotels in South Florida.'

Joseph chose not to answer. He suspected the Senator was not anticipating a reply.

Senator Rourke picked up the thread of the interrogation. 'Would it be closer to the truth to say that your real purpose in visiting Zurich so often was to deposit money with the Leinberg Bank? Money that represented the profits of the vast gambling operation that was controlled from the Jalo Cab Company building. Money that could not be shown in this country because you wished to avoid paying taxes on it.'

Joseph felt the warning touch of the lawyer's hand. 'I refuse to answer that question on the grounds that I may incriminate myself.'

'Thank you, Mr Granitz,' Senator Rourke said. 'That will be all.' He knew he'd scored points with that line of questioning. He would score even more when he got Benny Minsky and Lou Levitt in front of him.

When the hearing recessed for the day, another meeting was held in Joseph's office in Granitz Tower. This time, the mood was not so upbeat. Levitt was worried. Senator Patrick Rourke Junior and his brother, John, had done their homework well, knowing every date that Joseph had made the trip to Zurich. They must have checked with airlines and immigration people to be so thorough. Levitt wondered what surprises the committee would have for himself and Benny Minsky when their turn came to testify.

'Okay,' Levitt said when everyone was seated in Joseph's office. 'So they've knocked us back a bit on our heels. They're making assumptions, but they haven't got a damned bit of proof. If they had, we'd all be facing criminal charges by now. To get us, they've got to have corroborating witnesses, and there's no way they're going to pull that off.'

'What do you think they're going to ask me?' Benny Minsky wanted to know.

'Probably questions about the trucking company. And about the hotels. You went down there after Phil was out of the picture.'

'They haven't brought up Phil's name,' Joseph mused. 'Think they missed something? They know all about me going to Zurich, they know all about the hotels in Florida, but they haven't mentioned Phil.'

'Don't worry about it, they will,' Levitt said with grim certainty. He noticed Leo agitatedly checking his watch. 'You got a date or something?'

261

'We'll miss the news,' Leo answered. 'I want to see how I look on television.'

Levitt grinned at the answer, and some of the tension disappeared. 'You looked like someone who was mad enough to kill a whole bunch of United States senators. Go on, get out of here. We'll see you back at the hearing tomorrow.'

Leo left. Instead of returning to Scarsdale, he went to his apartment on East 59th Street. The news was just starting when he turned on the television. He pulled a chair close to the screen and sat down to watch. The Senate hearing was the fourth item to be covered. The emphasis was on Joseph's testimony about the trips to Switzerland and Leo felt disappointed. Then his mood lightened when his own angry face filled the screen, shouting at Senator Rourke that he had no damned business persecuting a widowed woman.

The moment the piece finished, the telephone rang. Leo answered. 'I just saw you on the news,' an accented voice said. 'Such anger, such fury . . . I do not think I would want to cross you.'

Leo smiled as he recognized Mahmoud Asawi's voice. The Jordanian youth never identified himself by name when he called Leo; it was part of the game, the urge for secrecy that Leo had instigated when he'd started seeing Mahmoud. He wanted no one to know of this relationship. That was even more important now, with this investigation taking place. God forbid that Senator Patrick Rourke Junior should throw up the spectre of homosexuality as well. 'Where are you calling from?'

'A pay phone, of course, outside where I live. Do you want to see me tonight?'

'Come to the other place.' Leo even refused to mention Scarsdale by name; when he played the game, he played it to the limit. 'I'll be there by nine o'clock. No, better yet, I'll pick you up at the north-east corner of Columbus and West Seventy-second Street at eight-fifteen.' With the investigation, he had no way of knowing if his house was being watched. Someone might see the number of the car he'd given to Mahmoud. Secrecy . . .! Secrecy . . .!

'I look forward to seeing you,' Mahmoud said before breaking the connection.

Leo returned his attention to the television, switching from station to station to catch other news broadcasts. There was nothing else on the committee. He would have to wait until the morning papers came out before seeing more of himself. Perhaps there would be a photograph of his furious expression, something he could cut out, frame as a souvenir. His mother was proud of him, he knew that, proud of the way he had leaped to her defence. This Senator Rourke would think twice before he attacked an elderly widow again.

Benny Minsky was the first witness to be called the following morning. Levitt sat watching, hold Pearl's hand as Minsky was sworn in. Neither the twins nor William Minsky were present; they were back at work, their roles in the committee hearing finished. Levitt had not wanted Pearl to come either, Senator Patrick Rourke Junior had put her through enough already, but she wanted to be present for when Levitt's time came. Like himself, she had little doubt that he was really the star attraction. She wanted to give him all the support she could.

'How do you think Benny will do?' Pearl whispered.

'As long as he listens to the lawyer and keeps his mouth shut when he's supposed to, everything'll be fine. The last thing we need is for him to go bursting a blood vessel now because he gets riled up.'

'He isn't that way anymore,' Pearl sai 'He's grown out of it, matured.'

Levitt gave a cynical laugh. 'everyone else matures at twenty or twenty-five. Our Benny, bless him, he has to wait until his mid-sixties.' He squeezed Pearl's hand as Senator Rourke asked the first questions of Minsky, and Pearl decided that Levitt's dislike of the dark-skinned man had not really changed ovr the years. He still found fault with Minsky quicker than he found fault with anyone else. It was as though, for some reason unfathomable to her, he'd held a grudge against Minsky all these years. Most times he managed to disguise it. Occasionally, though, he could not stop it from showing.

At the witness table, Minsky sat perfectly still, confident that he could field any question that the committee threw at him. 'Mr Minsky,' Senator Rourke said, 'let's go back to a question I asked your son. When you started B. M. Transportation, where did the trucks come from?'

'I bought them, fitted them out with rails and started by hauling dresses for manufacturers in the Garment District.'

'But *where* did you buy them?'

'From a truck shop!' Minsky exclaimed. 'Where else do you buy trucks . . . from Gimbel's or Macy's?'

Senator Rourke's voice turned to ice. 'Please remember where you are.'

'Some guy sold them to me. He had trucks and no money. I had money and no trucks. So we struck a deal.'

'Were they trucks that had been used to haul liquor, illegal, bootleg liquor during Prohibition?'

'They could have been,' Minsky admitted grudgingly. 'I didn't ask their pedigree. I was buying transportation, not championship dogs.'

'These manufacturers you hauled merchandise for, dresses . . . did you have a financial interest in any of them?'

'I may have done. I had a lot of interests in those days.'

'How did you acquire those interests?'

'I bought them.'

Senator Rourke quickly realized that he was getting nowhere by asking about the origins of Minsky's transportation company. More than thirty years had passed; a man could be forgiven for having a sketchy memory of events so long ago. He looked to his left at the Senator for Florida, who had his own questions to ask.

'You head the Palmetto Leisure Development Corporation now?'

'I do.'

'I shall not ask you about casinos in the two hotels operated by the corporation. You would undoubtedly tell me, as your son did, that casino gambling is illegal in Florida. What I would like to hear from you is something about the man who built those hotels. Tell me about Philip Gerson.'

Minsky licked his upper lip clean of the beads of sweat that had suddenly appeared. 'A smart cookie.'

'A smart cookie,' the Senator for Florida repeated. 'What happened to this . . . this smart cookie?'

Minsky's upper lip was sweaty again. So was his entire body. 'He died.'

'How?'

'He was in a boating accident, him and his girl. The boat burned up while they were out at sea.'

'And immediately afterwards, a memo was sent to all the staff at both hotels that you were taking over Gerson's responsibilities. The memo was sent out so quickly that one could almost believe it had already been prepared.'

'That memo was sent out the morning after the Coast-guard spotted the wreckage of Phil's boat. The moment we heard about Phil, we had to move into action fast. Sure we grieved for him, he was too clever a guy to lose like that, but the hotels had to keep on running. So I stepped in.' Damn! Minsky thought, what the hell was the matter with him? He never sweated as a rule. He was never scarced. Yet these questions were making his sweat glands work overtime, his heart beat like a jackhammer.

'And you've been there ever since?'

'Ever since.'

The Senator for California motioned to Minsky. 'I believe that a former associate of yours was once resident in my state.'

Minsky regarded the man blankly.

'Your wife, Mr Minsky.'

'My late wife. She died years ago.'

'Miss Kathleen Monahan. She started her career by singing in a club, did she not?'

'Sure. A club me and my partners owned.'

'A club that served illegal liquor?'

'That may have been one of the attractions, I don't remember.'

'Never mind that. When Miss Monahan got her big break on Broadway in – ' the Senator for California consulted notes – '*Broadway Nell*, was it solely because of her voice, her talent, or – was it because you coerced a certain producer? *Leaned* on him to give Miss Monahan the role?'

'I leaned on Irwin Kuczinski?' Minsky burst out laughing and his heart pounded even more wildly. He swung round to look back at Levitt and Pearl. They were smiling, they could

265

see the joke as well. 'It was Kuczinski who did the leaning! He leaned so far over the goddamned stage that he had Kathleen's boobs stuck in his eyes!'

Senator Rourke hammered with his gavel. 'Mr Minsky, I must ask you again to remember where you are. Such language will not be tolerated – '

Minsky cut the Senator off. 'Can I help the way I speak? I wasn't educated all fancy like you were. I came up the hard way, in the streets. When you and your hoity-toity family – ' Senator Rourke banged again with the gavel and Minsky jumped to his feet, shouting – ' 'were being wheeled around by your goddamned governesses, I was sweating blood to make a nickel or a dime so my family could eat and pay the rent on the shithole tenement we lived in! Maybe if I'd have had a rich father to send me to Harvard or Yale or wherever, I'd be a senator too. But I didn't, and I'm not! I came up the hard way, and I'm goddamned proud of it!'

Again and again, Senator Rourke slammed the gavel down. It was hopeless to continue. Minsky had made a mockery out of the entire proceedings. All Senator Rourke could do now was adjourn, take a break in which to discuss with his brother and fellow committee members how to approach the next and final witness, Louis Levitt.

The adjournment was called. Minsky started to walk away from the witness table, hands clasped above his head like a triumphant boxer. Levitt himself would not be able to do any better when his turn came! Minsky took no more than half a dozen steps when his legs buckled. His arms flailed for balance, and with a muted cry of pain at the searing bar of fire that ripped across his chest, he fell to the floor. Within twenty minutes, he was in intensive care, the victim of a massive heart attack. . . .

The television news that night concentrated on the final confrontation between Senator Rourke and Benny Minsky, the six steps Minsky took before the heart attack hit him. Patrick and John Rourke watched the report together in the hotel where they were staying. Neither brother thought their case had been well served by the day's events.

'It's a goddamned circus,' John said disgustedly as he watched a close-up of Minsky being carried from the hearing.

'The press is making out that it's our fault for pushing a man with a heart condition.'

'I never knew he had a weak heart!' Patrick exclaimed.

'And that bit about governesses and university . . . a rich father!' John slammed his fist against the palm of his hand. 'We're trying to get you the Democratic nomination, and that bastard Minsky rams it down everyone's throat that we're members of a privileged class!'

The telephone rang. The caller was old Patrick Joseph Rourke from his home in Boston. 'I suppose I should congratulate the pair of you on your first success,' the old man said sarcastically. 'At least you put one of those bastards in the hospital. You'll cost him medical bills if nothing else.'

'Dad, we're doing all we can,' Patrick protested. 'But the stuff we've brought up, it means nothing. There's a statute of limitations.'

'What about Switzerland?'

'We can't get proof! Swiss banks don't talk about their depositors.'

'For God's sake, are you going to let those Jews walk away after what they did to me? To our family?'

'We'll get Levitt when the hearing resumes.'

'You'd better!' Rourke snapped. 'Or else you're no sons of mine!'

Patrick heard the receiver being slammed down in Boston. He stared helplessly at his brother. 'If we don't get Levitt, we're no sons of Dad.'

'We'll get him,' John said. 'We'll get him good.'

Lou Levitt took his seat at the witness table, carefully lifting the trousers of his dark suit to avoid creasing them. With his slight stature, lined face and grey hair, he looked like someone's grandfather. Hardly the image, Senator Rourke mused as he studied the witness, of a criminal mastermind.

Although Levitt appeared outwardly calm, he could not rid himself of the memory of the previous day's events, the sight of Minsky falling to the floor, a look of pain and numb surprise etched on his face. Pearl had been tremendously upset by it, and Levitt had stayed with her at the Sands Point house, both waiting for news from the hospital. Early in the morning, William had called to say that his father was resting comfortably. Levitt had promised Pearl that if visiting were permitted he would take her to the hospital after today's session of the hearing, which she had again insisted on attending.

Senator Rourke's first question knocked all thought of Minsky clean out of Levitt's mind. He had expected the Senator to start off with innocent queries about his background, his early days, perhaps draw some references to the clubs and liquor business. Instead, the Senator went straight for the jugular.

'Mr Levitt, do you have financial interests in foreign casinos? Specifically, the Embassy Club and the Dominion Sporting Club in London, England, and the Belvedere Hotel in Freeport, the Bahamas.'

Levitt shifted uncomfortably on the seat. The Irish son of a bitch had dug deeply. 'I have no financial interest in these establishments whatsoever. Nor do I have any financial interests in any other casinos, in the United States or overseas.'

'You are under oath, sir.'

'I am perfectly aware of that.' Levitt made a rationalization to himself. A lie under oath was only a lie if it could be proved to be so. There was no way that Senator Rourke could prove his allegations. He could suspect it, but there was no black and white evidence. The financial involvement was too well concealed, money put on a handshake, a verbal promise. Nothing anywhere in writing.

'Have you ever been to any of the places I mentioned?'

'I have. I went to London on vacation with Mrs Granitz some time back. I took out overseas membership at the Dominion Sporting Club and the Embassy Club for the period I was in London.'

'Did you gamble?'

'I did not.'

'Did Mrs Granitz gamble?'

'Yes.' Levitt smiled coldly. 'She lost ten shillings.'

'Why would you take out a temporary membership at a gambling club and not gamble?'

'I find enjoyment in watching gamblers. I find no enjoyment in being one of them. They always lose eventually.'

'In how many places have you watched gambling? In Florida? In the room above the Jalo Cab Company garage? In the clubs you controlled during Prohibition? How many places, Mr Levitt?'

'I watch gambling wherever I can. I admit to being fascinated by it.'

'Let us forget London and the Bahamas for a moment, Mr Levitt,' Senator Rourke said. He no longer needed to dwell on those casinos. The damage was already done. The British authorities were so strict about whom they granted licences to that they would look hard at those two clubs now, so would the Bahamian government with the Belvedere Hotel. Senator Rourke had little doubt that the casinos would lose their licences through being associated – even if only allegedly – with Levitt. How much more could his father want? 'How much are you worth, Mr Levitt?'

'Offhand? I can't say.'

'A rough guess, a ballpark figure, will suffice. One million dollars . . . two million . . . five million?'

'That's being ridiculous. I live in a rented apartment. I drive a Pontiac. I buy my clothes off the rack. Does a man worth that much live in such a frugal manner?'

'Mr Levitt. . .' Senator Rourke's voice was condescending. 'You don't have to live high off the hog to prove you're wealthy. How much is in that account you have in the Leinberg Bank?'

Levitt felt sweat beginning to trickle down his armpits. 'What account?'

'The account you keep in Switzerland. The account from which you borrow money to finance the hotels in Switzerland, the buildings owned by Granitz Brothers. You're borrowing your own money, aren't you, and paying interest to yourself?'

For one icily terrifying instant, Levitt lost his composure. Had Walter Leinberg, or someone else working at the bank in Zurich been reached? No! Levitt relaxed. If Senator Rourke knew the truth, if someone had broken the vow of confidentiality, he would throw the codename in Levitt's face, demand to know what Blackhawk was. 'I have no idea what you are talking about, Senator Rourke.'

'Let me enlighten you a little.' Rourke knew the value of

such innuendoes. He didn't need to have proof. Allegations alone would cost Levitt his interest in the foreign casinos, just as allegations about a Swiss bank account would bring acute embarrassment. 'Before Joseph Granitz became your courier to Switzerland, Philip Gerson made the regular run. Was Mr Gerson also continually "sorting out problems" with an engineering firm in Zurich called A. G. Kriesel? You must have squirreled away a considerable sum of money during all those years, Mr Levitt. Is it thirty million dollars . . . forty million . . . a hundred million? And all of it tax-free from illegal ventures.'

'I repeat my last statement. I have no idea what you're talking about.' Levitt wasn't going to plead the Fifth Amendment to the Constitution. That route was for cowards, for people with little faith. He was going to keep on lying until he was blue in the face, brazen it out, dare the committee to prove him a perjurer. He knew they couldn't otherwise they would have done so already.

'Mr Levitt, will you tell this committee how much you are worth?'

'If you wish, you're perfectly welcome to inspect all of my holdings,' Levitt offered. 'I'll have bankbooks, lists of stocks, an inventory of personal possessions all ready for your scrutiny. You can figure it out for yourself.'

'Tell us about Switzerland, Mr Levitt. Tell us about the Leinberg Bank.'

'Ask the Leinberg Bank.'

'We did,' Senator Rourke admitted. 'They refused to yield any information about their depositors. They refused to say anything about you having a deposit account there.'

'Did you ever stop to think that was because I don't have an account there? Or isn't that what you wanted to hear?'

Senator Rourke never answered. He did not need to say any more; there was no need to ask another question. Whatever Levitt's character was like, this hearing had besmirched it. No matter what Levitt did or said in the future, the allegations made against him in this hearing would stick. He would never be free of them. The respectability he had laboured hard to build up was destroyed – by innuendo or solid, irrefutable evidence, it didn't matter. Senator Patrick Rourke

270

Junior had paid off his father's debt. Now he could concentrate on his own ambitions, take the Senate Special Committee across the country to give himself nationwide fame.

'Thank you, Mr Levitt. You have been most helpful. You may step down.'

Levitt left the witness table and returned to Pearl. She could see him holding back his temper. 'Let's get out of here,' he muttered. 'I stay here any longer, I'm going to explode.'

Pearl followed him outside. 'How bad is the damage?'

'Bad enough. Rourke dug deep and he came up with a ton of dirt. None of it can be proved, but just the allegations are enough. We dare not open the casinos in Florida again, and mark my words it'll be just a matter of time before our places in the Bahamas and London lose their licences. The smell of scandal alone will be enough to set the ball rolling on that.'

'What about the Granitz Brothers? What about B. M. Transportation?

'Oh, they'll be all right. They're rock-solid.'

'Is that so bad, Lou? The respectable businesses will still be there. We'll live more than comfortably from them.'

'Respectable!' His voice was venomous. 'You still want respectable? Is that all you're interested in? Take a look at what we just left inside. Senator Rourke and the rest of those squawking, pontificating *mamzarim*! That's respectable. My little finger – ' he raised it in front of Pearl's eyes – 'has got more life, more guts than all of those respectable sons of bitches!'

'Maybe London and the Bahamas will be all right,' Pearl said as she tried to placate Levitt. 'Maybe nothing will happen to them.'

'Maybe,' Levitt said, but he didn't believe it. He was certain that he was going to lose them. He'd already lost the Florida casinos. The Waterway and the Monaco would remain as they were now – legitimate luxury hotels. And soon he'd lose London and the Bahamas. He was just as certain that if such a thing happened, he wouldn't rest until he'd made Patrick Joseph Rourke and the whole damned Rourke family bleed again. Bleed until their veins ran dry.

Pearl and Levitt went straight from the committee hearing to see Benny Minsky. They found William and Susan already there, sitting in the waiting-room, holding hands as if to give each other strength.

'How is he?' Levitt asked William.

'We haven't seen him yet. The doctor says we might be able to spend a few minutes with him in half an hour or so.'

'Did the doctor give you a prognosis?'

William made a rocking motion with his hand. 'My father's a strong man, that's the ray of hope in this situation. The doctor said that anyone else would have been blown away. It was a major heart attack.'

Pearl went over to Susan. 'Who's looking after Mark and Paul?'

'A baby-sitter. How are you, after your ordeal this week?'

Pearl shrugged and smiled. Her own troubles seemed minor now.

'While William and I were sitting here, we watched the news.' Susan indicated a television set in the waiting-room. Pearl had not even noticed it. Now some man was pointing a stick at weather charts and talking about a cold front coming down from Canada.

Pearl dropped her voice to a whisper. 'Don't mention anything about it. Lou's very upset over what happened, to Benny, and to himself today.'

'I saw,' Susan whispered back. 'That Senator made a big show today. He won all the points he wanted to.'

A doctor entered the waiting-room, a young man with shiny black hair and horn-rimmed glasses. 'Mr Minsky, Mrs Minsky, you can go in now, but only for a few minutes.'

As William and Susan left the waiting-room, Levitt noticed the young doctor staring at him. 'You want something from me?' Levitt asked.

'No . . . no. . . .' The doctor was flustered, but unable to tear his eyes away from Levitt's face.

'See me on television before, did you? Want an autograph?'

'I'm sorry. I didn't mean to stare.'

Pearl stepped in. 'May we see Mr Minsky as well?'

'Are you family?' the doctor asked, relieved by her intervention.

Pearl was about to say no, until she realized that a man in

272

intensive care would only be allowed visits from immediate family. She was no longer under oath. 'I'm Mr Minsky's sister.'

'I didn't realize he had a sister.'

'Ask his son, William, my nephew.'

'And you, Mr . . .?' the doctor asked.

'You know damned well what my name is,' Levitt said. 'And you know what my connection is. I'm his business partner. I want to see him as well, to talk about all those millions we've got stashed away in some Swiss bank.'

'Two minutes. After his son and daughter-in-law come out.' The doctor walked away quickly.

'Marvellous, isn't it?' Levitt said to Pearl. 'I spent a lifetime staying out of the spotlight, and that *momzer* makes me into a celebrity overnight.'

'People'll forget, Lou. Next week, no one will know you.'

William and Susan returned to the waiting-room five minutes later. To Pearl's surprise, William was smiling, although Susan appeared downcast. 'He's sitting up in bed, talking about how he made a fool out of that committee,' William said. 'There can't be that much wrong with him.'

'He doesn't realize how sick he is, that's the problem,' Susan added. 'He won't realize it. He still thinks he's a young man, ready to take on the world.'

The doctor reappeared. Looking just at Pearl, ignoring Levitt completely, he held two fingers in the air. 'Two minutes, that's all. He needs rest.'

Pearl and Levitt entered the private room. Minsky was propped up on a pillow. His face was grey, but life sparkled in his dark eyes. 'Did you see how I took care of that son-of-a-bitching Senator? I put him in his goddamned place, didn't I?'

'You put yourself in this place as well,' Pearl said. She looked at the equipment adjacent to the bed, the machines that meant nothing to her, only that they were registering Minsky's condition.

'I heard what happened to you,' Minsky said to Levitt.

'How?'

'The doctor told me.'

'Which doctor? The one who showed us in here? When Minsky nodded, Levitt said, 'That little snot-nose was looking at me like I was something out of a freak show!'

'How long will you have to stay here?' Pearl asked.

'Maybe a week.'

'Then what? Will you stay with William and Susan?'

Minsky shook his head. 'I'm getting the hell out of this cold weather. This is what did it to me, having to be in New York during the winter. A couple of days in that Florida sun, listening to those dice click up profits, and I'll be as good as new.'

'I thought you said you heard what happened,' Levitt muttered. 'There won't be any dice. Ever again. We're all washed up. Those hotels stay as hotels from now on. We'll lose our London licences, we'll get kicked out of the Bahamas. We're out of business altogether.'

'So I'll just sit in the sun,' Minsky answered, refusing to let Levitt dampen his enthusiasm.

Levitt glanced at Pearl. 'Leave me alone with Benny for a moment, Pearl. We've got things to discuss.'

'Get well, Benny. I'll see you tomorrow.' She bent to kiss him on the cheek. Despite his protestations of how well he felt, his skin was cold and damp. Pearl wanted to wash the clamminess off her lips.

The door closed quietly behind her. 'William said you had a real big heart attack, Benny. Maybe you're kidding yourself about how good you feel.'

'Forget it, shrimp.' Minsky purposely used the derogatory nickname he'd called Levitt when they were young. 'You're talking me into nothing. I feel fine because I am fine.'

'Benny, don't kid yourself about your health.'

Minsky struggled to sit up. A little of the colour returned to his face. The pulse on the machine that measured his heartbeat jumped into urgent action. 'Listen to me, Lou, and listen good. You know what's going to keep me alive? You . . . you're the best medicine I could have.'

'Me?' Levitt's tight little smile was totally bereft of humour. 'How do you figure that?'

'If it wasn't for you, I'd say pull the plug, God, I'm ready. I've done all I ever wanted to do. I've had one hell of a good time. Most importantly, I've watched my son grow up to be the man I always wanted him to be. But he's no match for you,

274

Lou. No man living is, not even that fancy bastard Senator Patrick Rourke Junior. He may have made a monkey out of you today, cost you some – '

'Make your point, Benny,' Levitt said impatiently. 'Otherwise the doctor's going to be dragging me out of here before you get around to it.'

'No one's a match for you, Lou, except me. I'm going to stay around to see you don't rob my son blind and give everything to those twins of Pearl's.'

'You're crazy, Benny. You always were.'

'*I'm* crazy? Minsky laughed, and the pulse on the machine jumped again. 'You think after all these years I don't know what you're like, Lou? You always figured you were the only one with any brains, and because of that you were entitled to everything. If I go, you'll screw my son out of that money we've got stashed away with Leinberg. Not because you need it, or the twins need it, but because you think you deserve it more than anyone else.'

'Why shouldn't I think that way? Every deal that ever made money was my idea. What did you contribute, Benny? Name one thing.'

'Get out, Lou, before I ring for the nurse and have her throw you out.'

'Nothing, Benny. You contributed nothing. I did it all.'

'Maybe you did, but so help me God, I'm staying alive to see you don't get it all. I'll beat you by outliving you.'

Levitt left the room. 'I'll drive you home,' he told Pearl.

'What happened in there? You look awful. What did you and Benny have to talk about?'

'Nothing. I have nothing to talk about with Benny at all.'

Pearl asked no more questions. She believed she understood why Levitt was so distraught. The day at the hearing, the knowledge that his gambling days were over. So what? she wanted to ask him. Why do we need that kind of a business anymore? We certainly aren't short of anything. Even without all the money in Zurich, none of us would ever want again.

As they neared the end of the drive to Sands Point, Pearl began to rationalize the disaster at the hearing. It wasn't really so bad, she assured herself. Levitt was certain that nothing could be proven against them, none of the allegations. Even if the Internal Revenue Service put their affairs under the microscope, everything would stand up. All it meant was that the gambling days were over. From now on they would have to rely completely on the legitimate businesses they'd built up. The edge that Levitt had always looked for would be gone. But Levitt, like herself, was sixty-one. Why was an edge so important to him anymore? He had more money than he could ever spend, even if he should live to be a hundred and sixty-one! He should be content now, he should relax as he approached his last years. Enjoy life a little.

Or was it that the only thing in life he really enjoyed was the rattle of dice, the thrill of organizing, profiting from, a game of chance? Even after all these years, Pearl knew she didn't fully understand what mechanism, what motivation, controlled Levitt's life.

Chapter Five

Benny Minsky was discharged from the hospital eleven days after the heart attack. There was no question of his returning to Florida to look after himself, so he moved into the Forest Hills Gardens home of his son and daughter-in-law to convalesce for four weeks under the care of a nurse. Despite being so close to his family, especially his two grandsons, Minsky hated it there. The weather was still too cold for him to be allowed outside, and the nurse's constant ministrations made him complain that he might just as well be incarcerated in a maximum-security prison. Everyone told Minsky that such treatment was for his own good, including Pearl who visited him regularly at the house, although Lou Levitt never showed any interest in seeing his sick partner.

'Benny, you can't go back to Florida and start working again as if nothing had happened,' Pearl stressed. 'For God's sake, have a little patience.'

'Since when have you known me to have any patience? Besides, what work is there anyway? Running a couple of fancy hotels, that's all. Nothing else, not any more.'

'How upset will you be if the casinos don't reopen?'

Minsky gave the question some thought. 'I won't be upset if William's never involved in them. I never wanted him to be a part of the gambling side. I always saw him just the way he is. Upright, never having to look over his shoulder to see what's coming up behind.'

'Do you have to look over yours?'

'We all do, Pearl.' Just then, the nurse entered the room. She carried a tray on which was a cup of coffee for Pearl and a glass of warm milk for Minsky. He exploded. 'Warm milk! They're treating me like I'm a goddamned baby!'

The nurse, a flat-chested, middle-aged woman with a noticeable moustache, sent Minsky a glare that had terrorized her previous unruly patients. '*You* are *not* allowed coffee, Mr Minsky.'

'How about a walk in the garden then, Warden? The sun's shining.'

The nurse went to the window and looked at the thermometer that was fixed to the outside wall. 'It's thirty-one degrees out there, Mr Minsky. Far too inclement for someone in your condition. The cold, dry air will hurt your lungs, and any strain on them would be an additional strain on your heart.'

'You're a damned strain on my heart,' Minsky muttered, then, in a louder voice, 'I'm going to write to my damned Congressman.' But even that thread had little effect on the nurse.

'You'll have to get someone to look after you when you go home,' Pearl told Minsky. 'You can't live alone.'

'How can I live alone in a hotel full of people?' He thought for a few moments and his face brightened. 'You know what I'm going to do? That top floor of the Waterway in Hallandale . . . I'm going to take over the whole top floor for myself. Turn it into the fanciest suite of rooms you ever laid eyes on. Have my own private pool up there, even install my own nurse, a blue-eyed blonde with a figure like Venus.'

'A nuse like that would send your blood pressure through the roof.'

Minsky's face fell. 'Lou would veto it anyway. He'd say it'd cost too much money.'

'Benny, what is it between you and Lou? For a while you seemed to get on well together, but now you're both at each other's throats again.'

'Nothing's between us that was never there before. I could ask you the same question, Pearl. What's between you and him?'

Pearl lifted the cup of coffee to her mouth as if she could hide the blush that suddenly sprang to her face. 'How do you mean?'

278

'Pearl, I know he was in love with you.'

'He was? How do you know that?'

'Lou's warm feelings for anyone are so few and far between that when they occur they shine like a beacon on a black night. Did you ever feel anything for him?'

'I love him like I love you, Benny. As an old friend.'

'That's all?'

'That's all. If what you say is true, do you . . . do you think Jake ever noticed? About Lou? What was the point, she asked herself, of even thinking about it now? A lifetime had passed.

'No. Jake was too sure of himself to worry about anything. Not like me,' Minsky added ruefully.

'You?'

'Every time some guy would walk on the same side of the street as Kathleen, I'd start having fits. I was crazy jealous where she was concerned.'

'I know. She told me you held her out of the window once.'

'I wouldn't have let her go,' Minsky said, grinning.

'That's not what she thought at the time!'

The nurse reappeared. This time she carried two tablets and a glass of water. 'Time for your medication, Mr Minsky.'

'Time for your medication, Mr Minsky,' he mimicked. 'Dear God, let me get back home.'

'All in good time, Mr Minsky. All in good time.' The nurse waited for him to put the tablets in his mouth, then she held the glass to his lips as though he were a helpless child.

'I'll put in a good word for you with the parole board,' Pearl joked. There was nothing worse than sick men, she decided. The only thing you could do was humour them and hope they got better soon.

Minsky had been in Forest Hills Gardens for two weeks when Levitt received the bad news from his English partners. Following the allegations made by the Senate Special Committee in New York, a government inquiry was being launched in Britain to determine the infiltration of gaming clubs by so-called 'undesirable American elements'. Levitt took small comfort from the fact that neither the British press nor the government referred to him outright as a gangster or a

279

criminal. Just an undesirable American element. He wasn't even named. As a first step, the licences of the two London clubs referred to in the hearings were suspended. The principals were given thirty days to prepare arguments as to why they should be allowed to continue operating.

Levitt knew it made no difference to himself whether the clubs reopened or remained shut. His interest in them was no longer welcome. Nor, a week later, was it welcome in the Bahamas. Taking a lead from the British government, a Royal Commission of Inquiry ordered the Belvedere Hotel's gambling licence to be revoked. Senator Patrick Rourke Junior had repaid his father's debt in full.

At home in his Central Park West apartment, Levitt flicked on the television set and tuned into the late news. As if to mock him, the first topic was the Senate Special Committee on Organized Crime. It was sitting in Cincinatti that week, interviewing men who operated clubs along the Ohio River on the Kentucky border. Small people, Levitt thought as he watched. The clubs they ran, the illegal casinos, were pocket change compared with the operation he'd seen swept away from him. Senator Rourke would get more publicity, and some of those small fish would wind up facing prosecution because they weren't smart enough to cover themselves as well as Levitt had done. But Levitt understood that all this was an anti-climax for the Rourke family, nothing more than window-dressing. The main objective of the campaign had been achieved when the damned committee had convened in New York. It had destroyed the empire that Levitt had built up over the years.

News of the committee hearing finished with an interview of Patrick Rourke Junior. The camera zoomed in on that honest Irish face, and Levitt inched the chair closer to the television set. 'The people of this country,' the Senator was saying, 'have an unfortunate habit of forgetting quickly, and those who fail to learn from history are, as we well know, doomed to repeat it. Senator Kefauver exposed all this fifteen years ago, and people were interested for a while. But only for a while. Then they forgot, and the very people they had seen exposed as criminals of the worst kind slipped back once again into positions of power. This time, I am praying that their interest in the thieves and vandals who have stolen from this country lasts a little longer.'

For thirty minutes after the end of the late news, Levitt sat staring at the television screen. Commercials, programmes, more commercials flickered meaninglessly in front of his eyes. All he saw was that Irish face. That stinking, hateful Irish face with its unruly mop of hair. He became as obsessed with the Rourke family as he knew old Patrick Joseph Rourke to be obsessed with him.

While Levitt was staring at the television, Mickey Phillips was preparing to close up for the night. Every so often, he lifted his head from the cash register to say good-night to one of the waiters. It was past midnight and Phillips wanted to get home. He was tired, barely able to keep his eyes open. Wednesday was always one of the busiest days of the week for Mickey's Deli on Seventh Avenue, what with the theatre matinées. He refused to complain, though. Without matinée day, takings would not be anywhere near as high.

Leaving the cash register open, so that anyone peering through the window could see it was empty, Phillips checked around the delicatessen one final time before turning off the lights and locking the front door. He walked briskly along Seventh Avenue, enjoying the cold wind that shook off some of his sluggishness. He started to feel more awake. Just as well, he decided. He had a long drive to his home in Paramus. He'd leave the heater off, a window open. He didn't want to fall asleep at the wheel and drive off the road.

Leaving the bright lights of Seventh Avenue behind him, he turned into West 54th Street where his car was parked. At first, he thought that the set of footsteps dogging his own was nothing more than an echo. When he decided otherwise and turned around, it was already too late. Hymie Glass had a piece of iron piping raised high in the air. Phillips tried to duck and weave as he had once done in the ring. The pipe cracked down across his shoulder. Only the thickness of his coat saved him from having the bone broken. Nevertheless, the blow made him stagger. He came up quickly, fists clenched. He never saw Stan Kaye slip out of a shadowy doorway, a sawn-off baseball bat clasped in both hands. The weapon smashed into the side of Phillips' head. Without a sound, he dropped to the pavement. Glass and Kaye half-carried, half-dragged him to a black Cadillac that waited at the kerb with its engine purring. Behind the wheel sat Harry Saltzman. The moment the doors slammed, Saltzman dropped the car into gear and sped away.

Phillips regained consciousness to see a bright light glaring into his eyes. He was tied to a wooden chair. His feet were cold and damp, difficult to move. Squinting against the light, head throbbing, he looked down. Saltzman was squatting in front of him, gazing raptly at an old tin bath into which Phillips' feet were wedged. The damp coldness Phillips felt was freshly mixed cement that oozed above his ankles. He tried to wriggle his feet to break the cement's hold before it could set.

'Move all you like, Mickey,' Saltzman said in a genial tone, 'because where you're going soon, you won't be moving for a long, long time.' Phillips watched in horror as Saltzman lifted a bucket and poured more fresh cement into the bath. Slowly, the level crept up to the midway point of his shins, reaching the bottom of his rolled-up trousers.

'You ruined a house for me, Mickey, stunk it out so it smells like some shithole in a Bowery flophouse. Had to burn everything. The house still stinks, and I've got to spend good money to stay at the Statler Hilton.' Saltzman ran a finger across the surface of the wet cement, leaving a groove. 'Should be hard in a couple of hours, Mickey, and then you're going for a swim. Any preferences? East River? Hudson River? Harlem River? The condemned man's final wish.'

Phillips struggled in the chair but Hymie Glass and Stan Kaye held him still. All he could do was watch. And wait.

'Could have been so simple, Mickey. All you had to do was join my guild. For nothing I offered to let you join. But no, you were too hardheaded, too much of the tough guy. You had to do things your way, didn't you?'

Phillips wanted to shout that Saltzman would never get away with it. You didn't get away with murder, no one did. But the gag stuffed into his mouth cut off all sound. He looked around, wondered where he was. The place looked like a garage, or maybe a warehouse. Was it a warehouse? Was he

282

on the docks already? He thought he could smell the water.

'You're just going to disappear, Mickey. All people are going to remember about you is your ring career. And soon they're even going to forget that. You think the police will get involved? Forget it. You'll just be a missing person, that's all. Maybe you ran off with a piece of skirt. Maybe you were in some kind of trouble and you split for the Coast. Without a body, that's all the police can do: guess. And no one's ever going to find your body once this cement sets. You'll be standing on the bottom, giving traffic directions to the fish, Mickey.'

Saltzman looked up and gave an almost imperceptible nod. Behind the bound and gagged man, Hymie Glass lifted the iron pipe. It descended in a short, swift arc, and Phillips' consciousness departed once again.

When he came to the next time, he knew he could smell water. Arms and legs still bound, feet fixed firmly in hard cement, he was on a dock. It was eerily quiet, nothing but the lapping of the waves below him. How deep was it here? Twenty feet? Thirty? The water was so damned murky that he'd never be seen. Ignoring the pain that battered his skull, he looked straight out. The opposite shore was far away, almost pitch black, only an occasional light lifting the gloom. He made a guess. The Hudson, high up, close to the Tappan Zee Bridge. There was a small rowing boat. Hymie Glass and Stan Kaye lifted him into it, held him fast on a narrow bench. Saltzman took hold of a pair of oars and began to row swiftly into mid-river. Saltzman was humming to himself, and Phillips wanted to scream when he recognized the popular tune: 'Up A Lazy River'. That son of a bitch was finding it funny!

'This'll do,' Saltzman said, and Phillips felt a perverted sense of gratitude that the big man was breathing heavily. Maybe the strain of rowing would give him a coronary! 'Tip him over, boys.'

The gag was ripped from Phillips' mouth and he heard Saltzman say, 'You can save your last words for the fish, Mickey.' Strong hands gripped his arms and legs. The boat rocked. Before he could gather strength for a scream, the freezing water shocked his system. He tried to flail his arms, and couldn't. He tried to move his legs, and couldn't. The icy

283

water closed over the top of his head, and he sank rapidly. His eyes were open, his mouth jammed closed in one final, desperate attempt to avoid the inevitable. Blood roared in his ears. His chest pounded as he settled on to the bottom of the river. For an instant, he remained upright until the undercurrent's steady surge toppled him over. He lay on his back in the cold water, mouth still shut. The pressure on his lungs grew greater until they were ready to explode for want of air. His mouth popped open in a reflex gesture. Water flooded in. The roaring in his ears became louder. His eyes burned as he sought oxygen and found only water. The darkness became even blacker as his sight dimmed. Slowly, the roaring subsided to a dull hum. And finally, mercifully, he drowned.

Benny Minsky returned to his suite of rooms at the Waterway Hotel in mid-March. Both his son and daughter-in-law were reluctant to let him leave, but he assured them that he felt well enough to travel. A doctor who examined him expressed surprise at the recovery. Minsky's strength and resiliency had made a mockery of a heart attack that would have destroyed many weaker men.

Minsky took life easy when he reached home. With no casino gambling to oversee, he was in bed each night by eleven o'clock, and rose promptly at seven each morning to walk along the beach before eating breakfast. He knew that he was nothing more than a hotel manager now, and Palmetto Leisure Development Corporation had more than enough competent hotel management staff. Minsky had all the free time he could ever want. For the first time in his life he took up golf, spending hour after hour with a professional at a local course as he tried to make up in weeks the experience that other players had taken years to gain. To his own surprise, he found he had a natural aptitude for the game, and a fierce competitive spirit. He learned to become angry with himself for missing an easy putt, but when he realized what it was doing to his blood pressure he thrust his anger on the back burner. He had taken up golf for exercise and relaxation, not to give himself another heart attack.

Under a doctor's direction, he went on a special diet to lose twenty pounds, the excess weight that Pearl had noticed on her sixty-first birthday four months earlier. The Waterway's kitchen, along with preparing its regular menu, catered to Minsky's diet. A special tray was sent up every mealtime to his suite. He never ate in the restaurant with the hotel guests but tried to keep a respectable distance between himself and them. The Senate Special Committee on Organized Crime had bequeathed him a certain fame – compounded by his verbal assault on Senator Rourke, and then his heart attack on camera – and Minsky often felt that guests were looking at him, talking about him, as he walked through the hotel. He didn't want to discuss his appearance before the committee. He didn't want to talk about the past. He only wanted to relax, play golf for exercise, and religiously stick to his diet.

More than anything, he wanted to remain healthy, realize his boast that he would outlast Lou Levitt. That was the only thing that Minsky had to live for. Everything else he had wanted to do, he had already accomplished.

Harry Saltzman had never worked on a building site in his life, and that lack of knowledge led to his downfall. Reading the directions on the bags of cement he'd bought from a hardware store was not enough. Experience would have told him to leave the cement longer to set.

The Hudson River, which Saltzman believed would serve as the last resting place of Mickey Phillips, went to work on the bath full of cement the moment Phillips sank beneath the surface. At first, the deterioration of the cement was virtually unnoticeable. The water did nothing more than weaken the top layer, certainly not enough to free Phillips' corpse from its anchor. After a couple of weeks, the damage became more apparent. The top surface of the cement began to break up, and the water searched deeper. The bottom layer of the cement, where Phillips' wriggling feet had hampered the setting process, was more receptive to the water's probing. The cement began to split; small pieces initially, then larger chunks were swirled away by the Hudson's undercurrent. Finally, the tin bath floated free. Phillips' body banged along the river bed like a sodden log, hands and legs bound, skin bloated, hair rising from the scalp like fine streamers. The current carried the body towards the ocean. Past Yonkers on the New York side of the river. Past Englewood Cliffs and Alpine on the New Jersey bank. Under the George Washington Bridge. Past Fort Lee and Washington Heights. Until finally, abreast of the Cunard Docks on the West Side of Manhattan, it popped up to the surface.

A sergeant on board a New York police launch was the first to spot Phillips' body. It was after midnight, and the launch's spotlight picked out a white shape floating in the water fifty yards away, a small, round white disc that could have been a paper plate discarded by some litterbug, or a Frisbee skimmed across the water by kids. The sergeant looked closer, ordered the boat to be swung around. Paper plates and Frisbees did not have the bloated features of a face that had been underwater for a month. Engines cut back to a low rumble, the launch edged nearer. A boathook was thrust into the water. It caught hold of Phillips' coat, pulled the body a few yards before tearing free. The body disappeared beneath the surface and the crew of the launch waited. A minute later, Phillips rose again, twenty yards further downriver. The launch positioned itself again, the boathook was thrust into the water a second time. It ripped through the coat, jacket, shirt and flesh. Phillips' body was hauled on board, and the men on the launch radioed in that they were bringing home a floater.

Identification was simple. The murder was not connected to any robbery. Harry Saltzman and his two henchmen had not even bothered to go through Phillips' pockets. Even the roll of cash he'd taken from the cash register at Mickey's Deli was still in his trousers. The identification papers, his driving licence and Social Security card wrapped in protective plastic, were dried out. Within an hour of fishing the body from the Hudson, the police knew that the drowning victim was a man who had been reported missing almost a month earlier by his wife. The fact that he wore no shoes, and that some fragments of dried cement clung tenaciously to his trousers, assured the police that the drowning was not accidental.

Inquiries began, and ended, early the following morning at Mickey's Deli on Seventh Avenue. The delicatessen was still open, managed by Phillips' widow. The waiters there were only too willing to talk of the heavy-set man who had been thrown out by Phillips when he tried to coerce the delicatessen owner into joining the New York Guild of Restaurateurs and Victuallers, the visit later by two men with a bottle of butyric acid, and finally Phillips' poetic if ill-conceived revenge.

Saltzman was easy to trace. After checking at the house in Fort Lee, the police learned there was a forwarding address: the Statler Hilton in New York City. Before noon, two detectives – Lieutenant Derek Mulholland and Sergeant John O'Brien – arrived at the hotel to make the arrest. Showing their shields to the desk clerk, they asked for the number of Saltzman's room.

'He's out,' the clerk said.

'How do you know?'

'He goes out every morning to a gymnasium in Times Square. He's a fitness nut, comes back in a huge sweat every day.'

'Give us the key.' The clerk did so. Lieutenant Derek Mulholland and Sergeant John O'Brien went up to Saltzman's room, let themselves in and looked around. There was nothing in the wardrobe but three suits, some shirts, underwear and socks Saltzman had bought to replace the wardrobe he'd lost at the Fort Lee house. They went into the bathroom, closed the door, and waited. . . .

Saltzman returned to the hotel an hour later, his cheeks still glowing from the exertion of his morning exercise routine. He entered the room, closed the door and sat down heavily on the edge of the bed. The sound of the bathroom door opening made him swing around, and he found himself looking down the barrel of a revolver held by Mulholland. Behind the lieutenant stood O'Brien. 'Harry Saltzman, you're under arrest for the murder of Mickey Phillips.'

'Not a chance,' Saltzman said without even getting off the bed. 'I didn't murder any Mickey Phillips. I don't even know a Mickey Phillips.'

'Is that so? Then how come you were so gung-ho about getting him to join your restaurant guild?'

'*That* Mickey Phillips!' Saltzman exclaimed. 'He's dead?'

'You know damned well he is.' Mulholland waited while O'Brien stepped forward with a pair of handcuffs. Saltzman stood up, held out his hands unresistingly. 'We've got witnesses who saw him throw you out of Mickey's Deli, witnesses who saw him beat up the two men you sent to stink-bomb his place, witnesses who saw him on his way to your home in Fort Lee with the same stink bomb.'

Saltzman started to laugh. 'If you've got witnesses to all that, why the hell aren't you arresting Phillips? I'm the injured party, not him!'

'I already told you . . . he's not injured, he's dead. Murdered.'

'Says who?' Saltzman asked belligerently.

'We fished his body out of the Hudson this morning.'

'That's crap!' Saltzman burst out. 'He had enough cement around his – !' He gulped as he realized what hc was saying. He looked at the handcuffs, felt himself being pushed from the room. His mind started to race down avenues of escape. Not physical escape, that was out of the question. A trade-off! Whom could he trade for his own safety? Hymie Glass and Stan Kaye who'd helped him? Why should the cops be interested in two helpers when they had the crew chief? Money . . . could he bribe these two cops? Money always worked, everyone had their price. Saltzman had learned that from Levitt. But who else would he have to bribe? The whole goddamned police department? If it were just these two, perhaps . . . but everyone? Even a clever little bastard like Levitt wouldn't be able to subvert an entire police department.

Levitt . . .!

The germ of an idea began to shine in Saltzman's mind as he was helped into an unmarked car outside the hotel.

Levitt . . .!

Saltzman didn't have to use money to bribe his way out of trouble. He'd use Levitt. He was a much more valuable commodity than mere cash, in some quarters anyway. Did the Federal Government carry more weight than mere city cops? Saltzman tried to remember the television newscast he'd seen the previous evening. Where was the Senate Special Committee on Organized Crime sitting now? Where was Senator Patrick Rourke Junior campaigning for votes with his little circus? Los Angeles, that was it. The committee was sitting in Los Angeles.

288

'I've got a right to make a phone call,' Saltzman said the moment he was taken into the precinct house.

'You'll get that right,' Mulholland assured him. 'No one's going to stop you from calling your lawyer. Just make sure you get the best money can buy, because you're going to need him.'

'You're wrong,' Saltzman said. 'I'm not going to call a lawyer. I'm going to call someone with more pull than F. Lee Bailey and Clarence Darrow put together.'

'Who?'

'I want to make a long-distance call. To Los Angeles. To Senator Patrick Rourke Junior. I've got a deal to offer him that's going to make anything you've got on me seem like a parking violation.' Saltzman bathed both detectives with a smug smile. 'I'm going to walk right out of here, boys. And there won't be a single thing you can do to stop me.'

Lou Levitt ate dinner that night at Joseph's. During the meal the children were present at the table, so the conversation covered inconsequential subjects. The moment dinner was finished, and the children went to watch television for an hour before going to bed, the topic switched to Harry Saltzman, whose arrest for the murder of Mickey Phillips had made the front pages of the late editions. Even Pearl and Judy delayed clearing up from the meal, so shocked were they at the news which brought different memories to all of them.

Pearl remembered most of all Saltzman's gruff kindness when Leo had been ill with diphtheria. How many other men, complete strangers, would have done as Saltzman had done? He had gone about it in his own peculiar way, driving across the George Washington Bridge to kidnap the first doctor he found. A hundred dollars in one hand and a gun in the other, Pearl recalled the doctor saying when he'd been brought blindfolded to the house in Fort Lee where they were hiding out from Saul Fromberg. Saltzman had looked like a brute in those days, a coarse man who couldn't have cared less if a child was dying, but his actions had belied his gross appearance.

'Is there anything you can do for him?' Pearl asked Levitt.

'Like what? According to the story in the paper, they've got witnesses that he tried everything to get this Mickey Phillips to join his restaurant association racket. Phillips hit back by wrecking Saltzman's house with the stink bomb that had been intended for the delicatessen.'

'I remember him at my wedding,' Judy said. 'He was one of the men who went looking for Leo and the ring. Him and Phil Gerson.'

And Leo and Saltzman finished up by killing Gerson, Joseph mused, because he'd been caught once too often with his finger in the till. Not that Judy or Pearl knew that. They believed the story about the boating accident.

'Couldn't you talk to some of those waiters, perhaps?' Pearl asked. 'Maybe you could get them to change their minds, lose their memory?'

'Bribe them?' Levitt shook his head. 'Pearl, believe me when I say that if I could do anything for Harry, I would. God knows, he's helped us enough in the past. But I can't afford to get involved in anything now, not so soon after those damned committee hearings. Harry carried on like he was still living in the Twenties. He didn't use his brains, whatever little God gave him. He's going to go down the river, and there's nothing anyone can do for him.'

'Does he present a danger to us?' Joseph asked.

'No. We never got ourselves involved in those stupid protection rackets like Harry did. The New York Guild of Restaurateurs and Victuallers . . . where the hell does he come up with a name like that? He must have eaten a dictionary before he dreamed that one up. No, Harry's no danger to us at all. He's just going to draw a life sentence, and at Harry's age that shouldn't last for too long.' For a moment, Levitt wondered on whom he could call in the future for those special jobs at which Saltzman had been so efficient. Then he struck the worry from his mind. After the mess the Senate Special Committee had made of the gambling empire, there would never be a need for a man like Saltzman again. . . .

Levitt's belief that Saltzman posed no threat changed dramatically when he arrived home later that night. The telephone was ringing. He lifted it from the hook. 'Hello?'

'Lou, Derek here. I've been trying to get a hold of you all evening. I've got to see you. Urgently.'

Levitt's eyes sharpened as he pictured the caller. Derek Mulholland. Tall, grey-haired, distinguished-looking. Always turned out in fine custom-made suits, which was hardly surprising as he had been on Levitt's payroll since he'd been a patrolman along Houston Street when the bookmaking and numbers action had been heavy. Mulholland had risen far since then, a detective lieutenant who still received two hundred dollars a week from Levitt just for keeping his eyes and ears open. It was a ten thousand dollar a year investment that was about to pay enormous dividends.

'What is it?' Levitt refrained from using any name at all. After the Senate Special Committee, no man knew what line was safe anymore.

'Meet me. I'm parked on the East side of Second Avenue, just south of Fifty-second Street. A white sixty-four Impala.'

'I'm on my way.' Levitt left the apartment immediately and drove to the meeting place. He saw the white Impala and pulled in behind it. There was not one man inside, but two. Derek Mulholland was behind the wheel; a younger, solid man with jet black hair in the back seat.

'This is my partner, John O'Brien,' Mulholland greeted Levitt. 'Today we arrested Harry Saltzman.'

'So?' This wasn't why Levitt paid the lieutenant ten thousand dollars a year, to be told news he was already aware of. Okay, so the papers hadn't mentioned the names of the arresting officers, but knowing it was Mulholland and his sidekick wasn't worth anything to him.

'Saltzman made a phone call.'

'He's entitled.'

'We thought you might be interested in knowing who he called,' O'Brien said from the back seat. 'He made a long-distance call to Senator Patrick Rourke Junior in Los Angeles, California.'

'We've got special orders, Lou,' Mulholland said. 'All of a sudden, Saltzman's no longer a prisoner facing a first-degree murder rap. Now he's a goddamned VIP. He cut himself a deal with Senator Rourke.'

'What kind of a deal?'

'I was there when he made the call. He didn't seem to want any privacy, like he wanted the whole wide world to know how powerful he was. Like he wanted us to know that the cops, the evidence we had, didn't mean shit to him. But your name came up, Lou – '

'What kind of a deal?'

'Saltzman told Rourke that if he got a break with this Phillips murder rap, he could deliver you, Benny Minsky, Minsky's son and the Granitz twins to Rourke on a silver platter with apples stuffed in your mouths.'

Levitt did not need to hear more. He knew exactly what Saltzman could say about them all. He'd been associated with them too long. He knew too much. He'd been involved in too many heavy things. 'Where is he? Rikers Island? The precinct house?'

'Neither place. He's been billeted in some fleabag hotel on Times Square. Under guard the whole time. A couple of detectives always with him.'

'How come?'

'Rourke apparently can't get back from the Coast for a couple of days, because of this investigation of his. He wants us to keep Saltzman on ice.'

'Has he made a statement yet?'

'No. He's saving it for the Senator.'

Two days, Levitt thought. Today was Monday. Rourke would be in New York on Wednesday, Thursday at the very latest. He'd see Saltzman, get his statement, and have himself a witness far more powerful than any he had subpoenaed during his entire committee hearings. A witness who could explode a bomb under Levitt, the Granitzes and the Minskys, put them all behind bars from now until the Messiah came. 'This hotel he's in, can he be reached there?'

Mulholland gave Levitt a grim smile. 'I thought you'd never ask. John and me, we've got the four p.m. to midnight shift. Cushy detail because we were the arresting officers.'

'How much?' Levitt said. He was on firm ground, offering a price for a service.

'How much for what?' O'Brien asked from the back seat.

'What do you think? For tucking him into bed? For reading him a bedtime story? For putting him out of his misery, of course.'

'That's putting us both on the line,' O'Brien complained. 'I've never received a red cent from you.'

'Okay, consider yourself on the payroll as of now.' Levitt knew he was being shaken down. He didn't care. All that mattered was that Mulholland had come to him, had offered him this one golden opportunity to redeem everything. 'Fifty thousand dollars apiece. I'll pay you fifty grand each to shut Harry Saltzman up before he has the opportunity to spill his guts.'

'You've got it,' Mulholland said.

As Levitt started to leave the Impala, O'Brien said, 'That's a lot of dough for doing away with a slug like Saltzman. What's he got on you?'

Levitt swung around and impaled O'Brien with his sharp blue eyes. 'I'm paying you to commit murder for me, not to be my confessor.'

'Hey, I was kidding around, that's all. None of my business what's between you and Saltzman.'

'Kid around all you like when you're taking from someone else. When you're on my payroll, you're serious the whole damned time!' Levitt slammed the Impala's door and hurried back to his own car. Saltzman, who'd been connected with him for forty years, was going to die because he was trying to use what he knew to save his own skin. By Levitt's own convoluted code of ethics, Saltzman was doing nothing blameworthy in threatening to betray an old associate. Levitt would do exactly the same in a similar situation: bargain someone else's neck for his own. If there was any blame at all, it rested with the Rourke family. Like some ancient curse, they'd risen again to plague him.

Sitting behind the wheel of his own car, Levitt watched the two detectives drive off in the Impala. The name of Rourke thundered through his mind, distorting his vision, obliterating the noise of the street. Cars and buses drifted past silently, like ghosts on Hallowe'en. Lights flashed on and off in front of Levitt's eyes. Rourke! It was only because the Rourke family had tried to use Levitt as a political stepping stone that Saltzman possessed such a powerful negotiating tool. Without the Rourkes, Saltzman would have no bargaining power; he would not be able to cut any kind of a deal with a local

293

district attorney. Only with a senator. . . . Levitt could imagine the bargain Saltzman would strike. In return for spilling everything he knew, Saltzman would want a huge payment, a change of identity, the opportunity to live out his remaining years in some spot where no one would ever find him. The Rourkes would have no problem in putting up the money. Plastic surgeons could do wonders with a man's appearance. Saltzman would just vanish.

And still Levitt could find no fault with Saltzman's actions! Levitt had just contracted the murder of a man he'd known for forty years, an ally from the old days. He'd arranged to have Saltzman killed, all because of the goddamned Rourke family! Destroying his entire gambling empire, sullying his reputation in front of the entire nation . . . that was not enough! Now they were forcing him to kill Saltzman!

Levitt knew that if he returned home he would never sleep. He would sit up all night, thinking, imagining the worst. Imagining Senator Rourke changing his mind, returning immediately to the East Coast, getting to Saltzman before Mulholland and O'Brien could earn their money. Would the Senator do that, drop his precious committee work, the opportunity to gain a few more votes, just to rush back and destroy his father's enemies for ever? For once, Levitt's mind was unclear. A jumble of confused thoughts clashed inside his head. He was unable to make sense of it all.

He started the car. Instead of returning to Central Park West, he headed out to Long Island again. Misery and uncertainty, like happiness, should be shared around. To air his troubles would lighten the load on his own shoulders. It was time for others to carry some of the responsibility; he'd carried it alone for far too long.

Twice he had to hammer on the door of Joseph's home before a light came on. Levitt heard the barking of the two Dobermans, the scratching of paws around the base of the door. Footsteps, then the door cracked open to reveal Joseph in pyjamas and a heavy woollen dressing-gown. Behind his legs, the Dobermans strained to see the identify of the late-night caller.

'What are you doing here?' Joseph asked.

'I've got to talk to you.'

294

Joseph shooed away the Dobermans and Levitt entered the house, heading towards the library. As he walked across the entrance hall, Pearl appeared at the top of the stairs. She asked the same question as Joseph, and Levitt beckoned for her to come down. It would lighten his load even more if he could share his misery with two people instead of just one.

They sat down in the library. 'It's Harry . . . Harry Saltzman,' Levitt began. 'I just passed a death sentence on him.'

'You did what?' Pearl's voice was hushed.

'He made a deal with Senator Rourke to save himself. Spill his guts on what he knows about us to get himself off the hook for this Mickey Phillips murder. The Senator's flying back from the West Coast in a couple of hours to meet with him.'

'How did you arrange it?' Joseph asked.

'Saltzman's locked up in a hotel, under guard. The two cops who made the arrest are pulling one of the shifts. For fifty thousand each, they'll arrange a suicide.'

'Lou, Harry helped to save Leo's life when he was ill,' Pearl protested. 'How could you do this?'

'You think I've forgotten all the things Harry's done for us?' Pearl's face swam in front of Levitt as he looked at her. He was losing control of himself, losing control of the whole situation, and he did not know how to regain it. He only understood that he had carried them all for years. They'd ridden to prosperity on his coat tails, on his brain power. And still they wanted more. They couldn't lead themselves, they couldn't help themselves. Babes in the goddamned wood! If he weren't there to guide them, they'd be lost, floundering. Suddenly Levitt felt nothing but contempt. He wanted them to know how much they owed him, how much they'd been made to rely on him. 'Would you rather,' he asked Pearl, spacing out his words, 'see Leo in jail for life instead?'

'Leo? What do you mean? What did he do?'

'Harry could give testimony that Leo helped to get rid of Phil Gerson and his girlfriend.'

'Get rid of them?' Pearl's face wrinkled in puzzlement. 'They . . . they died in a boating accident, didn't they?'

'That was no accident. Phil and his girlfriend took the boat out. Harry and Leo were waiting for them.'

Pearl did not know which shocked her more – that Phil Gerson and Belinda Rivers had been murdered, or that Leo could have participated in such a terrible thing. All she could say was: 'What did Phil and his girlfriend do to deserve . . . to deserve being killed like that?'

'Why don't you tell your mother?' Levitt asked Joseph. Let the older twin get a piece of the grief that was going around wholesale tonight!

'They stole a couple of million dollars from us,' Joseph said softly. 'They were given warnings and they continued to steal.'

'*You* knew? Joseph, you knew about this?'

'Of course he knew!' Levitt snapped. 'He's on the board of directors, isn't he? We all took a vote on what should be done to Phil.'

'Joseph, Phil was your friend. You wanted him as best man at your wedding. And you knew? You voted?' When Joseph turned his face away, unable to look his mother in the eye, she swung back to face Levitt. 'And you . . . Leo is your godson! How could you allow him to be involved in something so terrible?'

'Because he was good at it, that's why!'

'Good at murder?'

Levitt wanted to grab hold of Pearl, grab hold of her and shake her, ask where she'd been living all these years? Where she'd been hiding? But it wasn't her fault. She wasn't to know any better. Levitt had made sure that the dark side of the business was kept from her. She knew only what he wanted her to know. And maybe, just maybe, that had been a mistake. 'Just before William and Susan got married, some Italian thugs tried to muscle in on the trucking company. William got badly beaten up. I was down in Florida at the time with Benny, trying to get to the bottom of the Phil Gerson mess, so William went looking to Leo for help.'

'That night William telephoned me, when I was living on Central Park West,' Pearl recalled.

'Leo got hold of Harry Saltzman and they took care of the problem between them – they burned three guys in a crematorium over in Jersey.'

'Lou, what's happened? What have you done to my family? To my sons? What have you done?'

'I've done nothing. I just carried on business the way it was always carried on.'

'But Leo? Did you have to drag Leo into it?'

'Leo dragged himself into it!' Levitt shot back. He knew that Pearl had always blinded herself to Leo's peculiarities, but had she blocked out everything else as well? How in God's name did she believe they'd all got on so successfully? By going to work from nine to five every day, taking two weeks vacation a year, attending the company Christmas party and the annual softball game? 'If it hadn't been for me and Harry, Leo would have been where Harry is now thirteen years ago!'

Pearl's face turned ashen. In the centre of her forehead, a tiny vein began to pulse. 'Did Leo kill someone thirteen years ago?'

'If he did,' a woman's voice said, 'it wouldn't surprise me in the least.' The three people in the library swung around to see Judy standing in the doorway, a robe covering her nightgown.

'This is a private conversation,' Levitt said.

'Then you should have closed the door. I heard every word upstairs.'

'Okay, you want to hear more? Come in. You might as well know, seeing as it happened on your wedding night. Remember Leo went missing? He wound up in the Village, drunk, and got himself picked up by some *faygeleh*. They went back to the queer's apartment. Afterwards, the queer tried to put the arm on Leo for some money. Leo went crazy and strangled the guy. That's when he called me, to come and bail him out. I contacted Harry, and Harry made the whole thing look like a gas leak. A big explosion which blew the apartment to pieces, burned it out along with a hardware shop that was downstairs. A little while later, he killed a barman who'd seen Leo with the *faygeleh*. And I invented some story for you, Pearl, about Leo being drunk and getting into trouble with the cops.'

'Why did you bother helping him?'

'You think I'd let that kind of trouble come home to roost? I bothered for the same reason that I just paid a couple of cops a hundred thousand dollars to take care of Harry. To keep us . . . this family . . . out of trouble.' Levitt suddenly felt very tired. The wild emotions that had shattered his logic were

297

dissipating. 'That barman could have fingered Leo. Harry can point the finger at us all. One kind act to Leo as a child doesn't balance the books.'

Pearl breathed deeply to steady herself. Her younger son was a killer, a murderer, a man who took life. Joseph had the brains, the education, the skill to run a large corporation. Leo possessed the strength and viciousness to make sure no one got in the way. They were equal partners. Levitt had made them so. What was it he'd once said . . . would he give one lox and the other pickled herring? He'd made certain to treat them equally, pushing each in the direction dictated by character. And without Levitt? Would Leo have been convicted of murder thirteen years earlier, a killing done on his twin brother's wedding night?

'This business with Harry, having to do what you did – it would never have happened without those hearings, would it?'

'I don't know, Pearl.' Levitt closed his eyes, wanting only to rest. He could not even be certain what he had told them. The urge to sleep was overpowering, making him forget.

'No, it wouldn't,' Pearl stated firmly. 'The Rourke family set out to destroy us. They think they failed because they couldn't make anything stick at the hearings. They won't get Harry to talk now, either. But they succeeded all the same, didn't they, Lou? They succeeded beyond their wildest dreams.'

'They succeeded,' Levitt agreed softly. He opened his eyes, forced them to focus on Pearl. At that moment, Joseph and Judy did not exist for him. Only Pearl, a tiny, tearful figure who had seen her cherished illusions shattered into a million fragments. Levitt knew he should never have told her everything, but it wasn't his fault. He'd been too distraught for cold reason, for common sense. It wasn't his fault, just like Harry Saltzman wasn't to blame for trying to save his own skin. It was the fault of the Rourke family. No one else. Just the Rourkes, those goddamned stinking Irish bastards!

The ten-storey hotel in Times Square where Harry Saltzman was installed under guard had been chosen because it catered to a transient trade. Rarely did its guests stay more than two

298

nights. Usually, they stayed only one, military personnel on pass, salesmen in town overnight. The different faces of the three shifts of detectives who shared the guard detail would not stand out among a sea of changing faces.

Saltzman was located on the eighth floor, at the very end of a long corridor leading from the lifts. He had what the hotel termed a suite – a bedroom barely big enough for the double bed it contained, a toilet and shower, and a tiny area with a table, three chairs and a television set that was referred to as the living-room.

When Lieutenant Derek Mulholland and Sergeant John O'Brien arrived for their watch Saltzman was sitting at the table, playing cards with the two detectives who shared the eight-to-four shift. The two newcomers exchanged notes with their predecessors before settling down for their eight-hour watch.

'Play some cards?' Saltzman said to O'Brien.

'Sure. Why not?' O'Brien pulled himself into the table while Saltzman shuffled the deck. Mulholland took a chair over to the door and sat with his back against it as he read the newspaper.

'Hope you guys aren't sore at me,' Saltzman said conversationally.

O'Brien picked up his cards. 'Why should we be sore at you?'

'Well, you make a big murder arrest and it's not going to stand up. I'm going to walk.'

'Don't worry about it. If you've got enough pull to slip out from under a murder-one charge, more power to you. Right, Derek?' he asked Mulholland. The lieutenant just grunted, without even lifting his eyes from the newspaper.

At six in the evening, when the shift was two hours old, Mulholland ordered dinner from a take-out restaurant. Prisoner and guards ate in silence, using plastic cutlery and paper plates which were discarded the moment the meal was over. Afterwards, Saltzman watched the news on television, while the two detectives started a game of gin rummy. When a report of the latest hearing of the Senate Special Committee on Organized Crime came on, Saltzman seemed more attentive, as though he now had a personal stake in the proceedings.

'You must really have some clout with that guy,' Mulholland commented as Senator Rourke's face was displayed on the screen. 'Fancy accommodation like this, the finest food.'

'Never met him in my life,' Saltzman answered. 'Never thought I would. Just shows you how things work out, eh? A big guy like that thinking so much of a little guy like me. America . . . the land of opportunity!'

'Don't knock yourself, Harry,' O'Brien said as he dealt cards to his partner. 'I hear the Romans thought a lot of Judas as well. I just hope you get more out of the deal than he did.'

'What did he get?'

'Thirty pieces of silver.'

'What's that worth?'

O'Brien chuckled and started to sort out his hand.

Saltzman spent the entire evening watching television. At ten-thirty, he covered a yawn with a beefy, hairy hand and announced, 'I'm going to hit the sack.'

'Wish we could do the same,' Mulholland replied. The lieutenant was feeling the first twinges of nerves. The shifts changed in ninety minutes; he and O'Brien did not have that much time. They had to get Saltzman now, as he was preparing for bed. His defences would be lowered. They could not risk a frontal assault while he was in the living-room. With the damage such a ploy would cause, there would be no way of faking a suicide.

'Yeah, we've got to stay on our toes for another hour and a half,' O'Brien added. 'Make sure your ex-pals don't come looking for you with a machine-gun.'

'You make sure you do that,' Saltzman said. 'Senator Rourke won't be very happy if he loses his star performer.'

Mulholland and O'Brien continued to play cards while Saltzman went into the bedroom. There, he slowly undressed, slipping his thin snakeskin belt out of his trousers and hanging it with the suit he would wear the following day. For fifteen minutes he sat by the bedroom window, looking down at Times Square, smoking as he tried to come to terms with his new life. The life of a rat! What else, he asked himself, could he have done? He was in a hole and he possessed the bargaining chips with which to get out. What man

300

wouldn't have done as he had done? Besides, what did he really owe Levitt and the rest of them? Levitt, Saltzman was certain, would have done exactly the same if the situation were reversed. Except Levitt would never have gotten himself into this kind of a fix. Levitt was too smart to get involved with a protection racket like the guild. Levitt had too much brains! That made Saltzman angry, not with himself but with Levitt. If Levitt had so much goddamned brains, let him think his way out of this one!

Stubbing out his cigarette and wearing only his underpants, Saltzman returned to the living-room where the two detectives were still playing cards. He watched a couple of hands and then went to the bathroom. He did not bother closing the door. If the cops wanted to play nursemaid, they'd have to put up with the sound of his taking a leak.

He was standing in front of the toilet bowl, looking down at the water as he shook himself free of the last few drops, when he heard a sound. As he started to turn around, the snakeskin belt was looped over his head and pulled tightly around his throat. Eyes bulging, he fought against the belt held by O'Brien, while in the living-room Mulholland turned up the volume of the television. Voices singing the praises of Coca-Cola drowned out the sounds of struggle from the bathroom.

O'Brien dug his knee into Saltzman's back and pulled as hard as he could. It was like fighting a bull. Despite his own strength and the thirty years difference in ages, O'Brien wasn't sure he would win. He called out Mulholland's name. The lieutenant came in to join the fight, pinioning Saltzman's arms while O'Brien continued to apply pressure with the belt. Slowly, the struggle diminished. Saltzman's eyes rolled up into his head. His body collapsed, his knees buckled and he dropped to the floor. O'Brien went down with him, continuing to squeeze tightly with the belt for another full minute.

'Is he dead yet?' O'Brien whispered. From the living-room came voices singing of Maxwell House.

'If he isn't now, he never will be,' Mulholland answered as he checked Saltzman's pulse. 'Get him in the shower stall.'

Together the two detectives hoisted Saltzman into the stall. Mulholland pulled on the shower head, grunting in satisfaction when it held his weight. He pulled the snakeskin belt

301

tightly around Saltzman's neck and tied the free end around the shower head. When O'Brien let go of Saltzman, the heavy body swayed from side to side, knees bent, weight on the toes.

'Determined guy to hang himself like that,' O'Brien muttered. 'He must have been scared shitless of what his pals would do if they ever caught up with him.'

O'Brien left the bathroom. Mulholland locked the door from the inside and knocked gently on the wall. Moments later, O'Brien's size eleven Oxford smashed into the lock from the other side. A second time, then a third. Wood splintered. The lock gave, the door smashed back. Mulholland came running out of the bathroom, heading for the telephone.

'Saltzman just locked himself in the bathroom and hanged himself!' he yelled when he got through to the precinct house. 'You'd better get a blood wagon up here quick!'

Senator Patrick Rourke Junior had expected to return to New York on Wednesday and meet a star witness who would give him chapter and verse on his father's old enemies. Instead, the Senator came to New York to confront the two detectives who had allowed that witness to commit suicide under their very noses.

The Senator met with the two detectives in an interrogation room at the police station. His brother, John, was also present. They were determined to find out exactly what had happened.

'When we took over the watch, Saltzman was fine,' Mulholland explained to the Rourke brothers. 'He was playing cards, joking with us. Then after dinner, he seemed to get a bit depressed.'

'Did he say anything?' the Senator asked.

'Not at first.'

'What do you mean – not at first?' John Rourke demanded.

'It was while he was watching television, that's when he seemed to change. You were on, Senator . . . it was a report about your committee hearings. Saltzman watched it and he started to talk about being a Judas, like he suddenly wasn't happy about what he'd done.'

'Did he specifically say he'd done the wrong thing?'

'Not specifically,' Mulholland answered. 'But you could see he was having second thoughts about any deal he'd struck with you. The lowest of the low, he kept muttering. Only the lowest of the low sold out their friends.'

'Then what?' John Rourke asked.

'Around ten-thirty he decided to go to bed. First he took a leak, went through the bedroom to the bathroom – '

'And you let him lock the door?' the Senator asked incredulously.

'We didn't know he'd locked the door. We heard water running, the toilet flushing. We didn't think there was anything wrong.'

'Why didn't one of you go into the bathroom with him?'

'For Christ's sake!' O'Brien shouted. 'We couldn't deny the man the basic right of going to the toilet alone!'

'You stupid flatfooted sons of bitches!' Senator Rourke yelled at the two hapless detectives. Followed by his brother, he stormed out of the room, his one clear-cut opportunity of destroying Levitt gone for ever. And all because of two stupid detectives, and a murdering moron like Harry Saltzman who had suddenly succumbed to an attack of conscience. The lowest of the low . . .! Selling out his friends . . .!

No man living was ever going to get Levitt. Patrick Joseph Rourke in Boston would go to the grave unfulfilled. Senator Rourke was beyond that now. He had wasted too much effort on this witchhunt. It was time now to put his own ambitions first.

Chapter Six

For six weeks after Harry Saltzman's death, Levitt lived in the depths of depression. Not because of Saltzman; his initial shame at ordering the killing soon passed, replaced by the certain knowledge that it had been the safe, logical decision to make. It was Pearl who lay at the root of Levitt's misery, her shock at learning of Leo's involvement in murder. All these years Levitt had managed to hide the truth because he wanted to protect her. Until, in one violent outburst, he had blurted out everything.

During those six weeks, Levitt spent much of his time around the apartment, reading, watching television, listening to music. He ventured out only for meals in local restaurants and daylight walks in Central Park, where he would sit by the lake and talk to the elderly men who always seemed to be there, watch children sail boats, or wander through the zoo and stare at the animals. It crossed his mind that this was how it must feel to be retired. Nothing to do but eat and sleep and walk. Retired! He detested the idea, and despised himself for even thinking of it. He wasn't retired. He was simply taking a break, a vacation, that was all. Soon he would pick up the pieces and start to live again.

Several times Pearl telephoned with invitations to dinner, as though she understood the pain Levitt was suffering. Each time, he refused. He could not return to the house in Sands Point. Not yet. But Pearl remained insistent.

'Lou, I don't blame you for anything, can't you understand that?' she asked after yet another refusal.

'You asked me what I'd done to your family, to your sons. If that isn't blaming me, what is?'

'Whatever I said was in the heat of the moment, just the same way you told me about Leo.'

'Have you spoken to him at all?'

'Yes.' A pause followed before Pearl said, 'He took me out to dinner over the weekend.'

'Did you say anything to him?'

'Of course not. He's still my son.'

'Of course not,' Levitt repeated silently. Somehow or other, Pearl would never find fault with Leo. She had always managed to explain away his strangeness. Was she still using the diphtheria as the eternal panacea – finding excuses in the childhood disease and its possible after effects on the nervous system – to absolve Leo of everything he did? Maybe she was right. The diphtheria might be responsible, a delayed action bomb exploding years after it was dropped. Who was he to know anymore?

'Judy left the house before Leo came to collect me,' Pearl volunteered. 'She took the children with her and returned after he'd left.'

'Did she say anything?'

'She didn't have to. It was obvious that she didn't want to be around Leo. Didn't want him near the children.'

Levitt was not at all surprised. Judy had always claimed that there was something wrong with Leo; now she had all the proof she would ever need. Unlike Harry Saltzman, she could never – would never – use it. To harm Leo would harm everyone, including herself and the children. Judy had to live with the knowledge that her brother-in-law was a murderer as well as a homosexual. 'What did Joseph say?'

'She told him and he accepted it. She refuses to be in the house when Leo's around. Have you spoken to Leo at all?'

'No. I haven't been to Granitz Tower. I haven't done anything. I may as well take up golf like Benny.'

'You?' Pearl laughed. 'You and I, we could never play golf, Lou. Too many people would mistake us for the clubs.'

Levitt laughed as well. Knowing that Pearl held no animosity made him feel a little better; some of the self-pity he'd been nurturing began to dissipate. 'Maybe I'll come over to dinner one night soon.'

'Good. You let me know when and I'll make something special for you.'

Levitt hung up the telephone and went to the window. Looking out over the lake in the park, he recognized two frail old men sitting on benches in the late May sunshine. They were always there, just sitting, whiling away the time. Both were retired with nothing better to do than watch other people carry on with their lives. What did they do in the winter or when it rained? What would he do in the winter? Suddenly, Levitt sensed that he was looking at himself. He must have appeared just like that these past few weeks. Perhaps not so old, but certainly just as aimless, a man with no motivation, no reason to get up in the morning. He had to change.

The change came a week later when war erupted in the Middle East. Pearl and Judy instantly became busy with the Hadassah chapter to which they belonged, organizing fund-raising events for Israel. Levitt took another direction completely, one with which he was quite familiar. Although he had a reputation for carefully watching every cent, he had always been a philanthropist where Israel was concerned, constantly claiming it was the duty of every Jew in the world to help the Jewish state. At the start of each autumn, around the time of the Jewish New Year and the Day of Atonement, Levitt would send a percentage of the casinos' take to agencies acting for Israel, much like a man in a synagogue would make a pledge on a UJA card. The casinos were not in existence anymore, but the hotels were. Even if it was the wrong time of year for all the big spenders to be down from New York, Levitt was certain he could make a success of a gala night for Israel.

News of the war reached the United States first thing on Monday morning. By early afternoon, Levitt was in Hallandale, marching into the Waterway Hotel and demanding to see Benny Minsky. When he was told that Minsky was out playing golf, Levitt went looking for him. He found him lining up a putt on the third green.

'What are you doing out here?' Levitt yelled.

His concentration shattered, Minsky dropped his putter on to the grass. 'What does it look like I'm doing? What the hell business have you got down here anyway?'

'There's a war on.'

'I listen to the radio, I read the papers. You didn't have to come all the way down from New York to tell me that.'

'You're running a hotel corporation, Benny. You've got the facilities for dances, shows, banquets – anything to raise money for Israel.'

Minsky's enthusiasm was at the opposite end of the scale to Levitt's. 'You want to put on a dance? You want to arrange a show? Fine! Help yourself, just let me get on with my game.' He picked up the putter and lined up the shot. Levitt snatched it from him and tossed it clean off the green.

'Up in New York, Pearl and Judy are busting a gut with their Hadassah work. I dare say your daughter-in-law, Susan, is doing much the same. I've flown all the way down here to make use of the hotels. And all you can think of is your damned golf game?'

'Lou, we've got a banqueting manager, we've got an entertainments director. We've got managers for this, directors for that. They're all overpaid. Go see them. Leave me alone to play my damned game, will you?'

Levitt marched off the green, disgusted with Minsky. This was the man who, twenty-five years earlier, had moved heaven and earth to see his son *bar mitzvah*ed. Being a Jew had been important to Minsky then. For the first time in his life he'd found some pride in it. Now, when his fellow Jews were fighting for their very existence in a land they'd carved from the desert, all Minsky wanted to do was play golf! Ah . . . what did you expect from a man who'd married a blonde *shiksa* anyway? Decency?

In the Waterway, Levitt located the heads of banqueting and entertainments, and the public relations officer. 'This Saturday, five days from now, I want the Waterway to put on the biggest dinner, dance and show that's ever been seen in Florida. Get the top stars from Vegas. I don't care how you do it, I just want it done. The cost is coming out of the hotel's pocket, and every penny we make is going to Israel. So you know what kind of people we want as guests.' He turned to

307

the public relations officer. 'Get something in the Miami *Herald*, the Ford Lauderdale and Palm Beach papers tomorrow. A big advertisement. A story. And run an ad up in New York. Maybe some of our old customers will come down for it.'

'What about applying for a licence to run a Monte Carlo night?' the entertainments director asked.

'Are you crazy? This place and the Monaco couldn't get a licence to hold a horseshoe pitching contest. No gambling. Just good food, good music and good entertainment. A gala for Israel, five hundred dollars a plate. How many people can we fit in?' he asked the banqueting manager.

'At a pinch? Four hundred. Forty tables of ten.'

'Make the necessary arrangements.' Four hundred people at five hundred dollars a plate. That was two hundred thousand dollars. A good sum. How many bullets would that buy? How many guns? How many gallons of fuel for tanks and aircraft? Suddenly, Levitt felt blood surging through his veins. His head was clear. He was alive again. 'Ill take the first table, right by the stage,' he told the banqueting manager. 'And put Benny Minsky down for one. The other thirty-eight tables are your responsibility. See they're filled.'

Levitt left the banqueting, entertainments and public relations people feeling that their jobs were on the line.

Minsky heard the news when he returned from the golf course after completing a full eighteen holes. He found Levitt settled in a suite of rooms, avidly watching the news reports of the first day's fighting. 'You've got some nerve putting me down for a table.'

'Is it that you're hard up for five grand, Benny, or haven't you got enough people to invite?'

'What's the point? You're not going to put all this together in five days. It can't be done.'

'We need to raise money, Benny. We used to do it. Remember in fifty-six, the Suez Crisis? We raised money for Israel then.'

'We passed the hat around the two casinos. The big winners felt generous. This isn't the same. You're not holding your hand out to gamblers now. You're asking five hundred bucks a head from regular people.'

'Gamblers are regular people.' Levitt held up a hand for Minsky to be quiet as the newcaster gave the latest details of the first day's fighting. Each side claimed to have inflicted heavy losses on the other; the number of destroyed aircraft was in four figures.

'Jesus,' Minsky murmured, 'they're slaughtering each other. They go on at this rate, and there won't be any need for you to hold a gala night on Saturday. There'll be no one left to send the money to.'

'You believe the Arabs' claims?' Levitt asked. 'Or do you believe our claims?'

'*Our* claims? I'm no part of this.'

'You're a Jew, that makes you a part of it.'

'I'm an American,' Minsky countered. 'I hope the Israelis win because they're in the right. I don't hope they win because I think I'm one of them – I'm not.'

'You don't know what you're talking about,' Levitt said angrily.

'I know that I don't make a living out of being a Jew like you do.'

'What's that?' Levitt swung away from the television to stare at Minsky. 'What's that supposed to mean?'

'You've been playing a game all your life, or haven't you realized it yet? Always you've been stressing how important it is to remember that you're a Jew. You've been using it as a weapon, as a defence, as a crutch. Anything ever went wrong, like this Senate Special Committee on Organized Crime, and you brought it up. I knew we got investigated because of the gambling, because of what happened to old man Rourke years ago. But you . . . you had it fixed in your mind that the whole thing was cooked up because the Rourkes were a bunch of Jew-hating bastards.'

'They are.'

'Maybe the old man is, but you've got no proof to hang that label around the necks of his sons.'

'Are you sticking up for them?'

'No way. I'm just pointing out the truth to you. For God's sake, Lou, if a damned dog bit you in the ass, you'd say it was because its owner was an anti-Semite! You thought you were better than me because I fell in love with Kathleen, and then

309

you sneered at me because I wanted to see William *bar mitzvah*ed. You were the one who was so hot to see Pearl's twins get *bar mitzvah*ed . . . the stories you told them about standing up and being counted. You haven't used being a Jew as a religion. You've used it as a goddamned career!'

Levitt turned his back on Minsky and looked at the television screen again. There was never any point in talking to Minsky. How could you argue, discuss any point, with a man who had nothing between his ears but solid bone?

While Minsky continued to play golf and go about his normal routine, Levitt pestered the hotel corporation's department heads. Full-page advertisements appeared in newspapers. The catering staff worked overtime. The entertainments director was constantly on the telephone to agents, trying to line up talent for Saturday night. Levitt arranged for Pearl, Joseph and Judy, Jacob and Anne to fly down from New York for the weekend as his guests. Minsky made the same arangements with his son, daughter-in-law and grandsons.

By Thursday night, the banqueting and entertainments heads were ready to face Levitt with grim news. 'We think you'd better cancel this gala night,' the banqueting manager said. 'Out of thirty-eight tables, we've sold three.'

'What about the show?' Levitt asked the entertainments director. 'Get the big names, publicize them, and people will flock here on Saturday night.'

'I've been on the telephone for two days solid. You don't get top-rate singers and comedians on five days notice. Every Jewish entertainer – every entertainer who even claims he's sympathetic to Israel – is already booked doing some charity show or helping some Israel Bond drive.'

'How come they got booked up so quickly for other Israel functions? How come you were so slow?'

'The war may have started this week, but there's been a threat of war out there for more than a month. All the Jewish stars have been taking bookings for the past four weeks.'

'Wait until tomorrow,' Levitt said. 'Give it one more day. I'll make a decision tomorrow night.'

When the Granitzes and Minskys arrived on Friday evening, Levitt was in a jubilant mood about the progress of the war, but

310

his spirits were dampened by the continuing failure of his big gala night. Only three more tables had been filled, sold to wealthy Floridians who had once been regular patrons at the gambling tables on the top floors of the Waterway and Monaco hotels. All the entertainments director had been able to book were second-string acts, and even then he'd been forced to promise exorbitant fees for their services.

Pearl was quick to spot Levitt's disappointment. She knew him too well for him to hide his feelings. When he told her the reason, she urged him to do what the entertainments and banqueting heads had already suggested. 'Cancel it, Lou,' she advised him gently. 'Admit it was a mistake and walk away.'

'It should have worked. There's no reason for it to flop like this.'

'Cancel it,' Pearl said again. 'You let your emotions override good sense. You didn't have a hope of putting something this big together in just five days.'

On Saturday morning, Levitt held one more meeting with the department heads. Including his own table and Minsky's, ten tables of the forty had been taken. Grudgingly, as if still expecting an eleventh-hour miracle, he gave the order to cancel. Whether he had thought for once with his heart or not, failure in any form did not sit well with Levitt.

Instead of a gala night on Saturday, Levitt settled for dinner with Pearl and her family. Minsky, who had spent the day on the golf course with his son, took his own family to Miami for dinner. Levitt was glad that his partner was absent. He could not have stood for Minsky rubbing in the failure of the gala night. Or even worse, God forbid, commiserating with him, offering sympathy.

Late at night, Pearl sat with Levitt in his suite to watch the news on television. The main story was still the Middle East where, after six days, the war had ended with Israeli forces having achieved the strategic objectives of the Suez Canal, the Jordan River and the Golan Heights. Levitt watched dispassionately as reports were made from the capitals of the combatant countries. Next, the focus switched to the huge drive for funds in the United States. Feeling that his own inadequacy was being thrust in his face, Levitt started to get up to switch off the set.

He froze in mid-stride as a scene was flashed on the screen. A gala dinner, just like the one he had planned. Only this one was in Boston. There were no singers, no dancers, no comedians. Just a solitary speaker.

'What is *he* doing there?' Levitt shouted at Pearl while his finger pointed at the screen. 'What is that bastard Rourke doing at a dinner to honour Israel?'

'Quite, Lou,' Pearl said. 'Let's hear what he has to say.'

Quivering with rage and indignation, Levitt dropped back into his seat. He could not believe his eyes. There, standing in front of American and Israeli flags, was Senator Patrick Rourke Junior, pledging to a hall full of people his support for Israel, his willingness to fight in Washington for increased aid in money and armaments. As the camera swung around the hall, Levitt saw that there were no empty spaces. Here, in Florida, there were vacant tables, but in Boston every seat was taken.

The newscaster's face returned. Levitt heard the man say that more than one hundred thousand dollars had been raised at the two hundred dollar a plate dinner. Further pledges by those attending were expected to increase the amount to more than a million dollars.

'That shitbag!' Levitt yelled out. 'That anti-Semitic Irish *shtikdreck* has got the goddamned nerve to show himself at a fund-raiser for Israel! It's because of him that we raised no money here tonight!'

'Lou, Pearl said softly, 'don't you think you're becoming a little obsessed with him?'

'Obsessed?' Levitt laughed. 'I've every reason to be obsessed. If he hadn't stuck his face into our business, the casinos would still be open. We'd have gone around with the hat again, just like we did in fifty-six. We'd have taken in a fortune. And now he's got the damned nerve to stand up in front of five hundred people, five hundred Jews, and say he supports Israel!

'That *shtikdreck*! He should rot in hell!'

In the basement of his Scarsdale home, Leo also watched the news. He would have preferred to see a movie; he even had the reel containing *Scarface* ready in the projector. But

312

Mahmoud Asawi, who was spending the weekend at Leo's home, had asked that they watch the news. Leo sat back comfortably on the leather couch, barely interested in what was happening in the Middle East. He felt it did not affect him at all. Only if the Arab nations should ever cut off their oil would he feel involved. Mahmoud, however, was tensed up on the edge of the couch, chin resting on his clenched hands as he watched and listened.

When the focus of the report switched to the Jordanian capital of Amman, Mahmoud rose from the couch and stood right in front of the television, as if he could enter the screen, travel along the airwaves and be home.

'What are you getting so wound up about?' Leo asked.

'My family.'

'I thought you didn't give a damn about your family.'

Mahmoud swung around angrily. 'Just because my father does not send me money any more does not mean I have no feelings for him. I have a mother as well, and a brother who is in the army. He is a captain of infantry.'

'It's over. It only lasted for six days. How much harm could have come to your captain-of-infantry brother in six days, for crying out loud?' Leo wondered why Mahmoud had never mentioned his mother and brother before. Had the abrupt ferocity of this odd little war stirred something in his memory, shaken up his emotions? Even after seven months, Leo felt that he knew little about Mahmoud's inner feelings. The Arab youth was a hedonist, interested in nothing but his own pleasure for which Leo paid dearly. His talk, until this moment, had only been of pleasure, of himself. If anything, it had left Leo feeling cheated. He had paid for the body but never for the inner soul. And now that he caught his first glimpse of Mahmoud's inner self, he was not very sure that he welcomed it. Mahmoud's preoccupation with the war was throwing a wet blanket over the weekend for Leo. Why couldn't the young man forget his family just for this weekend, remember them when he was back in his own West Side studio apartment, where he would impose on no one but himself?

'It is easy for you to say the war is over,' Mahmoud said hotly. 'Your side won.'

'My side? Leo was puzzled.

'Your side. The Israelis. You're a Jew, they are your side.'

Leo stared blankly at the young man. In seven months, Mahmoud had never made any reference to Leo being Jewish, to himself being an Arab. Nor had Leo ever commented on the fact. It was as though they were both enjoying the forbidden aspect of their relationship. While other Jews and Arabs fought, spilled blood, they were building a tender, loving relationship. Leo remembered thinking only a few weeks earlier, when the newspapers had been full of a story about two Israeli aircraft shooting down five Syrian jets, that he and Mahmoud could teach the rest of the world a thing or two about coexistence.

'Switch off that garbage,' Leo said at last. 'Let's watch a movie, have a little fun.'

'Your movie is the garbage. You live in the world of your movies. This – ' Mahmoud's eyes flashed as he pointed agitatedly at the screen, where a reporter was speaking from Damascus – 'this is real life. The real life where *my* people are dying so *your* people can steal their land.'

Again with the *your*. *Your* side . . . *your* people. What was it that Lou Levitt had once told the twins? It didn't matter if they forgot they were Jews because sooner or later a *goy* would remind them. Was an Arab a *goy*? Or did the word *goy* cover only whites? Christians? 'Mahmoud, you're beginning to bore me. I pay you well for your company. I don't pay you for your neuroses.'

'You hang a painting in the hall of your mother. It is the first thing you see when you enter this house. Am I not permitted to show some concern for my mother, for my brother?'

'Of course.' Mahmoud had found the surest way to reach Leo. A son's love for his mother was sacred. 'Go ahead, watch the news. Afterwards I can show the movie.' He clasped his hands behind his head, staring at the back of Mahmoud's slim body. The word *your* kept going around in his mind, bouncing off the inside of his skull like a ping-pong ball rattling across the floor. Your . . . your . . . your. . . . For seven months he'd felt as close to Mahmoud as he had ever been to anyone. Mahmoud had been the lover, the mistress, Leo had always dreamed about. Their basic difference, the knowledge that

314

the relationship must remain secret, had added spice. Now Mahmoud was displaying the width of the rift that really existed between them. Leo had mistakenly believed that he had bought and paid for the Jordanian youth, and now Mahmoud was telling him that money meant nothing. Perhaps seven months was long enough. . . . Leo dropped his hands to his side and smiled. The itch didn't come in seven years. It arrived in seven months.

Mahmoud took one step to the side, allowing Leo to see the screen. The newscaster's face was back again. Leo caught words about fund-raising drives in the United States, and he wondered how Levitt had gotten on with his gala night in Florida. Levitt should only know whom his godson was entertaining, Leo thought with a sly smile. Pearl, too. Levitt was busting his back to send a small fortune to Israel, Pearl had worked like mad all week with her Hadassah chapter, and Leo had been the lover of a Jordanian youth for the past seven months!

A picture of a hall full of tables flashed on to the screen, and Leo heard a familiar, hateful voice. Instead of saying, 'It's quite a switch from driving a cab to being vice-president of a thriving real estate company,' the voice was now pledging support for Israel, promising to fight in Washington for increased financial and military aid.

'There!' Mahmoud spat as he spun around to face Leo. 'That man who tried to disgrace you! Even he is on your side!'

Leo sat gaping at the picture. Only when it finally faded did he seem to notice Mahmoud glaring at him. 'Did you hear what I said? That man who tried to disgrace you is on Israel's side. He wants to fight in Washington to get the Israeli expantionists more guns, more bombs, more planes with which to kill my people!'

A spark of sadistic mischief took fire in Leo. He wanted to tease Mahmoud, see how far he could push the young man. 'Oh, he'll do it. He carries a lot of weight in Washington. He wants to be the next President of this country and he's got a lot of friends in influential places. When he gets in, this country will supply Israel with nuclear weapons.'

Mahmoud's lips were stretched tight. His eyes blazed and his body trembled. He had no idea that his lover was goading him; he took everything Leo said at face value. 'My people

315

get no help at all. Israel gets help from everyone. Do you know what my people call your President Johnson?' Leo shook his head. He didn't know and he didn't really care. 'They call him Johnson the Jew because of all the support he gives to Israel. And this man, if he becomes President, you say he'll give even more.'

'No. I didn't say *if*,' Leo replied, fanning his sadism to fresh flames. 'I don't think there's any *if* about it. Senator Rourke will be our next President.'

Mahmoud spat drily at the television. 'That for Senator Rourke. And that for his influential friends in high places. My people will fight on for ever to regain the land that has been stolen from them. We will kill the Israelis and we will kill those who aid them. Even those in high places in America. That way we will show the Americans how costly is their support of Israel.'

Leo turned the screw another notch. 'It wouldn't show Americans a thing. Murders here are a dime a dozen. Even if you shoot the President, ten seconds later the vice-president steps into his shoes and nothing really changes. The policies remain the same.'

'Maybe nothing would change here, but in my country it would change. It would give my people great strength to know that they are not completely impotent.'

'It would give them a hero, is that what you mean? What use is a hero if he's locked up in jail?'

'He would be a martyr. A martyr to a worthwhile cause.'

Abruptly, Leo's streak of sadism burned itself out. Replacing it in his mind was a picture of his mother, her anguish at the Senate Special Committee hearings. He had seen her reduced to tears and he had been unable to do anything about it. And the casinos in Florida, London, the Bahamas. . . . 'Would you,' he asked Mahmoud softly, 'want to become such a hero?'

Mahmoud gazed stupidly at Leo for several seconds. 'Are you proposing what I believe you are proposing?'

Leo just smiled.

'Why would you want to see a friend of your people killed?'

'I keep telling you . . . the Israelis are not my people. My people are right here in this country.'

Mahmoud turned towards the television again. When he saw an advertisement, he snapped off the set. 'You yourself pointed out the difference between a hero and a martyr. I do not wish to become a martyr for anything.'

Leo appeared crestfallen. His face fell and his voice, when he eventually spoke, was laced with sorrow. 'I thought I saw something in you, Mahmoud. I thought I saw fire, a desire for justice, the courage to right a wrong no matter what the cost.'

'You would like to see that man dead, would you not?'

'Whether he lives or dies is of little concern to me,' Leo lied easily. 'He tried his hardest to hurt me and my family, and he failed miserably.'

'Nonetheless, you would like to see him dead.'

'Let's just say I wouldn't wear sackcloth and ashes for him.'

'That is what I thought. I have no desire to be a martyr. The robes of a hero would suit me well, but not the rags of a martyr. I have too much living to do, and I do not intend to waste my life behind bars.'

'No one said you had to be a martyr.'

Interest flickered in Mahmoud's dark eyes. 'Escape would be possible after committing such a deed?'

'It would be possible.'

'How?'

Leo shrugged his shoulders. 'There are ways.'

'You are serious, are you not?'

'Only if you are.'

Mahmoud seemed disconcerted as the enormity of the proposition suddenly became totally clear to him. The killing of an enemy . . . the killing of a United States senator, a man who was heading for the top position of the mightiest country in the world. 'A man who did such a thing and escaped would have to leave this country. Where would he go?'

'With half a million dollars, such a man could live anywhere he chose.' Leo was certain that the Jordanian was motivated by money, and he was not wrong.

'Half a million dollars.' Mahmoud relished the sound of the amount on his lips. 'A very wealthy hero. But if such a thing came about, what would happen to us?'

'We lived before we met each other. We'd live again.'

'No, I do not mean that. There would be a connection.'

No, there wouldn't, Levitt wanted to say. No one would ever connect me to you, or you to me. Leo had initially insisted upon the secrecy to protect himself, but now he could see it possibly yielding an infinitely more valuable result. 'There might be a connection only if you were caught and identified. Like I said, there are ways to avoid that.'

Mahmoud stood in front of the television set, rubbing his index finger across his bottom lip. Leo watched expectantly, then his optimism plummetted when Mahmoud shook his head and grinned. 'No, Leo, no. Why are we even discussing such a thing? Let us watch your movie instead. What was it tonight? *Scarface*?'

He sat down on the couch while Leo turned on the projector. . . .

Mahmoud left Leo's home late on Sunday night to return to his studio on West 72nd Street. Leo stayed awake, sitting in his basement cinema while *White Heat* unfolded on the screen in front of him. He had seen the movie countless times, and still that ending never failed to thrill him. The last of the great old-fashioned gangster films, a blazing, roaring apocalypse of a finale.

The telephone rang and Leo stared at the instrument with annoyance. Who could be calling at this hour? Despite having seen the movie so many times he was still loath to stop the projector and answer the call. Leave it alone, he told himself. Half a dozen rings and the caller would give up.

Half a dozen rings were followed by another half dozen. Disgusted, Leo answered with a petulant 'Yes!'

'I am coming back to see you.'

'Why?'

'My brother . . . my brother, Hussein, is dead.'

Leo could hear the tears in Mahmoud's voice. After a week of watching reports on television, Leo felt that the war had struck home. Not with the death of a friend, but with the death of an enemy.

The Cadillac convertible that Leo had paid for swung through the gates thirty minutes later. Leo figured that Mahmoud must have broken every speed limit to make the journey in that time. The youth's face was streaked with dried

318

tears. His hands clutched a Western Union telegram. The block capitals looked so impersonal, Leo couldn't help thinking. News of a death in the family should be carried in copperplate, some fancy script. Not block capitals.

'From your father?' Leo asked.

Mahmoud nodded. 'The first time he has contacted me in almost a year. And this is what he has to say.' He repeated the words he'd memorized. 'Your brother Hussein killed Jerusalem June seven.'

'Were you and your brother close?'

'He was my brother,' Mahmoud answered in a tone that inferred nothing more needed to be said. 'Were you really serious before?'

'About Senator Rourke?'

'About the enemy of my people. About the half million dollars. About the escape.'

'I can arrange it all.'

Mahmoud stood silently for several seconds, balancing the death of his brother, the opportunity for revenge, the half million dollars against the enormity of the deed. 'Show me how well you can arrange it all, Leo, and then I will give you my answer.'

Leo contacted Lou Levitt the moment he returned from Florida. 'Uncle Lou, I've got to see you right away. Can you come into Granitz Tower?'

Levitt was still feeling depressed about the Waterway gala-night fiasco. Never mind what Pearl had told him about letting his emotions get the better of him, he continued to believe that the gala should have worked. Ten tables out of forty, including two that had been booked by himself and Minsky! The humiliation of having to cancel something he had planned! The entertainments director hadn't worked hard enough to pull in the big names. The public relations officer hadn't broken his back hard enough to get his stories everywhere. The advertising department had used the wrong creative people. Levitt could find fault with every one but himself.

'Leo, is it really important, or can it wait?'

'It's important, Uncle Lou. You'll want to hear this.'

'Okay.' After replacing the receiver, Levitt looked through

the window at the park and the lake. That's where he'd like to be, sitting on the bench talking with the old men. The only topic in New York these days seemed to be the Six Day War, as the media had dubbed it. He could have told those old boys a thing or two; he'd have had them believing that his big gala night in Hallandale had been a roaring success. He might even have had himself believing it as well.

He arrived at Granitz Tower forty minutes later and was shown in to Leo's office. At first he looked around, expecting to see Joseph. 'He's not here,' Leo said. 'This isn't Granitz Brothers business. It's strictly between me and you.'

'What's between you and me?'

Although there was no one who could overhear, Leo dropped his voice to a mere whisper. 'Did you see the news on Saturday night, Senator Rourke at that fund-raising dinner in Boston?'

'What about it?' The question was snapped out. Levitt didn't need to be reminded.

'How would you like to see him dead?'

Levitt regarded Leo as though he were mad. 'Don't you ever listen? I've told you a thousand times that you don't kill a United States senator.'

What Leo had to say next took courage, because it would destroy the veil of secrecy with which he'd protected his affair with Mahmoud Asawi. I know someone who'll do it for us, provided he's assured of half a million dollars and an escape.'

'Who is this someone?'

'A young man named Mahmoud Asawi.'

'An Arab?'

'A Jordanian. He's from Amman. He came over here to study.'

'How do you know him?'

'He's a friend.'

'You're friends with an Arab?' Levitt's eyes registered total disbelief. 'How the hell could you be friends with an Arab? Wait a minute. Have you been –?'

'Having an affair with him? Yes, I have.' Leo saw no shame in admitting it now. Levitt would overlook such an indiscretion when he fully realized its ramifications.

Levitt's reaction was exactly as Leo had imagined it that

first night with Mahmoud. 'How could you . . . how could you have . . .?' Levitt's voice trailed off, unable to speak the horrifying thoughts that pounded in his brain.

'Have been lovers with him? Lovers with an Arab?' Leo asked. There was nothing wrong in using the term.

'You said it, not me. How could you do it? He'll stab you in the back as soon as look at you. He'll cut your stupid throat while you're asleep. Has he called you a goddamned filthy Jew yet?'

'No. Nor will he.'

'How come you're so sure about that?'

'Because I've shown him sympathy. Because I've pointed out that Senator Rourke is my enemy as well as his enemy.'

'And just because of that,' Levitt said disbelievingly, 'he'll go out and kill the Senator for you.'

'No, not because of that. Mahmoud spent the weekend with me. I put the idea to him then. He toyed with it, interested but not committed. When he left me to return home, something happened to make up his mind.' Leo told Levitt about the cable that had been waiting for Mahmoud, and the little man's scepticism changed to interest.

'You told him you could arrange the escape?'

'Yes.'

'He believed you?'

'I think so.'

Levitt stroked his chin. 'I don't know. Half a million dollars . . . that's a lot of money, Leo.'

'It cost us a hundred thousand to shut Harry Saltzman's mouth. Surely a United States senator, a presidential hopeful, is worth five times what Harry was worth. Especially when that half million is only in the form of a non-recourse promissory note.'

'What about your connection to him? How many people have seen you together?'

'Uncle Lou, if I kept this relationship secret from you, even God wouldn't know about it.'

'I want to meet him. I want to make the final judgement for myself.'

'I can have him over at my place whenever I want. I pay him enough.'

321

'You do that. Let me see if this Arab boyfriend of yours is really as gullible as he sounds. Or whether you're the gullible one.'

'Not me, Uncle Lou,' Leo said proudly. 'There's nothing gullible about me.'

We'll see, Levitt thought, still unconvinced that Leo could have manipulated this Arab into such a position. We'll see. 'As you're so proud of your secrecy, don't breathe a word of this to anyone. Especially not to your mother. This'll be between me and you, Leo, okay?'

Leo felt a trace of disappointment. This would be the achievement of his life, getting even with the man who'd hurt his mother in front of millions of eyes. And he wouldn't be able to tell anyone.

Not even his mother.

Mahmoud approached his meeting with Levitt cautiously. He had seen the little man on television during the Senate Special Committee hearings and knew that he, like Leo, wanted to see Patrick Rourke Junior dead. But Levitt was another Jew, and since learning of the death of his brother, Hussein – killed by Jews while defending East Jerusalem against the invading Israeli army – Mahmoud was naturally wary.

The meeting was held late at night in Leo's home. Watching Mahmoud's car swing right into the grounds where no one would be able to see the licence plate or the driver, Levitt was able to appreciate first-hand the careful manner in which Leo had gone about the relationship. Levitt had never even guessed that such an association could be taking place. Leo and an Arab. For seven months yet! Leo had even got the Arab to go to Florida over Christmas, register in Miami under a false name. If I don't know about it, Levitt mused, even God doesn't know. The deception gave him a new understanding of Leo. He could plot and scheme with the best of them. Even with me, Levitt thought, and could conjure up no finer compliment for anyone.

After Leo made the introductions, both men stood facing each other silently. At last, Levitt offered his hand. He wasn't happy about shaking the hand of an Arab, but it was a small price to pay if Leo's claim was true. The final, devastating blow to the Rourke family. A blow struck not by an American, but by a Jordanian. A blow struck by an Arab at a United States senator who was loud in his support of Israel. A double-edged sword. A shattering disaster for the Rourke family, and the reason for a wave of anti-Arab sentiment in the United States. Levitt did not know whether Leo had forseen this added benefit. It didn't really matter. Leo had laid the groundwork, and for that alone he deserved all of Levitt's admiration.

'I was sorry to hear about your brother,' Levitt said.

'Do you really care?'

'I do. War is a waste, and this is a war that should never have happened. Jews and Arabs could coexist peacefully if bigger powers left them alone to do so.'

Listening, Leo was taken in completely by Levitt's air of sincerity. The little man wasn't pushing his ideas or his sympathy. He was speaking in a calm, matter-of-fact tone that dared anyone to contradict him.

'All I understand is that you hate this Senator Rourke as deeply as I do,' Mahmoud said. 'And you would pay me half a million dollars to do this thing.'

'We would pay you. We would help you.'

'Help me? How?'

Levitt looked deeply into Mahmoud's dark eyes. Fire burned there. Flames of fanaticism, of revenge. Most importantly, flames of greed. Levitt knew of Leo's arrangement with the Arab. Money to purchase luxury was this young man's sole motivation. Like everyone else, he had a price. Levitt was reassured that his lifelong dictum still held true. 'Before I can tell you that, we have to decide where this act will be committed. Only after we learn that – see the surroundings, the area involved – will we able to plan.' He saw doubt begin to flicker in Mahmoud's eyes and added quickly, 'I am a man of my word. If I say these things will be done, they will be.'

Mahmoud looked at Leo, who slowly nodded his head. They had Mahmoud exactly where they wanted him. Revenge and greed – an infallible combination to leave a man dangling at the end of a thread.

'Leo will stay in touch with you,' Levitt said. 'When the time is right, we will meet again.' He offered his hand. Mahmoud shook it more readily this time. 'To our mutual ambition, to our mutual revenge.'

The moment Mahmoud left the house, Levitt turned to Leo. 'Drive me to Flushing.'

'Why?'

'It's time to see a friend in the police department, Lieutenant Mulholland.'

The two men made the long journey from Scarsdale to Flushing. Mulholland lived with his wife in an unprepossessing duplex, half of which was rented out. At the end of the street was a payphone. Levitt dropped in a dime and dialled the detective's number. Mulholland's voice was blurred with sleep when he answered, but he snapped alert the moment he recognized Levitt's voice.

'We're parked at the end of the street. Come out, we're going for a ride.'

Mulholland threw on some clothes, let himself out of the house and walked quickly along the street. Leo's car was parked in the shadows, far from the nearest streetlamp. The detective climbed in, sharing the front bench seat with the two other men.

'I've got a proposition for you,' Levitt said as Leo drove. 'It'll make you look like the biggest hero since George Washington.'

'I've already got a chest full of citations.'

'There's a hundred thousand dollars that goes with this particular citation.'

'Maybe I can find the space for one more.'

'First, I want you to find out for me if Senator Patrick Rourke Junior is making any appearances in New York. He was at a big fund-raising dinner for Israel in Boston the other night. Find out if he's going to be doing anything here.'

'That should be easy enough.'

'Next, I want you to be near him while he's in New York.'

'Me?' Mulholland laughed. 'If he saw me, he'd have a fit.'

'I'm not telling you to put yourself in his pocket. Just be in the general area, understand?'

'If he's somewhere in Midtown, I can always find a legitimate reason to be there.'

'Good. Then I want you to meet a friend of ours.'

'That's it?'

'The rest comes later. Leo, drive Lieutenant Mulholland home and let him get back to sleep.'

The detective was dropped off at the end of his street and left to wonder what the meeting had really been about. A hundred grand to be a hero? Levitt must have something big up his sleeve this time.

Three weeks passed before Mulholland discovered the information Levitt needed. A pro-Israel rally was scheduled to be held the following Sunday outside the United Nations Building on the East Side of Manhattan. Among the speakers would be the Israeli Ambassador to the United Nations, the Mayor of New York, and several congressmen and senators. A late addition to the list of speakers was Senator Patrick Rourke Junior.

Leo was told to summon Mahmoud to the house in Scarsdale. When Levitt arrived, he had Mulholland with him. 'This is the man who will help you to escape,' he told the Jordanian youth.

Mahmoud regarded the detective quizzically. 'How will you do that?'

Mulholland gave an easygoing smile. With his carefully groomed grey hair, tanned, open face and tall, athletic build, his reassuring all-American looks had always been his greatest asset. Three of the commendations he'd earned during his twenty-nine years with the department stemmed from his ability to talk an armed man into surrendering. 'I'm going to show you,' he said, and pulled a hand-drawn map from his pocket.

'This is United Nations Plaza. There'll be a platform erected there, that's where all the hotshots will sit. We figure there are going to be about fifty thousand people there on Sunday. That's a lot of people, a lot of confusion and noise. To get to the platform, the speakers will have to walk from their limousines which are parked here.' Mulholland's finger jabbed the map at the point where First Avenue and East 46th Street intersected. 'There'll be police barriers up to protect the speakers from the crowd, but they'll stop to shake a few hands on the way. Never knew a politician who could pass up the opportunity of shaking hands.'

'Where will I be?'

'Right here, right at the start of the aisle that the police barriers will form. With this.' Mullholland lifted a small case he had brought to the house. Opening it, he displayed a double-barrelled shotgun. The butt had been shortened and shaped like that of a handgun. The two barrels had been sawn right down. 'Ever use one of these?'

Mahmoud picked up the weapon and examined it. 'Never.'

'Don't worry. Even a blind man couldn't miss with one of these. All you've got to remember to do is press down with your front hand. Don't let it kick up and spray into the air Now, as Senator Rourke passes close to you, you call his name. Evcryonc's going to be calling him, wanting to shake his hand. You do the same. And when he looks in your direction, you do this.' Mulholland took the sawn-off shotgun from Mahmoud, levelled it at the wall and pulled both triggers. The click of the hammers falling on to empty chambers was deafening. Mahmoud jumped back. Even Leo flinched. Only Levitt showed no emotion, other than a grim smile as he envisioned Mahmoud squeezing the triggers on a loaded gun, with Patrick Rourke Junior right in front of him.

'Where does that gun come from?' Leo wanted to know.

'Evidence room. Used in a bank hold-up a long time ago.'

'Can it be traced?'

'No way.'

'What happens after I fire?' Mahmoud asked.

'There'll be pandemonium like you never saw before. I'll be standing within a couple of yards of you and I'll arrest you. You'll hand me the gun. I'll put the cuffs on you, get you out of there. Only you'll never see a squad room. You'll be in my car so quickly, no one'll know what really happened.'

'What about the money, the half a million dollars?' Mahmoud asked Levitt.

'It'll be waiting for you. Name a bank, name a drop-off point. Wherever you want it to be.'

Mahmoud took the shotgun from Mulholland examined it again. His heart was racing, his brain in turmoil. Was it really this simple to kill such a powerful figure in America? Walk right up to him, call him by name? Watch as, hand outstretched, his face collapsed in shock and disbelief? And

326

then this policeman would perform the fake arrest, spirit him away before anyone had a chance to work out what had really happened.

'Well?' Levitt asked. 'You wanted your chance to make a hero out of yourself. A rich hero. We've given it to you.'

Mahmoud looked past Levitt to Leo. In Leo's eyes he would find the truth. Leo had loved him. Leo would not lie. What he saw in Leo's eyes was trust and tenderness, a reflection of the love they had shared these past eight months. It was enough. Clasping the shotgun tightly to his chest, Mahmoud said, 'I will do it.'

Sunday dawned bright and clear. The weather forecast was for continued sunshine with a high in the afternoon of eighty-five degrees. To the workmen erecting the platform on which the speakers would sit, it felt like a hundred and twenty degrees by ten in the morning.

At eleven-thirty, the platform was ready, gaudily draped in the red, white and blue of the American flag, and the pale blue and white of the Israeli colours. Police barriers went into position. By midday, three hours before the rally was due to start, the first listeners drifted in to claim a good position. Many carried flags, Israeli and American. The entire area soon became awash with red and white and two shades of blue. There was a carnival atmosphere to this outpouring of support for Israel that would undoubtedly be seen by those inside the United Nations Building who were hostile to the country; that was part of the idea of staging the rally there.

Mahmoud Asawi approached United Nations Plaza at twelve-thirty. He wore heavy sunglasses and a white cotton hat. Pinned to the front of the hat was an enamelled pin of crossed American and Israeli flags. From his left hand hung a bulky shopping bag. In the bag, hidden beneath a sweater, a thermos flask of cold soda and a book, was the sawn-off shotgun that Mulholland had provided. A single shell rested beneath each hammer.

Instinctively, Mahmoud felt out of place the moment he reached the edges of the gathering throng. He found himself surrounded by men and women, young and old. Some of the men wore hats or *yarmulkes*, a few even sported the

327

flourishing beards and sideburns of the orthodox. Mahmoud realized instantly how dark his skin looked in comparison with everyone else. Surely it would be an immediate give-away. All the police had to do was look at him and they would know he was an Arab. He would be dragged from the crowd, his bag searched. The shotgun would be found. He would be flung into jail. What kind of a hero would that make him? And how would Leo and the little man he referred to as Uncle be able to help him then?

A yell ripped through the air to Mahmoud's right. He spun around, expecting to see accusing fingers pointed at him. Instead, he saw a group of young people linking arms around each others shoulders. They were dancing! Singing at the tops of their voices and dancing! Were these people utterly mad? He had come here to commit a political assassination, and all around him these maniac Zionists were dancing.

Slowly, Mahmoud's panic passed. The dancers, the singers, they all signified that his own arrival had gone un-noticed. He even saw men and women with skins darker than his own. Oriental Jews, Jews who had fled from Arab countries to live in Israel. Now they were in New York, demonstrating in front of the United Nations. Mahmoud prayed that none of them spoke to him. He could converse only in Arabic and English. He didn't understand more than a smattering of Hebrew; if someone mistook him for an Oriental Jew, spoke to him, he would be doomed.

The crowd grew larger as Mahmoud pressed himself towards the police barrier in the exact spot that had been pointed out to him on the map. He felt bodies crushing in behind him and looked around wildly. He saw a snap-brimmed hat made of straw with a wide, colourful band around it. Beneath the hat were sunglasses. Despite them, Mahmoud recognized the face he had seen in Leo's Scarsdale home, the police detective who would escort him from this crowd, assist in his escape. He felt Mulholland's gaze sweep over him and then on. Mahmoud tore his own eyes away from the tall detective. There was to be no liaison between the two men, no opportunity for anyone in the vast crowd to notice a connection, to remember. . . .

At two forty-five, the limousines started to arrive. The

328

Mayor of New York was first, passing along the narrow aisle within two feet of where Mahmoud stood. Hands were thrust out, and the Mayor took pains to shake every single one. Mahmoud saw a light brown hand in front of him, the Mayor's white hand grasping it over the police barrier. Only when the handshake had been broken and the Mayor had moved on did Mahmoud realize that the hand had been his own. He had shaken the hand of the Mayor of New York. The Mayor had accepted him as one of the crowd. So, too would Senator Rourke when he arrived. He would reach out to shake Mahmoud's hand just as the Mayor had done. It would be the last hand the politician would ever attempt to shake.

More people passed along the aisle between the police barriers. Mahmoud had seen their photographs in newspapers, on television, but he could not put names to the faces. It didn't matter; he was interested today in only one face. Anger suddenly gripped him as he identified one of the speakers, the portly, bespectacled figure of Israel's Ambassador to the United Nations, the man who lied so eloquently in front of the General Assembly. It took every ounce of Mahmoud's self-control not to reach into the bag there and then and abort his mission by killing the wrong man. The moment passed as the Ambassador continued on up to the platform and took his seat.

Mahmoud looked around to see that the straw hat and sunglasses had moved closer, no more than five yards away, no more than half a dozen people separating the detective from himself. His confidence grew until he could feel it bursting through his chest. He was on wings, soaring above this crowd, untouched by all the madness, the noise, the Broadway atmosphere. He was a man with a mission that would rectify all the injustices his people had ever suffered.

He heard a roar of applause, the clapping and cheering of thousands. Turning away from Mulholland, Mahmoud saw another limousine disgorging its occupants. Two men, obviously brothers by their shared bushy light brown hair, their fresh, ageless Irish faces. Mahmoud had seen both men on television; he had no trouble recognizing them. Senator Patrick Rourke Junior, and his brother, John Rourke. Mahmoud's hand snaked into the bag, past the book, the thermos

329

flask of cold soda, past the sweater until it gripped the smoothly shaped wooden handle of the sawn-off shotgun. . . .

The narrow aisle between the grey-painted police barriers stretched before the Rourke brothers. The crowd crushed forward on either side of the barriers but the space remained intact, leading up to the platform like Moses' parting of the Red Sea. Bodies hung over the barriers, hands were outstretched, to pat, to shake, to applaud. Senator Rourke felt an overwhelming flow of emotion. All these people, these thousands of people, cheering him. So what if the Primaries were still almost a year away? The popularity he was gaining here would not fade by then. Nor would the positive publicity he'd achieved through his Senate Special Committee hearings across the country. The Six Day War could not have occurred at a better time, right on the heels of these hearings, and he'd been able to use it to keep his name firmly in the headlines. He'd get the Jewish vote, whether his father approved or not. To a degree, he could understand his father's bitterness, his anti-Semitism, but all that had been so long ago, in the Thirties. This was the Sixties. It was a different world completely, and Senator Patrick Rourke Junior was a different Rourke to his father.

'Make it good,' John Rourke whispered to his brother as they started the walk towards the narrow aisle leading to the platform. 'Fifty thousand votes right here.'

Patrick grinned. 'Have you counted them already?'

The grin was returned. 'A good photographer's supposed to be able to wet his finger, stick it in the air and come up with the right shutter speed and lens opening. I can do the same with votes. That's why I run your campaigns.'

'I don't want you to run my campaigns. I want you to win them for me.'

'Consider it done. Don't forget to shake a few hands on the way up there.'

Senator Rourke reached out to the first hand that came close to him. An Israeli flag was thrust in his direction. He took it, waved it above his head to draw even more cheers. Vote-getting had never been so easy. Everywhere he heard his name being called. Wherever he turned he saw a smiling

330

face, a hand in his own. Never had the Senator seen such an enthusiastic crowd. Even if it had poured today, he was sure the crowd would have been just as large, just as cheerful. American support for Israel was a highly emotive issue. Votes were given, or denied, because of emotions. And the Senator, when he finally spoke to this wonderful crowd from the flag-festooned platform, would be as emotional as any Oscar-winning actor had ever been.

'Senator Rourke! Over here! A big smile!'

The Senator looked to his left, straight into a camera lens. He waved his hand, made his smile even broader as the shutter was released. Cameras seemed to be appearing everywhere. He wondered why. All these people had to do was write to his office in Washington. They'd get an official portrait of far higher quality than the snapshots they'd get here. Signed no less.

He looked directly ahead into the beckoning lens of a television camera and gave his big confident smile for the six o'clock news.

'This way!' another voice called out. 'This way!'

Senator Rourke looked to his right, into a light brown face, eyes that were shaded by sunglasses, hair that was covered by a white cotton hat. He saw the enamelled pin of the American and Israeli flags pinned to the hat. What kind of a camera was that the young man held? Twin lenses. He hadn't seen a stereo camera for years; he didn't know that people still used them. In all the excitement, the Senator did not even recognize the twin barrels of the sawn-off shotgun for what they were.

Mahmoud's lips parted in a wide, victorious smile. His teeth gleamed in the sunlight. Two barrels. Two brothers so close together. Remembering to hold the weapon down, he pulled one trigger and then the next. Two booming explosions, so close together they sounded like one, rose above the shouting of the crowd. The Senator flew back against the police barrier, his chest and stomach ripped open. His brother, John, fell on top of him. On the dry, baked concrete, their blood mixed in an ever-widening scarlet pool.

Next to Mahmoud, a girl screamed. All round him the crowd scattered. Suddenly he had space in which to move, in which to escape. Everything was happening just as he had been told it would happen. He swung around, the shotgun still held in front of him. Five yards away, now separated by no one, was Mulholland in the straw hat and sunglasses. He was crouched in a shooter's stance, a heavy revolver gripped by both hands in front of his face.

'Drop it!' Mulholland yelled.

Mahmoud's fingers started to open. The revolver in Mulholland's roared, flame spurted from the muzzle. Mahmoud felt no pain as the bullet smashed into his head to give him a tiny blue-rimmed eye directly between the other two. He felt only surprise. His final thought as he crashed through the barrier and fell on to the blooded corpses of the Rourke brothers was: Why?

Chapter Seven

News of the assassinations of Senator Patrick Rourke Junior and his brother interrupted regularly scheduled radio and television programmes, including the Sunday afternoon concert to which Leo was listening. An announcer, voice charged with emotion, broke in to say that Senator Rourke and his brother, John, had been shot to death by an assassin during a pro-Israel rally in front of the United Nations Building. The so far unidentified assassin, while trying to escape, had been shot and killed by a New York City detective who had been on the scene.

Leo waited for the music to resume. He felt no sadness about the death of Mahmoud Asawi. His fling with the Arab youth had run its course. There would be other attractive young men to take his place. Perhaps that very evening, Leo would begin the search for a replacement. Mahmoud, like Harry Saltzman before him, had served a purpose. When that purpose was no longer necessary, he had become expendable.

The announcement finished with the promise of an update later in the programme. The music picked up again. Leo leaned back and hummed along, quite content with the world.

He had planned, he had schemed, and he had succeeded. With a smug smile wreathing his face, he wondered how high he had climbed in Lou Levitt's estimation. Leo understood that his twin brother, Joseph, had always held the edge. He'd had the education. He possessed the ability to manage a large corporation, keep his finger firmly on the pulse of every

333

department. But that edge was blunted now. Surely Uncle Lou would recognize Leo's value as well. . . .

Lou Levitt heard the news while at Joseph's home in Sands Point, where he was spending the day. He was sitting outside with Joseph and Judy, watching the children play on the grass with the Dobermans, when Pearl came running out of the house. She had been in the kitchen, preparing dinner. As was her custom, she had a small radio playing popular music.

'Someone just killed the two Rourke brothers, the Senator and his brother John!' Pearl exclaimed.

'Where?' Joseph asked.

'In front of the United Nations Building. There was a rally today, they were speaking at a pro-Israel rally. Everyone was there, the Mayor, the Israeli Ambassador to the United Nations, everyone.'

'Was anyone else killed?' Joseph asked.

'No. Just the Rourkes.'

'Did they catch the murderer?' Levitt asked.

'He was shot by a policeman. Killed. How terrible.'

'What, that the murderer was killed?' Levitt asked.

'Everything,' Pearl said.

Levitt led the way inside the house. There was a big radio in the library, along with a television. He chose instead to go into the kitchen and listen to the small radio that had been playing. Bending over it, he paid rapt attention. Pearl, Joseph and Judy crowded in close. The children, outside with the dog, were forgotten.

'Who could have done it?' Pearl asked.

'Don't tell me you're sorry they're dead,' Levitt said.

'Lou, how can you say such a thing at a time like this?'

'You won't see me crying for them. They tried to pillory us. Why should any of us be sorry?'

The four of them remained in the kitchen for another fifteen minutes until an update was given. The assassin had been identified as Mahmoud Asawi, a Jordanian national living in the United States as a student. The detective who had shot him down was Lieutenant Derek Mulholland, a twenty-nine-year veteran of the force with many commendations for bravery.

'So now he'll get another one,' Judy remarked drily. 'He'll

be called a hero, and no one will ever know for sure why this Jordanian student killed the Rourkes.'

'Don't you know that already?' Levitt asked.

'Do you?'

'Of course I do. These Arab *mamzarim*, they aren't satisfied with trying to push the Israelis into the sea. So they come over here and murder our leaders who are sympathetic to Israel.'

'*Our leaders*?' Joseph asked incredulously. 'You just said you wouldn't shed any tears for Senator Rourke, and now you're calling him your leader.'

'You know what I mean. The Arabs bring their dirty war over here. They got their butts kicked in face-to-face battle, so now they come here and gun down unarmed politicians who've said they were wrong to start the war in the first place. It's going to backfire, Joseph, you mark my words. By this time tomorrow, there'll be so much revulsion, so much anti-Arab sentiment in this country that the Arabs will need a microscope to find a friend over here in the future.'

The news was repeated; this time it included an interview with Lieutenant Mulholland. Sounding breathless, a little flustered by all the fame that had suddenly been thrust upon him, the detective answered questions.

'What was I doing there? New York in summer is a haven for dips. Dips . . . that's what I said. You know, pickpockets. City full of tourists draws them like a magnet. We had a special detail going today, big crowd, lot of confusion, perfect situation for pickpockets. So we were on the look-out for them.'

'What did you see?' the interviewer asked.

'Nothing, until it was too late. The Senator and his brother, they were walking between the barriers, heading for the platform. All of a sudden there was this tremendous roar. Two roars, but so close together they could have been one. Two barrels of a shotgun. I didn't see the shooting, I only heard it. People started screaming, diving out of the way, and then I saw this man in sunglasses and a white cotton hat. He was holding a sawn-off shotgun. That was when I got my first look at the Rourke brothers, both of them on the ground and covered with blood. This man with the shotgun, he started to swing around towards me. I unholstered my own weapon and yelled at him to drop the shotgun. He didn't listen. He kept on turning. The shotgun was pointing directly at me.'

'But you said you'd heard two roars, two barrels of the shotgun,' the interviewer pointed out. 'Why did you fire? Surely you knew the shotgun was empty.'

'Some guy's holding a sawn-off shotgun . . . I don't know anything and I don't take any chances. I let him have it right between the eyes. Blew that son of a – '

The interview was cut as Mulholland, in the excitement of the moment, lapsed into obscenity. Levitt held back a grin and announced he was going for a walk in the grounds.

He passed Pearl's grandchildren and continued walking. A stiff breeze was blowing in from Long Island Sound to cool the air, bringing with it a hint of the sea. As the breeze swept over him, Levitt experienced an enormous wave of satisfaction, like a mountaineer who looks down at the world from the peak of Mount Everest. With Leo's help, Levitt had conquered his personal Everest. He had put to eternal rest a ghost that had haunted him remorselessly. It seemed that at every turn these past few months the Rourke family had been waiting. The hearings, the forced closure of the casinos in Florida, the loss of the gambling licences in England and the Bahamas. And finally, the fiasco of the fund-raising dinner at the Waterway, while Senator Rourke had been speaking at a dinner in Boston which had been as successful as Levitt's had been abysmal. That was all paid off now. The two hundred thousand dollars Levitt had hoped to raise for Israel was a mere spit in the ocean compared to the wave of anti-Arab feeling that would surely follow the murders of the Rourke brothers. Such sentiments in America would benefit Israel more than money.

'A stroke of genius,' Levitt said softly to himself. Leo had come up with an absolute stroke of genius. He had manipulated the Arab youth as he had once manipulated his twin brother and their mother.

Levitt turned and looked back towards the house, Joseph's house. All these years he had been convinced that only Joseph showed his own personality, the quick mind, the attention to detail, the ability to grasp any situation

336

immediately. Now, with one deft piece of thinking, Leo had placed himself on the same plateau. To cap the comparison, Levitt imagined the twins playing chess. Joseph would follow accepted strategy, build up his position move by move, piece by piece, until he had overwhelming strength on the particular file or diagonal which he had pinpointed as his opponent's weak spot. Leo would work a different game altogether. Out of the blue, he would indulge in a piece of wild, innovative play that would end a game abruptly, a move that would be rewarded by the critics with the double exclamation point, the highest accolade in chess.

Leo was ready, Levitt decided, to be told the truth about the death of the man he believed to be his father.

That night, as Leo was preparing to drive into town to begin the search for Mahmoud's successor, the telephone rang. It was Levitt, offering an invitation to his apartment on Central Park West. The invitation was delivered tersely, and not for a moment did Leo consider saying he had other plans. Levitt's tone implied that all other plans should be placed immediately on the back burner.

Leo had little doubt that the summons concerned the events of that afternoon outside the United Nations Building. Shock waves were being felt throughout the country, throughout the entire world. As one, politicians on both sides of the House had risen to cry out against the killings of the Rourke brothers. President Johnson, it was even rumoured, was going to make a condolence call at the Boston house of Patrick Joseph Rourke.

Levitt had the television on when Leo arrived. Silently, they sat down in front of the set for a few minutes to stare at the footage taken by the cameraman who had been tracking the Rourke brothers along the aisle towards the platform. Levitt showed no emotion as the drama unfolded, but Leo watched hungrily. Mahmoud's outstretched hand . . . instead of a handshake, the sawn-off shotgun's double blast . . . the Senator and his brother reeling back. And then the finale, Mahmoud turning around to face Mulholland, believing that the detective in the straw hat would afford him escape. Another roar of gunfire, and the drama was over.

'Sweet,' Leo said, surprised to find himself breathing hard.

'Revenge always is,' Levitt remarked evenly. 'It's the purest motive in the whole world, and when you achieve it, you can actually taste the sweetness. Too bad your mother couldn't taste that sweetness, you know.'

'What do you mean?'

'When she heard this afternoon, she was upset. Can you believe that? Upset that two *mamzarim* like that should have died. But you. . .' Levitt leaned forward and patted Leo affectionately on the knee. 'You, you're like me. You know how to take enjoyment from the sweet things of life.'

Leo was puzzled. Levitt's talk sounded to him like a come-on, an approach he might use to a young man, to another Mahmoud Asawi. Was Levitt – the question shrieked at Leo – like himself? No. No way. Levitt had been genuinely shocked when he'd learned of Leo's homosexuality. If he had shared the inclination, he would never have been so surprised. But still it sounded to Leo like a come-on. . . .

'I've been waiting a long time to see how you and Joseph turned out,' Levitt continued, unaware of the consternation his approach was causing. 'I've been waiting a long time to see which one of you, you or Joseph, was the man to tackle an important task. A task that will right a wrong committed many years ago and restore the honour of your family.'

'Restore the honour of my family? I don't understand, Uncle Lou.'

'Listen to me, Leo, and you will.' Levitt patted the younger twin's knee again. 'It's appropriate that I should tell you this on the day that Patrick Joseph Rourke's sons died, because this story begins with Patrick Joseph Rourke. That old Irish bastard contracted with Saul Fromberg to kill me and Jake.' Levitt was unable to describe Jake to the twins as their father, not when he firmly believed himself to be that; he always used Jake's first name. 'The men Rourke sent to do the job were Irishmen like himself. No brains. They blew their chance and we all went into hiding.'

'That time I had diphtheria.'

Levitt nodded. 'While we were in hiding, we arranged the murder of Saul Fromberg. Bogus Internal Revenue agents threw him out of his office window, faked his suicide, just like

338

we did with Harry Saltzman. Only Gus Landau, the man who was Fromberg's lieutenant, he escaped. We thought he'd run and we made the mistake of forgetting all about him while we evened up the score with Patrick Joseph Rourke.'

'That night my father went up to Massachusetts?'

'That's right, the night Jake hijacked old man Rourke's convoy and killed a dozen of his guards. But Gus Landau came back. He tried to get me and Jake again, outside your grandma's restaurant on Second Avenue. Instead, he killed her.'

'Uncle Lou, I know all this. Landau ran again. He disappeared, until the day of my *bar mitzvah*, when he came back.'

'No!' Levitt allowed the sharp rejection to hang in the air while he studied the amazed expression on Leo's face. 'That is not what happened at all. What I'm about to tell you is the truth of what happened. Landau was hiding out for years in Canada, in Toronto. You remember Canada entered the war two years before we did, they were with England. So in 1940, Landau wanted to come back. But he was scared to show his face in New York because he knew we were still looking for him. He was between a rock and a hard place – Canada, a country at war, or the United States where we'd get him. So he came up with a deal to buy his way back here.'

'What kind of a deal?'

'In Canada, he was involved in a new business. He had good drugs connections. The stuff used to come into Canada from Spain and some of the Middle East countries, countries that were neutral during the war or on the Allies' side. Anyway, in September 1940, a few weeks before you were *bar mitzvah*ed, Landau contacted Benny Minsky and asked for a meeting. A one-on-one meeting to discuss this deal he wanted to make.'

'And Benny Minsky met him?'

Sombrely, Levitt nodded. 'Benny didn't tell any of us beforehand. He just took off one day, met Landau in Niagara Falls on the Canadian side. Only when he came back to New York and met up with me, Jake and Moe Caplan did he have the balls to say he'd been with Landau.'

Leo clenched his teeth in anger. The man who'd killed his

grandmother – and Benny Minsky had met him! Left the country to meet him! The man who had eventually killed his father!

'The deal Landau offered to Benny was this: we would forget what had happened in the past, let bygones be bygones, and Landau would turn over his drugs connections to us. We could sell the stuff in New York through selected small shops that handled the betting for us. Benny was all for it. I've never seen him so enthusiastic about anything other than that blonde *shiksa* nightingale of his. There was a vote. We voted on everything in those days, the four of us. Jake was dead set against it, and me and Moe, we voted with Jake. But that didn't stop Benny. To him, the democratic process didn't mean a damned thing.'

'You mean, he kept pushing for this deal with Landau?'

'You bet he did. There were tremendous arguments between Benny and Jake over Landau's offer. The two of them would be shouting and screaming.' Levitt closed his eyes for an instant, as if to bring to life the scene – the two partners arguing violently in the office of the Jalo Cab Company. 'It reached a point where Jake, one day, he stood up, jabbed a finger at Benny and said, "So help me God, but if I ever see one packet of white powder in any of our handbooks, I'm coming looking for you with a gun!" That's what Jake threatened Benny with, Leo, and he meant it.'

'Why was my father so against drugs?'

'Two reasons. Landau himself, obviously. Landau had killed Jake's mother-in-law, your grandmother. He wasn't going to let that be forgiven and forgotten. No way. And the second reason was you and your twin brother. Jake said that kids got hooked on dope and he wasn't going to be involved in anything that preyed on kids. Jake wanted to know if Benny didn't give a damn about his own kid.'

'Obviously he didn't.'

'Benny said he could control what his own kid did. The truth is, Leo, Benny was more interested in making bucks than he was in his own family. As if the money we made from the gambling wasn't enough.'

'What happened then?'

'I acted as peacemaker. I persuaded Benny to cool it. I kept

340

saying we had a good enough business without drugs – why did we need something that could get us into hot water? Things quietened down, returned to normal. I never thought Benny would double-cross us. I didn't think he could scheme his way from the toilet to the shower stall without tripping over something, but he did. While Benny was sitting next to Jake in the synagogue that day, listening to you and Joseph do your *bar mitzvah* pieces, he had Gus Landau cruising up and down the street outside. He'd brought him down from Canada, accepted his proposal with a rider. Benny would let Landau come back to New York in return for the drug connections, *and* if he killed Jake.'

'Why? Why was it so necessary to kill my father?'

'Benny knew that Jake meant every word of his threat. Jake would have gone looking for Benny with a gun in his hand once drugs started popping out of those small shops. Benny was just protecting himself. And Landau wasn't shy about that part of the deal. He hated Jake like the plague. He had orders from Benny to hit Jake as he came out of the synagogue after your *bar mitzvahs*.'

Leo's eyes burned with fury. 'That bastard! He brought William around to our apartment. He got me and Joseph to explain how important it was to be *bar mitzvah*ed because he wanted William to be *bar mitzvah*ed too. And then on the very day he had our father murdered!'

'Now do you see what I mean about restoring the honour of your family?'

'What about Moe Caplan and Landau shooting each other?'

Levitt answered the question obliquely. 'Once Moe and I realized that it was Landau sitting in that car outside the synagogue, we knew what Benny had done. He'd gone against the vote. So Moe and me had a choice – either we threw in with Benny, or we fought him. We pretended to throw in with him, that way we could pick our own time to even Jake's account. Only Benny wanted a sign of good faith. He wanted Moe to go with him to some abandoned building in the Bronx where Landau was holed up. Benny wanted Moe to help him kill Landau. Moe went along. They killed Landau, and as Moe walked out of the place, Benny fired a couple of shots into his back. Then he stuck the gun in Landau's hand. The scenario was easy for the police to understand. Moe Caplan had shot Landau. Landau, with his dying breath, had squeezed off a few shots through the door and gotten lucky.'

'How do you know all this? Were you there?'

'No. Benny came to see me right after.'

'To kill you?'

Levitt shook his head. 'I was the one person he couldn't kill. I was the person he had to make his peace with.'

'Why?'

'Because I could have sent Benny to the electric chair any time I wanted to. I still could, if this state practised capital punishment, and if any jury would convict Benny for a murder he committed forty years ago.' Levitt stood up, walked to a table where he picked up a folded sheet of paper. 'This is a photocopy of an affidavit I swore to forty years ago. It concerns the death . . . the murder . . . of a man called David Hay.'

'Who's David Hay?'

'A rich socialite who was fool enough to make a pass at Benny's girl, Kathleen Monahan; she wasn't his wife then. Hay was stupid enough, and unfortunate enough, to get lucky with her. Benny and Jake were driving down to South Jersey to meet a shipment one night. Jake fell asleep at the wheel, ran the car off the road before they even got out of New York. So Benny went back to Kathleen's place, looking for a little sympathy for his cuts and bruises. Instead, he found that she was playing around. Benny found out about this David Hay character and plotted to murder him. But, being Benny, he didn't follow through, like planning how to get rid of the body. He was trying to dig a hole in Flushing Meadows in the middle of winter – the ground was frozen like granite – when I found him. I helped him to ditch the body in the ocean when we picked up a shipment of liquor. Ever since then, I've held that over his head like the Sword of Damocles. I swore an affidavit about the murder, and left it locked up with a lawyer. That law office is still in business, with instructions to turn over the affidavit to the police if I should die by . . . let's say mysterious means while Benny Minsky is still alive.'

342

Leo read through the photocopy of the affidavit. It was all there: Levitt being suspicious of Minsky's desire to rush down to the Jersey shore, following him to Flushing Meadows, the eventual disposal of David Hay's body. Leo was uncertain how much weight the affidavit carried now, forty years after the event, when both men were in their sixties. He had little doubt, though, that at the time of Jake Granitz's death, the affidavit was pure dynamite. He handed the photocopy back to Levitt.

'He knew he couldn't kill me, not without himself going to the hot seat because of my insurance, so he put a deal to me,' Levitt said. 'If I didn't fight him, we'd split fifty-fifty on everything. Two weeks later, drugs started getting pushed from twenty or so of the small shops where we had the handbook and the numbers drops.'

'You went in with him?' Leo asked in disbelief. 'He killed my father, he did all this, and *you* went in with him?'

Levitt lowered his head a fraction as if admitting shame. 'Leo, what could I have done? What choice did I have? I never made a living with these – ' he lifted his fists – 'like Benny did. Violence was second nature to Benny. He was a *chaye*, a wild animal. I made a living with my head. I had to go in with him because it was the only way I could protect you, your brother and your mother. Who knew what that maniac Benny would do if I went against him? He'd backed himself into a tight corner over this drugs business. If I went against him, it would be all or nothing for him.'

'But you still went in with him.' It was no longer a question. It was an accusation filled with sorrow.

'I still went in with him. I'm sorry, Leo, but there was nothing else I could do.'

'There were no drugs when I started working for Jalo. When I began making the rounds with Phil Gerson, none of the places were pushing drugs.'

'Five years, that's all Benny did it for. That's all the time he needed to make a killing.'

'Why five years?'

'Benny was bringing his son up on his own then, and maybe what Jake had said about drugs had lodged in his mind. He didn't want William seeing how his father made money with drugs. I didn't want you and Joseph seeing it either. We agreed that the moment the first boy left school and started working – that was you – the drug business would cease. Benny kept his word. As you were finishing high school, the drug trade was killed off. The owners of the shops where the stuff was being pushed were paid off. A big payoff. And just for good measure, Benny promised that he'd kill anyone who ever mentioned a word. But that was always Benny's way of doing things.'

'That money in Zurich?'

'A lot of it came from drugs.'

'And I thought it was all from gambling.'

'That's what you were supposed to think. I didn't want you or Joseph believing that the money rested on filth like drugs.'

Leo stroked his chin with his hand. 'All this time you waited. All this time you did nothing. My father was murdered by Benny Minsky, and you did nothing!'

Levitt's temper flared with sudden fire. 'I did plenty, damn you! I kept you, your brother and your mother alive! And I kept that memory alive!'

'What is it you want me to do?'

'Make Benny crawl and scream, just like he did to us. Do you remember your mother after Jake was killed? Do you?' When Leo nodded, Levitt said, 'I want Benny just like that. I want him climbing the walls because the son he had with his blonde *shiksa*, his precious son, is dead.'

Leo looked up sharply. It had never occurred to him that William would be the means of vengeance. 'Why not just go after Benny himself?'

Levitt dismissed the suggestion with a wave of the hand. 'Too easy. He'll hurt for a minute, maybe not even that, and then it'll be all over. Like the Rourke brothers hurt for a minute. But their father's pain will go on for the rest of his life, and I hope he has a long life in which to remember and regret it. That's the revenge we want against Benny. Leave him to live out his days with a gaping hole in him. Make him bleed like you made that Irish bastard Rourke bleed today.'

Leo turned to gaze at the television set. He was surprised that the set was off; he couldn't remember either Levitt or himself flicking the switch. It didn't matter. Leo's imagination

344

provided the only picture he needed. A scene outside a synagogue, Leo and Joseph admiring the gold watches Levitt had given to them. And Jake, walking on ahead with Isaac Cohen, the elderly man who had taught the twins their *bar mitzvah* portions. Jake leaving Cohen to come back and look at the watches. His name called, just as Mahmoud Asawi had called the name of Senator Rourke. Even the same weapon, a shotgun.

There was a chilling coincidence to that. The use of a similar weapon to kill both Jake Granitz and the Rourke brothers. Leo's mind explored another coincidence. A *bar mitzvah*. Benny Minsky's older grandson, Mark, was due to take the step into manhood in two years time.

'How's Benny's heart, Uncle Lou?'

Levitt looked at Leo in some shock. 'How do I know?'

'Will he last two years?'

'Why is it so important that he should?'

Leo told him. At first, Levitt just nodded in agreement. Then he began to laugh, a low chuckle that finally erupted into a loud, appreciative roar of laughter. 'It's poetic, Leo. Snatch the joy from Benny's mouth, just the way he snatched it from Jake's.'

Leo just smiled. He had two years in which to prepare. When a man had that much time to plan, he rarely made a mistake.

BOOK 3

Chapter One

Richard Nixon's defeat of Hubert Humphrey in the election of 1968 gave rise to a string of haunting hypothetical questions. What would have happened if Senator Patrick Rourke Junior had been alive? What would have happened had he won the Democratic nomination? Would the slim margin of victory that Nixon enjoyed have been transformed, instead, into a margin of defeat? The assassination of Senator Rourke and his brother by a fanatical Jordanian youth named Mahmoud Asawi had left an indelible question mark over the immediate course of American politics.

A side story to the election was the death in his Boston home of old Patrick Joseph Rourke. When the butler went into Rourke's bedroom to rouse him on the day after the election, he found the old man dead in bed, eyes staring sightlessly at the ceiling, hands gripping the top of the sheet like two stiff claws. Rourke's two daughters-in-law, Grace and Rose, both agreed that it wasn't old age that had killed the former ambassador – he had died from a broken heart after having seen his dreams swept away in a hail of gunfire. He had nurtured tremendous ambitions for his sons, and those ambitions had been stolen from him just as they were about to be turned into reality. As if wanting to see the final chapter of his dream, he had held on to life until after the election. Then he had given up.

Despite her own harsh feelings towards old man Rourke, Pearl was saddened when she read of his death in the *New York Times*. Rourke had allowed his life to be compelled by two driving forces: vengeance, and the need to see his sons in

Washington. Neither ambition had come true. She wondered if he had actually taken any joy in his family, real joy as she did in her own, or was his familial concern based only on self-serving interest? It surprised her that she felt she knew him so well, she who had never even met the man.

When she mentioned seeing the story to Lou Levitt, he advised her not to waste her sympathy. 'The only thing wrong with that *momzer*'s death is that it didn't happen seventy years earlier. Remember, Pearl, he took money to kill Jake and me.'

'And if he hadn't taken it, does it mean that no one else would have?'

'It doesn't matter. Just be glad he's dead and don't squander your tears on him.'

Pearl supposed that Levitt was right. Why should a man like Rourke be the beneficiary of her sorrow? Still, she continued to dwell on what she considered Rourke's wasted life. What had he really gotten out of it? Nothing; he had just reaped the hatred he'd sewn. And for that reason she felt sorry for him. Despite Levitt's advice, she wasn't glad that Rourke was dead. There was no one whose death gladdened her. After all these years, she even found it difficult to muster up hatred for Gus Landau. Was that one of the benefits of growing older? Passions seemed to lose their sharpness. As she realized that the time left to her was diminishing, she wanted to waste none of it by dwelling on hatred. To do so would mean that those she had hated would have won.

And then she felt a trace of sympathy for Lou Levitt. Not because he lived alone, and no man of sixty-three should live alone. She had decided long before that solitude was the way of life that Levitt preferred. She felt sorry for him because, in this bout of introspection, she noticed many alarming similarities between Patrick Joseph Rourke and the little man. Levitt's hatreds seemed just as strong, just as long-lasting as Rourke's had been. Levitt had allowed his loathing of the Rourke family to become an overwhelming obsession. Even after the tragedy which had befallen the Rourkes, Levitt could find no compassion for them. Why wasn't the aging process affecting Levitt, Pearl wondered, in the same manner as it was affecting her? His passions were still as sharp, as violent, as they had ever been. He could find forgiveness for no one who had ever tried to harm him.

Approaching old age, Pearl was seeing shortcomings in Levitt that she had never recognized before. Or did the fault lie within herself? Was her willingness to forgive, and not continue to hate as Levitt did, the real flaw?

Had Pearl asked those questions of Levitt, he would undoubtedly have answered yes, the fault was her own. You never forgave, and you never forgot – that was the maxim by which he had lived. To forgive, he would have told her, was simply an invitation to those you had forgiven to go ahead and hit you again. Turning the other cheek meant that you got that one slapped as well.

There was little doubt in Levitt's mind that had Senator Patrick Rourke Junior lived to run as the Democratic candidate, public admiration for the Massachusetts Senator would have swept him into the White House. He'd had everything going for him: drive, glamour, a vibrant personality. The only mistake he'd ever made was in listening to his father. He could not be blamed for his parentage, Levitt reflected wryly. On the other hand, if the Senator had not taken it upon himself to avenge his father, he'd be getting ready to take up residence in the White House now. One way or the other it was his fault, and he'd paid for it in the only coin that Levitt knew. Like Harry Saltzman had paid before him. Like Saul Fromberg and Gus Landau had paid. Like Benny Minsky would soon pay.

Pearl, Joseph, Judy and the two children spent the Christmas and New Year following the election at the Waterway Hotel in Hallandale. Benny Minsky's family was also there. Only Lou Levitt and Leo refused to travel south for the holidays.

Minsky was a genial host. During the day, he played golf with William and Joseph. In the evenings he took everyone out to dinner. One day, he hired a small fishing boat and its crew. No one caught anything but that did not spoil the outing. As Pearl watched Minsky show the children how to cast, she wondered how different he would have been if Levitt had made the trip to Florida with them. Apart and together, Lou Levitt and Benny Minsky were two different men.

The Waterway celebrated New Year's Eve with a gala party. Minsky took a table for both his own and the Granitz family. All four children stayed up until midnight, holding hands with the adults in the centre of the dance floor as 'Auld Lang Syne' was sung.

'That makes two years since the casinos were closed, Benny,' Pearl said as she clutched his hand on one side of her, Joseph's on the other. 'Do you miss them?'

'I thought I would, but I don't. This is like a retirement for me. I'm sixty-six, Pearl, I've earned it. I play golf, do a little fishing – '

'And catch nothing,' Pearl reminded him.

'What would I do if I caught anything? All of a sudden I'm going to start supplying the hotels with fresh fish? I enjoy being out on a boat, that's all.'

The singing of 'Auld Lang Syne' finished and it was 1969. The hotel guests returned to their tables where, while 'Auld Lang Syne' was being sung, bottles of champagne had been placed. Minsky picked up a bottle. 'Can the kids have champagne?'

'Why not?' Joseph asked. 'Jacob's fourteen. Anne's eleven. A drop of champagne once a year isn't going to hurt them.'

'William . . . Susan?' Minsky looked at his own son and daughter-in-law, then answered the question for himself. 'Mark's getting *bar mitzvah*ed in less than six months – of course he can have a glass of champagne! And if we give Mark some, we can't leave out Paul. Let's just check it's the real stuff, the good stuff – fresh off the boat.' He pulled a pair of spectacles from his pocket and slipped them on. 'Taittinger, *Comtes de Champagne. Blanc de blanc Chardonnay*,' he read from the label, and everyone laughed at his atrocious pronunciation. 'Don't make fun of the way I talk,' he protested. 'Remember what I told Senator Rourke, *alav ha-sholom*. I was brought up on the streets, not in some fancy university with a grim-faced governess.'

'They certainly weren't the streets of Paris,' Susan said.

'Never mind what streets they were.' Minsky bent forward to pour the champagne. The spectacles slipped off the end of his nose and dropped on to the table. Setting down the bottle, he retrieved them and pushed them back towards his face. Pearl watched, puzzled, as he placed them upside down on his nose.

'Are you playing games, Benny?' she asked uncertainly. Minsky's mouth worked as he tried to answer. His words were slurred, running into each other. Horrified, Pearl watched as the left side of his face sagged. Muscles collapsed to drag down the eye and one corner of his mouth. The entire left side of his body seemed to shrink and he began to fall.

As realization dawned on Pearl, she reached out to grab Minsky. Simultaneously, William held him from the other side. Together, they lowered him into a chair. 'Get a doctor, quickly!' William hissed at Susan. 'My father's had a stroke.'

Pearl saw Minsky the following day in the hospital. He was sitting up in bed, the left side of his face twisted as though he had no control over it. What made it worse was that the right side of his face was normal. He recognized Pearl and tried to smile at her when she entered his room. The expression made his face even more bizarre, a grotesque mask pulled simul- taneously by two opposite poles. As Pearl sat down next to the bed, he said something which she had to ask him to repeat. His words were still slurred, malformed by his ina- bility to control the muscles on the left side of his body.

'I . . . said. . .' Slowly, Minsky forced the words out of the side of his mouth, and Pearl could see the frustration in his eyes at having to speak like this, at not being understood. '. . . Happy . . . New . . . Year.'

'You sure started it off on the wrong foot,' Pearl answered, and realized that she, too, was speaking slowly, pushing out each word with extreme care.

Minsky said something more and, again, Pearl did not understand. He stared at her, his lopsided face a mixture of anger and frustration. She felt terrible as she watched him reach out his good right hand for a notepad and pencil which rested on the bedside table. Pearl mouthed the words he wrote in big block capitals.

'It'll go away? The paralysis will go away?'

Minsky nodded, pleased that he had got the message through. The pencil started to move again, and Pearl read out each word. 'The . . . doctors . . . told . . . me . . . that . . . the . . .paralysis . . . is . . . temporary.'

Minsky set down the pad, ripped off the top sheet and started on a fresh page. 'Exercise. Therapy. Good as new.'

'By when?'

'June,' Minsky wrote. 'Got to be June. *Bar mitzvah.* Mark.'

Pearl patted his hand and removed the notepad. Even writing a few words was exhausting Minsky. He needed to rest, otherwise his dream of being fully fit again when his older grandson was *bar mitzvah*ed would remain just that.

Pearl returned to New York that night with Joseph, Judy and the children. When Levitt met them at the airport, Pearl told him of Minsky's stroke. Levitt's concern on hearing the news surprised her. 'Is he going to be all right?'

'The doctors say he is. With therapy, the paralysis in his left side should disappear.'

'Will he get back the use of everything? What about his mind? Is that affected? Does he understand what's going on around him?'

'He recognized me when I went to see him.'

Levitt relaxed, but only a little. Leo had wanted two years, and Levitt had been content to wait because Leo's scheme would snatch away the pleasure that Minsky would reap from his grandson's *bar mitzvah*, take that pleasure and turn it into the most devastating grief. But it would all be wasted if Minsky wasn't fully cognisant of what was taking place. A stroke! Was nature – was God – going to foil the revenge that Levitt so desperately wanted?

Levitt didn't give a damn about Minsky's physical shape. Just the brain, the senses, the mind. Those senses had to be sharp so that Minsky would register every moment of pain that Levitt would cause him. The senses had to be as acute as they had been on that day in 1940, when Minsky had surprised Levitt by demonstrating just how well he could think and plan.

Minsky's recovery was a slow, frustrating affair. Only after a month of rigorous exercise was he able to bring back some movement to his left side. He was able to stagger a few steps with the aid of a walker, and the prognosis of a virtually full recovery was modified. If Minsky were fortunate he would regain eighty per cent of his physical faculties. He would be able to walk, but not without a cane. He would be unable to drive, nor would he ever be able to play golf again.

Minsky accepted the news stoically. Since the stroke he had resigned himself to living one day at a time. If, each morning when he woke up, he could walk a step further than he had been capable of the previous day, he was satisfied. Most important to him was that his brain had not been damaged by the stroke. He remembered everything – people, places, dates. Even if he had to be helped into the synagogue when his grandson was *bar mitzvah*ed, he would be happy. Just as long as he could see and hear.

In Minsky's mind, the *bar mitzvah* of his older grandson became as important as that of his son, William, had been. It was the coming of age of the third generation, just as William's *bar mitzvah* had signified the coming of age of the second. And more. Whenever Minsky thought back to those days he could feel a lump forming in his throat, a churning of the stomach, a wetness in his eyes. If he could point to one act he had committed during his lifetime and say he was proud of it, it was that. He'd grabbed the opportunity of Kathleen's being out West to steal his own son back. Levitt had laughed at him, but Levitt had always mocked everything Minsky had done. Minsky had found a friend, though, in Pearl. With her help, he had overcome.

Minsky thought a lot about Pearl while he was going through the tedious business of regaining the use of his body. It seemed that he had always gone to her. Her and Annie. Whenever there had been trouble, whenever he'd needed help from a woman – usually because of Kathleen, he recalled ruefully – it was always to Pearl that he had turned. Getting Kathleen on to the stage of the Four Aces; trying to persuade Kathleen to keep the baby she so desperately wanted to be rid of; seeing William *bar mitzvah*ed; and, finally, those last few weeks when Kathleen had returned to New York, broke and dying. Always Pearl was there to help. Minsky felt remorseful about some of the comments he'd made, some of the thoughts he'd had, about the twins. He knew he shouldn't feel so badly

355

about them, even when he compared them to William. They were Pearl's twins. How could he hold a grudge towards her children? It was just that Levitt was so damned fond of them, and anything Levitt liked Minsky instinctively disliked. And vice versa. The two men had fought all their lives. The twins were something special to Levitt, the way he'd helped to raise them after Jake's death. Just like a father. Christ! Anyone could be forgiven for thinking that Levitt believed they were his own!

The physical improvement continued slowly. Four months after his stroke, Minsky could walk fifty yards with just a cane for support. He was realistic enough to understand that this was probably the best he would ever achieve. His left hand and arm were sufficiently strong to grasp the cane. That there had been improvement at all was cause enough for gratitude. Those first few hours, when he understood about the stroke, had been terrifying. He'd had visions of never being able to move again under his own steam, being confined for ever to a wheelchair, needing help with everything. A cripple. God forbid!

Only Minsky's facial muscles showed no improvement. The downward, twisted slant remained on the left side of his face, as though his expression had been frozen into a grimace. He hoped that when Mark was *bar mitzvah*ed, the boy did not look at his grandfather. He might think Minsky disapproved of the job he was doing.

Despite Minsky's protests, William flew down from New York to spend every weekend with his father. William watched while Minsky took his few steps, listened attentively as he spoke his slurred words. At the beginning of May, four months after the stroke, Minsky asked, 'Are you planning on coming down every weekend until I fly up for Mark's *bar mitzvah*?'.

'Of course.'

'In that case, I'll come up to New York for the month before, otherwise Susan's going to be citing me as the reason for a divorce. You're married to her, William, not me.'

'Okay. You call me with your flight number, and I'll be waiting to pick you up.'

Minsky flew to New York in the middle of May. An elderly

man, obviously the victim of a stroke, he was assisted on to the aircraft, pampered during the flight, and helped off. William was waiting by the baggage carousel. 'How was the flight?' he asked as he carried his father's two bags to the car.

'Everyone was wonderful. They treated me like I was some bone china ornament.' Words were still difficult to form, and William listened with extra care. The last thing he wanted was to annoy his father by asking him to repeat something.

'That's how we're going to treat you when we get you home,' William said. 'Susan's made up a room for you on the first floor. You won't have to climb any stairs, you'll be able to get around just fine.'

Minsky settled himself into the car. 'Do me a favour, William. When you go into Long Island City to work, take me with you.'

'What for?'

'I only came up here to stop you flying down all the damned time. But I'll go crazy if I'm stuck around the house all day long. Besides,' he added with a lopsided grin, 'I want to see what kind of a mess you made of that business I gave you.'

'Sure.' William reached out and squeezed his father's arm. It would do Minsky good to be back among the rumble of trucks again. Be like old times, Benny Minsky and Son. As William headed out of the airport parking lot, he found himself looking forward to working with his father again. Until this very instant, he had not realized just how much he'd missed him down in Florida. . . .

When William took his father to the depot the following morning, Minsky hobbled around with his cane, inspecting the fleet of trucks. For half an hour he watched a mechanic working on an engine, until William came over to see how he was faring.

'In my day, all you needed to strip an engine was a screw-driver and a monkey wrench,' Minsky told his son. 'For these damned complicated things you've got to have a degree in nuclear physics!'

'They might look more complicated, but they sure work better.'

'Do they?' Minsky asked dubiously. 'Let me tell you some-thing – if we ran out of gas, the damned things we drove would have run for ever on the booze we were hauling. Can this?'

'We don't haul liquor.'

'Too bad. Make sure your drivers keep an eye on the fuel gauge.' Awkwardly, Minsky hauled himself up to look into the driver's cab. 'Luxury, that's what these things are. Limousines pretending to be trucks. When we drove, we didn't have a heater. We didn't have soft seats like this, no power steering. Didn't even have a damned roof half the time, just a canvas top flapping over our heads. Truck drivers today are spoiled.'

Smiling, William helped his father down. 'Maybe they are, but they don't make the money you used to make with your truck runs.'

For lunch, William took his father to a diner close to the depot. It was a diner that Minsky had frequented when he was working in Long Island City, and he was pleased to see it was still in business. Even the owner, Minsky noticed, was the same; fifteen years older, but the same man none the less. When Minsky called him by name, though, the man just stared uncomprehendingly.

'You remember my father, surely,' William said quickly to the diner's owner. 'Benny Minsky, he used to come in here all the time.'

'Benny Minsky, sure, but. . . .' The man's voice trailed off in embarrassment. One side of the face he recognized; the other, deformed side was that of a total stranger. 'Hey, Mr Minsky, I know you now. I thought you were living down in Florida, running those hotels we heard all about during the Senate investigation.' He tried to keep his eyes away from the left side of Minsky's face, but they were drawn there as if by a magnet.

'I am, but I came up for my grandson's *bar mitzvah*,' Minsky answered proudly.

The owner of the diner was Greek, but he knew enough of Jewish culture to wish Minsky '*Mazel tov!*' and shake his hand.

Minsky sat back, satisfied that he had not been forgotten. The comfortable familiarity of the diner, the feeling of *déjà vu* as he'd sat in William's office that morning, were all bringing the memories flooding back.

358

After eating lunch, father and son left the diner to return to the depot. As William swung his car into the parking lot, a motorcycle roared past, its rider swathed in leathers and a black helmet with a dark visor. The rider turned at the end of the street and coasted to a halt beside a pay phone. Taking off his helmet to reveal a sharp face topped by long, curly blond hair, he dropped a dime into the phone and began to dial.

In Leo Granitz's office at Granitz Brothers, the telephone rang. Not the line that came through the switchboard, but a private direct line that Leo had ordered installed four weeks earlier. He answered it immediately.

'Chris here,' the motorcyclist said. 'Our friend just had lunch at the Pantheon diner close to the depot. Now he's gone back to work. By the way, he wasn't alone.'

'Who was with him?' Leo asked.

'Old guy, walked with a cane. Had a bad limp on his left side and his face was all out of whack.'

Benny Minsky, Leo thought. He knew about the stroke, but he hadn't been aware that Minsky was in New York. Had he come up early for the *bar mitzvah*? 'Call me again if anything happens. I'll be here until six.' Leo hung up and leaned back in his chair, hands clasped across his stomach. Perhaps Minsky coming north early was an added benefit. Instead of hearing about William through a long-distance telephone call, and then having to make the hectic rush north, he'd be on hand. The shock would be that much greater.

Leo wondered if this was how Napoleon had felt at the outset of a campaign. Or Alexander the Great, Eisenhower, Rommel, any one of those military leaders. Receiving intelligence reports, sifting, evaluating the news brought in by the spies. That's all Chris was, a twenty-two-year-old spy. Leo did not even know his last name, nor did Chris know Leo's. He had met the young man a month earlier in a bar and had bought him a drink. Chris was just out of the army, drifting while he looked for a way to make some money. Leo had offered him the means to do so. A game, he explained to Chris – a game that would last a couple of months or so. Follow a man during the day, let me know where he goes. Call me every time he makes a move. Chris hadn't asked any questions; he didn't even know the location of the telephone number that Leo gave him. Nor did he know the identity of his quarry, only that he worked at a trucking firm in Long Island City that traded under the title of B. M. Transportation. All he cared about was the money Leo gave him, the promise of a large bonus when the game was over.

Leo decided to see Levitt that evening and apprise him of the situation. So far, Levitt had shown scant outward interest in what Leo was doing. He had set Leo the task of avenging the murder of Jake Granitz and had let him get on with it. Levitt's confidence in him built up Leo's own. The smartest man Leo had ever known was saying to him: go ahead and get the job done in your own way, I have all the faith in the world in your ability to do it right.

When Leo went to Levitt's home, the little man suggested they walk in the park. Two hours of daylight remained, two hours before the muggers and rapists took over. Wandering through the zoo, the two men stopped to watch a keeper hosing out the gorilla's cage. The gorilla hung sideways from the bars, trying to catch the stream of water in its mouth.

'Benny's come up from Florida,' Leo said, staring at the gorilla. 'He was in the depot with William today.'

'How do you know this?'

'My spy,' Leo answered with a smile. 'Young guy on a motorcycle who keeps me informed of everything William does during the day.'

'Such as?'

Leo decided to boast. 'Did you know that he goes into Manhattan every Tuesday morning, takes a cab over to an address on Madison Avenue and the Fifties?'

'Advertising agency that handles B. M. Transportation's account,' Levitt answered. 'Probably goes over the schedule once a week.'

Deflated, Leo continued to stare at the gorilla. Levitt looked up at the younger man. 'I knew he went there. I didn't know when, though.' After waiting a few seconds, he said, 'Figured out how you're going to do it yet?'

'Kidnapping. Make Benny bleed three times that way. Once when he finds out William's been kidnapped. Second time when he pays the ransom. Third time when he doesn't get William back.'

360

'Three-time loser,' Levitt said approvingly. 'And then we pray that Benny has a long time left in which to think about it. Not like that old bastard Rourke. A year, fifteen months, wasn't enough for him. He should have been tortured for all eternity thinking about his sons.'

As Leo watched the gorilla continue to drink from the keeper's hose, he tried to equate Levitt's emotions with his own. The little man's feelings for Benny Minsky and his son were strong enough to be visible, a sheen of hatred that hung around Levitt like a cloak. Leo's own feelings were more obscure. His loathing of Minsky was fresher than Levitt's; it hadn't been given time to mature. Towards William he felt nothing at all. He was going to kill a man who aroused no emotions inside him whatsoever. Philip Gerson's murder had been like that; and the killing of the Italian uncle and nephew who had tried to extort money from B. M. Transportation, along with their driver. William's murder would not be a killing brought on by passion, as the Rourke brothers had been. As a young man named Tony Cervante had been. It would be a game, just as he had explained it to Chris. Put together the game plan like a football coach. Or, an analogy that Leo preferred, a general. Put it together, and then execute it.

'Can you trust this spy of yours?' Levitt asked.

'Could we trust Harry Saltzman to keep his mouth shut?'

'In the end we could.'

'We'll be able to trust my spy as well.'

'Funny thing. . .' Levitt turned away from the gorilla's cage as the keeper cut the water. 'I got my invitation to Mark Minsky's *bar mitzvah* the other week.'

'So did I. How come you were sent one?'

'Keep up appearances. Minsky's son and daughter-in-law don't know what's between Benny and me. Anyway, I said I'd be able to come. Even sent the boy a gift already. Too bad there won't be any *bar mitzvah*.'

'Too bad,' Leo concurred. 'Think the kid'll return the gifts?'

Levitt laughed and clapped Leo on the shoulder. Together, they made their way towards the park exit. It was beginning to get dark, and there was no sense in hanging around longer than necessary.

361

Chapter Two

Mark and Paul Minsky, William's two sons, loved having their grandfather around. He fascinated them with stories of how New York City had once been, told them to their disbelief of the manner in which he had lived when he was their age. He wove tales of bitter poverty, rats and roaches, of more people crammed into a single building than now lived in an entire street. Having known nothing but the secure comfort of Forest Hills Gardens, the boys found their grandfather's stories of the Lower East Side difficult to accept, so one Sunday Minsky made William drive the entire family down there. He showed his grandsons the streets and buildings, and when he saw them grimace at the dirt and squalor of the area, he was quick to point out that in his day the people who lived there had shown more pride than the current residents.

'It sure as hell wasn't heaven,' he told the boys, 'But we didn't turn it into no garbage pit either. You know, we used to have six, eight, sometimes ten families sharing one toilet.'

'And the shower?' Mark asked.

'Shower? What the hell was a shower? Public baths, that's all we knew. Baths you had to pay for.'

The younger boy, Paul, gazed uncertainly at his grandfather. 'You had to pay for a bath every day?'

This was too much for Minsky. He threw back his head and roared with laughter. 'Once a week people used to have a bath – Friday night for *Shabbes*. The rest of the time you washed out of a basin, and we were still cleaner than these people,' he said, indicating the blacks and Puerto Ricans who jostled each other on the litter-strewn sidewalks that had once been the domain of the Jewish wave of immigrants from Eastern Europe. 'There. . . .' He indicated a shop that sold luggage. Suitcases were piled high inside the shop and on the sidewalk outside. 'That place there, it used to be a bakery. Me and the other kids, we'd each bring our family's dish of *cholent* down there, and the baker would leave it in the oven overnight to cook. We'd pick it up the following day. We used to pay the baker a nickel for what.'

'What's *cholent*?' Mark asked.

Minsky looked at the boy as though he came from another world. Then he stared at William and Susan. 'This kid's going to get *bar mitzvah*ed soon, and he doesn't know what *cholent* is?'

'Who cooks *cholent* anymore?' Susan asked in return.

'I bet you Pearl Granitz still does.'

'Pearl Granitz is your generation, not ours.'

Minsky dismissed his daughter-in-law's rationalization with a wave of the hand. He turned back to his grandsons. '*Cholent* was meat and potatoes and onions and hard-boiled eggs, baked overnight.' He lapsed into silence, staring at the grimy buildings that were simultaneously so familiar and yet so strange. For a moment he could even smell the dish of *cholent* as he carried it back from the baker for the Sabbath feast.

Another Sunday, Minsky took his grandsons to a ball game. Because the loss of movement in his left side precluded him from driving, William had to chauffeur them the short distance to Shea Stadium and pick them up after the game. While the boys watched the play, Minsky talked about the baseball celebrities of his day, men with names like Ty Cobb and Babe Ruth, names which meant nothing to the boys as they started in awe at a new hero called Tom Seaver working on the pitcher's mound.

'Cobb, Ruth . . . they would have hit this college boy a mile,' Minsky said after the pitcher had put down the side in order.

'The hell they would,' Mark fired back. 'Seaver throws pitches those guys never knew existed.'

Minsky didn't answer. He just sat back in the spring sunshine and smiled. What did you expect from kids who didn't know what *cholent* was? He reached out and hugged both boys, marvelling at the wonderful joy of being a grandfather. That was something Lou Levitt would never know. The little man's preoccupation had always been with turning a buck. He'd done that well enough, but in doing so he'd cheated himself of everything else.

For three weeks after Benny Minsky's arrival in New York, his son's working habits were monitored by the young blond-haired man named Chris. Sometimes Chris would wear motorcycle leathers. At other times, when the sun shone warmly, he would be dressed in blue jeans and a cotton shirt. Always the helmet obscured his face and hair. Often he would change two or three times during a single day, just so William would never become suspicious of the motorcyclist who dogged his every move from the moment he arrived at work each morning until he went home at night.

Leo carefully studied the information he received from Chris. William's daily trips to the diner with Benny Minsky were useless. Leo needed William to be alone. Also useless were visits William made to a barber in Long Island City, to a dry cleaner, and to an employment agency in Manhattan. All these journeys were irregular; there was no way of knowing in advance when he would make such trips again. Only one activity stood out, William's Tuesday-morning taxi ride to the Madison Avenue advertising agency. According to Chris, you could set a clock by that. It had to be a standing appointment, a regular weekly meeting with the account executive who handled B. M. Transportation's advertising. Every Tuesday morning at ten-thirty, William would climb into a taxi. The meeting was for eleven. At eleven-thirty, he would be outside the building on Madison Avenue, looking for a taxi to take him back to Long Island City. Maybe he was frightened to drive in Manhattan, Leo mused. Or perhaps he just didn't need the aggravation of battling the heavy traffic. He had to be fresh for his meeting at the advertising agency; he didn't want to walk in there looking like he'd been through a mangle.

Tuesday morning it would be then.

*   *   *

On the Tuesday before Mark's *bar mitzvah*, William drove his father to the truck depot as usual. While Minsky wandered around, talking to drivers and mechanics, William went through some paperwork. At ten-fifteen, he instructed his secretary to order a taxi for ten-thirty.

'I'm going over to Manhattan,' William told his father. 'I'll be back at midday for lunch.'

'Your advertising people? That's a side of the business I never knew much about. It's something new, all these advertising types with their statistics and charts.'

'I know. In your day all you needed to run a trucking company were some trucks, a serviceman and a place to park them. Times change.'

'It might be time I changed with them. Today I think I should come with you. In all my business life, I never so much as went inside an advertising agency.'

William considered the idea then he shook his head. 'What would you do there? All we do is okay the future ads, go over the copy, see what new markets we should go after. You'd be bored out of your mind.'

'I would, wouldn't I? Go. Go ahead and see your advertising people. I'll be waiting for you when you get back.' Minsky returned to watching the mechanics at work, while William, briefcase in hand, walked out to the parking lot where the taxi was just pulling in. It was beginning to rain, and he wondered how much trouble he would encounter in finding a cab to bring him back.

Leo was nervous. Sitting in the back of a Cadillac limousine with darkened windows, he looked along the length of Madison Avenue, trying to spot one yellow taxi among the many that could be carrying William Minsky to his regular Tuesday morning appointment. At the wheel of the Cadillac sat Chris. He no longer wore the motorcycle outfit. He was dressed today in a dark grey chauffeur's uniform, the long blond hair seeming out of place as it dropped below the peaked cap to hang just above his shoulders.

'Maybe he put it off today,' Chris said. 'Didn't like the rain.'

'Was it raining any of the times you tailed him here?'

Chris tried to remember. 'Once. It was coming down in buckets.'

'Then he'll be here today.' Leo glanced at his watch. Ten fifty-five. A taxi pulled up in front of the building where the advertising agency was housed and Leo leaned forward eagerly. To his disappointment, a woman alighted. Two more taxis pulled up. Neither carried William. Leo swivelled agitatedly in his seat, trying to cover the street and both sidewalks in one sweeping glance.

'There he is,' Chris said.

Leo swung forward again. Another cab had stopped. William jumped out and ran through the rain to the building entrance; a woman who had been waiting for a taxi took his place, and the vehicle moved away into the stream of traffic.

'Now we wait,' said Leo. He dug his hand into his coat pocket and pulled out two lengths of string which he ran between his fingers. This was the worst time, the waiting. All his planning was about to be put to the test. Leo was confident that he had overlooked nothing. Nothing . . . except the waiting, knowing that William was inside the building but being unable to do a damned thing until he showed his face. What did opposing military leaders do while they waited for the battle to commence? Did they review their plans a final time, make sure they had taken every possibility into consideration? It was a strange question. No matter how certain each general was, one of them had always overlooked something. That was why he lost. What was it, Leo tried to remember, that he had once read in the biographies of great military men? What quote? A battle wasn't won by the most prepared army, it was won by the least confused. Something like that; he couldn't remember it word for word, but he had the gist. Well, he wasn't confused right now as he sat in the Cadillac limousine and waited. His mind was clearer than it had ever been before.

'Eleven-thirty,' Chris said from the driver's seat. 'Should be surfacing any minute now.'

Leo craned forward. The Cadillac's engine was ticking over. The transmission was in drive, ready to roll at a moment's notice. The wipers swished monotonously across the windshield. Fifty yards away was the building that housed the advertising agency. How long would it take to cover that distance? Five seconds? Ten? Would William have found a cab in that time? The first doubts started to eat away at Leo's confidence. 'Move up a little bit,' he told Chris.

'If we get any closer than this, he'll see we've pulled out from a parking spot,' Chris answered.

Leo opened his mouth to rebuke the younger man until he realized that Chris was right. The general having something pointed out to him by the lieutenant. It happened. The whole idea was that William would believe the Cadillac was just passing by – not that it was waiting for him.

'Here he comes,' Chris said. In a quick movement, he slipped his foot off the brake pedal and on to the accelerator. The Cadillac surged forward. As William glanced along the street for an empty cab, Chris braked the Cadillac to a halt in front of him, and Leo threw open the rear door.

'William, which way are you heading?'

William stared blankly across the wet sidewalk at Leo and the invitingly open door. He'd been looking for a cab, cursing the rain because it would be that much more difficult to find one, and the sight of the chauffeur-driven limousine with the darkened windows threw him completely off balance.

'Get in!' Leo called across the sidewalk. He was grateful for the rain. Not too many people were out. Those who were walked quickly, or ran, heads down, as they tried to dodge the rain. No one seemed to take any notice of the limousine. 'You'll never find a cab in this lousy weather.'

William darted across the sidewalk and slid into the Cadillac. 'You're a godsend, Leo. I'm heading back to Long Island City if you're going in that direction.'

'No problem,' Leo said grandly. He leaned forward to give Chris directions for the truck depot. 'What are you doing in town?'

'Meeting with our ad people. You sure this isn't taking you out of your way?'

'Don't worry about it. I'm early for a lunch meeting.'

William laughed. 'If you hadn't turned up, I'd be late for one! I told my father I'd be back at the depot by midday, and we'd go to lunch together. He's a stickler for having lunch exactly at noon. Must be something to do with getting old, having to eat at regular hours.'

'You'd know that better than I would. I never saw my father get old.'

William appeared not to hear. He was staring through the windshield as Chris headed north along Madison Avenue. At the intersection with East 57th Street, he swung west. 'Hey, where's this driver of yours going, Leo? We need the Queensboro Bridge.'

Leo slammed his right elbow hard into William's chest, right over the heart. Above William's sudden gasp of pain, Leo shouted: 'Did you hear what I said about my father?' His elbow slammed into William's chest again. The snap of cracking ribs could be heard clearly 'He never got old, and do you know why?' Leo swung around in the seat to send a huge fist smashing down into the side of William's face. William slid across the seat to crack his head against the darkened window. 'He never got old because your father double-crossed him and set him up for Gus Landau! That's why my father didn't get old!' Leo dived across the seat, lifted William up by the lapel of his raincoat and smashed his right fist into his face again and again.

After the fourth punch, William's eyes rolled up in his head. Leo released his hold and dropped the unconscious man on to the seat. He glanced in front, saw that Chris was concentrating on the driving, and pushed William on to the floor. Kneeling beside him, Leo pulled out the two pieces of string with which he had been playing earlier. He tied William's wrists and ankles, pulling the string tight until it bit harshly into flesh. Lastly, he stuffed a rag into the unconscious man's mouth.

The Cadillac sped through the Holland Tunnel and into Jersey City. The rain began to fall more heavily, and by the time the limousine reached a disused warehouse close to the river there was hardly a pedestrian to be seen. The warehouse doors were open. Chris drove right inside, stopping when he reached the far wall. Leaning against the wall, hidden by a tarpaulin, was his motorcycle.

'Shut the door,' Leo said. While Chris ran to drag the warehouse door closed, Leo slipped on a pair of gloves. He lifted William from the back of the limousine and carried him up a flight of wooden steps to a room that had once been an

368

office. Its windows were broken, the rain blew in to wet the dirt and debris that covered the floor. Without any ceremony, Leo dropped the body on to the floor. Returning downstairs, he found Chris removing the chauffeur's uniform. Leo watched as the young man slipped into the dark leather trousers and jacket he wore when he rode the motorcycle.

'You know what you've got to do?'

'Sure,' Chris answered. 'Tonight at six o'clock, I call the number you gave me. Then again at seven.'

'Do everything just like I told you. It's foolproof. Once we get the money, a third of it's yours. That's your bonus.'

Before slipping on the crash helmet with the dark visor, Chris nodded. He thought he was in on a kidnapping, nothing else. Meeting Leo in the bar had been the answer to a prayer. Just out of the army and needing some easy money, and opportunity had knocked. A partnership in a quarter-of-a-million-dollar abduction. He'd never realized when he'd accepted the proposition that his partner wasn't in the least interested in any money, or that his own participation was only intended to be a very temporary affair.

Leo watched Chris sit astride the motorcycle and kick it into life. He roared across the warehouse, stopped by the door to push it open far enough to pass, and then disappeared into the rain. Leo walked after him to pull the door closed again. For a few seconds, he stared at the rain, regretting the waste that Chris represented. He'd liked to have met Chris under different circumstances. The young man's North Carolina accent appealed to Leo, his wiry but strong body, the tales he'd told of his service in Vietnam. There would be others, though. Many more. Dismissing Chris from his mind. Leo returned upstairs to where William lay. His eyes were open. His breathing, forced through the rag stuffed into his mouth, was ragged. Leo stuck in two fingers and pulled the rag free. William immediately coughed blood from a lung that had been punctured by his broken ribs.

'Why are you doing this?' William asked. Each word was an effort. Each movement of his lips sent pain searing through his chest.

'Why did your father have my father murdered?' Leo asked in return. 'That's the question you should be asking. Not of

369

me, but of your father.'

'I don't know what you're talking about. My father thought the world of Jake Granitz.'

'Did he? Or did he think more of the money that he could make from the drugs deal he set up with Gus Landau?'

William coughed again. Blood and saliva dribbled down his chin. 'You're crazy, Leo. You're as mad as they come if you believe that.'

Leo's eyes altered shade, changing from hazel to a steely grey. His heavy eyebrows lowered into a furious scowl. 'Don't . . . call . . . me . . . mad!' he spat out, punctuating each word with a savage kick to William's chest. 'It's your father who was mad! Mad to do what he did! Mad to think he could get away with it! And now you're going to pay for what he did. You ever hear about the sins of the fathers being visited on the sons? That's what this is, William. With your last breath, you can curse your goddamned father for what he did!' Leo stuffed the rag back into William's mouth. On the floor was a ball of twine. Leo picked it up, looped it around William's ankles, drew it tightly around his neck, then around the ankles again before tying a knot.

Leo rose to his feet and stared down. William lay on his stomach, body arched into a bow, the twine running from his ankles to his neck providing the string. He could still breathe, but any relaxation of his muscles would cause the twine to tighten around his throat.

'Strangle yourself, you bastard,' Leo said, and closed the door.

At twelve o'clock exactly, Benny Minsky stood sheltered from the rain in the doorway of the B. M. Transportation office. William was supposed to be back by now to accompany his father to the diner for lunch. Minsky glanced anxiously at his watch, then at the rain. Maybe he couldn't find a cab. You never could when it was raining like this. Everyone knew that New York cab drivers went on a coffee break the moment rain began to fall, and stayed there until the sun shone through again.

Returning inside, he forced himself to sit down and wait. When twelve-thirty came, however, he knew something was

370

wrong. If William was going to be half an hour late – if he'd been delayed in his meeting with the advertising people, or if he'd been stuck looking for a cab – he would have called. William was considerate. He would never leave his father dangling on the end of a string like this.

'What's the number of that advertising agency?' Minsky asked William's secretary. The woman dialled the number and Minsky waited for the telephone to be answered. 'I'm looking for Mr William Minsky of B. M. Transportation,' he said. 'He had an eleven o'clock appointment with someone at your place.'

'He left here an hour ago.'

'Thank you.' Minsky replaced the receiver and went back outside. Even allowing for a half-hour wait for a cab, William should have been here already. In his bones, in his stomach, in his heart, Minsky knew that something was terribly wrong.

At one o'clock he telephoned the police, only to be told that a man could not be listed as missing after only an hour. 'I know that!' Minsky snapped back. 'I just want to know if there have been any accidents in Manhattan that might have involved my son.' He was advised to try the hospitals. Every admissions desk he contacted had no record of a William Minsky. At three o'clock, he tried the police again.

'I know something has happened to my son!' he yelled into the mouthpiece. 'I want your people to do something about it!'

'Mr Minsky, three hours doesn't warrant a police investigation. I'm sorry.'

Minsky went back to the secretary. 'Is there anywhere else he could have gone! Any other business meeting he might have forgotten to tell me about?'

The secretary scanned through William's appointment book. Only the advertising meeting was scheduled. None the less, she telephoned every business contact William had – insurance agents, the bank, parts suppliers. No one had seen or heard from him that day.

At four-thirty, Minsky telephoned Susan in Forest Hills Gardens. Somehow, he managed to sound reasonably calm. 'Susan, I'm worried about William. He went to his advertising meeting this morning, and he hasn't returned yet. Do you know of anywhere else he might have gone?' The wild notion of William's having a girlfriend crossed Minsky's mind. No . . . even if his son were fooling around, he'd be more discreet than to give his father reason to suspect. Minsky felt ashamed for even thinking of such a thing.

'I don't know of anywhere. What places have you tried?'

Minsky reeled off the list. 'There's no record of him being involved in any accident or crime. He's just disappeared.'

'That's not like him,' Susan said. 'Every time he goes anywhere, he tells his secretary.'

'There's probably a reasonable explanation behind this whole thing,' Minsky assured Susan. 'But just in case, I want you to stay at home until you hear from me. Something might have happened, an accident, perhaps, and there'll be a call to the house. In the meantime, I'll stay here in case someone tries to contact the depot.'

'Do you think – ?'

Before she could finish her question, Minsky said, 'I don't know what to think, Susan. All we can do is stay calm.' He hung up and then mocked his own advice by savagely slamming his fist on to the desk again and again. Where the hell was William? What had happened to him? Not this week of all weeks, for Christ's sake!

At six o'clock, Minsky was alone in the depot office. He had sent the secretary home, telling her that there was nothing she could do, no point in her staying. Now he wished that she was in the office with him. Facing the unknown alone was terrifying.

The telephone rang. It was Susan, her voice a mere whisper that was filled with fear. 'William's been kidnapped.'

'What?'

'I just had a phonecall. A man. He said William's been kidnapped. I tried to ask him what he meant, and he hung up.'

'I'll be home as soon as I can find a cab.'

Kidnapped! The uncertainty was gone. His only son had been kidnapped. A ransom. Money didn't mean a damned thing. Minsky would pay it and not even bother calling the police, just to get William back. And afterwards, when William was returned to his family, Minsky would take his own revenge. He still knew people. He'd find out the identity

372

of these kidnappers just as surely as the police would. More surely. All the police could do was dig for clues. Minsky could do much more. He could offer such a reward that the kidnappers of his only son would never be safe from treachery. That was it, he decided as he waited for a taxi. Keep the police out of it. Do it all on his own.

Such hopes were dashed the moment the taxi swung into the driveway of the house in Forest Hills Gardens. A police car was parked there, a garish advertisement that something was amiss. Tucked in behind it was an unmarked Plymouth. Minsky paid off the cab and hobbled towards the front door. It was opened before he could reach it by a man in a dark blue suit. Minsky had seen enough federal agents in his life to be able to recognize them at first glance. 'Who the hell called you here?'

The agent showed no response to Minsky's hostility. 'You would be William Minsky's father, I take it. I'm Frank Hopkins, from the New York office of the Bureau. Your daughter-in-law called the police the moment she received the telephone call. They informed us.'

Pushing his way past the FBI agent, Minsky came face to face with a uniformed sergeant. 'Where's my daughter-in-law?'

'In there.' The sergeant pointed to the front room. Minsky opened the door and saw Susan sitting on a couch. Her sons were on either side of her.

'Why did you call the cops?' Minsky demanded. 'I could have handled this.'

'It's a kidnapping,' Susan answered. 'A police matter.'

'The hell it is! I can take care of it, just like I've taken care of everything where William's concerned.'

'This isn't the Twenties anymore!' Susan retorted. 'You don't just pick up a gun like you used to do and go out looking for someone to shoot full of holes.'

Minsky started to say something in return, then closed his mouth when he noticed his grandsons staring at him. Both were frightened, uncertain. They weren't alone. So was he. But he knew he had to take charge. 'Don't worry about a thing,' he told them. 'Your father'll be home safe and sound for the *bar mitzvah* on Saturday. You'll see.'

There was a knock on the door. Frank Hopkins entered. 'Mr Minsky, I'd like to speak with you and your daughter-in-law. Just the two of you, please.'

Reluctantly, Susan sent the boys out of the room.

'Is your husband a wealthy man, Mrs Minsky?' Hopkins asked. He felt it was a rhetorical question; the house alone told him the answer.

'He's comfortable.'

'And you, Mr Minsky?' Hopkins asked.

'I can put together a couple of bucks.' Minsky wondered when the FBI agent would point a finger and say he remembered Minsky from those damned Senate hearings. Or were FBI men more tactful?

'You've been contacted once, Mrs Minsky. No demands, nothing but a short message to let you know your husband's been abducted. The kidnapper will call again. When that happens, we'd like to trace the call.'

'Supposing you do?' Minsky butted in. 'Supposing you catch the kidnapper that way? What happens to my son then? The kidnapper keeps his mouth shut, and my son rots away somewhere? Nothing doing.'

'It's more than likely that we could reach an agreement with the kidnapper once he was in custody. A trade-off. He could lessen his own problems by helping us.'

'Sure. And just supposing he's got a pal who's guarding William? That pal doesn't want to get caught in a double-cross, so he takes it on the lam . . . after taking care of William. Forget it. When we get a ransom demand, I'll come up with the money. Once we get William back, it's your affair. But only then.'

'I think I should point out that many kidnappings where the ransom is paid end up with the abducted party being killed. That's if he hasn't been killed before the ransom was paid – before the first contact was even made.'

'If you're trying to scare me into letting your guys take this thing over, you've got another think coming.'

'Why don't you listen to him?' Susan pleaded. 'He knows what he's talking about. He's been involved with kidnappings before.'

'Not where my son's concerned, he hasn't.'

'You're forgetting that he's my husband as well.'

Hopkins stepped in between them. 'Nothing is going to be solved by the pair of you arguing.' Both Susan and Minsky swung on him, as if to demand what right he had to interfere. Before a word could be spoken, the telephone rang.

'Answer it,' Hopkins said.

Susan hesitated, fearing what the call would be. Minsky touched her on the arm and walked over to the telephone. He resisted snatching the receiver from the hook, waited until another full ring had gone by.

'Hello?'

'That's not Mrs Minsky, is it?' a man's voice asked.

Minsky thought he detected a Southern accent. 'This is Benny Minsky, William Minsky's father.'

'You've got until tomorrow morning to come up with two hundred and fifty thousand dollars, Benny Minsky.'

'Who is this?'

'Two hundred and fifty thousand dollars. Tens, twenties and fifties. Used bills. No consecutive numbers. We'll be in touch again at ten o'clock tomorrow morning.' A sharp click was followed by the dial tone. Minsky stood staring at the mute instrument for a few seconds before replacing it.

'They want a quarter of a million dollars by ten in the morning.'

'Can you arrange that?' Hopkins asked.

Minsky nodded. 'I'll get hold of the bank that my son's company uses.'

'If you'd prefer, we could handle the money. We have funds we can call on for these emergencies.'

'And mark it? Stick a tear-gas bomb or some dye spray in the bag? No thanks. You're not getting my son killed.'

The FBI agent tried one more time. 'Let us tap your line. When he calls tomorrow morning, we'll trace it.'

'What the hell's the use? You couldn't have traced that call. It was too short.'

'Tomorrow morning's call will be longer. They have to supply details of where the money is to be taken.'

Minsky looked at Susan. He knew what she wanted. To let the police, the feds, in on the act. She didn't come from the same background as he did. To her, the police symbolized security. Not to Minsky they didn't. He knew all about police graft and incompetence. If she was ever going to see William again, this would have to be done on his terms.

'You don't tap anything,' he told the FBI agent. 'Afterwards you can do whatever you damned well like, but until that money's delivered, until William's safe back here, you keep your face out of it.'

The story of the kidnapping was in the following morning's newspapers. Before eight o'clock, Lou Levitt telephoned the house in Forest Hills Gardens.

'Benny, is this true? About William? It says in the paper that he's been kidnapped.'

'It's true, all right.'

'How much money do they want?'

'A quarter of a million.'

'You need help in raising it?'

'No. I was on to William's bank manager last night. They're shipping the money up here before ten.'

'Okay. If you need any help, you know where to reach me.'

Despite himself, Minsky felt a sudden burst of warmth towards Levitt. Sometimes trouble brought out the best in people. 'Thanks, Lou. I'll remember.'

On Central Park West, Levitt hung up the telephone and smiled to himself. It was always easy offering another player an extra card when you held all the aces yourself. . . .

Pearl telephoned the house at nine-thirty, shortly after a bank messenger had delivered the ransom money. 'Benny, this is terrible.'

'You don't have to tell me that. We're going crazy here, waiting for the bastards to call and tell us what's what.'

'How's Susan?'

'Bearing up.' He glanced at his daughter-in-law who was bringing in coffee for himself and Frank Hopkins, the FBI agent. Despite being told he wasn't wanted, Hopkins had insisted on staying.

'And the boys? What's happened to them?'

'They've gone to friends. Susan sent them last night. Look, Pearl,' Minsky said as he saw the agent gesturing towards his

376

watch. 'I've got to get off the phone. We're expecting a call soon from the kidnappers.'

'All right. Benny, if there's anything you need, let me know. I'll come over and stay with Susan if that'll help.'

'I'll let you know.' He hung up.

At ten o'clock, the telephone rang again. It was the same voice, the same Southern accent that had spoken to him the previous night.

'Have you got the money?'

'I've got it.'

'Listen good. By ten-thirty, be at the pay phone on the corner of Jewel Avenue and Queens Boulevard. By yourself. You'll be under surveillance the whole time. We see a cop within half a mile of you, and you can kiss your son goodbye.'

'I can't drive,' Minsky said, suddenly remembering his own condition. 'I'll have to have someone with me.'

'Take a taxi.' The caller broke the connection. Minsky snatched the directory from beside the telephone and looked up the number of a taxi company. As he started to dial, Hopkins pressed down the receiver rest.

'One of our men'll drive you. He'll be the cab driver.'

'Forget it. This guy so much as smells a cop and my son's dead.'

'How do you know your son isn't dead already?'

'I don't. I'm just praying that he's not.'

'Think of yourself then. Have one of our men as a driver for your own protection. You'll be carrying a fortune around with you.'

'Screw my protection! Can't you get it through your fucking thick head that I want you and your FBI to butt out?'

The taxi came. Minsky handed the driver two one hundred-dollar bills and said he was hiring the vehicle for the day. 'I don't know how long I'm going to need you. I've no idea how many miles we'll cover. Let me know when that two hundred runs out.'

'What is this – some kind of a mystery tour? A treasure hunt?'

'It's a kidnapping. I'm delivering a ransom.' He pointed to the small blue suitcase which he had brought into the taxi. That's what's in there, two hundred and fifty thousand bucks worth of ransom money. And just in case you get any crazy ideas, there's a whole gang of cops and FBI men inside that house who've got your licence number. Understand?'

'Where to?'

'Corner of Jewel Avenue and Queens Boulevard.'

The taxi reached the pay phone with five minutes to spare. Precisely at ten-thirty, the telephone rang. The voice Minsky had come to know so well was mocking as it said: 'Glad you could make it. Now I want you to go to Jackson Heights.' Minsky scribbled feverishly with a pencil on the back of an envelope. 'Thirty-seventh Avenue and Eighty-second Street. There's a pay phone outside a men's clothing shop. Be there in twenty minutes.'

Returning to the taxi, Minsky gave the new destination to the driver. He understood perfectly what William's kidnappers were doing. They were going to run him all over the city, follow the taxi to make sure that he wasn't being tailed by the police. He twisted in the seat to check whether one vehicle hung too long on the taxi's tail. he looked forward again immediately. Whoever was keeping him under surveillance might decide that his curiosity was too dangerous. Under surveillance . . . the term stuck in his mind. It was a military term. Whoever had kidnapped William had been in the military. Christ! He hoped the cops weren't stupid enough totally to disregard the kidnappers' and his own demand to be left alone.

From Jackson Heights, Minsky was sent to another pay phone at Queens Plaza. There, he received instructions to go into Manhattan, to Grand Central Station. Slowly, the Southern voice at the other end of the line drew him west across the borough, and then north, until, at just after two o'clock, Minsky was laboriously climbing the stairs from Broadway to the George Washington Bridge bus station in Upper Manhattan. He prayed this was the last stop. He was exhausted, his heart beating wildly, sweat covering his face and body. Twice during the long walk up the stairs – cane and small suitcase clutched in his right hand, while he used his left to claw at the rail – he stumbled. Both times he just wanted to sit there on the cool stairs, let the case and cane go tumbling down to Broadway. He didn't care anymore, he was too tired

378

to worry. Until he thought about William, and remembered the promise he'd made to his grandsons. *William would be home*. In three days time, on the Saturday, the entire family would be sitting in the synagogue for Mark's *bar mitzvah* – sitting there as if nothing had happened! He hauled himself up and continued the climb, praying to God for the strength to see this thing through. William was relying on him like never before.

As he reached the top of the stairs, Minsky reviewed the last set of instructions he had received at a pay phone on Amsterdam Avenue. Go to the George Washington Bridge bus station. Climb the stairs. You'll see two banks of telephones, one with six booths, one with only two. On the smaller bank will be a telephone with an out-of-order sign hanging from it. That is the telephone where you will receive your next orders.

Christ, Minsky thought, as he headed towards the bank of two telephones, whoever was behind this had planned the whole thing like some kind of military campaign. Under surveillance . . . all the fine detail. What next? His heart leaped when he noticed that one of the two telephones was in use. A man in motorcycle leathers was standing there, his back to the second telephone as he talked into the mouthpiece. He was wearing a crash helmet with the dark visor lifted so that he could hear and speak. Between his feet was a red suitcase, slightly larger than the blue case Minsky carried. Was that the telephone he was supposed to use? Had something gone wrong? Then Minsky spotted the out-of-order sign hanging from the telephone next to the leather-clad man, and he breathed easier. Standing next to it, he waited for the summons.

In the adjacent booth, Chris had seen Minsky emerge at the top of the stairs, face flushed and sweaty. 'He's just arrived,' he said softly into the mouthpiece. 'Looks like he's going to have a heart attack at any moment.'

In his office at Granitz Brothers, using the direct line that bypassed the switchboard, Leo digested the information. Everything was working like a charm. He'd planned as carefully as any tactician had ever done. Chris had made all the telephone calls so far, watched while Minsky sped by taxi from one destination to the next. With the mobility of the motorcycle, Chris had always been there first, ready to put the next step of the plan into operation. Now, Chris's participation was almost over. The next voice that Minsky would hear would be Leo's. Minsky would spot the difference immediately, the switch from the slower speech of North Carolina to the abruptness of New York City. That would throw him enough to avoid recognition. But just in case. . . . Leo draped a handkerchief over the mouthpiece.

'You sure no one followed him?' he asked Chris.

'What's the matter with your voice? I can hardly hear you.'

Leo removed the handkerchief. So much for that worry. He repeated the question. Chris said no; he'd watched the stairway leading down to the street carefully. By the wildest stretch of his imagination none of the people who had reached the top of the stairs after Minsky could have been police or federal agents. Old women, young women struggling with prams, kids, old men. But no cops.

'I'm going to hang up now and call the other line,' Leo said. 'You stay on, pretend you're still speaking until I've given him the instructions.'

'Okay. Anything else?'

'No. We'll meet tomorrow night as planned.'

'Got you.' Chris heard the line click, the dial tone return. Leaning against the wall, he engaged in a one-sided mock conversation, pausing as though listening to someone, then talking again. Beneath the crash helmet, his ears strained for the ringing of the out-of-order telephone.

Thirty seconds later it rang. Minsky leaned forward to lift the receiver from the rest. 'I'm here!'

'Good. What I want you to do now,' Leo said through the handkerchief, 'is leave your suitcase on the floor right where you're standing. I want you to walk away. On the other side of the bus station are local bus schedules. Go over to them, pretend you're studying them. Whatever you do, don't look back. Stay there for five minutes. After those five minutes are up, you go home. The message regarding your son will reach you at home. Once we've got the money and are certain that you've kept your end of the bargain, you'll be told where to find your son.'

380

'Is he all right?'

'Walk away. If you look back, your son's going to wind up looking like Lot's wife when she looked back. Understand?'

The line went dead. Minsky replaced the receiver and looked down at the blue suitcase. Dare he leave it there, right in the middle of the busy bus terminal? There was a quarter of a million inside. He glanced at the adjacent booth, at the back of the man in motorcycle leathers. He was still carrying on his conversation, totally unaware of anything that was going on outside his own little world. Didn't he understand the drama that was taking place only feet away? Minsky left the case on the floor and walked towards the local bus schedules. It took every ounce of willpower and determination not to turn his head and look back.

Still clutching the receiver to his ear, Chris angled his head just enough to see Minsky's back. His foot snaked out, caught the edge of the blue case. With a deft movement, he lifted his own, slightly larger red case and dropped it over the blue one. The red case was hollow and had no bottom. It fell over Minsky's blue case like a glove fitting a hand. The handle of the blue case came through a space in the top of the red case. Chris gripped it, replaced the receiver and walked quickly towards the stairs. As he started down, he risked one backward look. Minsky stood at the schedule board, apparently engrossed. Quickening his pace, Chris reached the street, strapped the red suitcase and its load on to the rack of his motorcycle, jumped aboard, kicked the engine into life and sped off along Broadway. To a casual observer, he was a messenger making a run, or a man going away on a biking vacation.

A quarter of a million dollars! Excited, Chris gripped the handlebars of the motorcycle as he thought of the vast sum. In thirteen months of risking his neck in Vietnam he'd barely made one per cent of that. Getting shot at for fifty bucks a week plus combat pay, and now he was sitting on a quarter of a million. A bike with a full tank and thousands of miles of open road stretched seductively ahead of him. He could head anywhere, keep the money for himself, do whatever he liked. The man he knew as Leo would never find him. Who the hell was Leo anyway? Just a fag who prowled the bars to see whom he could pick up. Fags always got taken once in a while. It went with the territory, a little risk in return for their fun and games. Chris grinned . . . if he split with the entire quarter of a million, Leo would get taken for a lot.

For a minute, while he battled the Broadway traffic, slipping in and out of different lanes, Chris ran the idea through his mind. Leo would turn up at the meeting place tomorrow evening, expecting to be handed the ransom so he could turn a third of it over to Chris. Why, Chris asked himself, should I get only a third of it? Sure, Leo did all the planning, but I did all the work.

A stop light loomed red in front of him. Chris slowed to a halt. To his left was a police cruiser. He gave the vehicle the once over, and the two police officers surveyed him through narrowed eyes. Come on and change, Chris whispered to the traffic light. Change before these bastards get nosey or bloody-minded. He froze on the seat of the motorcycle as the police car's siren suddenly burst into life. Lights flashing, it moved into the intersection, swung left and sped away to an accompaniment of squealing tyres. Chris wanted to laugh. A traffic accident, probably, or some dumb bastard getting mugged. And those stupid cops had torn off to that when they'd had the biggest crime of the week sitting right beneath their noses.

The light changed and Chris rolled forward. Steering with one hand, he felt quickly beneath his leather jacket, caressed the butt of the automatic that was stuck in his waistband. Souvenir from Vietnam. Now it would come in useful. Chris knew he had to go back to Leo, keep the appointment with him. Leo was the only link between Chris and the kidnapping. The man they'd abducted and left in the Jersey City warehouse was someone Leo knew. Chris had seen that much when they had picked up William outside the building on Madison Avenue. But there was no link between that man and Chris. No connection at all, except for Leo.

Chris would keep all of the money, and when he met with Leo the following night he would sever the connection completely.

Minsky counted off seconds while he stared at the bus schedule board. Times flashed in front of his eyes, joined to names like Englewood, Dumont and Teaneck. All around him, people jotted down platform numbers and departure times, but Minsky just stared. And counted. At two hundred and forty, he glanced down at his watch. Three minutes and fifty-three seconds had passed since he'd arrived at the schedule board; he was only seven seconds out with his count. Dare he look around yet? He had little doubt that the case would be gone, its collector long since departed from the bus station. The five-minute waiting period was meaningless. He could be on his way back to the taxi already, heading back to Queens, to Forest Hills Gardens to learn where William was being held.

'Hey, mister . . . are you going to stand there all day?'

Minsky felt an elbow dig him in the back. He swung around, and a tiny middle-aged woman dived past him to the board. The bank of two pay phones flashed before Minsky's vision. Both were empty. The blue suitcase was gone. Gripping the cane in his left hand, he walked towards the stairs.

'Where to now?' the cab driver asked.

'Back to where you picked me up.'

'You finished running around for the day?'

'I've finished.'

'Where's that case?'

'Why don't you just shut the fuck up and drive?' Minsky leaned back as the taxi moved off. His breathing was still coming hard and he could feel his heart pounding in his chest. That would be the final irony, another goddamned heart attack or stroke. He closed his eyes and, by some miracle, went to sleep.

He awoke just as the taxi pulled up behind the unmarked Plymouth belonging to FBI agent Frank Hopkins. Minsky climbed out and walked towards the front door. Hopkins opened it. Behind him stood Susan.

'Did you make your delivery?' the agent asked.

'At the George Washington Bridge bus station. They ran me all over town, one telephone to the next. Have they called here yet? They're supposed to let me know where William is.'

'No calls at all.' Hopkins stepped aside as Minsky entered the house.

'Are you okay?' Minsky asked his daughter-in-law.

'When William comes back, I will be.'

'He'll be back. I did everything they told me to do. Where are the boys?'

'They're still away.' She noticed how tired he seemed. 'Do you want something? A cup of coffee, a sandwich?'

'Coffee'll be fine.' Minsky went into the living-room and sat down, hands clasping the top of the cane in front of him. Where were they? Why didn't they call? Any time he had made a bargain in his life, he'd kept to it. Weren't these bastards cut from the same damned cloth?

Susan brought in three cups of coffee, for Minsky, the FBI agent and herself. Over the top of his cup, Minsky glared at the agent. 'I suppose you're going to tell me how I should have let someone from your office drive me around. That way we'd have the pick-up man by now.'

'I'm not going to say anything, Mr Minsky. You made your choice, did what you thought was best for your son. My active participation will commence the moment your son is released.'

'Look, I'm sorry. I know you've got a job to do. . . .' Minsky was suddenly aware of how badly he'd treated the FBI agent. Hopkins was there in good faith, prepared to do his best to obtain William's release and the apprehension of the kidnappers, and Minsky had put him down at every turn.

'Don't apologize, Mr Minsky. Believe me, I understand perfectly what was going through your mind. You didn't care about the kidnappers being caught, all you wanted was your son back. That's fine. I just hope they keep their word.' Hopkins lifted his head inquisitively as the telephone began to ring.

Minsky put down his coffee and took the call. It was the same voice that had told him to walk away from the money in the suitcase, the muffled New York accent.

'Welcome home, Mr Minsky,' Leo said.

'Where the hell's my son? I paid you the damned money just like you said. I walked away to study those bus schedules. I left the case and I didn't turn around for five minutes. I kept up my end of the bargain.'

'We know,' Leo said. 'Here's where you'll find him. In Jersey City, there's a warehouse close to the river. . . .'

Minsky scribbled down the address on the pad next to the telephone. The moment the call finished, he ripped off the piece of paper and handed it to the FBI agent. 'I'll call this in,' Hopkins said. 'My people will be waiting when we get there. With a bit of luck, they might be able to pick up something.'

Feeling far better than he had done earlier, Minsky kissed Susan goodbye and climbed into the back of Hopkins' Plymouth. As the car began to move, he rolled down the window and called back to Susan, 'Get the boys back! William's going to want to see them. They're going to want to see him.'

'You know, Mr Minsky,' Hopkins said from the front of the car, 'only in very few cases do we ever get back all of the ransom money once a kidnapping's over. If we grab the man who makes the pick-up, that's one thing – the money's still in our sight. But once we lose sight of it, it's a different matter altogether. By the time we apprehend those behind your son's kidnapping, the money could have been spent a thousand different ways, hidden, who knows . . .?'

'Who cares?' Minsky responded. 'I'm just glad to get my son back. The quarter of a million I can afford.'

'Whoever took your son sure knew that.'

As they exited from the New Jersey end of the Holland Tunnel, the Plymouth's radio crackled into life. Hopkins picked up the microphone. In the rear of the car, Minsky was unable to hear what was being said above the hum of the tyres and the sound of traffic. But he knew it was bad the moment Hopkins pulled the car over to the side of the road and turned around.

'What is it? My son? What's happened? Isn't he there, at the warehouse?'

'He's there all right, Mr Minsky. Or, at least, a man answering his description is. But he's dead.' He stared sympathetically at Minsky for a few seconds, then swung around, put the car in gear and continued the journey.

Four cars were parked at the deserted warehouse when Minsky and Hopkins arrived. Two wore the insignia of the local police department. The other two, like the Plymouth, were unmarked. Minsky got out of the Plymouth and walked towards the entrance. Hopkins pulled him back.

'Are you certain you want to go in there, Mr Minsky?'

'Someone's got to identify the body, right?'

'Someone has to, yes. But you don't have to do it right away.'

'I may as well get it over with.'

Accompanying Minsky into the warehouse, Hopkins decided that his haste was prompted by the slender hope that the body might not, after all, be that of his son.

A medical examiner was at work in the small room upstairs that had once been an office. The twine had been removed from William's ankles and neck, and the examiner had little doubt that the cause of death was strangulation. A vivid red line encircled William's throat. His eyes bulged sightlessly, the skin on his face was dark, his swollen tongue protruded grotesquely from his mouth. Minsky walked into the room and rested his weight on his cane as he stared down at the body.

'Is that your son, Mr Minsky?' Hopkins asked.

'That's William.' He moved his gaze to the medical examiner who, totally oblivious to the grief of the man standing next to him, continued with his work.

'Been dead a full day, I'd guess,' the examiner said to no one in particular. 'Be able to get a better handle on the time of death when we do an autopsy, but twenty-four hours seems like a reasonably accurate estimate.'

A reasonably accurate estimate . . . that was how they talked about William now, Minsky thought. Been dead a full day . . . get a better handle on the time of death . . . autopsy. 'He was dead when they first contacted me,' Minsky murmured. 'all this time they had me running around, and he was dead all along.'

The medical examiner carried on talking as though he had an interested audience; he could have been discussing a particularly interesting case with medical students. 'These marks on the victim's face – they could be the signs of a struggle. He may have put up a fight, either when he was abducted or when the string was looped around his throat and ankles. On the other hand, though. . . .' The medical examiner lifted William's hands in his own. 'There are no abrasions, no bruises on his hands. Maybe he was just beaten up before he was murdered. And this. . .' He indicated dried blood on

William's face. 'He was spitting blood before he died. The interior of his mouth isn't marked so it suggests internal bleeding.' Prodding William's chest, he added, 'I'd surmise broken ribs, more evidence of a beating.'

'Come away, Mr Minsky,' the agent said. He had been proven right, yet he felt no pleasure. Seeing this elderly man just standing there, gazing numbly down at his son, removed any satisfaction at being proved correct.

Minsky refused to move. He remained in the room until William's body was taken downstairs to a waiting ambulance. As the medical examiner prepared to leave, Minsky touched him on the arm with his cane. 'Excuse me, sir. How long will it be before I can bury my son?'

'There has to be an autopsy. It shouldn't take long, though. A formality, really. Perhaps we'll be able to release him to you by tomorrow.'

'Thank you.' Minsky did not even want to think about the further abuse his son's body would have to suffer under an autopsy.

All the way back to Forest Hills Gardens, Minsky tried to think of a way to tell Susan and the boys. He had broken his promise to his grandsons. He'd told them William would be coming back, and it wasn't true. They would not all be sitting in the synagogue this coming Saturday for Mark's *bar mitzvah*. They would be mourning William instead. Just like the Granitz family and Jake, the twins and Pearl mourning for their father and husband when there should have been celebrating.

Susan knew the truth the moment Minsky stepped out of the Plymouth in front of the house. She had been watching through the front window, her mind made up about what would happen. If the telephone rang, everything would be all right. Minsky would call the moment William was found unharmed. He would put William on the line to reassure her. But if Minsky did not telephone . . . if he returned to the house without calling first . . . it would be because he had bad news. News he could only impart personally. News that William was hurt. Or worse.

She came running out of the house before Minsky could reach the front door. One look at the iron set of her father-in-law's dark face was enough to tell her the worst. 'He's dead, isn't he? William's dead.'

There was no way to soften the blow. 'Yes, Susan,' Minsky answered in a voice that was as expressionless as his face. 'William's been murdered. He was dead all the time. Where are the boys? I should be the one to tell them.'

Chapter Three

The meeting place chosen by Leo Granitz was a tiny rest area with no facilities on Route 17, close to the Wurtsboro exit in Sullivan County, some eighty miles north-west of the centre of New York City. Late at night, the road was lightly travelled. A car and a motorcycle with lights off, parked well away from the road, stood a one-in-a-thousand chance of being noticed.

Just before midnight on the day following the discovery of William Minsky's body, Chris sped west along Route 17 on his motorcycle. He was careful to stay within the speed limit. The last thing he needed was to be pulled over for speeding, if there was such a thing as a policeman patrolling this deserted stretch of four-lane highway so late at night. A cop might take it into his mind to see what Chris was carrying in the leather grip strapped to the motorcycle's luggage rack. A quarter of a million dollars was bound to raise even the dumbest hick cop's suspicions. And then Chris would have to shoot the cop.

As he followed the road illuminated in the white beam of the headlight, Chris considered the impending meeting with Leo. They hadn't collaborated on a kidnapping, they'd collaborated on murder. The discovery of William's body had been in all the newspapers, on radio and television. It became even more imperative for Chris to sever the link that bound him to the crime. Not that he should have been surprised at learning William was dead. It was the obvious outcome of the whole affair. Leo and William had known each other. You didn't kidnap someone you knew, and then let him go when the money was paid. The first thing he'd do was identify his abductors.

389

When had Leo committed the murder? While Chris was still in the warehouse, changing from the chauffeur's uniform into his leathers? String tied around William's ankles and neck so he'd choke himself. Despite the cloudy, humid June night, the heavy clothing he wore, Chris shivered. It took a certain cruel bent to kill a man that way, leave him to choke himself to death. Chris knew he would have to be extra careful when he arrived at the meeting place. He had under-estimated Leo, thought he was just some middle-aged fag. Now he knew better.

Chris passed the exit to Wurtsboro and started to look for the rest area sign. Glancing down at the luminous hands of his watch, he saw it was a few minutes after twelve. Was Leo there already? Waiting for him? The sign for the rest area loomed up, flashed past. Chris cut his lights and touched the brakes. At the beginning of the entrance ramp, he killed the engine and coasted silently.

The rest area did not even boast a light. It was nothing but a narrow paved area set well back from the highway with dense trees to its rear. For a moment, the cloud broke and the moon shone through. Parked right at the far end of the rest area, off the paved surface and almost in the trees, Chris saw a white Cadillac convertible, its roof up. Chris braked and ran the motorcycle up on to the grass at the entrance to the rest area. He jumped off, dropped the motorcycle silently on to the grass, following it with his helmet. Then, gun in hand, he started to run. Not towards the Cadillac but towards the trees.

Ten yards into them, he cut left, using what he had learned in the army to find his way in the darkness. Each step was an adventure, foot and hand thrust out in front, using them as a blind man uses a white stick. He made agonizingly slow progress. After eight minutes, he estimated that he must be level with the white Cadillac. He turned left again, moving by inches in case he snapped a twig, disturbed an animal. Was he being overcautious? Leo was just sitting in the Cadillac, waiting for him. Or was he? The brutal killing of William Minsky – never mind that it should have been obvious to Chris from the moment Leo called William's name outside that building on Madison Avenue – was forcing him to be careful.

390

He reached the edge of the trees, staying in their shadow while he surveyed what lay ahead. The boot of the Cadillac was only five yards away. A single shot – he raised the gun to eye level – through the rear window and his connection to the kidnapping and murder of William Minsky would be cut. Wait! The night was dark, the moon again concealed by clouds. The rear window of the Cadillac's convertible roof was difficult to see through. Chris could not be certain there was even anyone sitting in the Cadillac.

Emerging from the cover of the trees, he took a step closer. He dropped down on to his knees and elbows, crawled like they had taught him to do in the army. He could feel the warmth of the Cadillac's exhaust system. Skirting the side of the car, he made his way to the driver's door.

From behind Chris came a soft whisper. 'I knew you'd come here tonight, Chris. And I knew why.'

Chris spun around in his crawl position, the gun coming up. Before he could raise it fully, exert pressure on the trigger, a heavy steel bar crashed down across his right shoulder. He screamed in pain. The gun clattered on to the concrete. His scramble for it was stopped when Leo slammed his foot down on the young man's wrist. The steel bar descended again across the side of Chris' head, and blackness followed it.

Leo picked up the pistol and slipped it into his coat pocket. He ran towards the other end of the rest area where Chris had left the motorcycle. After unstrapping the grip full of money, he returned to the Cadillac. Chris was just beginning to regain conciousness. Leo squatted next to him, took out the gun and pointed it at Chris's face. The metallic click of the hammer being pulled back could have been the sound of a cricket.

'I must have looked like a dumb bastard to you, Chris. I let you pick up a quarter of a million dollars from the bus station, didn't I? You could have just cut and run, but I knew you'd come to this meeting. You know how I knew?'

'If you're going to pull the trigger, get it over and done with, you fucking fag!' Chris spat out.

In the darkness, Leo's smile was barely visible. 'Quarter of a million. Easy pickings. But no, you wanted to get rid of me first, didn't you? You had to. I could connect you to what happened in Jersey City. You didn't want that, did you?

That's why I knew you'd come, to kill me before you took off with the money.' Leo pushed the gun a few inches closer to Chris's face, until the muzzle was staring directly into his left eye. 'I could read you like a book, Chris. Forewarned is forearmed, did you ever hear of that saying? I was forewarned all right. That's why I was up at the other end of the rest area when you coasted in with your lights off. For every silent step you took through those trees, I was taking one right behind you. You should have seen how stupid you looked, waving your hands and feet in the air like some insect probing with its antennae. Now you look even more stupid, don't you?'

Chris tried to black out the waves of pain that pulsed through his entire body from his shattered shoulder. The gun was so close. If he could gather the strength, time his move, push himself up and make a grab for it. . . .

'You know what makes you even more stupid, Chris? This money, it doesn't mean a damned thing to me. Here. . .' Leo unzipped the grip, felt inside and pulled out a fistful of bills. He threw them up into the air like confetti, let the wind carry them away towards the road. 'Little windfall for someone. I'm going to burn the rest. This money doesn't mean shit to me.' He broke off, lifted his head curiously as the sound of an engine carried through the night air. A truck in low gear struggling up a hill. Headlight beams danced across the sky like searchlights. The beams levelled out, and Leo turned towards the source of the noise. There, approaching the far end of the rest area after having completed its climb up the hill, was the truck.

Chris took a deep, silent breath and lunged at Leo. His left hand slammed against the gun barrel, shoved it back and up. A booming explosion echoed across the rest area. Leo catapulted back, hands clutched to his head. For a few seconds he lay writhing and groaning, then in one convulsive movement his body jerked into a rigid line and he became perfectly still. As Chris approached him, the truck rumbled past the the rest area, engine revolutions dropping as the driver shifted into a higher gear.

The gun lay on the ground. Chris picked it up, levelled it at Leo's head, then lowered it. Even in the dim light supplied by the hidden moon, Chris could see the copious flow of blood that cascaded from Leo's temple, filling his right eye before running off his cheek on to the ground. Another shot was not only unnecessary but risky. The report of the first shot had been concealed by the grinding of the truck's engine as it reached top revolutions. A second shot might be heard. Chris dropped the hammer, slipped on the safety catch and concealed the weapon in the waistband of his trousers. He picked up the grip full of money in his left hand, spent a few seconds looking around to see if he could spot any of the bills Leo had tossed into the wind. They were gone. Why did he need them anyway? He had more than enough in the grip.

The moment he started to lope towards the motorcycle at the far end of the rest area, his right shoulder screamed in agony. Excitement, danger, had acted like an anaesthetic, killing the pain in his broken shoulder, numbing the ache in his head. Now the anaesthetic had worn off. The pain in his head he could live with, but every movement was like having sharp knives thrust into his shoulder and right arm. He gritted his teeth, tried to remember what it had been like in airborne training at Fort Bragg before he'd ever gone to Vietnam. Mind over matter . . . that's what the drill sergeants had said. We don't mind, and you don't matter. If he could live through the hell of airborne training, the further hell of Vietnam, he could live through this.

He reached the motorcycle, struggled to raise it. After strapping the grip on to the luggage rack, he jumped up and down on the kick start. The engine roared as he opened the throttle. God . . . his shoulder was on fire! Every degree of steering, every gear change, every braking motion, was rewarded with a spasm of agony that ran from his fingers to his head. How many bones had that fag son of a bitch broken with the damned steel bar? He pointed the motorcycle towards the rest area exit, lights off until he reached the sanctuary of the highway. He'd fake an accident, that's what he'd do. Find some place to stash the money and then fake an accident to explain away his injuries while he sought medical help.

The motorcycle picked up speed. Chris passed the Cadillac, the motionless figure of Leo. Didn't need the money! *Rich* fag son of a bitch! He sure as hell wouldn't be needing it now. Reaching the highway, Chris flicked on the lights. He'd keep heading west, get well away from this spot. Try to hold on for a couple of hours. Ditch the gun, hide the money, then fake the accident. A hospital would set his shoulder straight.

The front wheel wobbled uncertainly. Chris caught it just in time. He was having difficulty steering. Despite the pain, he gripped tighter with his right hand. He could hang on. A couple of hours, that was all. Two hours to put a hundred and thirty miles between himself and Leo's body. He could tough it out for that long. Sure he could, when he had a quarter of a million dollars to look forward to spending.

After five miles, red lights danced in the blackness ahead of him, the tail lights of the truck that had passed the rest area when Leo had held the gun on him. The truck that had saved his life and cost Leo his. Chris pulled out to overtake. As he roared past, he raised his good left hand in the air. He was thanking the truck, thanking the driver, not that the man would ever understand. The front wheel wobbled again and Chris dropped his left hand back on to the handlebar.

He saw no more westbound traffic until he reached the long hill leading up to Monticello. Halfway up the incline, he spotted a battered old truck staggering along in low gear. Chris sped by as if the truck was stationary. He reached the crest of the hill. Down to his left was Monticello Raceway. Ahead was a steep downward gradient. The needle of the speedometer swept up to eighty miles an hour as Chris opened the throttle. Caution fled on the wings of excitement, the speed of the powerful motorcycle on the open road, the knowledge that he had defeated a man who'd thought he'd outwitted him. How long would it be before the police were notified? Would Chris have hidden the money, staged the accident that would account for his injured shoulder, the bruise and abrasions on his head, by then?

The gun! He still had to get rid of the gun! Steering with his right hand, feeling the pain shoot up his arm to his shoulder, Chris plucked the gun from his waistband and flung it as far as he could to his right, aiming for the dense undergrowth that bordered the highway. The sudden movement cost him balance. He felt the motorcycle sway sickeningly. Too late he tried to correct the situation. The back end of the motorcycle swung out. Centrifugal force overcame friction. At eighty miles an hour, the motorcycle skidded off the road, across the hard shoulder and into a deep ditch filled with shrubs and small trees. Flung off, Chris soared through the air like a tree uprooted by a tornado, arms and legs flailing as though trying to fly. A flight that was stopped abruptly by the sharp, spiky tree branch that impaled him through the centre of his chest.

Hanging upside down, ten feet above the ground, Chris's final thought was of waste – the criminal waste of the quarter of a million dollars he had carried on the back of the motorcycle.

Leo had been right all along. The money didn't mean a damned thing.

Leo wasn't dead. The bullet from Chris's gun had only grazed his forehead, leaving a deep furrow across his right temple that merged into his hairline. All around the cut were minuscule black dots, powder burns from the weapon that had been discharged so close to his head.

The noise of the motorcycle starting permeated Leo's unconsciousness. Lying on his back, face covered in blood, he listened to the sound and knew that he should do something. He had to stop Chris, kill him as he'd intended to do before the solitary truck had diverted his attention for a fraction of a second. Urgently, his brain sent out messages to his body. They went unheeded. He heard the motorcycle pass by where he lay, and he could do nothing but listen to its engine note grow fainter and fainter. For another five minutes he lay on his back, moving only to dab away some of the blood that closed his right eye like glue.

Chris was gone. There was nothing Leo could do about it now. He had to save himself. Summoning all his strength, he rolled over on to his hands and knees. The effort sent hammers ringing inside his skull and he almost passed out again. Screwing his eyes shut with pain, forcing his mind to focus, he pushed himself on to his knees. Next, he attempted the most difficult feat of all: standing up. The world swayed. Feeling his legs starting to buckle, Leo guided himself in the direction of the white Cadillac. He fell against the door, fingers clawing for support. Gradually the dizziness passed. He opened the car door, fell on to the seat. Where were the keys? He searched through his pockets, each movement sending signals of pain to his brain. In the ignition! He'd left the key in the ignition. He turned the key, listened gratefully to the engine crank into life. Home. He had to get home to Scarsdale. There, in the safety of his own house, he would clean up his head, wash away the blood, clean the wound. He couldn't got to a hospital. No matter what lies he told there, no one would believe him. The powder burns – he turned on the interior light and examined his forehead in the mirror – were a giveaway. Even a first-year medical student would be able to spot the gunshot wound. The police would be summoned. Leo could not afford that.

He turned on the headlights, put the Cadillac into drive and headed slowly toward the rest area exit. The next exit was four miles west. Four miles here and four miles back. Eight extra miles on his journey home. The hell with that, he muttered, and drove right across the two westbound lanes and on to the grass separating them from the eastbound traffic. The Cadillac dipped into the soft ground and came up on the tarmac on the other side. Leo turned the steering wheel to the left and headed back to New York City. He had no idea which way Chris had gone. He just hoped – the irony of it almost made him laugh – that the young man got clean away. Next to being dead, the safest thing for everyone was for Chris and the money to disappear completely.

The journey home seemed to last for ever, yet when Leo arrived at Scarsdale and checked the dashboard clock he saw that only sixty-five minutes had elapsed. Entering the house, he went to the bathroom and took the first aid kit from the cupboard. First he washed the blood from his face and right eye. Gritting his teeth, he cleaned the wound. The iodine caused even more pain than the bullet had done, burning its way into open flesh. As Leo looked at the raw furrow in the mirror, he realized for the first time that he had been shot. Shot, and he'd survived. Not only that, but here he was, standing in his own bathroom, cleaning the wound. Someone had been watching over him tonight.

Once the wound was clean, he covered it with cotton gauze

396

and a large patch of plaster. The powder burns still showed. He picked at them with a pair of tweezers, ripping off the burned spots of skin, leaving the area with a raw, shredded appearance. He would say he'd stumbled, slipped on the gravel driveway of the house and grazed his temple. That would account for the raw patchiness. No one would disbelieve him; no one would have reason to.

After taking aspirin, he went to the telephone. Two o'clock in the morning or not, Leo knew that he had to tell Lou Levitt what had happened. More than anything else, he dreaded apprising the little man of his failure.

William was buried on Friday afternoon. Pearl rode with Joseph to the chapel in Forest Hills. Lou Levitt travelled in Leo's Cadillac. Minsky rode alone. Susan did not attend the service, nor would she be at the interment. She remained at home, with Judy keeping her company. Susan's two sons were staying with friends of the family, as they had been during the period of the abduction; they were considered too young to attend the funeral of their father.

Leo's head still throbbed excruciatingly from the gunshot wound. Regular doses of aspirin had done little to alleviate the pain. If anything, they had contributed to the dull ache in his stomach. The patch of plaster was partially concealed by the hat he wore. Nonetheless, questions were asked when he arrived at the chapel. He responded with the story he had concocted – a fall on the gravel driveway of his home, a bad graze. Everyone offered him sympathy. Everyone except Levitt.

'You're damned lucky you didn't get yourself killed,' he said as they took their seats in the chapel. 'How could you let yourself be distracted like that?'

'I thought the truck was coming right into the damned rest area,' Leo replied in an angry whisper. 'That's all I needed, for some truck driver to see me there with a gun.'

'You've no idea where this Chris went?'

'He just took off, that's all I know.'

'While we're here, you'd better pray that he gets swallowed up by some hole in the ground. Him and the damned money.'

Some of Levitt's anger abated as he looked at Benny

Minsky leaning on his cane. Minsky seemed to have aged dramatically since the last time Levitt had seen him. He looked like a man in his eighties, not his late sixties. He wore his grief like a piece of clothing, on the outside for the entire world to see. When Levitt had gone over to shake his hand, he had seen dried tear stains on Minsky's dark, wrinkled cheeks.

When the service was over, the funeral procession headed out to the cemetery on Long Island. Leo drove behind his twin brother's car, in which Pearl rode. At the cemetery, he parked next to Joseph. Levitt took Pearl's arm and walked with her towards the freshly dug grave. 'Your place isn't here,' he said gently. 'You should have stayed with Susan and Judy at the house.'

'Benny's my friend, Lou. I couldn't let him face this alone. Look at him. . . .' She gestured with her head towards the lonely figure. Minsky was refusing any assistance to get to the grave. He plodded on, dragging his left leg behind him. 'Outside, he might look alive, but inside he's shrivelled up and dead.'

'I know. He thought the world of that son of his. What happened to William makes me worry about the twins. Some lousy place we live in, eh? A guy puts together a few bucks and immediately he becomes a target for animals.'

'The police said William was killed even before the ransom demands were made. He was tied up and left to choke to death.' Pearl's voice faded. Levitt held her arm tightly and turned to the twins.

'Why don't you get your mother out of here? Let her sit in the car until it's over.'

Before either Leo or Joseph could move, Pearl said, 'I'm all right.' Levitt felt her arm stiffen and he let go. She marched on ahead to join Minsky at the side of the grave. Levitt's eyes turned bleak as he watched her. She had no business standing next to that bastard.

The prayers were said, the coffin lowered. One by one, the burial party stepped forward to shower a spadeful of earth into the pit. Levitt followed Joseph. He lifted the spade to send earth cascading down on to the top of the casket. To his ears, the noise of earth and stones hitting the wood was like applause. Struggling to hide an expression of satisfaction, he turned around and passed the spade to Leo.

Leo dug the spade in deeply, twisting free a huge mound of earth. He straightened up too abruptly. Blood roared in his ears, his head felt empty. Levitt and Joseph reached out simultaneously to grab hold of him as he tottered back and forth at the edge of the grave. The spade fell from his hand into the pit, bouncing off the top of the varnished casket.

'Carry on like that and you'll join him,' Levitt said. 'You'd better get yourself home, get some sleep.'

'I'll be okay.' Leo breathed in deeply, waited for the moment of dizziness to pass. He stood in line at the small fountain to ritually rinse his hands, shook them in the air to dry.

While Joseph took his mother back to the Minsky home in Forest Hills Gardens, Leo returned Levitt to Central Park West. Levitt no longer talked about the young man named Chris. His worry over Leo's mistake had been replaced by a sensation of victory. 'You see Benny's face back there?' he asked Leo. 'That's what you call defeat. Total, utter defeat. When you can do that to a man, you've crushed him like an ant.'

'I saw. He looked so bad I thought we were going to get two funerals for the price of one.'

'Don't wish that, Leo. Wish instead that the bastard lives for a long time yet, so he can think about this. He set Jake up for Gus Landau, and now he's going through what you, your brother, your mother all went through. What I went through as well.'

'You?'

'Sure, me. Jake was the closest friend I ever had. From schooldays, even. Too bad your mother can never know the truth, never know who was responsible for Jake's death, never know how we paid him back.' He shook his head at the injustice of it all. 'How's your head holding up?'

'Still there.' Leo took one hand off the wheel, touched it to his temple. Was it his imagination or were the aspirins beginning to have some effect? The pounding seemed to have lessened. Gunshot wound. It was an injury, just like any other. It was nothing special. Given time, it got better.

'You know,' Levitt gave a dry chuckle, 'the rabbi back there, he went on about the *shivah* starting tomorrow night, after *Shabbes* goes out. He never made any mention, though, of Mark's *bar mitzvah*. You paid Benny back well, Leo. He thought he'd be getting a barrel full of pleasure tomorrow. Instead, he's going to be sitting on a wooden chair, mourning his son.'

Leo smiled in satisfaction. Levitt had forgiven him for allowing Chris to escape. The money didn't matter at all – it wasn't even their own money to begin with. It was Minsky's. Chris would just disappear, be swallowed up somewhere. It was a big country. Leo was convinced that he had nothing to worry about at all.

After dropping Levitt off outside his building on Central Park West, Leo drove north to Scarsdale. He removed the dressing on his temple and inspected the wound. The tiny tears where he'd ripped off the spots of burned powder were already beginning to fade. The bullet wound itself was also paler. He applied a fresh patch, took two more aspirin and lay down in his bedroom. He'd do as Levitt had suggested, get some sleep. If he felt better when he awoke, he'd go into town.

Just becuse Benny Minsky was in mourning, it didn't mean that Leo had to forgo his own pleasure.

Pearl, Joseph and Judy stayed the remainder of the day at the Minsky home. At five o'clock in the afternoon, Minsky's two grandsons were returned to the house. The family sat in a sombre group in the living-room, while Pearl busied herself in the kitchen. They had to eat. Cooking dinner for them would take her own mind off the tragedy. It was a tried and trusted remedy. She only wished that she could prescribe a similar cure for Minsky, Susan and the boys. As she prepared the meal, she wondered how well Susan would stand up to the loss. To have it happen so close to her older son's *bar mitzvah* as well. There was something uncanny about that. Pearl had lost Jake immediately following the twins' *bar mitzvahs* twenty-nine years earlier. Now, history had repeated itself.

Pearl prepared dinner, but she did not stay to share it with the Minskys. With the promise to be back the following day, she left the house with Joseph and Judy to return to Sands Point.

Susan served the meal. It was eaten quietly, without enjoyment. Afterwards, when the boys helped Susan to clear the table, Minsky walked out to the patio in the rear of the house. He wanted to be alone, to review the day he had buried his only son.

Sitting there in the warm June night, Minsky questioned what he could have changed in his life to avoid this dreadful day. How . . . he gazed up to the heavens as though asking God . . . could it have ended in this manner? He saw a picture of Kathleen trying to abort the child, terrified that its birth would ruin her career. He saw a picture of himself holding a gun to Kathleen's head, swearing to pull the trigger if she didn't go through with the pregnancy. Later, he'd brought the boy up on his own after Kathleen had decided that the limelight was more alluring than motherhood. Minsky had taken more pride in his son than in anything he'd ever done, because William was the only thing in Minsky's life that he was truly proud of. And to have it end like his! A stupid, senseless murder when he'd been prepared to hand over the money for William's release. A quarter of a million dollars. He would have given ten times that much for William's safe return; he would have given every penny he could beg, borrow or steal.

He thought of Kathleen again, not as he had last seen her, with her body eaten away by cancer, but as he had known her in the early days of their tempestous love affair. How much grief could he have been spared if he had not threatened to kill her? If he'd allowed her to go through with her craziness and lose the baby? He would have suffered short-term pain, the loss of a son he never knew, a boy who never entered life. Surely that pain would not have been as acute as the anguish he was suffering now. To have watched William grow into such a fine young man with a family of his own, and then be torn away so cruelly.

Footsteps sounded. Minsky swivelled around in the chair to see Susan standing by the French windows that led to the dining-room. 'The boys have gone to bed.'

'Already?'

She gave him a weary smile. 'You've been sitting out here for almost two hours.'

Minsky looked at his watch, surprised to see it was almost ten o'clock. 'So I have.'

'They want you to go up and say good-night to them.'

'Of course.' Minsky eased himself to his feet, entered the house and laboriously climbed the stairs. First, he went into Paul's room. The younger boy was sitting up in bed. 'Good night, Paul.' Minsky bent forward to kiss his grandson on the cheek. 'I'll see you in the morning.'

From Paul's room, he went next door to Mark. The older boy was not in bed. Wearing pyjamas, he was sitting in a chair by the window, looking out over the street. When he heard Minsky enter the room, he turned around.

'I can't believe it, Grandpa. I can't believe that my father's dead.'

Minsky sat down next to him. 'Neither can I, Mark.' He hoped the boy wouldn't remind him of the promise he had broken.

'I keep looking out of the window, expecting to see his car pull into the drive. Like he used to come home when he worked late at the truck depot, and I'd be watching out of the window for him.'

Minsky put an arm around the boy's shoulders, held him tightly. 'I know how you feel, Mark. Each time I hear a car, I think it's him.'

'Will the police ever catch the people who did it?'

'I don't know.'

'I hope they do,' Mark spat out with sudden vehemence. 'I hope they catch them and kill them.'

Minsky said nothing because his thoughts were too close to his grandson's. On this day of all days, he did not want Mark to see the ugliness that welled up within him. Minsky wanted the police to apprehend whoever was responsible. And then he wanted them turned over to himself. Old man or not, partially disabled by the stroke, it didn't matter. Lock him up with William's murderer . . . murderers . . . in a room for ten minutes, and he'd make them wish they'd never left the secure comfort of the womb.

He kissed Mark good-night and returned downstairs. Susan said that she, too, was going to bed and did he need anything? Minsky told her no. He just wanted to sit, to be alone.

Instead of returning to the patio, he sat in the downstairs room at the front of the house which had been turned into his bedroom for the time he was in New York. Watching through the window, he understood only too well how Mark felt. Each time a car came along the road, Minsky could easily think it was William returning home after working late. Soon, one of the cars would turn into the driveway. Its lights and engines would die. The driver's door would open and Wiliam would step out. He'd see his father sitting in the window and give him a cheerful wave, and the nightmare would be over.

Another set of headlights probed the darkness of the street. Minsky's imagination took over completely. The car did not go past the house. The headlights turned full on the window through which Minsky was looking, illuminating his face, almost blinding him. He had to shield his eyes with his hand until the car had swung around in front of the house. The lights dimmed. The sound of the engine died. The driver's door opened. Minsky almost cried out William's name. He stopped only when he realized it was not William who stepped out of the car. It was Frank Hopkins, the FBI agent who had stayed at the house and begged to be allowed to tail Minsky when he made the ransom drop; the same man who had driven him to the warehouse in Jersey City where they found William's body.

The agent saw Minsky sitting in the window and lifted a hand in greeting. Minsky opened the window. 'What do you want?'

'I need to speak to you, Mr Minsky. We have information, important information.

'Come around to the front door. I'll let you in. Please be quiet, my daughter-in-law and grandsons are sleeping.' Minsky limped to the front door and opened it. The agent stepped inside and led the way to the front room where Minsky had been sitting.

'What is this important information?'

'Do you know of a man named Christopher Latham?'

'Christopher Latham?' Minsky repeated the name mechanically. 'Never heard of him. Who is he?'

'Was. He's dead. A Vietnam veteran, out of the army two or three months. From Sanford, North Carolina, originally, but he'd been living in a hotel in Times Square. He was killed in a traffic accident either late last night or early this morning on Route Seventeen up in Monticello. Drove a motorcycle. Came off it at high speed and was impaled on a tree.'

'What does this have to do with me?'

Hopkins held up a hand, signalling for Minsky to be patient. 'It may have everything to do with you, with your son. Latham's motorcycle was wrecked, but at the scene of the accident the state police recovered a leather grip. Inside it was almost a quarter of a million dollars.'

Minsky's dark eyes sharpened. 'Wait a minute. When I went to the George Washington Bridge bus station, I was supposed to wait by a telephone that had an out-of-order sign hanging from it. In the next booth, talking on the telephone – ' Minsky saw it clearly, every single detail – 'was a man in motorcycle clothes. You know, the leather pants and jacket, the helmet. He had a suitcase on the floor by his feet. A red suitcase. I didn't pay any attention at the time, but now I remember.'

'Of course, we don't have any proof that the money this Christopher Latham was carrying on his motorcycle was the same money you left at the bus station. The ransom stipulation was for tens, twenties, and fifties. That's what was found in the grip, but they were all used bills, no way to trace the money, no way to say definitely that it was the ransom. However. . .'

'However what?'

'The state police found this among Latham's possessions.' Hopkins produced a slip of paper. It was a photocopy of a list of telephone numbers, eight in all.

'What's this?'

'The first seven telephone numbers corresponded to the pay phones where you were sent. This one – ' Hopkins pointed to the first number – 'that's the telephone at the corner of Jewel Avenue and Queens Boulevard. The next one's Jackson Heights, and so on and so on. We've located seven of these numbers. It's the eighth number that's interesting.'

'How come?' Minsky ran the information about Christopher Latham through in his mind. Sanford, North Carolina

. . .how could he have missed that? 'The man who spoke to me most of the time, he had a Southern accent.'

'That's right,' Hopkins said. 'But let's get back to this eighth number. There's no area code to tell us which city it's in, so we assumed it was two-one-two like the rest of them, a New York number. This number in New York presents us with an intriguing scenario. It's a recently installed business line, but it doesn't go through any switchboard. It's a direct line to an office in a real estate company called Granitz Brothers.'

'Granitz Brothers?' This time, Minsky's repetition of a name was filled with amazement.

'The installation order was placed by Leo Granitz.' Hopkins sat quietly while he watched a whole flood of expressions flash across Minsky's face. Surprise was first, dumb amazement as though Minsky could not comprehend such an involvement. Shock gave way to acceptance. Slowly Minsky's face clouded over until it was filled with nothing but rage and hatred. His body started to tremble, and he grasped the cane until his knuckles turned to ivory.

'Mr Minsky, we don't know what the connection is. We don't know why this Christopher Latham would have Leo Granitz's private office number in his possession. We don't even know if it is Leo Granitz's number that Latham had. The two-one-two is just a guess.'

'It is,' Minsky said with grim certainty. 'It's Leo's number. And that money is the ransom money.'

'Please allow us to do our job. Our men are at Scarsdale now, at Leo Granitz's home. We want to question him. He's away at the moment, but when he returns we'll question him. Believe me when I say we'll arrive at the truth of this matter.'

'Have you tried looking anywhere else for him?'

'At his twin brother's home in Sands Point? Yes, we've been there.'

'What about Lou Levitt, Central Park West? He might be there.'

'I'll get on to that right away. When we learn anything, I'll be in touch.' Hopkins stood up, ready to leave. As he looked down at Minsky sitting in the chair, he felt a perverse gratitude that the man was a partial cripple. The agent had never

405

seen such fury as that which was etched on Minsky's face. If Minsky were fit, the agent was sure, he would certainly take matters into his own hands.

Minsky remained in the chair for ten minutes after the FBI agent had left the house. Christopher Latham, fresh out of the army with a quarter of a million dollars and the direct-line number of Leo's office in his pocket. Was Latham – the Southern-accented voice on the other end of the line – the murderer of Minsky's son? If so, he had already paid the penalty. Minsky felt cheated, the bastard had gotten off too damned easily. Or was it Leo who had tied the string around William's ankles and throat, left him to choke to death? Broken his ribs and pounded his face to pulp? The hell with what Hopkins said about finding out the connection between Latham and Leo! Minsky did not need a degree in criminology, or whatever education modern-day cops had to get before they could strap on a shield and a gun, to know what the score was. He could see the connection perfectly. Not the connection Hopkins was chasing, but the *real* connection. A little runt of a double-dealing bastard named Lou Levitt!

He rose from the chair. Very cautiously, he climbed the stairs to the upper level of the house. By each door he stopped to listen. Susan and the boys were sleeping soundly. He returned downstairs and went into the kitchen. On a hook above the counter were Susan's keys. Minsky took the key to her car, and prayed that he could drive without full control and strength in his left arm and leg.

The driver's seat of Susan's car felt strange. Minsky had not sat behind a steering wheel since the stroke on New Year's Eve. Six months without driving. For a moment he came close to getting out of the car, leaving the police to do the job they were paid to do. No! This was something he alone must do. Levitt! That sawn-off, two-faced little shitbag had even possessed the gall to come to the funeral, to walk right up to Minsky, shake him by the hand and offer condolences. Minsky turned the ignition key and peered up at the house. No lights came on. Carefully, he guided the car along the driveway to the street. The power-assisted steering and automatic transmission made driving feel easy. He did not even need his left hand and foot.

Confidence deserted him the instant he reached Queens Boulevard. The heavy Friday night traffic swept at him from all directions. Horns assaulted his ears as he dithered over which direction to take. He was a stranger in the city where he had been born, grown up. Headlights flashed as he wandered from lane to lane. He followed signs to the Long Island Expressway. A car horn screamed when he entered the eastbound side without first checking for traffic. A sports car flashed past, its driver punching the air angrily with his fist. Minsky ignored him. He stayed in the inside lane, slowly picking up speed until he reached forty-five miles an hour. His was the slowest vehicle on the road, but he was not prepared to go faster. Driving was a new experience; he felt like a learner approaching his test.

Leaving Queens behind, he entered Nassau County. After a while, he saw signs for Sands Point. He left the expressway and took the crowded road north towards Long Island Sound.

He reached Joseph's house. Lights blazed in almost every window. The house was as bright as the one he'd just left in Forest Hills Gardens was dark. The Minsky house was black with mourning, and here, the Granitz home appeared as though a party were in progress. Climbing the steps to the front door, Minsky rapped on it with the head of his cane. Immediately, the hollow barking of the family's two Dobermans echoed from inside.

Joseph swung the door open, pushing with his leg to keep the powerful dogs inside the house. 'Benny, what are you doing here? How did you get here?' He looked past Minsky, expecting to see someone else. 'Who brought you?'

'I brought myself. Where's your mother?'

'In the library. I thought you weren't able to drive.'

'Never mind that.' Minsky waited for Joseph to stand aside and let him enter. The two Dobermans – Solomon, the larger male, and Sheba, the smaller female – sniffed his hands and legs before deciding he was a friend. Pearl appeared in the large entrance hall to confront Minsky as he stepped into the house. There was no air of gaiety about her, no brightness to reflect that of the house. Her face wore lines of worry which deepened the instant she recognized the late-night visitor.

'Benny, the police were here, men from the FBI. They

were asking about Leo. They wanted to know where he was.'

'Do you know?'

'I thought he'd be at home. He wasn't well. You saw at the funeral, the bandage on his head, the accident he'd had.'

Minsky hadn't even noticed what Leo looked like at the funeral. He'd had eyes only for the casket that had contained his son. 'Leo's not at home. The police have already checked Scarsdale.'

'How do you know what the police have and haven't done?' Joseph asked.

'I just left an FBI man at Forest Hills Gardens, that's how I know. He came to tell me that the ransom money had turned up. A motorcyclist who got killed in an accident upstate had it. He also had Leo's office number on him.'

'What number was that?' Joseph asked. When Minsky told him, Joseph shook his head and said, 'That's not one of our numbers. The police have made a mistake.'

'Don't sound so pleased, they didn't make any mistake. It's a direct line to your brother's office, only installed recently. Even you, his goddamned twin, don't know what he gets up to, do you?'

'Do you believe the police?' Pearl asked fearfully. 'Do you believe that Leo could possibly have been involved in William's . . .?'

'In William's murder?' Minsky finished the question for Pearl. 'You're damned right I do.' The cane tapped on the floor as he walked towards Pearl. Reaching the entrance to the library, where she stood, he looked inside and saw Judy with Jacob and Anne. The entire household was up! No wonder all the lights were on. 'Yes, I believe Leo had something to do with my son getting killed, and I know why. It's that bastard Lou Levitt. In all of the world, I'm the only person who ever got the better of him, and he never forgave me for it.'

'What the hell are you talking about?' Joseph demanded.

'Your godfather, that's what I'm talking about! The slimiest son of a bitch who ever drew breath!' The abrupt fury that Minsky directed at Joseph made the two Dobermans growl menacingly. Joseph grabbed hold of the dogs, opened the front door and pushed them outside. Minsky waited for him to return. 'Lou put your twin brother up to this. God alone knows what lies he told him, but your brother's nuts enough to listen to anything. To believe anything!'

'Benny, William and Leo were friends!' Pearl protested. 'Leo would never have done such a thing!'

'Don't bet on it,' came Judy's voice from inside the library. 'You know full well what Leo's done in the past. Lou Levitt told you himself. Phil Gerson and his girlfriend, Belinda. Those men who beat up William.' She touched a hand to her mouth as she mentioned the name of Minsky's dead son. 'And the man who picked Leo up on the night Joseph and I were married.'

Joseph swung around on his wife. 'Don't be satisfied with saying it in front of the kids! Why don't you take a full-page ad in the *Times*, let the whole damned world know!'

Judy bit her bottom lip. Grabbing her son and daughter by the hand, she led them through the entrance hall to the door that connected the house with the guest wing. Both Jacob and Anne kept their faces averted from the people standing in the hall. They were confused, unable to comprehend what was going on. Only that voices were being raised, and that their Uncle Leo, and the man they regarded as their grandfather, were the cause of the argument.

Minsky looked from Pearl to Joseph. 'The police are convicned that Leo's mixed up in William's murder, but I don't blame Leo, can you understand that? Even with all the terrible things that were done to my son before he died, I don't blame Leo. I know what he's like. He was always a little crazy, not really responsible for his actions. A child who could be persuaded to do bad things. That's why I blame Lou Levitt, because he could manipulate Leo like some kind of a hypnotist. For twenty-nine years Lou's had a grudge against me, he's hated me because I wasn't as dumb as he liked to think I was. That's why I'm still alive. That's why I didn't die in that week when Jake and Moe Caplan died, when Gus Landau died. I stayed alive because I had more smarts than Lou gave me credit for. And what he's always thought should have been all his, he's had to share with me all these years.'

Joseph glanced at his mother. Both wore the same puzzled expression. Neither could make any sense out of what Minsky was saying, yet they made no attempt to interrupt him.

'That two-faced little worm, he wanted to see me crawl. My heart attack, my stroke – they weren't enough for Lou. He wanted to take away the only thing I ever did that was worthwhile. He wanted to take my son. Pearl, call him . . . call Lou! Have him come over here now and explain to you and Joseph what he's done. Have him come over here now and face me, if he's got the guts to do that.'

Pearl found her voice. 'I don't have to call him. He's on his way. The moment the police left here, I telephoned him.'

'You told him they were looking for Leo?'

'Yes.'

'And? What did he say?'

'He told me not to worry. He said he'd keep Leo out of trouble just as he has always done.'

'And you asked me if I believed that Leo was involved? There's your proof right there!' Minsky walked into the library and sat down. 'I'm going to wait here because I want to hear the lies that scheming bastard uses to explain away why he got your son to murder mine. And when he's finished his lies, I'll tell you some truths.'

Leo drifted from bar to bar, staying only long enough to have one drink while he surveyed the young men who stood alone. He didn't know whether it was the dull ache in his head that was responsible, but his appetite was blunt tonight. Perhaps the youths he saw did not attract him physically. But then he studied a young man with dark wavy hair and warm brown eyes, and he knew that the headache wasn't the cause. Any other time he would have moved in. Tonight he felt that he could not be bothered.

At eleven-fifteen, he began the drive home to Scarsdale. Was he growing old? That was an interesting possibility. He considered it while he waited for a traffic light to change in his favour. He would be forty-two this year, the start of middle-age. Did a man's sexual drive start to fade when he reached the middle period of his life? Again, he knew that the answer was no. Only three days earlier, as he had watched Christopher Latham change from the chauffeur's uniform into his motorcycle leathers, Leo had felt a tremendous sexual urge.

410

It was just a bad day, that was all. Driving to the funeral and back, the heavy doses of aspirin he'd taken to numb the pain in his head. . . he should never have gone out tonight. He should have stayed in, perhaps watched a movie in the basement cinema. That would have done him more good. He'd put one on when he got home. *White Heat*, that's what he'd watch. That Cagney could act, and whoever had written the story knew all about the love of a son for his mother.

He had his first inkling of trouble when he neared the house. A police car was parked by the corner of the street where he lived. Instead of turning into the street, Leo carried straight on. The car could be out on regular patrol, or answering a call. But why were its lights off? Why was it tucked away, almost out of sight behind a clump of bushes? To catch motorists speeding at this time of night? No. A policeman taking a break? Leo shook his head. The sight of the car unnerved him. He had to find out for certain.

He drove back to the centre of town, found a pay phone and dialled the number of the local taxi company. Ten minutes later, the taxi collected him. Leo gave the driver instructions to take him along the street in which he lived. One look at the house was all he needed to know. Lights were on inside. Cars were parked with little care for concealment. He instructed the taxi driver to return him to his point of origin.

Back in his own car, Leo sat quietly for several minutes. If the police were at the house it meant they had a warrant. A search warrant . . . and a warrant for his arrest? He didn't question how they could have latched on to him; his only concern was escape. He began to perspire. The ache in his head increased. He had to run. But where? The police would be looking for his car. A white Cadillac convertible, it was conspicuous. How many of them were around? Damn . . . why hadn't he bought a Chevvy or a Ford like everyone else? Why did he have to be different?

He drove the Cadillac to a dark alley and left it there, running away as though it carried disease. He entered another telephone booth and dialled the same taxi company he had used earlier. 'I want to order a cab.'

'Destination?' asked the woman dispatcher.

411

'Sands Point, out on Long Island.' The woman told him there would be a special rate for a journey of that length. 'I don't care!' Leo yelled back. 'Just get me the damned cab!'

'One'll be with you in fifteen minutes.'

Leo stood in the shadow of a shop doorway while he waited. Sooner or later, the police would find the white Cadillac. By then he'd be long gone from Scarsdale. He would be hiding in the only place where he would be safe, the only place in the entire world where he had ever felt safe.

He would be with his mother.

Chapter Four

Benny Minsky sat immobile on the chair, hands clasping the top of the cane that stood between his parted legs. He was thinking about a New York socialite named David Hay. More than forty years had passed since he had killed David Hay, and for all that time Lou Levitt had dangled the spectre of that murder over Minsky's head. For the past twenty-nine years, since the death of Jake Granitz, the weight of Levitt's blackmail had been excruciating, forcing Minsky to loathe himself. Tonight he hoped to cleanse the stain from the little soul he had left.

Pearl sat on a couch on the far side of the library from Minsky. Her thoughts concerned both Levitt and Leo. Was it true what Minsky had said, that Levitt had told her younger twin lies? What lies? Why? And what did it all have to do with William being killed? She no longer knew what to think. She could only hope that Levitt, when he arrived, would explain the situation to her. Just like he always did.

Joseph stood, arms crossed, in front of the library door. He could have been a guard, ensuring that none of his charges escaped.

Pearl and Joseph swung their heads towards the window as they heard the sound of a car drawing up. Only Minsky failed to move. He remained sitting like a statue, unmoving, unblinking. A car horn sounded. Joseph, walking towards the hall to let Levitt into the house, swung around and looked out of the library window. Levitt was sitting in his car, pointing at the two Dobermans which stood by the driver's door.

'Call off these hounds of yours.'

Joseph went to the front door and whistled for the dogs. While he held on to their collars, Levitt left the safety of the car and hurried into the house. The moment he was inside, Joseph pushed the dogs out and closed the door.

Leaving Minsky sitting alone in the library, Pearl walked out into the hall to join her son and Levitt. When Levitt saw her, he said, 'Pearl, I don't want you to worry about a thing. Leo's going to be all right. I'll get him the best defence lawyer, I'll fix him up with rock-hard alibis that'll prove he was nowhere near where William was found. He'll have an alibi for every moment of the time William was missing. You can rely on me.'

'Just like I've always relied on you, right, Lou?'

Levitt angled his head. Had he detected an odd tone in her voice? 'Sure. Have I ever let you down? For one moment since Jake died, did I ever do wrong by you or the twins?'

'Why, Lou?' was Pearl's plaintive question. 'Why did you have to get Leo involved in something like this?'

'For Jake, that's why. Leo was evening the score for what Benny did to Jake.'

Finally, Minsky moved. The motion was only minimal, just his head so he could see Pearl as she stood in the hall talking to Levitt. The real action took place in his eyes. The hatred and fury that had earlier frightened FBI agent Frank Hopkins were back again, lending the eyes a dark fire.

'What Benny did . . .?' Pearl asked.

Levitt's voice became softer, and Minsky had to strain to hear the words. 'Who do you think set Jake up outside the *shul* that day? Who do you think arranged for Gus Landau to come back to New York from Toronto? Who do you think cooked up a drugs deal with Landau to grab hold of that business? It was Benny, that's who! And who do you think was responsible for Moe Caplan's death?'

'Liar!' Minsky screamed from inside the library. 'Goddamned filthy lying bastard!'

'Benny?' Levitt's voice dropped to the faintest whisper as he stared at Pearl. 'Benny's here?'

'In the library,' Joseph said. 'He's waiting for you.'

Levitt walked to the library door and looked inside. Minsky was struggling to his feet. In his right hand, the cane was

414

brandished like a sword. 'Liar!' Minsky screamed again. 'Is that the poison you told Leo to make him kill my William? To kill him, and make it look like a kidnapping? Is that how you get back at me after all these years?' He stumbled towards Levitt, thrashing the air with the cane. Levitt ducked, and the cane cracked against the doorframe. Minsky lost his balance and toppled to the ground. When he tried to get up, Joseph stepped in between the two elderly men.

'Look at yourself,' Levitt sneered. 'A foolish old man who still can't accept the truth of the evil he did.'

'The truth? What would you know about truth? Every time you open your mouth, a lie pours out.'

'What was it you told my brother?' Joseph asked Levitt.

'I told him what this piece of garbage did to Jake. What he did to Moe Caplan, and what he would have done to me if he could have gotten away with it. Leo took that truth and used it to avenge Jake, to avenge this family.' He swung around to face Pearl. 'That's why I used Leo. That's why I involved him. Because it was his duty to pay this maniac back for what he did.'

'You paid me back for still being alive!' Minsky shouted. 'You paid me back for outsmarting you. Your ego couldn't stand that, could it? You couldn't cope with someone who was as smart as you.'

'If you lived to be a thousand,' Levitt shouted back, 'You wouldn't have ten per cent of my brains.'

'Shut up!' Pearl shrieked. Her head was going around and around with their yelling. She couldn't think anymore, couldn't concentrate.

'What about Gus Landau?' Joseph asked Levitt. 'What about Benny bringing him back from Toronto? Tell me the whole story you told my brother.'

'Tell us all,' Minsky invited, his voice quieter now. 'Let us all hear your lies, and then we might go out and kill innocent people for you as well.'

'I told Leo only what happened,' Levitt said to Minsky. 'I told him how you met with Landau, Benny. I told him how Landau offered you the drugs business if he was allowed to return unmolested to New York. I told him how the idea was put to the vote, and you were outvoted, three to one. And you still went ahead with it. You brought Landau down and you set Jake up for him, because Jake had sworn to kill you if he ever saw drugs being pushed from our shops – '

'Don't listen to him!' Minsky shouted at Pearl and Joseph. 'He's lying. All his life he's been a liar, a cheat, a thief! And now he's telling the biggest lie of all.'

'Am I, Benny?' Levitt asked softly. 'You remember, surely, the way you took Moe to that place where Landau was hiding out after shooting Jake. You were going to close Landau's mouth, and you closed Moe's as well.' He turned to Pearl. 'Me he couldn't kill, because I'd protected myself.'

'How?'

'Years before, Benny murdered a boyfriend of Kathleen's. I found out about it. I swore an affidavit that was kept in a safe place, because I didn't trust Benny. If anything happened to me, that affidavit would be sent straight to the police. Benny would have burned, just like he should have done.'

Pearl remembered the night she had sat in the bedroom she had shared with Jake, toying with the ivory-handled revolvers and contemplating suicide. The knock on the door that had saved her life. Minsky and Levitt waiting outside to tell her that Landau was dead, killed by Moe Caplan who had died himself. They had wanted her to break the news to Annie. She had, and the news had made Annie take her own life. 'The pair of you came around to see me. You told me that Landau and Moe had killed each other. What is the truth? How did Moe die? And what is all this about drugs? And Landau . . . who was it who arranged for him to come back to New York?'

'Do you have to ask that, Pearl?' Levitt wanted to know. 'Didn't you just hear what I said?'

'I heard Benny as well.'

'Who are you going to believe? Him or me?'

Pearl shook her head. 'I don't know anymore, Lou.' She placed a hand to her temple. It was burning. In minutes, a blinding headache had enveloped her. Movement was pain, but that pain gave her a clarity of thought she could never recall having before. Suddenly, everything in her thoughts, in her vision, seemed so sharply defined. She could see things to which she had been blind before.

416

Without a word to anyone, she left the library and climbed the stairs to the second floor. In her own bedroom, she locked the door and approached the heavy bureau that stood against a wall. That piece of furniture had travelled more than some people ever did, she couldn't help thinking, from the apartment at the bottom of Fifth Avenue to Central Park West, and then on to Sands Point. She remembered how Joseph and Judy had wanted her to get rid of all her old furniture when she moved to Sands Point. They offered to buy her new. She had scorned the offer; what was the point in spending money on new furniture when the old was still serviceable? It was more than a waste of money, though. These old pieces held memories for her. They were part of life's scrapbook.

She opened the bottom drawer of the bureau and withdrew a polished walnut presentation box. Lying on top was the card signed by Benny Minsky more than forty years earlier: 'If you've got to protect yourself,' Pearl read, 'protect yourself with style.' Fingers working mechanically, she inserted ammunition. Would it still be good all these years later? Hadn't she just read somewhere of the United States using ammunition in Vietnam that had been manufactured for the Second World War? Bullets weren't milk or bread; they didn't go sour or stale.

When she returned downstairs, she was carrying a large handbag. Levitt and Minsky were just as she had left them, as though her temporary absence had suspended life. The puppet master had taken a break, and the puppets lay lifeless until their strings were picked up again. Minsky stood in the centre of the library, leaning on his cane. Levitt stood just inside the doorway, glaring at the dark-skinned man. Even Joseph had not moved. He remained in between the two men, keeping them apart.

Pearl's right hand dipped into the bag. When it emerged, she was holding a revolver. 'Sit down, both of you.'

'Ma, give me that!' Joseph reached out a hand to remove the revolver from his mother's grasp. She snatched the weapon away from him. 'Where did you get that thing from?'

'It was your father's.'

'It's been in this house all the time?'

'Under lock and key.'

'Hey, that's one of the guns I gave to Jake for his twenty-fifth birthday!' Minsky exclaimed. 'A matching pair – '

'I said, sit down.' Pearl motioned towards the couch, and Minsky sat. Next, she pointed the gun in Levitt's general direction. 'You, too.' She watched him take a seat on a straight-backed chair. Pearl switched her gaze from one seated man to the other. 'All I've heard tonight is a single word: *truth*. Now I'd like to hear some.'

'I just told it to you!' Levitt's voice had lost some of the calm reason that Pearl had always associated with it. This wasn't the first time she had heard him shout, but there was a timbre to his voice that she had never noticed before. It was a quaking . . . a shivering. . . . Of fear?

'I've listened to you already, Lou. I've listened to you all my life. Now I want to listen to Benny.'

Minsky sat back. He had no fear of the revolver in Pearl's hand. All he felt was relief. After all these years, he could finally tell the truth to someone. As damning as it would be to himself, the truth would hurt Levitt even more.

'Well, Benny?' Pearl said.

'Lou came to us with a proposal,' Minsky said. 'He called a meeting late one night in the office above the Jalo garage on the West Side. And there he told us he'd come to an arrangement. An *arrangement*, that's what he called it, with Gus Landau.'

Pearl listened, and as Minsky went further into his story she felt acid burn her stomach. . . .

It was raining the night Levitt called the meeting above the Jalo garage. The big room was empty, the book-keepers and runners gone for the night. There was noise only downstairs from drivers in their taxis, mechanics working on engines and transmissions.

While Levitt waited for his three partners, he sat behind his desk and listened to the radio with its war news from Europe. For once there was a ray of optimism. Although the bombing of England was continuing with unabated ferocity, the number of destroyed German aircraft was steadily growing. The Nazis were learning that their conquest of Europe was not to be without cost.

418

Jake and Moses Caplan arrived together, having driven in Jake's car from their apartment building at the bottom of Fifth Avenue. The three men sat listening to the radio for ten minutes until Benny Minsky walked in. The moment Minsky sat down, Levitt flicked off the radio.

'You know, I've been doing some thinking,' he began. 'Those small shops where we run the books, the numbers – we could push a million different kinds of things through them.'

'Such as?' Jake asked. He doubted that Levitt was fishing for ideas; he probably had one of his own already.

The answer came back in one word. 'Drugs.'

'You're crazy.'

'Am I? What we're making in those shops right now is *bubkes* compared with what we could be making. I don't mean use every single shop. Maybe twenty, that's all. One in each area.'

'And twenty shops would get raided by the cops so fast that we wouldn't know what hit us,' Caplan argued.

Levitt dismissed the objection. 'We'll make more money pushing drugs through those twenty shops than we do in taking bets, so our payoffs to the cops will be proportionally larger. They'll be paid well enough to look the other way.'

'Where are these drugs coming from?' Jake asked.

'Gus Landau.'

'Landau?' It was Minsky who repeated the name with a mixture of surprise and disgust. 'Where the hell did you drag up that scumbag from?'

'Canada. Landau's been living up there since he ran from New York. In Toronto. He's worked himself up a good little business with junk. Now he's willing to turn it over to us as long as we let him come back to New York. He's paying for his own safety with his drug connections.'

'How do you know all this?' Jake asked.

'I met with him.'

'You met with Landau?'

'In Niagara Falls last weekend. I went across the Canadian border to see him. He drove there from Toronto.'

'How did you know to go to Niagara Falls to see him?'

'He wrote to me.'

'How come you never said a word to us?'

'Because I wanted to see what he had to say.' Levitt leaned forward, his expression intent. 'Landau wants to come back here badly. Canada's fighting a war and he doesn't want any part of it. Turning over his drugs connections for us to use in New York will be worth a fortune to us.'

'When you get around to giving him an answer,' Jake said quietly, 'make sure you tell him no. If he knows what's best for him, he'd better not show his scarred face around here.'

Levitt missed Jake's meaning completely. 'He doesn't have to worry about the cops. He's got himself a new identity, everything.'

'I don't mean the cops, Lou. I mean me. He shows his face in New York and I'm going to blow it off for him!' Jake's voice rose as anger filled him. 'Where the hell do you come from going up there to see the likes of him?'

'Jake, think with your head, not with your guts. Don't you know how much this money could mean to us? Landau has built up a whole business. He'll turn over his connections so we can do the same thing down here.'

'Is money the only thing that damned well matters to you? He killed Pearl's mother, remember? And just in case you've forgotten, he killed her while he was trying to kill you and me!'

Levitt regarded Jake with an icy stare. 'It's just as well that there are four of us. Maybe Moe and Benny won't think the same way you do.'

'Go ahead and put it to a vote,' Jake responded. 'I couldn't care less how much I'm outvoted by. If Landau comes back here, I'll kill him. And I'll fight you all about drugs getting pushed from those shops. We don't need any part of that business. It stinks. It's the kind of filth that only a rat like Landau would get involved in. What the hell do you want to get mixed up in it for?'

'Money,' Levitt answered simply. 'The same reason I get involved in any business.' He looked at Caplan and Minsky. 'Well?'

'Count me out,' Caplan said.

'Me, too,' was Minsky's answer.

Levitt looked like a man betrayed, a man who finds himself cuckolded by his best friend. 'Christ, where are your brains?

We've been offered a fortune on a silver plate, and all you can do is shake your stupid heads! If I'd have thought this was how you'd react, I wouldn't even have bothered going all the way up to Canada.'

'Who asked you to go?' Jake said. 'You had no damned business going up there without talking to us first.'

'I had every damned business! Remember, everything that we ever did that made money was my idea. The three of you would still be living in some shithouse on Delancey Street if it wasn't for me, pushing rails around Seventh Avenue for a living, or in jail for robbing nickels and dimes.'

'Maybe we would,' Jake concurred. 'I'll tell you one thing, though, little man. We just took a vote here, a democratic process. You were outvoted three to one. That puts an end to it. Maybe you've got some other ideas, but if I ever see one ounce of Landau's junk coming out of one of our books, I'm going to come looking for you with a gun in my hand.' He stood up, glanced at Caplan and Minsky, and the three men left the office. . . .

When Minsky paused for breath, Pearl turned her attention to Levitt. As small as he was, he had shrunk even more, pressing himself against the back of the chair as though trying to become a part of it. His face was devoid of colour, his eyes nothing more than slits through which icy sapphires gleamed with hate. Pearl wondered how wise it was for Minsky to narrate the tale with Levitt sitting there. It looked as though something might snap within him at any moment, if it hadn't done so already. She gave a signal to Joseph, who took a step closer to Levitt, ready to restrain him should his trance-like state suddenly turn to violence.

'It was the first time I'd ever seen an argument between Jake and Lou,' Minsky continued, not even noticing Pearl's momentary preoccupation with Levitt. 'The first time Jake had ever raised his voice to any of us. But he had a thing about drugs – he was scared of them because of the twins – and he hated Landau because of what he'd done. He couldn't believe that Lou would have gone to see Landau to talk about such a deal.'

Pearl tried to recall those weeks leading up to the twins' *bar mitzvahs*. 'Jake was edgy,' she said. 'I couldn't understand why. I put it down to nerves on his part, getting worried for the boys' sake. But Lou kept on coming around to the apartment for dinner just like he always did. He seemed to get on well with Jake.'

'That's right. The day after we had the meeting and the vote, Lou called us all together again. He apologized, said we were right. He'd been outvoted and that was the end of it. He even apologized for what he'd said to us, claimed that it was all in the heat of the moment. But,' he glanced over at the still figure of Levitt, 'you saw what happened outside the *shul* as well as I did, Pearl.'

'Landau. So Lou did bring him down.'

'Lou went right ahead and disregarded the vote. He got back to Landau, told him it was okay. But turning over the drug connections wasn't enough anymore. He wanted Landau to do something else. He wanted Landau to kill Jake.'

Pearl closed her eyes just long enough to conjure up the scene outside the synagogue. Levitt with the twins, giving them gold watches. Jake walking on ahead with Isaac Cohen. And herself calling out to Jake to come and see the watches – when all she was doing was giving Landau a clear field of fire. 'Why, Benny? Why? Jake and Lou had been friends since they were small, just like you all were. Why would he turn like that?'

'Why don't you ask him yourself?'

Levitt found his voice, and when he focused his eyes on Pearl the sheen of hatred had softened. 'I was in love with you, Pearl. You're the only woman I ever loved, you know that.'

'To prove you loved me, you killed Jake? Had him killed? For me, or for the money this drugs deal with Landau could have earned?' Levitt fell back into his motionless, silent state. Pearl knew the truth now, there was no point in going on. Levitt's admission of love had sealed it. He'd told her before of his feelings. Once, his confession had thrown her into turmoil, when they were young, before she married Jake. And later, after Jake was dead, his avowed feelings for her had brought comfort, letting her know that she had such a

422

staunch and trusted friend. To hear him say he loved her, now brought only shame. She returned her attention to Minsky. 'You and Moe, didn't you know what had happened?'

'We knew, all right. Once that old boy who taught the twins their *bar mitzvahs* said he'd never seen such a scar on a man's face, we knew exactly what had happened. Lou had double-crossed us. There was chaos outside the *shul*, people running everywhere – '

'I can see it as though it's happening right now,' Pearl interrupted. 'I ran to look at Jake, and Lou – ' she gave him the briefest of glances – 'caught hold of me. He buried my head in his shoulder so I wouldn't be able to see what had happened . . . what he had caused to happen. Annie, she was holding the twins. And Benny, you were holding William and Judy, pulling them away.'

'That's right. Lou pushed you on to Harry Saltzman – '

'Did he have anything to do with it?'

'Nothing. Harry was an outsider, he had no role in our business. Lou pushed you on to Harry and yelled at Moe to get on the telephone for an ambulance. Moe made the call, and while we waited for the ambulance, Moe went up to Lou and told him he knew the truth. There and then, outside the *shul*, while Jake's blood was pouring on to the sidewalk, Moe told Lou that he was going to kill him. He didn't know where, he didn't know when, but he was going to kill him for what he'd done.'

'Why didn't you just turn him over to the police when they arrived?'

'What evidence did we have? An argument about drugs? Lou would have waltzed his way around any murder charge based on that. You saw what he did at the Senate hearings. This was a family affair, something we'd sort out between ourselves. Moe wanted justice, and so did I. And all Moe got – ' Minsky dabbed at his eyes; Pearl was surprised to see he was crying – 'was a taste of what Jake got. Betrayal by a friend. Me. . .'

Throughout the week-long *shivah* period for Jake, Levitt was constantly at Pearl's side, doing all he could to help her through the painful time. Whenever Caplan and Minsky were present in the apartment, Levitt ignored them. Only when the mourning period ended did he acknowledge their existence. As Pearl removed the cloths that covered the mirrors, Levitt noticed that Caplan had returned to his own apartment next door. The little man inclined his head towards the twins' bedroom, indicating for Minsky to follow him.

'What's on Moe's mind these days?' Levitt asked.

'Nothing new. He's going to kill you.'

Levitt didn't seem in the least perturbed. 'Too bad he feels that way.'

'I'd sound a damned sight more worried if I were you.'

'Worried?' Levitt laughed. 'I don't have to be worried, Benny. Not when I've got you on my side.'

'Me? I wish Moe luck. A bullet in the back of the head's all you deserve.'

'Is it? And what do you deserve, Benny? A few thousand volts of electricity running through your veins? Your blood boiling before your head explodes? I've heard that you can even smell yourself burning before the lights finally go out. I've got my affidavit about you and David Hay all locked up nice and safely, but it won't take much for someone to turn a key and bring it out. Remember, Benny, something happens to me, and something just as bad is going to happen to you, whether it's you who pulls the trigger or whether it's Moe.'

Minsky flinched as though he could already feel the current coursing through him. Levitt smiled. 'That's better, Benny. Now you look like a man who's ready to act sensibly. I know where Gus Landau's hiding out. Do you think Moe will be satisfied with Landau? Do you think if you led him to Landau, he'd call it quits?'

Minsky was powerless. He remembered a stupid poem from schooldays, a story about a pied piper who cleared the town of Hamelin of rats. He felt like one of those rats right now, dancing to a tune played by Levitt, unable to do anything but follow. Nevertheless, he tried to wriggle free of Levitt's spell. 'That affidavit isn't going to stand up in any court so long after David Hay's murder. Where's the body, for one thing?'

'At the bottom of the Atlantic. Just a skeleton now, Benny. Sharks come pretty far north in the summer. But are you

424

prepared to take a chance on my sworn testimony *not* standing up in court? If you are, all you've got to do is walk away from me right now. Let Moe put a bullet in me. That's all you've got to do.'

'Where is Landau?'

'Sensible, Benny. Sensible. He's holed up in an apartment in the Bronx, off Fordham Road.' Levitt handed Minsky a folded slip of paper. 'There's the address. Not tonight. Wait three or four days. Let me get it set up. And while you're at it, keep Moe off my back.'

The three or four days that Levitt asked for was the only thing Minsky liked. He knew there was more to it than just killing Landau, closing a mouth that could incriminate Levitt, trying to satisfy Caplan's desire for justice and revenge. Minsky was being asked – asked, hell! – he was being forced, coerced, blackmailed into setting up Moses Caplan, removing another threat to Levitt. In three or four days, however, he could create a barrier of protection for himself from the little man. Levitt had always sneered at him. No brains . . . crazy Benny. But he wasn't that dumb that he could not learn a thing or two parrot-fashion from the master of deceit. . . .

The building in which Landau was hiding was slated for the wrecker's ball. The last tenant had left a month earlier. There was already an air of decay about the building that hit Minsky and Caplan the moment they entered the lobby, a damp stench that caught in their noses and their throats.

'Third floor,' Minsky said, and led the way to the stairs. The handrail was loose and trembled in his grip.

'How did you find out about this place, about Landau being here?' Caplan asked.

Minsky pretended not to hear the question. He could be forgiven for being temporarily hard of hearing. About to betray a friend, his heart was pounding loudly enough to drown out any other sound.

'There.' Minsky reached the third floor and pointed to a door at the end of a long hallway. A gun appeared in Caplan's hand and he crossed the intervening space in long, running strides. His foot smashed into the lock to send the door flying back. Caplan charged into the apartment with Minsky on his heels. There, right in front of them, sitting in an armchair that faced the door, was Gus Landau. His eyes were fixed wide open, and a crimson stain covered his shirt front. Caplan's hopes of revenge were smashed, for Landau was already dead. But standing next to the chair, holding a silenced Colt automatic that seemed almost as big as himself, was Levitt. The weapon was pointed unerringly at Caplan's chest.

'You son of a bitch!' Caplan shouted as he spun around to confront Minsky. 'You double-crossing son of a bitch! You're in this with him!'

More than anything, Minsky wanted to tell the truth to Caplan. He wasn't allying himself voluntarily with Levitt. He was being forced to do this. Didn't Caplan understand that? But his own sense of self-preservation overrode all else. He knocked the gun from Caplan's hand and shoved him away. Caplan banged against the open door and bounced out into the hallway. As the door rebounded off the wall, Levitt fired two shots with the silenced automatic. Both bullets tore through the wood of the door. The first ripped through the fabric of Caplan's coat as he fought to regain his balance and run. The second bullet smashed into the back of his head, killing him.

The gun in Levitt's hand described a slight arc until it was pointing directly at Minsky. Levitt's index finger tightened, and Minsky wondered how much more pressure was needed before the hammer dropped. He tried to find his voice but his throat and mouth were dry. The words that could save him refused to come.

Just when it seemed that the hammer must slam forward, Minsky managed to croak: 'You pull that trigger, Lou, and you go right down the drain.'

Levitt's hand remained rock steady. The gun never wavered. But a flicker of interest – or was it, Minsky hoped, apprehension? – appeared in his blue eyes. 'How's that, Benny?'

Minsky's voice became stronger. 'I know lawyers as well, Lou. I know what an affidavit is, just like you do. You taught me.'

'I taught you what?'

'How to cover myself. I know how you set up Jake, and I knew you were using me to set up Moe. I couldn't fight you,

426

Lou, not with what you've got hanging over my head. But I could make damned sure I had something just as heavy hanging over yours.'

'You swore an affidavit about Jake, about this?' Levitt couldn't believe it. Never in a million years would he have credited Minsky with such forethought.

'Damned right I did! Once I brought Moe here, there was no way you were going to let me walk. Not unless I had protection.'

'Where's your lawyer, Benny? What's his name?'

'Go fuck yourself, shrimp,' Minsky answered confidently. 'Go fuck yourself.'

To Minsky surprise, Levitt laughed. 'I underestimated you, Benny. I never even gave you credit for having the brains to copy anything I did. What do you know . . .?' While he spoke, he wiped the automatic clean of his own fingerprints and pressed it against Landau's hand. Then he dropped the weapon on to the floor beside the corpse. Next, he took another gun from his pocket, a revolver, wiped it clean again and went into the hallway to press it against Caplan's fingers.

'Is that the gun you shot Landau with?' Minsky asked as he watched Levitt slip it into Caplan's pocket.

'That's right. The police will think they shot each other,' Levitt answered. 'Now let's get out of here and leave the police to clear up this mess.'

'Where are we going?'

'We'll drive around for a while, we've got things to discuss. We're partners now, and partners always talk about what they're going to do. After a while we'll go and see Pearl. She might want to know that Jake's killer is dead. Too bad about Moe, though.' Levitt shook his head sadly. 'He should never have gone looking for Landau on his own. Landau was too tough to be taken by one man alone. Moe should have called us first.' He walked past Minsky, heading towards the stairway. Minsky followed automatically, Faust following Mephistopheles to eternal damnation.

Late at night, they knocked on the door of Pearl's apartment. Both men wore expressions of mourning. Like each other or not, they were together for ever now, as close as Siamese twins. They were bound to each other for life, each protected by the sworn testimony that could send the other man straight to the electric chair. Neither man had any idea that by calling on Pearl to tell her of the deaths of Gus Landau and Moses Caplan, they had prevented her own suicide.

Pearl opened the door and flung her arms around both men. 'Lou . . .! Benny . . .! What are you doing here?'

'We found Landau,' Levitt said after kissing her on the cheek and entering the apartment. Minsky followed him inside.

'Where?'

Levitt checked that the twins were sleeping, closed their door and walked on into the kitchen. 'Landau was holed up in some apartment in the Bronx, off Fordham Road. He's dead, Pearl.'

'Lou, it doesn't make me feel any better. I don't feel anything at all.'

Levitt took her in his arms as she burst into tears. He waited for a minute, until the crying tapered off. 'Pearl, look at me. This is very important, and I want you to listen carefully. I didn't come here to make you feel better, Pearl. I came because I need your help.'

'What is it?'

Levitt dropped his arms and leaned against the sink. He looked as though all of his energy had suddenly evaporated. Minsky saw the beads of sweat that appeared on Levitt's upper lip and forehead, the pallor of his skin, the bleak hollowness of his eyes. Pearl would think the news Levitt had to tell was making him ill. Minsky knew better. It was a delayed reaction on Levitt's part at having Minsky outsmart him. These were visible signs of the dent the little man's ego had taken.

'It was Moe who found him, Pearl,' Minsky said softly. 'We had a tip that Landau was hiding out in this apartment. Moe went in after him, all by himself.'

Levitt seemed to recover his poise. 'Maybe he wanted to pay him back real bad for what he did to Jake,' Levitt said. 'Who the hell knows why he did it on his own? We don't know all the details yet, only what our friends in the police up there have told us. It looks like Moe surprised Landau, burst into the apartment and shot him. That's the way the police found

Landau when they got there. He was sitting on a chair, facing the front door, and he'd been shot through the chest.'

'There were two bullet holes in the door,' Minsky added. 'Not fired from the outside, but from the inside. There was a gun on the floor by Landau's chair, two bullets had been fired. The police figure Landau had just enough strength left in him before he died to fire those two shots through the door. He must have fired as Moe left, after he'd closed the door on the way out. One of the shots . . . one of them hit Moe in the back of the head.'

'Oh, God. Annie!'

'Yes, Annie,' Levitt said. 'Moe's gone as well as Jake. Now you've got to be doubly strong because Annie's going to need your help.'

'Have you told her? Has anyone? Does she know?'

'I can't tell her, Pearl,' Levitt replied. 'Will you?' When Pearl hesitated, Levitt urged, 'Do it quickly, before the police get here.'

Leaving Pearl to tell her best friend that her husband was dead, Levitt and Minsky departed. They drove to the Jalo garage on the West Side, walked up the stairs to the office that Levitt had shared with Jake.

'You appreciate irony, Benny?' Levitt asked.

'What the hell's so ironic about this?'

'You and me being here together. We never got on since we were kids, and now we're stuck with each other. There's your irony.'

'I don't like it any more than you do.'

'Like it or not, it's the truth and we've got to make the best of it. There's only two of us left, Benny. We've got to stick together, otherwise everything we worked for gets washed down the sink. You've got a son you've got to take care of.'

'And you?'

'I'll take care of the twins, they're my responsibility. I'll look after Jake's share of the business.'

'And Moe's share? Who'll look after that for Annie and his daughter?'

'I'll make sure they don't go hungry. We owe that to Moe.'

'Yeah, we do.' Minsky fidgeted on the seat, uncomfortable as he thought of Moses Caplan and his own part in his friend's

429

murder. Better to think of something else. 'Are you going to make a move on Pearl?'

Levitt looked up sharply. 'What's that supposed to mean?'

'Exactly what I said. Maybe Jake wasn't smart enough to see how you feel about Pearl, but I saw it. I saw it all along, the way you had those big blue eyes of yours following her wherever she went. Christ, you even look on those boys of hers like they're your own.'

'Benny, you surprised me once by having more brains than I gave you credit for. Don't push your luck and try to do it twice.'

'How do we split up the business now?'

'Right down the middle. Is that fair enough for you?'

'You're not going to haggle, say you should get more because you'll be looking after Pearl and the kids, and Moe's family?'

'Equal partners, that's what we always were, and that's the way it'll remain. Because we've both got the same to lose. Expenses don't enter into it.'

'Okay.' Minsky offered his hand to Levitt. 'Equal partners.'

'Just as long as you realize it doesn't mean we have to be friends.'

'We never were,' Minsky said. 'Why should we change now?'

Minsky fell silent again, gazing at Pearl and waiting for her questions. He felt as weak as a baby. confessing the betrayal of his friend had drained him of every ounce of physical and emotional strength. Pearl watched him for a while before looking at Levitt. Some of the colour was returning to his face, a man beginning to recover from the traumatic shock of having his life exposed as one gigantic lie. Benny, too, was another man who had lived a lie. Their unholy partnership had been based on the murder of Jake and the subsequent murder of Moses Caplan. Pearl could feel a degree of sympathy for Minsky. He hadn't acted out of greed, out of envy. He had acted in this manner because he had become entangled in the web of Levitt's deceit. Just as they had all been, Pearl thought. One way or the other, Levitt had ruled all their lives. They were all his victims.

'Ma, please let me have that thing.' Joseph stepped forward to remove the revolver from Pearl's hand. She looked down, surprised to see it there. While listening to Minsky she had forgotten all about the weapon she had taken from the walnut presentation box.

'Take it, Joseph. Take it away from me.' She handed over the revolver to the older twin, relieved when she was no longer encumbered by its deadly weight. She could not even remember now why she had gone up to her bedroom to fetch it. Joseph held the gun as though it were something distasteful, thumb and forefinger around the barrel, letting the butt hang down by his knee. He retreated to his former position beside Levitt's straight-backed chair.

'That affidavit you made out,' Pearl said to Minsky. 'Is that what you meant when you said you were the only one who had ever gotten the better of Lou?'

Minsky nodded. For an instant his eyes met Levitt's. The gleam of hatred was back in those blue eyes. 'I had him tied down just like he had me, and he hated me for it. I'd proved to him that I was his equal in deceit, in trickery, and he couldn't handle that. The only thing that mattered to Lou was being smarter than anyone else, being a step ahead. Some crazy drive to prove he was the best. It robbed him of every feeling, except what he had for you.'

Joseph spoke up. 'He must have had some feelings when he killed my father and then killed Moe Caplan. You don't kill without emotion.'

'Lou does. It was just business to him, the same as adding up the money from the books, the same as going to Scotland that time to work out the booze deals. He was as cold and clear about a business decision – whether it was buying liquor or arranging to have someone killed – as a surgeon is when he's doing an operation. It was a piece of work, and Lou didn't let himself get excited about work. But to have someone get the better of him, his ego couldn't stand that. A giant-sized ego in a half-pint midget. He's hated my guts ever since that day, hated them even more than he did before. Not only did I best him, but I took half of the money he thought he'd get all for himself.'

'What about those drugs Landau offered?' Joseph asked.

'They went on sale through the small shops. Lou took care of the police just like he said he would. He carried on with the drug trade until Leo was getting ready to finish school, and then he stopped the supply. He didn't want Leo – or you when you joined the firm – to know where the money was coming from. He considered drugs too dirty for you and your brother to be involved with.'

Levitt interrupted in a low, hollow monotone, a ghost speaking at a seance. 'That was because my sons' interests were always closest to my heart.'

The three other people in the room swung their heads to look at him. Minsky and Joseph were stunned, perplexed. Pearl's face was a picture of fright. It was her turn to have her past exposed, the shame she had concealed for forty-three years.

'What did you say?' Joseph's voice trembled as he asked the question.

'My sons!' Levitt's voice gained strength and authority. His body grew stronger. 'You, your twin brother Leo. Jake wasn't your father. I am!'

'You're crazy,' Joseph whispered.

'Ask your mother! Ask her about the night Jake was in the hospital after he'd smashed up the car on the drive down to the Jersey shore! Go ahead, ask her!'

Pearl remembered that night. So did Minsky. He had been in the car with Jake, injured slightly. Patched up, he had gone looking for Kathleen at the King High on Seventh Avenue and 55th Street, and then at her apartment. He'd wanted sympathy, affection. Instead, he'd learned that Kathleen was two-timing him. That night had ultimately led to this situation, led to him being blackmailed for more than half his life by Levitt.

'Ma . . what happened that night?' Joseph asked.

Pearl composed herself. So much else had come out that her own moment of indiscretion appeared trite in comparison. It didn't even seem worth admitting. 'Lou came around to the apartment with the news that *your father* – ' she stressed the words purposely, a deliberate snub to Levitt – 'had been injured in an automobile accident. I . . . I was upset, how else would you expect me to be?'

432

'Tell him everything,' Levitt urged. 'Tell him why you were upset. Not because Jake was in the hospital, but because you believed that you had put him there. Remember? Trying too hard for children, pushing Jake too much! And then you made love with me. I'm the one who got you pregnant with Joseph and Leo. It was never Jake!'

Pearl stared in horror at Levitt. She had been his friend for sixty years. Only now was she beginning to know him. And she despised what she saw. 'Lou, you're absolutely mad.'

'I looked after you, after the twins, better than Jake could ever have done. You never married me, but I was still the head of your family. I guided the twins. I brought them up to be something.' Levitt rose to his feet, stood beside Joseph, clapped him on the shoulder. 'Didn't you ever wonder where you inherited such brains from? Was your mother good with figures, with organizational work, as you are? She was a cook. Was Jake? No, he was a truck driver, a *shlepper*. It was me. My genes run through you.'

'They must run through Leo as well,' Minsky said in the same kind of sneering tone that Levitt had perpetually used to him. 'You turned Leo into a murderer. Did he inherit that from you?'

With a movement so swift as to take everyone by surprise, Levitt snatched away the ivory-handled revolver that Joseph held by his side. 'Your gun, was it, Benny? You gave this to Jake for his twenty-fifth birthday, did you?'

The sight of the revolver in Levitt's hand threw Minsky back down the labyrinth of memories he had navigated that night. The revolver changed into a Colt automatic with a longer barrel threaded for a bulky suppressor. He was no longer sitting in the library at Sands Point, partly crippled with a stroke. He was back in a condemned apartment building in the Bronx. Moses Caplan was dead in the hallway, and Levitt's gun was swinging around to seek a new target. Minsky knew that all he had to do was speak. Find his voice, tell Levitt of the reverse blackmail. Instead of death, Levitt would reward him with a partnership. And Minsky would have to live with the shame of the betrayal for the remainder of his life.

He thought about it. He'd gone that route once. He didn't want to journey it again. Last time, the gun in Levitt's hand had been a threat. This time it promised blessed relief. 'Fire, you twisted little bastard. Pull the trigger, and I'll be waiting down in hell for when you come.'

Levitt squeezed the trigger. The explosion rocked the library. Minsky's body slammed back into the couch. The cane skipped out of his grasp and rolled across the floor.

'You're mad,' Pearl murmured, her eyes riveted to the spread of crimson across Minsky's chest. 'You always called him crazy Benny, and it's you who was the crazy one all the time. It's not Joseph your genes run through – it's Leo. He's mad like you.'

Levitt continued to hold the revolver, the barrel pointing harmlessly down at the floor. He began to smile. 'Pearl, what's happened to you?'

'To me? Nothing's happened to me.'

'But it has. What about the diphtheria, Pearl? Every time Leo did something, you found refuge in the diphtheria. Diphtheria was to blame for everything. All his craziness. Don't you remember the things he did? Bursting in on Joseph and Judy in the bedroom when you all lived on Central Park West? The scenes he would throw, the temper tantrums. And each time you said it was the diphtheria.'

'What did you expect me to say, that he was crazy?'

'I recognized what he was, Pearl. On his tenth birthday I knew exactly what he was. Remember the dog I brought for a present?'

'The one Leo lost?' Joseph asked. He kept his eyes fixed on the revolver in Levitt's hand, wondering when an opportune moment would arrive to take it away.

'He didn't lose it. He took it for a walk to prove he wasn't scared of it. And then he smashed its head to a pulp against the wall of a building.'

Joseph blanched. He had known that Leo had done something to the dog. He'd thought Leo had deliberately lost it, but this . . .!

Levitt kept on talking. 'I promised you, Pearl, that I would make something of Leo, and the only way I could do that was to understand him, understand what drove him. I knew about his homosexuality long before you did. I accepted it, and because of that Leo trusted me. He trusted me enough to let me turn his craziness into a weapon.'

'You made him kill for you.'

'No! I made him strike against those who would harm this family! My family! And beneath that craziness was my ability to scheme, to plan!' Levitt licked lips that were suddenly dry. His heart was racing, the gun trembled in his hand. 'The whole world thinks that the shooting of the Rourke brothers was just a random act by some Arab student. . . . It was me who was behind it. With Leo. That boy who shot them, he was one of Leo's lovers. The Rourkes hurt us, and we paid them back!'

'You were behind the Rourke killings? Leo as well?'

Levitt nodded. 'The policeman who was on the scene, the one who killed that Arab, was paid by us to be there.' Levitt saw Joseph's hand reach out to take the revolver from him. He relinquished his grip on the weapon, no longer needing it. He had done what he should have done twenty-nine years earlier.

The library door flew back on its hinges. Judy stood framed in the doorway. 'I heard a gunshot!' She threw her hand to her mouth when she spotted the revolver in Joseph's hand, the body of Minsky on the couch. 'My God!'

'Where are the kids?' Joseph asked.

'I left them. You. . . .' She pointed at the gun. 'Why?'

Joseph dropped the revolver on to the floor. 'Not me. I didn't do it.'

'Lou did,' Pearl said. 'He killed Benny, just like he killed Jake, just like he killed your father when they went against him.' Her voice was the calmest it had been all night. She felt wonderfully serene as she sat down in an armchair. The large handbag was on the floor beside the chair. She slipped her hand inside.

'Lou, did you hear what Benny said before?' she asked.

'About what?'

'He recognized that revolver. He gave it to Jake.' Her hand began to come out of the bag. 'It was one of a pair, a matching pair. Here's the second one.'

Eyes bright like amber, she lifted the matching revolver clear of the handbag, aimed it at Levitt's face and squeezed the trigger.

Leo could not believe how long the journey was taking. Fifty, a hundred, no . . . two hundred times he must have made the drive from Scarsdale to Sands Point, in pouring rain, in fog, in snow, in all kinds of weather, all kinds of traffic, and never had it taken anywhere near this long. What kind of a driver had the taxi company sent him?

'For Christ's sake, can't you go any faster?' he asked as the taxi sped west through Queens on the Long Island Expressway.

'Take a look at my speedometer, mister,' the driver answered. 'I've been doing sixty-five, seventy, all the way. You want to get there any quicker, hire yourself a Phantom jet the next time, not a damned taxi. Just consider yourself lucky to find anyone who'd take you from Scarsdale all the way out here this time of night.'

Leo sat back and checked his watch for what he knew must be the fifth time in as many minutes. One-thirty. His mother would be in bed. She always went to bed early. He wanted, needed, her to help him, and she was asleep. A sweeping wave of self-pity washed over him. He was in trouble like never before, fleeing across New York in a taxi while police turned his home inside out, and the only person who could help him didn't even know of his plight. Sleeping soundly, unaware. And he had acted only out of concern for her. He had killed because his love for her was so strong. She didn't understand. She didn't care. She was asleep.

'You all right back there?' the taxi driver asked. He peered nervously into the rearview mirror as an oncoming car's headlights lit up the inside of the taxi. His passenger had his hands to his face; tears were streaming down his cheeks. Jesus, the driver muttered to himself, what kind of a nut did the despatcher send me to pick up? He just hoped the guy had the money on him to pay the fare.

Leo made no reply. He didn't even hear the question. He glanced out of the window, saw the sign that told him the taxi was entering Nassau County. He sniffed, wiped away the tears. Soon he'd be there. His mother wouldn't be asleep. She'd know that something was wrong. She'd feel it. She'd be waiting to comfort him like she had always done. She'd understand that whatever he had done was for her benefit. She always understood. She'd hold him, and all of his troubles would just disappear.

No embrace, not even that of the young men he had loved, could ever match the security that a hug from his mother brought.

436

Chapter Five

For fully a minute after shooting Lou Levitt, Pearl remained sitting rigidly upright in the armchair, the revolver pointing down to where Levitt had fallen as if she were undecided about administering an unnecessary *coup de grâce*. Joseph and Judy stood perfectly still, too terrified to move. Finally, the gun dropped from Pearl's hand on to the floor and she leaned back in the chair.

'Call the police,' she whispered. 'Tell them what's happened.'

Joseph leaped forward to snatch the revolver from beside his mother's feet. He saw Judy lift the telephone receiver and dial the emergency number. When the call was answered, she asked for both police and an ambulance.

'What about the children?' Pearl asked after Judy had made the call. 'You should see about the children.'

Judy glanced at Joseph, who nodded. Jacob and Anne must be terrified, alone in the guest wing, hearing the two shots, wondering what had happened. Judy left the library to return a minute later. Both children were asleep; by some miracle they had slept through everything.

Joseph squatted down beside his mother's chair. 'When the police come, what are you going to tell them?'

'The truth, of course. That I shot Lou after he had killed Benny.' Pearl made it sound so childishly simple that Joseph worried for his mother's sanity. He looked away from her to view the two bodies. Minsky on the couch, Levitt on the floor with the front of his face little more than a gaping, bloody mess. The bullet had struck him at the bridge of the nose, exiting through the back of his head. For the first time Joseph

437

noticed the hole in the plaster of the far wall, where the bullet had finished its journey.

'Ma, before the police get here, I can put that other gun next to Lou. Judy and I, we'll say you shot him in self defence. We'll say he was threatening everyone. We'll swear to it on a stack of bibles.'

'We'll back you up,' Judy assured her mother-in-law. 'We'll say whatever will keep you out of trouble.'

Pearl smiled at them both. 'What kind of trouble can an old lady get into? I just did what should have been done years ago, that's all.'

Judy walked across the room until she stood over Levitt's body. The sight of the blood and gore did not disturb her. All she could think of was that this was the man who had killed her father, caused her mother's suicide. Uncle Lou . . . Lou Levitt . . . the trusted family friend. Dear old Uncle Lou. And all he had done was cause havoc and tragedy.

'While we're waiting for the police,' Pearl said, 'perhaps I should make some coffee. Would anyone like a cup of coffee? There's even some fresh fruit cake and *mandelbrodt* to go with it.'

Joseph stiffened at what he considered the oddity of the suggestion. Two corpses, one killed by his mother, and all she could think of was making coffee, serving cake. Judy cut in quickly.

'That's a wonderful idea. I know I could do with something.' She caught Joseph's eye. Slowly, he understood. His mother's way of coping with a crisis, any crisis. Feed the crisis until it went away.

Joseph watched his mother walk out of the library, heard her footsteps as she crossed the entrance hall to the kitchen. 'Is she all right?' he asked Judy.

'She's in shock. She just killed someone, a man who was very close to her.'

'Closer than you think,' Joseph whispered. He told Judy of Levitt's claims to being the father of himself and Leo. Judy's eyes widened.

'Do you think that could be true?'

'What? His claim that he . . . he made love to Ma, or that I'm his son?'

438

'Both.'

'Ma didn't deny that she'd . . . you know.' He was unable to think or talk of his mother in those terms. 'But being his son . . .?'

'You're not,' Judy assured him. 'You couldn't be.'

'Thanks.'

'Go into the kitchen, stay with her. Show her she's not alone.'

Joseph left. Rather than remain in the library alone with the two bodies, Judy walked into the entrance hall. She'd listen for the police. After a couple of minutes, she heard the sound of an engine, a car door slamming. Before the bell could be rung, she pulled open the door. And stopped dead. There was no police car or ambulance outside. Only a taxi pulling away, and Leo climbing the steps towards the door.

'Where's Ma?' he demanded. 'I've got to see her!'

Judy stepped outside, pulled the door closed behind her. 'What do you want?'

'I want Ma. Wake her up. Tell her I'm here.'

'Go to hell. You're not setting one foot inside this house ever again, you murdering bastard.'

Halfway up the steps, Leo froze into immobility. His mouth gaped. He stared in disbelief at Judy. 'You can't stop me seeing Ma.'

'She doesn't want to see you, don't you understand that? She knows what you did. She knows what you're like. She knows what you are. She never wants to see you again. Now get away, before you bring her even more grief.'

'I've never brought Ma grief!' Tears started down Leo's cheeks as he made the denial. He'd never hurt his mother. Judy was lying, just like she always did. 'She loves me. How could I ever hurt her?'

'You've hurt her with every breath you ever took, you bastard.' Standing in front of the door, denying Leo entrance, Judy felt no fear. Only jubilation. At last, after years of having to accept his abuse, his insults, she could confront him. No longer would his twin brother or his mother stand up for him. No more would Pearl find excuses for his barbaric behaviour. On this night of tragedy, Judy was experiencing a heady triumph. 'She doesn't want to see you, don't you understand that? She doesn't love you, Leo. She hates you. Like poison, she hates you.'

Leo wiped his eyes with the sleeve of his jacket. Cunning appeared on his face. At last he understood. 'You made her hate me, didn't you? All along you worked on her with your lies to make her hate me. And my brother, my stupid brother who's supposed to be my twin – supposed to be closer to me than to anyone else – he let you fill Ma's mind with your lies.' He started up the steps again, determined to push Judy aside to gain entrance to the house. Determined to kill her if that was what it took.

'Lies?' Judy laughed. 'I didn't have to tell her lies.' She stopped talking for a moment, squinting in the light above the door as she tried to peer into the bushes behind Leo. Surely she had just seen something move out there. What was it? There, again. The bushes moved. Then she relaxed. It was Solomon and Sheba, that was all, the Dobermans foraging round in the bushes until they were called back into the house. She looked back into Leo's heavy face, the patch of plaster across his temple. 'Who do you think told your mother all about your place down on MacDougal Street? That wasn't a lie, was it? I didn't lie about you meeting your pretty little boy down there, did I?'

'You? It was you?'

'Damned right it was me.' From inside the house, she heard Joseph call her name. He didn't know she'd gone outside, or that Leo had arrived. He called her name again, and she ignored him. 'I followed you one night, Leo. One night when Joseph was in Switzerland, and I'd eaten around at Ma's apartment. I followed you because I so desperately wanted something to hurt you with. And you gave it to me. You and your little faggy boyfriend. Remember the cab driver who came banging on the door to see who'd ordered a cab? He saw your little boyfriend with you. And he believed you were my husband, can you beat that?'

'You're the one who told Ma about me? You're the one who told on me?' Leo's voice rose to a tortured scream. He ran up the remaining steps, hands reaching out for Judy's throat. She heard Joseph call her name again, but now that she wanted to answer, she could not. Leo's strong hands were

440

around her neck, cutting off sound, cutting off air.

'I'll kill you!' Leo shrieked. 'You bitch! I wish I'd let you die before!' The pressure around Judy's throat became greater. 'I wish I'd let you die with your fucking lousy mother. You should have died, you bitch!'

The bushes parted. Judy heard a deep growl, saw nothing more than a dark blur flying through the air. The pressure on her throat was eased. She leaned back against the door, chest heaving as she watched Leo stagger down the stairs with Solomon, the male Doberman, hanging from his right arm.

'Get him off me!' Leo screamed. He punched wildly at the large dog with his left fist. Despite the assault, the Doberman continued to hang by its teeth from Leo's arm.

Another blur of movement. Leo's screams soared to a pitch beyond human hearing as Sheba, the Doberman bitch, joined the attack, snapping her fangs into Leo's left thigh. Judy stood on the top step, frozen in fear and fascination as the two powerful beasts worried and tore at Leo as though he were nothing more than an old blanket, a toy, a plaything. In Judy's eyes, they were two contestants in a grotesque tug-of-war.

Pulling and ripping, Solomon and Sheba dragged Leo on to his back. For an instant, Judy believed that Solomon had given up the tug-of-war. The larger dog released its grip on Leo's right arm and backed off, tongue hanging out as it panted for breath, blood dripping from its muzzle. Then, staring at Leo lying helplessly on his back, while Sheba's teeth ground at his left thigh, Judy understood perfectly why Solomon had given up the arm. Leo's white, unprotected neck presented a far more tempting target. Judy closed her eyes, but not quickly enough to avoid seeing Solomon leap forward and sink gleaming fangs into Leo's throat.

At the far end of the driveway, lights appeared. Headlights, and the red and blue flashes of emergency vehicles. Behind Judy, the door opened, and she fell back into Joseph's arms. The nightmare was over, and she was just grateful that those she loved had lived through it.

Pearl refused to go to bed. She insisted on staying up all night to make coffee and serve homemade cake to the many officials who tramped through the house, taking photographs, asking questions, and making copious notes.

'Do you think that my mother really understands about Leo?' Joseph asked Judy nervously. 'She's walking around like she's the hostess at some party.'

'She understands all right. She's just treating this crisis like she treats any other. Be more worried about yourself.'

'It hasn't sunk in yet, none of it. Benny Minsky, Uncle Lou, Leo. . . . It's like a dream.' Joseph shuddered as he recalled the three bodies being removed, two from the library, and Leo's from the front steps. Of all three bodies, Leo's had been the hardest to look at it, savaged by the dogs. In comparison, the bullet wounds of Levitt and Minsky had been almost clinically clean. 'Judy, why did Solomon and Sheba attack Leo?'

'Because he attacked me. He tried to strangle me.'

'Why?'

When Judy did not answer, Joseph repeated the question. 'Did you provoke him at all, knowing the Dobermans were out there?'

'Of course not!' she fired back.

'He just tried to strangle you?' Even while Joseph asked the question, he tried to understand his own feelings about what had taken place. As if the deaths – the violent deaths – of three people so close to him weren't enough, he had to come to grips with the sickening betrayal of the entire family by Lou Levitt. Three deaths . . .? Four deaths! He'd forgotten all about William Minsky, whose abduction and murder had started the chain of events leading to the carnage in the Sands Point house. But the betrayal, and Levitt's absurd claim to being the father of Leo and himself . . . No matter which way he tried to approach it, he could not even begin to comprehend.

'Since when did your brother need a reason to wish me harm?' Judy wanted to know. She would never tell Joseph that she had deliberately taunted his twin brother with the information that she had been the one to tell Pearl about Leo's homosexuality. If she did, he might think she'd done so knowing the two Dobermans were foraging in the bushes, knowing that Leo would assault her, knowing that the dogs would come to her aid. She hadn't known, had she? Surely it had slipped her mind that Joseph had put the dogs out when Minsky had arrived? Or had it? Perhaps . . . perhaps the memory of Joseph pushing out the two Dobermans had been lodged in her subconcious, ready to be resurrected the instant Leo made one menacing move towards her.

A police officer approached Joseph and Judy. More questions were asked. Judy knew that the rush of official activity around the house was acting like a buffer to those involved. Only after all the inquests, all the legal matters, would she and Pearl and Joseph be able to sit down and think about the future. They'd have to move, of course. This house, once the home of so many happy memories, was now a horror chamber of ghosts. And the children, Jacob and Anne, would need a different environment, a school where they would not be known. Judy remembered too well the scenes at school after Jake Granitz's murder, the other children making Joseph and Leo the centre of attention. Joseph, she recalled, had shunned the attention. Not Leo, though. The younger twin had revelled in it. Violence had always been his shadow, from his youth to the moment of his death. . . .

One by one, the police and the technicians finished their work at the house in Sands Point. The last to leave was the medical examiner. As he placed his black bag in the trunk of his car, Pearl approached him.

'Excuse me, you are a doctor, aren't you? A regular doctor?'

'Yes, ma'am,' the medical examiner replied. 'Would you like me to prescribe something for you? A sedative?'

'No, thank you. I have my own family doctor should I need anything like that. It's just that I was wondering if you could answer a question for me.'

More than anything else, the medical examiner wanted to get home and go to bed. It was already six in the morning; he had been at work for four hours. Tomorrow, he would be busy performing three autopsies. Yet he could not bring himself to be abrupt to this sweet little old lady who had supplied coffee and cake all night long, treated all the members of the emergency services as though they were here own flesh and blood. 'What is it, Mrs Granitz?'

'It's about twins. Not identical twins, mind you, but fraternal twins.'

The medical examiner appeared startled. He had expected something very different, especially from a woman who had seen the horrors Pearl had tonight. 'What about fraternal twins?'

'Is it possible . . . oh, this must seem like such a silly question to a doctor like yourself . . . but is it possible for fraternal twins to have two separate fathers?'

'There's nothing silly about the question at all, Mrs Granitz. They can.'

'They can?'

'Yes. You see, the difference between identical twins and fraternal twins is this: identical twins are formed when a single egg splits in the mother's womb, whereas fraternal twins are formed when two eggs are fertilized separately. It's possible that a woman could have sexual intercourse – ' the medical examiner spoke in a crisp, dry tone, without any hint of embarrassment at having to explain such things to an elderly woman – 'with two separate partners within a very short period of time, and the sperm from each partner could fertilize a single egg. She would then be pregnant with twins from different fathers. Does that answer your question?'

'Yes, thank you, it does.' Pearl walked back towards the house. When she passed Joseph and Judy standing in the doorway, she gave them a slight smile and said she was going to bed. She was feeling tired, and she would sleep well now that she knew that Lou Levitt had been wrong. Imagine that, little Lou Levitt being wrong! And being wrong about the most important thing of all.

As she climbed the stairs to her bedroom, she recalled the times that Levitt had claimed he was the father of the twins. Tonight, of course, when he'd caused enough confusion to snatch the revolver from Joseph's hand. And more than forty years earlier, just after Pearl had given birth. And all those intervening years he'd believed wrong, Pearl thought with a savage joy.

Levitt wasn't the father of both twins, he was the father of just one: of Leo, who had inherited his father's madness. Joseph's father was Jake. Joseph was the only true child of her marriage to Jake. The only child that mattered.

Dawn flooded the room as Pearl climbed into bed. If only she'd known that snippet of information more than forty years earlier, she reflected as she closed her eyes.

Who would have thought it possible that twins could have different fathers?

444